Starheart

By the Same Author

The Iron Admiral: Conspiracy
The Iron Admiral: Deception
Starheart

Supertech
Morgan's Choice
A Victory Celebration
Morgan's Return
Ink
Kuralon Rescue

Black Tiger
White Tiger

To Die a Dry Death
A Matter of Trust

Greta van der Rol

Starheart

Starheart

Copyright ©2012 by Greta van der Rol

Cover by Greta van der Rol

ISBN-13: 978-1495340598
ISBN-10: 1495340597

This is a work of fiction. Names, characters, places and incidents either are the product of the authors' imaginations or are used fictitiously and any resemblance to actual persons, living or dead, business establishments, events or locales is entirely coincidental.

All rights reserved. No part of this book may be used or reproduced or transmitted in any form or by any means, electronic or mechanical, including photocopying, recording, or by any information storage and retrieval system, without written permission from the copyright owner except in the case of brief quotations embodied in critical articles and reviews.

First edition: Aug 2012
Second edition: 2013
Third edition 2014

Published in the United States of America with international distribution.

Chapter One

"We're gonna get boarded, Jess." Santh glanced up from his console, where Confederacy Battle Cruiser *Defender*, sleek, dark and weapons hot, dominated the display. Jess read the 'oh shit' in her first officer's eyes.

"Santh, we're chugging along on our way to the space station, minding our own business. It's got to be routine. Let me do the talking."

But even so, her heart hammered. She'd been boarded before, by teams from Nordheim Militia's patrol frigates, but this was the first time she'd ever seen a battle cruiser in this part of the Confederacy.

"*Saintly Maid this is Confederacy Battle Cruiser* Defender. *You will shut down all drives and prepare to be boarded. If you fail to comply you will be attacked.*" A crisp military voice barked instructions, sharp and to the point, no visuals.

"*Saintly Maid to Confederacy Battle Cruiser* Defender. *Message received and understood. Welcome aboard.*"

If they brought InfoDroids with them and they searched thoroughly... She pushed the thought away.

"Shut us down, Santh. I'll pop off and fix my makeup. Might as well look the part."

Jess headed out of the bridge, through the freighter's common room and into her own quarters. Let's see now, what did she have suitable for a military boarding party? She rummaged through her wardrobe and selected the dark green uniform. The pants accentuated her long legs and if she left the jacket unbuttoned over a white shirt, she'd give them something else to think about other than the cargo. She pulled out the clasp holding her hair back and let the blonde mane hang around her shoulders. A little bit of makeup, but not too much, and she was ready.

"Just in time," Santh said as she slid back into the captain's chair. "Their cutter has attached to our airlock."

The airlock status gauge flashed orange. Airing up prior to release. The numbers rose... seventy, eighty, ninety. The gauge glowed green. Jess pressed the hatch release. The boarding party appeared in her view screen, eight people, suited up in black, helmets on. The spheroid shape of an InfoDroid drifting beside them sent a shiver down her spine. Even her security couldn't beat one of those. Still, even an InfoDroid would need to scan the right place and they hadn't the other times. She crossed mental fingers and hoped her luck hadn't changed.

Three of the boarding party, InfoDroid in tow, clumped off to search the cargo hold. Two started searching the common room, and the other three... She rose to greet the trooper who stepped onto the bridge. The other two, both armed with laser rifles, stood outside.

The leader took off his helmet, revealing an attractive young man staring at her with unabashed admiration. "Er... ma'am... Are you Captain Jestinia Sondijk?"

Jess smiled. "Correct, Lieutenant..." She checked his name patch, "...Douglas. And this is First Officer Santhias Dekstra."

Douglas cleared his throat and stiffened into a more military posture.

"You and your first officer are to be transferred to *Defender* for interrogation, ma'am, while the boarding party makes a thorough search of your ship."

Her nerves twanged. "Oh? Is there some sort of problem, Lieutenant? We're on our way to the space station to dock. I wouldn't want to miss my arrival slot."

"Those are my orders."

"We'll comply, of course. Please," she thrust out a hand. "Lead on."

She followed the officer through to the airlock off the hold and into the cutter, Santh at her heels. This was unexpected. And scary. Usually they searched the ship, looked at the trade manifestos and left empty-handed. She exchanged a look with Santh. He'd know enough to keep his mouth shut. If this trip was intended to unsettle them the move had worked. The butterflies in her stomach were performing a salsa.

The warship's side loomed like an apartment block with a few lighted windows. The cutter aimed for the window with the flashing light and slid into the vessel's interior. A few minutes for the airlock to air up and they were out. Jess sniffed the air. Not even a hint of mustiness or cooking. Their filters were obviously better than *Saintly Maid's*.

Jess and Santh walked together, the troopers behind them, while Lieutenant Douglas led the way to a transit foyer, where he pressed a button to summon a car.

Jess stared around her at clean grey walls and floors, and a row of no less than ten lifts. Strewth. The buttons went up to thirty. Thirty levels. This ship was huge. A group of people appeared from a doorway, also heading for the transit foyer. Three senior officers. She fixed her 'not sure why this is happening but I'm being co-operative' expression on her face as they approached.

Well, well, well. The captain, a senior commander and a rather dishy admiral. Tall, thick brown hair, heavy eyebrows over blue eyes that right now were shifting his gaze over her body and most especially down the carefully-judged split at the front of her shirt. She smiled at him, taking care to adjust her hair while she did so. Now what would a Star Fleet admiral be doing at Nordheim?

Beside her, Lieutenant Douglas and the two escorts stiffened to parade ground attention.

The admiral stopped in front of her, still staring. "What have we here, Lieutenant?"

The look in his eye sent a sexy shimmy down her spine. No prizes for guessing what was on his mind right now. And under different circumstances, she wouldn't mind. No, not at all.

"Captain and First Officer of a suspicious ship, Sir. The *Saintly Maid.* They're here for interrogation."

Jess widened her eyes. "Suspicious ship? Oh, really, Lieutenant, you must have mistaken the *Maid* for some other vessel."

The admiral grinned. The transit car the senior commander had summoned arrived with a gentle ping. The captain and the senior commander both had their bodies pointed towards the open door but the admiral lingered, gazing down at her.

"Delightful to meet you, Captain…?"

"Sondijk .And equally delightful to meet you, Admiral…?"

"Hudson. Ullric Hudson."

She gave him a long, hard once-over, her gaze traveling slowly down his body and back up to his eyes. "Welcome to Nordheim, Admiral Hudson."

He chuckled, jerked his head down in a brief nod and followed the two officers into the transit.

***

Douglas herded her into the waiting transit car, then selected a destination on the key pad.

"Just visiting, Lieutenant?" Jess said as the car rose. "We've never had a battle cruiser on our patch before. I thought they were busy keeping the Ptorix hordes at bay."

His lips jerked in a smile. "The admiral doesn't share the orders from the High Command with the likes of me, ma'am."

No, he probably didn't. Admiral Ullric Hudson certainly looked like a man in charge. Those three wide bars on his shoulders denoted a fleet admiral, a very senior rank for a back-water like Nordheim. Interesting. She'd have to ask a few questions back home when she got a chance.

The transit car slowed, causing that familiar rising feeling in Jess' stomach. The door slid aside to reveal an anonymous grey corridor lined with doors at regular intervals. A large sign between each pair of doors announced 4-D in red to the left, in green to the right. They took Santh off into one room and marched her along to another. Grey walls, sensors in the corners, a desk with one chair on the side nearest the door, and two chairs opposite, both occupied. She suppressed the sigh. These two wore Nordheim Militia uniforms. She should have known the local planetary border control would be involved in this raid.

She didn't recognize these two. The middle-aged male commander's swift up-and-down revealed suitable appreciation of her presentation but the hard-faced female sergeant looked like she'd swallowed vinegar. Knowing Longford, their commanding officer, he'd probably chosen the woman specially.

"I'm Commander Harcourt," the man said," and this is Sergeant Box. Please sit down."

Jess walked the three steps to the chair on her side and sat.

"I expect you know I'm Jess Sondijk." Jess put on an engaging smile. "What would you like to know?"

"Perhaps you can tell me where you've been and what you've been doing in this last voyage," the commander said.

"I'm sure this warship's scanners have already pulled my navigation system and my cargo manifests, Commander. And you would have had my voyage plan and cargo manifests from the space station. But ... I left Nordheim with a cargo of local manufactured goods; vases, carvings, beads and jewelry, dresses, bolts of material headed for the markets at Kentor. I managed to sell most of my stock and came back with some precision cutting gear which should fetch a good price in the manufacturing sector here."

The man grunted. He clearly already knew this. She'd play his little game.

"How long were you there?" he asked.

Jess pulled a wry face. As if he didn't know? "Three days at the space station. It cost me a lot in docking fees, I can tell you."

And gave her enough time to shift the cases of fine wine and Pyrrhian silk that weren't on the manifest to the GPR ship parked in the level below.

"We have intelligence indicating you met with representatives of the Galactic People's Republic."

"Oh, 'met with' is a bit over the top. Exchanged a few words in a tavern, more like. When did that become illegal?"

"When the transaction involves smuggling."

Jess threw her arm over the chair back and crossed her legs. His gaze strayed to her breasts. "I've nothing to worry about."

"Your ship is being dismantled as we speak. If we find contraband you can expect a jail sentence."

"Yes, I kinda guessed that. I hope the boarding party has a good time. I'm an honest trader, Commander. If those people break anything on *Saintly Maid*, I'll send the Fleet admiral the bill. And a complaint to Longford."

He raised an eyebrow. "*Admiral* Longford."

She folded her arms. "Whatever. You report to him. I don't."

He jerked his lips. "In the meantime, you're under suspicion. I'll leave you with Sergeant Box," he said, rising to his feet. "She will perform a strip-search. I'm sure you'll understand."

Jess kept her face straight. A strip-search? Strewth.

The door swished closed behind the commander.

The sergeant smiled, if that screwed-up expression qualified, stood and pulled a pair of thin gloves out of her pocket.

Chapter Two

"Thanks so much for the lovely trip, Lieutenant Douglas." Jess smiled at the young man. The sarcasm flew over his head and evaporated near the bulkhead.

"My pleasure, ma'am." His ears flushed red.

She and Santh stepped out of the cutter, into *Saintly Maid's* airlock, through the hatch and into the hold. Santh sealed the hatch port and set up the venting procedure so the cutter could transfer back to *Defender*.

When he'd finished she shot him a look. Santh raised both eyebrows slightly. The ship would be bugged—and the bug would be able to pick up any conversations they might want to have via their implants. Confederacy citizens had the implant fitted to their skulls at a young age, allowing them to communicate with each other without a comlink. Many people didn't realize those conversations could be intercepted with the right equipment. Still, some things she didn't have to keep a secret.

"Should've known that creep Longford would be involved," she said. "Did they strip-search you, too, Santh?"

"Oh yes." His lips widened into a beatific smile.

Jess chuckled in spite of herself. "I got a crabby, hatchet-faced dragon."

"Maybe you should have asked if the admiral could do it."

She cuffed him around the ear. "Cheeky. I'll go get changed, you set course for the space station."

Jess ran up the steps and through to her quarters, where she changed back into her usual grey, spacer's overalls. They'd have set up a sensor here somewhere. She hoped whoever was running surveillance enjoyed the view.

She turned on music and cranked up the volume so they'd have something to listen to while she did her stuff, then slid open a drawer in the closet and pulled out her special laser light. It looked like the ordinary ones, silver, slim, with a slide to clip it onto a pocket. Now to see if it was worth the price she'd paid for it. She turned the device on, flicked the switch to activate the sensor detection function and slipped it into her top pocket. The ship graphic on her cranial implant showed the system's own sensors as green dots. A red dot appeared in the light fitting of her quarters.

She could disable the sensor but if she did, they'd know and she'd look suspicious. No. Let them look. For now, anyway.

She ambled through the ship's common room, noted the sensor in the corner and passed through into the cargo hold. Yes, one here in the main bay. But she'd expect that. There'd be one in Santh's quarters, too. She stuck her head in the door and pretended to search. Yep, a sensor in the light fitting. And there'd be another on the bridge. That would go without saying.

One more thing to check. She strode along the walkway past the rows of cargo bays and through the hatch into the engine room, where she made a show of checking the gauges. The drives throbbed behind their shields. No red dots.

Breathing a little easier, she moved on to the shift drive, isolated in its own compartment. She flipped down an inspection hatch and put her eye to the eyepiece for the retinal scan. A panel of the housing slid away, revealing a shielded case. Yep, still there. And she'd bet they hadn't found it, despite their superior detecting equipment. The GPR paid its bills with unpolished gems. They might look like dull stones but when the jewelers finished with them, they'd be worth a fortune. Tanaka would sell this little lot for a heap of credits, carefully laundered through a few businesses she didn't care to know about, and she'd get her cut.

Jess headed back to the bridge, her heartbeat restored to its normal rate.

***

By the time Jess slid back into the captain's chair in *Saintly Maid's* small bridge, Nordheim's single space station, in geostationary orbit above the planet's capital, dominated the scopes. A flutter of delicious expectation stirred in her stomach. Next stop home. The IS responded to the station controller's instructions, aiming for the flashing signal on the lowest of the stations six wheels.

Jess and Santh lay in their seats, harnesses secure, while the ship's IS made the final minute adjustments to match the station's slow spin. On the screen the image of the ship approached the docking tunnel, nosing gently between walls which altered to match her girth. A muffled clunk reverberated through the hull. That would be the tether attaching.

"*Ship secured, Jess*," the IS said in its soft, female voice. Jess had programmed her that way, to match her name. *Saintly Maid*.

The harness on Jess' shoulders and legs unclipped, withdrawing into the housing as the seat returned to upright. Whatever else, she was glad to be back. She'd call Tenna and finalize that country stay for the school holidays.

She and Santh left the ship carrying their bags over their shoulders and entered the station-side dock. Jess called a cheery hello to the boss of the station crew busy attaching hoses to replenish the air and water. He grinned and waved. She'd ordered detailed cleaning, too, including the light fittings and the usual engine and shift drive maintenance after a trip. That ought to sort out most of the snooper sensors. The others she'd deal with later.

They passed through the gate which sealed off their dock area from casual visitors, and jumped onto the pedolator running down the centre of the corridor.

"How many bugs?" Santh asked as they sped along.

"Common room, bridge, cargo hold, my quarters, your quarters. I left them on."

He nodded. She didn't have to say the rest, one of the nice things about working with Santh.

At the station's hub they transferred to the elevator terminal to wait for the next car taking people from the station to Nordheim, one hundred klicks below. The cars traveled up and down once every two hours, the next in twenty minutes or so.

A few travelers sat at scattered tables beyond the front counter of the departure lounge. The lounge's back wall had been fitted with an enormous screen which looked like a window, displaying the view from the station's outer hull. Nordheim glistened, a streaked, blue-and-white marble against the blackness of the void. Judging by the coil of cloud in the Varenic Ocean, the Outer Rim Islands were going to be saying hello to an enormous storm any minute now. Lucky them. Orham City, just appearing from the darkness of the terminator line, should be sunny.

The girl on the desk greeted Jess with a broad smile. "Hiya, Jess. Good trip?"

Jess threw her bag onto the counter's scanner platform. A network of blue lines marched across the bag as the tracker surveyed the contents. Negative, of course. The case containing the gems wouldn't register.

"G'day, Cynthia. Yes, we did pretty well. We were slightly delayed coming in, though."

"*Defender*? They've stopped most everybody. We got an announcement that the Government is sick and tired of smugglers not paying needed revenue."

"If they lowered their import and export duty there'd be less incentive to smuggle," Jess said.

Cynthia looked over the paperwork, already sucked from *Saintly Maid's* IS. "This looks fine, you can go home." She looked up. "Oh. Except for this." She pushed a sheet across the counter to Jess. "There's a reception on tonight at the Regent Hotel's Stargazer room. All captains are required to attend. President Ottenshaw's orders."

Jess read the document. Bloody hell. A reception? President Ottenshaw wants everyone to meet Admiral Hudson and his senior officers, does he? Well, too bad. She'd already met them, thanks so much.

"Thanks, Cynthia. See you in a month or so."

***

Engines humming, the elevator car slowed down for its final descent into the Orham City spaceport. Ah, the joy of homecoming. Jess' body positively tingled with anticipation. She bounced down the ramp into the main terminal where her enthusiasm drained away like water down a plughole. Uniforms. Four—no, six—armed Confederacy troops dressed in black strolled in pairs through the hall. They didn't appear to be doing much, apart from making a presence.

"What are they doing here?" Santh said over her shoulder.

"Looking for smugglers, I guess." She sighed. "I hadn't been expecting this. Ottenshaw must be making a stand. Pompous dork. A few thousand credits more or less wouldn't make a difference. He should be doing something about the state of the economy."

They walked on together, headed for the exit doors.

"Off home, Jess?" Santh asked.

"After I've seen Tanaka. I'd be interested to see what he makes of this military presence."

"Will you be going to this reception?"

"Not a chance. You?"

He grinned. "Yes, I think so. I've got nothing else to do."

"Sure. I'll see you later."

Santh walked away, his bag over his shoulder, while Jess paused for a few moments outside the terminal, tasting the air, smelling flowers and fumes, hot pavement and somebody's kaff. The sun felt warm on her face and a breeze carried the scent of the ocean, five klicks away. In a month's time when she was leaving, she wouldn't detect that sea smell anymore.

One of the autocabs parked on its holding platform trundled up at her call. She slipped into the seat and selected her destination on the map. The little vehicle rolled into the traffic for the short trip to Tanaka's wholesaling company's main office. The place looked like a warehouse but a lift in the foyer took visitors to the administrative offices from whence Tanaka held sway over a diverse manufacturing, mining and transport empire. Jess walked down carpeted corridors to Tanaka's office, where a receptionist ushered her through to the inner sanctum.

Tanaka was in, a bullet of a man perched behind an ostentatiously large, sumptuously-carved, desk. Ornate gold sculptures and holographic art lined the walls of his office, testament to his wealth.

Sitting in a visitor's chair, she took out the case of gems and handed it to him.

When he opened the case his normally expressionless eyes sparkled with naked, unadulterated greed.

"Magnificent." He lifted the largest stone, turning it in his fingers so that the blue glow at its centre shimmered and shifted. "You had no trouble?"

"Of course I had trouble. I was stopped, they took the ship apart and took us over to their ship for interrogation."

She didn't mention the strip-search. The thought of the horrible woman and the intrusive, probing fingers made her flesh creep.

"Ah, yes. Your wonderful security program."

"Even beat an InfoDroid."

His eyes hooded slightly. "Are you sure you do not wish to sell it?"

"I keep telling you, the program is tailored for *Saintly Maid*. It wouldn't suit any other ship."

He hadn't expected any other answer. "And you will not apply your talents to modify it? I'd pay you very well to do the job."

"I'm not that good, Tanaka. I can tweak a little—but only on my own ship." Perhaps a little more than that. Rabuka had taught her quite a lot before he died but he was an artist; she couldn't compare to his raw talent with machines. And even if she could, she wouldn't. Troy might have trusted Tanaka but frankly, he made her flesh creep.

Tanaka put the gems back, then put the case somewhere in the recesses of the desk. "I will have payment transferred to you in the usual way."

"Good. Look, I know it's none of my business but that seems like a lot of gems for what I delivered."

He raised dark eyes, his expression blank. "They owed me for a previous transaction. I was expecting it."

Like she said, it was none of her business. "Sure. I'll be off." She made to rise but he raised a hand.

"Will you go to the reception tonight?"

"The one for captains? No. I've already met the admiral. Quite nice, by the way." She smiled. Oh, yes, very nice. "To look at, anyway."

"Hm. I thought you might refuse the summons. It's not wise to cross Ottenshaw."

She snorted. "I'm not interested in politics."

"But the Confederacy Fleet should concern you. I, for one, do not want them too interested in me and my captains."

"Sure. Understood. I don't want sensors scattered all over my ship, either. But Longford's goons held the interrogation so I'd say they acted on his request. It's planetary, not the Fleet's problem."

Tanaka smiled his inscrutable smile. "Talk to their admiral. I hear he likes women. Perhaps you could see what you can find out?"

Huh. Her skin tingled at the memory of that hot gaze on her body.

"What? Prostitute myself?"

He chortled, not in the least embarrassed. "What you do with him is your business. I just want you to talk to him."

"They're trying to root out smugglers. What else is there to know?"

He inclined his head and his eyes took on that vacant quality which hid his thoughts. "How. Who they most suspect. What their next approach will be."

"You think he's going to tell me that?"

"Men say things when drunk, or relaxed. I'm sure you'll find a way."

"Oh, what the hell. All right." It might even be fun.

***

Jess heard the reception when she stepped out of the lift, a roar of voices. The captains had heeded the summons. She stood in the doorway, scanning the crowd before she ventured inside. Santh was probably here already.

Maybe sixty or seventy people filled the room. White uniforms were scattered about, the light glittering on varying amounts of gold on their shoulder boards. Nobody under commander, if she was any judge. Mostly men but a few women. The civilians had dressed for the occasion, too. Quite a few of the captains wore corporate uniform, their wives in cocktail or evening wear. Jack Hawkins, staid and stuffy captain of *Audrey's Gift*, looked like a doorman at a swanky hotel, gold-encrusted epaulettes, broad rings on his sleeves and a couple of lanyards brightening up a dark blue uniform. Jess fluttered her fingers in a wave and earned a flush from Hawkins and a glare from his sour-faced wife.

Admiral Hudson chatted with a group that included the Home Services Minister, Delia Marati, stunning in an iridescent gown. That dress must have cost a fortune and she did look good, every rejuvenated inch of her. You could always tell, though. Old eyes in a young head.

Santh, drink in hand, strolled up to Jess, looking her up and down.

"Jess, baby, he doesn't stand a chance."

Jess laughed. "Well, thank you, spacer but I don't know what you're talking about. You look lovely yourself."

The pale blue breeches molded to his slim and athletic form and he'd tied back his luxuriant dark-blond hair. He'd covered the white shirt with a sleeveless jerkin, giving him a dashing air.

She had made a special effort. The red dress was a favorite. The neckline plunged deep, affording everyone quite an eyeful. The rest clung to her waist and hips, accentuating her figure. The split up the front meant she was able to stride if she wanted and provided more than a glimpse of leg.

Santh flicked a finger at a waiter, who approached with a laden tray, his eyes following the plunge of her dress.

"Careful," Santh said, straightening the tray from a dangerous angle. "She wants to drink the wine, not wear it."

Jess selected a glass of pale yellow wine and watched the youth walk away. "Not your type?" she said to Santh.

"No. But I expect somebody will be." He winked.

"Have fun. Let's go and mingle."

Best to let His Admiralship find her. Men like him preferred to chase. Meantime, there were plenty of folk here she knew from the docks. She'd be interested to know what everybody else thought about the recent events.

She and Santh joined a nearby group of friends. Every one of their ships had been boarded and every captain returning from Kentor had been transferred to *Defender* for interrogation. She had no idea if any of them were smugglers or not, although she had her suspicions.

Sonja Brand, captain of *Thorbald*, leaned close. "Were you strip-searched?" she whispered.

"Yes," Jess muttered. "You?"

"Uh-huh. Nobody else, though." She shuddered. "I've never been so embarrassed."

"Nobody else?"

Sonja shook her head.

"Odd." Jess would swear Sonja was honest as the day was long. What was that about? Or were only female captains strip-searched?

She spied Tanaka in a group that included *Defender's* captain, left Santh talking to Sonja and insinuated herself next to the merchant.

"Good evening, Mister Tanaka, how are you?" she said.

"Ah, Captain Sondijk. Have you met Captain Sundra?" Tanaka said.

Jess looked past the captain, over his shoulder. Hudson's head had come up at the mention of her name. She caught his gaze for a nanosecond and turned back to Sundra.

"We've not been introduced, no. Although I did have the... er... pleasure of visiting his ship earlier today."

Sundra smiled, white teeth against dark skin. "It wasn't personal, Captain. I'm sure you appreciate we have a job to do."

"Well, I do so hope you can lay your hands on these smugglers so we honest traders can carry on."

Hudson, murmuring 'excuse me', stepped past Captain Sundra, the group shuffling aside for him. He kept walking until he stood right in front of her. "Captain Sondijk. I'm delighted to see you again." Again that sweeping glance which encompassed all of her and left that lingering, sexy shimmer. "I had wanted a private word."

He took her arm and led her away toward the tall doors leading out onto the terrace.

Nordheim's two small moons glimmered against the dark sky to the East while to the West, the dense stars of the inner arm blazed. The air, redolent with the fragrance of night-flowering junisters, felt cool after the warmth of the crowd inside.

"What about?" she said.

He leant against the balustrade, silhouetted against the soft lighting of the garden below.

"I trust you were not too inconvenienced today?"

He had to be joking, didn't he? "Oh, the interrogation was what one might expect. But a strip-search? After being physically scanned? A little excessive, don't you think?"

His lips stretched in a brief smile. "Not conducted by my crew. I expect these things are a necessary part of the job of a planetary militia but I can't see much point in antagonizing people." He waved a hand. "I wouldn't like you to judge me on an unpleasant sideshow. I'd like to get to know you better. Much better."

And get her into his bed. He still looked at her with that all-consuming gaze. He had an aura, something about him that radiated authority. This may prove to be a dangerous game. But it might be fun.

Footsteps rang on the tiles.

"Admiral? Ah, there you are. Miss Marati and I would like a word."

Ottenshaw. She'd recognize his prissy accent anywhere. He sounded like he had pebbles in his mouth.

"It seems we've been found," Hudson said, soft voiced. "Will you have dinner with me? I'm told the Mountain View is one of the better restaurants in town. Just nod. I'll have my adjutant call you."

Jess nodded.

He pushed himself away from the stone wall.

"But you'd better call me yourself."

The tiny smile widening into a grin, he swept her up and led her back into the room.

Chapter Three

The coptercab set down on the landing platform on the fifteenth floor of her apartment block long enough for Jess to alight before it swept off into the darkness, its bright green 'for hire' sign flashing.

"I'm home, Jeeves," she told her apartment's IS through her implant.

The doors recognized her approach, sliding aside to let her into the building and into her apartment.

"*Good evening, Jess,*" Jeeves said in his cultured, plummy voice. "*Did you enjoy your evening?*"

"Guess so."

She kicked off her shoes. They might look nice but they were hell to wear for any length of time if you'd been in spacer boots for a while.

"Have you booked me a call with Tenna?"

"*Yes. In twenty-three minutes.*"

"Okay."

Shoes in hand, Jess padded off to the bedroom. Better change into something a little less revealing. Thirteen-year-olds didn't need to see their mother dressed like a femme fatale. She hung away the red cocktail dress and changed into jeans and a loose shirt. La Delia had not been happy about the competition when she'd emerged from the terrace with Hudson's hand resting on her bare back. Too bloody bad. Still, from what Tanaka had told her, Admiral Hudson would favor more women than her with his company while he was here. Good luck to him. All she wanted was information. Although a roll in the hay might be nice; it had been a while.

She dropped onto the couch and propped her bare feet on the low table, ready for her chat with Tenna.

Right on time, the line to the school connected and she appeared, fresh-faced, blonde like her mother but with Troy's deep brown eyes. Jess blinked away moisture. Every time she saw her daughter she looked a little bit more grown up.

"Mum. You're back." The grin almost split her face. She sat in the booth the school used for holo-calls to parents, sitting on an upholstered sofa.

"Yes, babe. Oh, you look great. Been keeping fit?"

Tenna scowled. "I'm not a baby, Mum. I'm nearly fourteen."

No, she wasn't. Jess had heard the clichés, how time changed, how quickly your children grew up. It seemed like only yesterday when she learned to walk and talk and went off to school.

"Sure. Sorry. School still good?"

"Yes, fine."

But the enthusiasm was missing. "You sure?"

Tenna nodded. "Exams are the week after next."

That was true. "Hang in there, hon. I've booked us two weeks at Paradise Cove resort for the school holidays. Would you like that? Shopping, riding oliphaunts, surfing…"

Tenna's face lit up. "Oh, zoot, wonderful. Really, really brill, Mum. Um… any chance I could ask Sufi?"

"She's your friend, yeah?"

Vigorous nods that had her hair flying around her shoulders. "My best friend ever. Her parents don't have any money. She's never been anywhere. Please?"

Wide brown eyes pleaded. One day those brown eyes would melt the hardest man's heart. But not too soon, Jess hoped. "Sure. Provided her parents say it's okay. Can I call them?"

"Naw. They don't have tech. They live down in Burkesville."

Burkesville. Jess couldn't imagine anybody at Orham Girl's College coming from the slums. Tenna must have seen something in her expression.

"She won a scholarship, Mum. She's really smart and good at athletics, too."

"I don't care where she lives, hon, I'm just a bit surprised. What if I come down on the weekend? We can have lunch together. Bring Sufi with you."

"Brill," Tenna said, bouncing in her seat. "Can we go to the Mad Hatter? It's the new tea shop. It's great fun."

"Sure. I'll meet you there the day after tomorrow."

Some further discussion about sport and schoolwork and Tenna's allotted quarter hour was over. Jess blew her a kiss and Jeeves shut the system down.

After the noise of the reception and Tenna's rapid-fire description of life at school the silence was deafening. Only a whisper of traffic in the street below filtered through the open windows to the balcony. Jess poured herself a drink and flopped back down onto the couch.

"Play me some jazz, Jeeves. You know what I like."

Soft, modulated, mood music sung by a lady with a milk-chocolate voice.

Tenna reminded her of Troy. But it was funny, she could hardly picture him without having to look at a stored image. Her memory of him was fading, like morning mist evaporating with the sun rise.

***

Back in normal service black, Hudson sank into his chair in his office and waved a hand to indicate to Commander Mann that he should sit.

"Well, Commander? Have we helped our local brothers in arms?"

"A little. We found an unexplained stash of cash and some drugs on *Pot of Gold*, captain and owner William Smythe. Nothing on *Flash Harry* or *Saintly Maid*, despite what the Militia said. I've handed over the data to them."

"Good. I don't want to get too involved. It's their problem, not ours." He didn't mind doing the planetary militia a favor to cultivate a spirit of cooperation, but border control and smuggling were not part of the Star Fleet's jurisdiction.

He leaned back in his chair. "I must say, the whole notion of strip-searching seems strange to me. I understand the basic principle but Jess Sondijk doesn't strike me as the sort to care about intimidation. It's more likely to annoy her. I take it the scan was negative?"

"It was. On all of them."

"Oh, well. Longford doesn't work for me." He wasn't surprised the man was an admiral commanding a planetary militia, rather than a fleet. Now to move on to more attractive matters. "What can you tell me about Jestinia Sondijk?"

Mann accessed his data via his implant.

"A widow, has one teenage daughter. Does quite well for herself and appears to be above-board but is thoroughly distrusted by the Militia. She owns her ship, but like a lot of the freighter captains here she contracts for work through Enyo Tanaka."

An image appeared of a solid, slant-eyed man with arms too long for his body and one of those closed faces which were so difficult to read.

"He's a wheeler, a manipulator," Mann continued. "He has a finger in many businesses. She works for him casually but quite often. She's taken up where her husband left off. He used to work for Tanaka full time, usually captain of a ship called *Kimberley*."

"Oh, yes. What happened to him?"

"He was killed during a boarding a year and a half ago."

"Pirates?"

"No, a Militia boarding."

Hudson grunted. Why wasn't he surprised?

"It seems the patrol ship here received an anonymous tipoff that the ship was carrying illegal drugs," Mann said.

"Was it?"

Mann pulled a wry face. "Drugs were produced, yes. Apparently found in the cargo bay when this man Grimani was shot."

That wasn't impossible. Many a lovely exterior hid a rotten heart. "Do they have any reason to suspect her now? Or is this latest bit of derring-do about a beautiful woman captaining a freighter?"

"It might have," Mann said. "They only strip-searched the two female captains. But also, I think they hoped our InfoDroids would find something. I get the idea they think anyone associated with Tanaka must be doing something illegal but they haven't been able to pin anything on them. And, er, my informant suggested that the local militia admiral, a man named Longford, doesn't like Captain Sondijk."

Interesting. This date may well prove entertaining in more ways than one. "I have a date with Captain Sondijk—or at least I will have after I've called her. Get me the file and anything else we have on her."

Chapter Four

Jess jumped onto a city transit train for the trip across town and into the open spaces where the faux-classic black stone buildings of Orham Girl's College sprawled amongst well-tended gardens. She alighted from the train in the leafy shopping hub a klick or so from the school. No prizes for guessing which building was the Mad Hatter tearooms. Tall, deep pink and shaped like a top hat, the building occupied an area directly opposite the station. The front door, shaped to resemble a decorative buckle on the hat's brim, stood open, revealing a bustling interior, but tables and chairs were scattered about on a terrace surrounding the tea rooms. The place rang with laughter and chatter. Groups of kids surrounded most of the tables and if she was any judge, quite a few of the patrons were schoolgirls. Come to mention it, the young fellows dancing attendance were most likely from the nearby boy's school.

A figure dressed in jeans and a blue shirt jumped up and waved from a table under the dappled shade of an old tree. Jess grinned and waved back, weaving her way between the tables.

"Mum." Tenna engulfed her in a huge hug, her arms around her neck.

Jess breathed in the scent of shampoo, felt soft young skin against her cheek. Her little girl was beginning to blossom into womanhood.

"Sufi's not here. She hasn't come back to school," Tenna said before they'd even had a chance to sit down. A small frown creased a line between her eyebrows and the dark eyes reflected worry.

Jess scraped a chair back over the paving and sat down. "What do you mean? Come back from what?"

"She hasn't been at school all week. She's supposed to be sick."

Tenna picked up her disposable napkin and started to shred the material. "I worry about her. People are rude to her, Mum. Jenny Brixton says Sufi's a gutter cat because of where she lives. Adala Maher makes fun of her because her clothes are a bit worn. The teachers can be awful, too, as if she's not good enough. But she won their stupid scholarship and she's the prettiest girl in the class, too. This is her."

Tenna flipped open her comlink and displayed an image of herself and her friend, as dark as she was fair. Moccha skin, full lips, dancing dark eyes.

Her hair hung in soft waves around her shoulders. Yes, unusual as well as pretty.

"Let's have some lunch and afterwards we can go to Burkesville if you like, see if we can find out how she is and if she'll be able to come on holiday."

"Brill. Thanks Mum. Let's eat. They do a fantasmagorical chocolate mud cake. And a cheese cake to die for."

Jess laughed. "That's dessert taken care of." She tapped a finger on the menu in the table top. "What's worth eating for main course?"

***

Jess paid the lunch bill, then the two of them scampered over the road back to the train station. They strap-hung in the crowded carriage for a little way but at each stop a few more people disembarked and soon they were able to flop into a seat.

"*The next stop is Burkesville,*" the train's IS said.

The doors hissed apart and they alighted into the usual well-lit underground station. The place was clean enough but it looked … damaged. Chipped seats, a rubbish bin hanging drunkenly from a holder, crude graffiti on the walls.

They caught the escalator up to the ground floor and walked past grubby walls and dented ticketing machines to the outside. Jess gazed up and down the road past the station and along the narrower street in front of them. This place had never been anything but ramshackle. Grimy walls supported jerry-built buildings and more than one had boarded up windows. An alley overflowed with junk and the smell of long-abandoned litter fought with the sharp stink of urine. A couple of youths slouched down the pavement away from them, the clunking clatter of the can they kicked competing with the muffled music emanated from a tavern over the road. Jess couldn't help but feel the pall of sullen hopelessness.

Maybe this wasn't such a great idea after all.

"Tenna, maybe—"

"She's my best friend. I want to be sure she's all right." Tenna's jaw clenched tight.

Words like petulant and belligerent came to mind. What the hell. Jess would have been the same at Tenna's age. But now, Jess knew she wasn't Supergirl, that a punch could knock her out or even kill her, that there were bad people in the galaxy. And she wasn't armed, damn it, whereas she would have been in the backstreets of any other world. You relax at home. She mentally kicked herself.

"Have you been here before?" Jess asked.

"Yup. Sufi's mum met us at the station."

Oh, great. Sounding better and better. Already tense nerves tensed a little further. But they were just people, living in a less-than-ideal neighborhood. Just people. Yes, said that little voice in her head, desperate, out of work people who might do anything for a good pair of boots or new jeans.

"Honey, Sufi's family lives here; we don't. In a lot of places in the Galaxy, that's enough to make us a target." She held up a hand as Tenna started to open her mouth. "Don't start. We'll go, but we have to be careful. All right?"

Tenna jerked her head.

"Put your lip away, young lady. It's not a good look. This time, mother knows best. Which way?"

"Straight ahead," Tenna said.

Jess set a good pace; not hurried, not furtive; two people with somewhere to go, a destination in mind. At this time of day few people were out on the streets. She wasn't sure if that was good or bad.

Ahead of them four youths stood talking to a couple of slatternly-looking girls. They passed a bottle of something from hand to hand. One of the girls tipped the bottle and drank but some spilled down into her low-cut blouse. Amid ribald laughter one of the boys put his hand down her shirt to wipe the fluid away. Tenna baulked. Jess took her arm.

"Keep walking, Tenna. If we cross the road or run or anything else we're asking for it. How much further?"

"A couple more streets." Tenna passed her tongue across her lips.

One of the girls nudged the other and stared at them. They all stopped talking, watching them approach. Jess' heart hammered. Older teenagers, but six of them. She glanced around, looking for bolt holes or weapons. A chunk of broken wood hung off a fence nearby. She hoped she wouldn't need it.

She looked them full in the eye, gave them a smile and a nod, and held her breath, the sound of her own footfalls deafened by the thunder of her heart.

"Well, looka there, Seban," one of the girls said. "They's wearin' Benchmark jeans."

"O yairs. Bettin' she's gotta comlink, too. C'n sell 'em real good."

Behind her their footfalls beat a menacing tattoo on the pavement.

Jess shoved Tenna. "Run."

She spun around, grabbed the hunk of wood in both hands and kept turning.

"You goin' fer the girl, Mima," said one of the boys. "This one's gonna—"

Jess slammed the wood into the side of his head. "Fight," she said.

He dropped like a rock. One down. She ducked under a clumsy attempt to stop her and swung her weapon into a second boy's side. He doubled over with a satisfying 'oof' while she side-stepped another. She'd caught them unawares but it wouldn't be for long.

Tenna yelled. The girls laughed.

Fury charged up Jess' spine. She dragged an arm from an assailant's grip, kicked him in the crotch and raced towards Tenna. They'd thrown her to the ground and those two laughing bitches were trying to pull her jeans off.

"Get your filthy hands off her."

The girls backed off. Tenna struggled to her feet but the four had them surrounded, revenge in their eyes. And this time they were ready for whatever she could do. A knife blade glinted in the sunlight.

"Drop that now or I'll put a hole in your chest."

Jess almost dropped her makeshift stave but the man's words were for her attackers. They stared past her, over her shoulder, suddenly wary. One sneered. The zip-hiss of an energy bolt sizzled past Jess. The boy's knife clattered to the ground. Groaning, he clutched at his scorched arm. The smell of burnt flesh drifted in the air. Tenna whimpered.

"Go on, piss off. The lot of you." The man's voice dripped contempt.

The teens retreated, backing off, naked fear in their eyes. A few meters away they turned and ran, not even stopping to help their fallen comrades, who were left to straggle behind.

The adrenalin drained out of Jess' body, leaving her legs trembling. Too soon to say hurrah. Maybe they'd replaced six attackers with one. With a gun.

She turned around and faced a non-descript man, the sort who would be lost in a crowd. Not tall, not short, not handsome, not ugly.

"Not a good place for two well-dressed women to be stumbling around on their own." He put the gun back into a holster on his belt. Light sparkled briefly from a blue stone set into a ring on the small finger of his right hand. "Especially a pair of blondes."

"Thanks. I'm grateful." Jess scooped Tenna into her arms. The girl sobbed on her shoulder, while Jess ran soothing hands over her back in the way she had when Tenna had been small. "It's okay, babe, it's okay."

If this fellow meant them harm, now was the time. But he waited and watched until Tenna's tears subsided, and she stood blinking and wiping her nose with her sleeve.

"Where are you headed?" he asked.

"To the Wickram's house," Tenna piped up.

He smiled at her, eyeing her blonde hair in a way Jess didn't much like. "Sure. Up the street here and around the next corner. Come on, I'll take you."

"Friends of yours, the Wickrams?" Their benefactor strode soft-footed beside them.

"Yes," Tenna said. "Gee, Mum you were—"

"Thanks, mister...?" Jess said before she could say any more.

"No need, ma'am. Those young thugs could do with a proper beating." He stopped at the corner, pointing. "Down there, third on the right. Nice to meet you both. Not too often you see a pair of beautiful blondes in these parts." He nodded and walked away.

"Mum, you were awesome. Did dad teach you to fight?"

"No. If you choose to make a living on ships you learn pretty soon to take care of yourself in whatever way it takes." She grinned and draped an arm around Tenna's shoulder, drawing her down the street towards the third house. "Sometimes that means not going to the bad places in the first place. And sometimes that means grabbing a weapon and using it."

And sometimes it meant flashing your boobs if that was going to work. But Tenna could find that out for herself, all in good time.

The whole street exuded hopelessness, dilapidated buildings with peeling paint, dirty windows, verandas stacked with junk. Plants struggled through cracks in the pavement and most of the tiny front yards overflowed with what had to be vigorous weeds. Except this house. Peeling paint, old and cheap, yes. But a small garden flourished in front of a neat veranda.

"This is Sufi's," Tenna said.

"Yes, I'd guessed."

Jess couldn't find a buzzer, so she knocked.

After a few moments, the spyhole in the door slid open. "Who is it?" a female voice said.

"I'm Jess Sondijk and this is my daughter, Tenna. We came to see Sufi."

The door opened a crack and a dark-skinned woman gazed at them. A moment's hesitation and she stepped aside, smiling. "Come in."

Jess and Tenna followed the woman up a dingy hallway and into a room where sagging, mismatched chairs surrounded a table. A collection of old glassware artistically arranged on a side table drew the eye. The furniture might be old and worn but the room was neat and clean, and the small decorative features added a feeling of pride Jess hadn't encountered in this neighborhood before.

"Tenna, it is so nice to see you again," the woman said. "And you, Miss Sondijk. You could be sisters, you know. You look so young. Please to sit down."

Jess pulled out a chair. "Call me Jess."

"Thank you, Jess. I am Nulleni," she said. "Can I fetch tea?"

Jess hesitated. These people didn't have much.

"Is Sufi at home, Miss Wickram? I've really missed her," Tenna said.

The woman's face crumpled. She pulled back a chair, almost collapsed into it and put her head in her hands. Tenna shot an alarmed glance at her mother.

Jess reached out a hand. "Miss Wickram? Nulleni?"

Sufi's mother straightened up. Her shoulders heaved in a huge sigh. "I'm sorry. I've been so frightened. Sufi has been extremely ill; a stomach virus. I thought I would lose her, like my youngest." She cleared her throat. "There are so few doctors here. She is much recovered now. Would you like to see her?"

See her? What about that virus?

The expression on her face gave Jess away. Nulleni shook her head. "She is no longer contagious. The doctor told me yesterday." She smiled at Tenna. "You have been such a good friend to her. It meant so much. And for you to come here ... that is wonderful."

Tenna stared at her mother, challenging her to refuse. Jess nodded.

Miss Wickram beckoned Tenna to follow her. Soon, the unmistakable voices of two excited teenage girls drifted through paper-thin walls, punctuated with the inevitable giggles. Sufi's mother came back with a tray of tea things. A chipped pot, pretty mugs with a variety of designs, a few home-made biscuits.

"It's so nice for Sufi to have a friend at the school." She poured fragrant tea. "So nice to meet you. Thank you for coming."

"Not a problem. I wanted to ask you something. I'm taking Tenna away to Paradise Cove for the school holidays. She'd like Sufi to some with us, with your permission."

The woman's face closed over. "Impossible, no, it would be lovely for her but ... no."

"I'm paying, Nulleni. It won't cost much more to have two girls instead of one and it would be great for Tenna to have a friend with her. Please?"

Nulleni shook her head. "We cannot afford anything like that."

Poor, but proud. "I can. It would be a great experience for Sufi, to go to a different climate, swim, learn about other places. It'd be good for her health." Nulleni chewed at her lip. A little more and she'd be convinced. "Tenna says Sufi is very clever."

The pride shone like a beacon. "She is. She works hard to take advantage of the opportunity she has been given even though sometimes it is hard. Here, many girls of her age have boyfriends; they can't think past marriage and babies but not Sufi. She wants to make a better future for herself, go to university, become a scientist."

"Well, if I'm lucky some of that will rub off on Tenna, too. It sounds like a holiday together will do them both good." She set her empty mug down on the table. "Please let her come, Nulleni. I promise I'll look after them."

Tears shone in the woman's eyes. "You are too kind."

Fantastic. "Let's tell them together."

***

Jess called a coptercab to take Tenna back to school. The vehicle landed in the roadway outside the Wickram's front door in a maelstrom of dust and debris. Jess hugged Miss Wickram before she and Tenna climbed inside.

"I'll take Sufi off straight from school when the holidays start, and take her back to school again afterwards. Thank you so much for letting her come."

Nulleni blinked away the moisture in her eyes. "You are so kind. Thank you."

The cab took off into the late afternoon sky. Burkesville lay below, a rotting breeding ground for wretchedness and despair.

Jess wriggled her shoulders. Time to think about something more pleasant. "Okay, Tenna, spot the cloud types. What are those on the horizon?"

Jess kissed her daughter goodbye at the school gates, exchanged a hug and used the coptercab for the trip home. A journey on the train didn't appeal. How she felt for that poor woman, stuck in a dead-end hole like that, with no way out, and a sick kid; especially after already losing one to illness. Kids shouldn't die before their parents, it was wrong. At least when Tenna was ill she and Troy could afford to send her to a top hospital. It had stretched the budget almost to breaking point, but still.

Jeeves had the door open immediately she alighted. Late afternoon sun glinted off the balcony railings of the apartment block. Time to get beautiful for her date with Admiral Ullric Hudson.

Chapter Five

Jess checked her make-up one last time. Not a blemish. A hint of expensive perfume, earrings. Her heart throbbed like one of those native bands. Strewth, she hadn't been so nervous since her first high school date. Lack of practice. Outrageous flirting was one thing; sitting opposite an admittedly dishy male who had the power to have you arrested in a heartbeat was something else again.

"*A call, for you, Jess. Admiral Hudson awaits you at the landing pad,*" Jeeves said.

"Thanks."

The butterflies set up a conga line in her stomach. One last nervous swallow. She smoothed down the little black dress and walked out to the platform. Admiral Hudson stood, hands behind his back, beside a large black limo. He was out of uniform, dressed in grey pants and a blue shirt that accentuated the blue of his eyes.

"Good evening, Captain." Looking her over, he smiled. "Elegant and lovely."

He gestured at the vehicle's open door so she slid into the back seat. The smell of well-cared-for leather filled the compartment. He followed, bringing with him a hint of cologne.

"Carry on," he said to the driver.

The big vehicle lifted off with the merest hiss of its thrusters.

Jess stared out of the window, admiring the tapestry of illumination that defined the city, the lines and curves of streets and boulevards with their bluish-white lights, the red taillights of vehicles, the occasional strident brilliance of an advertising array.

"You don't get to see views like this when you spend a lot of time in space," she said.

"So true. Are you away a lot?"

"Quite a bit. It goes with the job. I expect you're the same."

He nodded. "Do you see your daughter often?"

He'd done his homework. Why wasn't she surprised? "Not as often as I'd like. But she's at a good school and she's doing well." She rummaged in her purse. "I have a picture."

She held the holo-projector disc on her palm to show him a picture taken almost a year ago, a tiny hologram of Tenna on her birthday, opening presents.

"She looks like you. In a few years she will be as lovely as her mother."

She smiled at him, clicked the disc closed and put it away. "Do you have children?"

"No." Hudson shifted his weight in the seat. "This mountain range is magnificent."

So he didn't want to talk about family. He was right about the mountains. The snow-clad summits of the Asgard range were usually lost in cloud but tonight moonlight glittered on the frozen peaks, while behind them the stars wheeled across the sky.

"Yes, it's a nice part of the world. I've never had an ambition to climb mountains but the lower slopes have lovely lakes and meadows, forests you can walk through. I love it there."

The limo angled gently downwards, beginning its descent to the hotel.

"Good hunting, I expect?" he said.

"Yes, if you like that sort of thing. Fish in the lakes, Stickhorns in the mountains, bears in the forest."

"I do like the countryside. But I always wanted to go to space."

"Are you from a military family?"

Hudson nodded, smiling. "Yes, indeed. Fifth generation. Son of a captain, grandson of an admiral."

"Did you have a choice?"

He laughed. "Of course. Tell me, what do you love about space?"

The remaining time passed quickly and pleasantly. Hudson was easy to talk to and a good listener. Jess was almost surprised when the limo settled in the parking area opposite the entrance to the hotel. The head waiter himself hurried forward to meet the new arrivals, nearly falling over himself to bow to Hudson.

"Admiral. We're delighted to see you. If you and your lady would follow me..." He stalked off before them, like a standard bearer.

Huh. Rank had its privileges, it seemed. The staff had been polite but hardly attentive when she and Troy had come for their tenth anniversary a few years back.

They were led to a private room where a glass wall afforded uninterrupted views of the mountains across the valley, now wreathed in deep shadow. Floodlights lit up a waterfall cascading down a rock wall to feed the invisible river far below. On the table set for two polished silverware lay beside fine porcelain plates on a cream tablecloth enhanced with hand-embroidered flower emblems.

Hudson deferred to her local knowledge, discussing suggestions with the waiter before deciding on food and wine.

Jess raised her pre-dinner drink in a salute. "Welcome to Nordheim, Admiral."

"A pleasure to be here."

"Tell, me," Jess said, "is it true you're here with a battle cruiser to stop a bit of smuggling?"

"You find that hard to believe?" he said, smiling.

"Well…"

"No, that's not why we're here. It isn't a secret. Nordheim isn't far from the Confederacy's borders and Lord Governor Anxhou has been flexing his tentacles despite his defeat at Forenisi. So we do some exercises with the local defense force to keep the troops busy and make sure his spies see us doing it."

"Oh."

His words made sense. Kentor, the closest planet to Nordheim, was an independent planet outside the human Confederacy. From there, you could easily stray into the Ptorix Khophirate. The battle of Forenisi a couple of years ago eased tensions for a little while but even Jess had noticed the exchanges had become more strident of late. So much for Tanaka's worries. The talk about smuggling was nothing more than window dressing.

"Yet you stop ships and help the Militia's border control efforts?"

He shrugged. "It keeps my crews busy and encourages a spirit of cooperation with the local military."

"Hmmm. Even if it doesn't impress the locals."

"Only the local captains. By the way, I thought the strip-search was foolishness. But it's not my command."

"Understood."

"This is your home planet, I gather. You grew up here?"

"Yes, I did. It's a lovely place, except that the economy is in dire straits. Ottenshaw should be addressing those problems, not wasting his resources on small-time smuggling."

"You said you know these mountains?" Hudson asked, waving his glass at the window toward the waterfall's silver stream.

"I used to go camping with my father when I was a child. Hiking, fishing, taking pictures of animals. I loved it." She grinned. "Dad was surprised when I went into commerce, but he was a merchant himself until he retired."

Relaxed and unselfconscious, Hudson told stories about his own childhood, the son of a serving Fleet officer. His mother had moved to different planets several times, taking the children with her. Several times he made her laugh, telling a story at his own expense. The lines around his eyes crinkled when he smiled. He made her feel comfortable.

The main course arrived, a lustrous game pie served with local vegetables. The aroma sent Jess' mouth watering. A specialty in this part of the mountains, the dish tasted delicious.

After the plates were cleared away she sipped at her glass of most excellent, very expensive wine and noted the strong lines of Hudson's jaw, the way his hair curled around his ears. She was enjoying herself, more than she would ever have expected. Would she fall into bed with him? The way he looked at her it was obvious that was where he'd like this evening to end. Those blue eyes smoldered, a laser blast aimed at melting her resolve. She hadn't been with a man since Troy had died close to two years ago, although she'd long since given up mourning. Hadn't met one that interested her; until now.

Change the subject, Jess. "You mentioned you were here because of the Ptorix situation?"

He nodded. "That's right."

"But I thought we had a treaty with them? After Forenisi?"

Hudson smiled. One of those humorless, introspective smiles. "Forenisi was a great victory, but we won a battle, not the war."

Jess was surprised. The media had been so certain. "You don't think the treaty will hold?"

He stared at her for a long moment before he answered, his eyes slightly narrowed. "Let's just say we don't trust Anxhou," Hudson said. "We think he's trying to get into a position to either split from the Khophirate and form his own independent system or become Khophir himself."

Jess had heard of Anxhou. If she remembered correctly he was the Governor of a Ptorix province adjacent to the Confederacy. "What, a coup d'etat sort of thing?"

"I suppose that's not such a bad analogy. He isn't the only one trying to topple the current Khophir. Which is good in one way, bad in another."

"In what way?"

"The Khophirate is weaker, of course, but on the other hand, the instability breeds warlords like Anxhou, which can be dangerous if they have ambitions to expand their borders." He leaned back in his chair, his fingers loosely holding the wine glass. "Speaking of Ptorix, you said you trade with Kentor. Tell me, how was it on this last trip?"

Jess blinked. It was a good question. A lot of Ptorix traded with Kentor, too. Shrugging, she said, "Kentor was Kentor. Busy, efficient, no nonsense. I couldn't say it was any different to before Forenisi, if that's what you mean. Not that I noticed, anyway."

He nodded. "Have you had much to do with the Ptorix?"

"Not much. You see them on Kentor, of course. But I've not traded with them. They're odd. Like cones moving on trolleys." They had four legs but they seemed to glide along under those floor-length robes they wore. "Besides, they keep to themselves most of the time. So do the humans." She chuckled. "I went past one of their food places, once. God what a stink."

"Yes, I've heard their food smells like rotting offal. Apart from that, though, do you like them?"

"The Ptorix? Look, I'm like most humans. They're strange and a little bit creepy." She shuddered. Blue fur, three swirling eyes, four strange, naked arms with writhing tentacles instead of fingers. "But they have that vast Empire, what d'you call it, Khophirate and they've been around longer than us. Live and let live, I say. But let's keep our distance."

He nodded.

"What about you?" she asked.

"Me? I've come across them once or twice but only in confrontations between ships." He fiddled with his wine glass. "Speaking of which, I heard about the loss of your husband. I'm sorry."

"Yeah." She looked away. It didn't hurt anymore. At the time she'd felt empty, without hope or direction but she had to go on for Tenna. And now Troy was part of history.

"What exactly happened? This was a Militia patrol ship that stopped him, was it not?"

"Yes. I wasn't there. The report said Troy made an aggressive movement, waved a weapon and he was killed."

"He was smuggling drugs?"

She shook her head. "Rubbish. Never drugs; never. Besides, they take Nervana up to Tabora to suck in bored miners. They don't bring it back."

He spread both hands. "But it was found."

What was this about? Maybe he was asking questions about the Militia and how they did things? Whatever. She had nothing to hide. "It was planted to cover up the botched raid. That's what I think, anyway. The officer got jumpy, thought Troy was pulling a gun and overreacted." She shrugged.

"So you don't believe any of it?"

"No. Not then, not now. An incompetent bully-boy covered up a fatal mistake. It wouldn't be the first time." She picked up her glass, sipped at her wine. This was uncomfortable. She didn't want to talk about it. It was over.

"True." Those blue eyes regarded her steadily. Well, if he was hoping for some sort of agony aunt confession, he could forget it. Emotional wasn't her scene.

"Look, it's in the past." She twirled her glass in her fingers, watching the wine swirl around the bowl.

"You weren't on this trip?"

She stared at him but couldn't see anything but polite interest in his expression. Jess found herself licking her lips. But why not tell him? It didn't matter, anyway. "I was at the hospital with Tenna, our daughter. She'd been taken ill, extremely ill."

Memories flooded. Tenna lying on a sheet, her face parchment-white, tubes, nanobots taking over her functions, drips, oscillating lines on screens. And then to top it off, Troy was dead.

"It must have been a terrible time for you. Is your daughter recovered?" Hudson's eyes reflected sympathy.

Jess glared at him. Getting all teary in front of a virtual stranger was not in her job description. "Yes, but learning her father was dead didn't help."

"No, I expect not. So he was alone on that trip?" Hudson had placed one elbow on the table, his chin resting on his fist.

"No. There has to be a first officer. Regulations. But it was an unusual trip. His first officer, his best friend, was bashed within an inch of his life on Tabora, so he had a stand-in co-pilot. Vera might be a competent navigator but she's a pain in the ass."

The memories flooded back. Hudson had burst the dam with all his questions, damn him.

"And this Vera was the replacement first officer?"

"That's right. Vera Quattro. She's a freelance, a locum if you like. She needed a trip home after taking a ship to Tabora. I heard she complained about getting boarded, too. Troy's dead and she's whining about her reputation. Stupid bitch."

"Did you ask for an investigation into his death?"

She met his gaze. "They did an investigation. I have the report. 'Dear Ms Sondijk, we're dreadfully sorry your husband was killed, it was an accident, these things happen, have a nice day.'" She pushed her fingers into her forehead. Damn it. She was over this. Over it.

"The case can be re-opened if you're not happy."

"What the hell for? It won't bring him back, won't change anything. No thanks." An investigation was the last thing she wanted. Who knew what else they might find on the way through?

This was getting personal and she was getting emotional. It was all she could do to stop the moisture messing with her eyes. Time to call a halt to this nonsense. "Look, I ought to be getting home. My body clock's still not in sync. I'm sure you'd understand."

Hudson looked as if he wanted to ask more questions but he didn't. "Of course." He paid the bill and the head waiter escorted them to the skimmer. On the flight home she gazed out the window, ignoring the Confederacy admiral sitting beside her.

"I seem to have stirred your emotions with talk of your husband's death. Forgive me," he said.

She glanced over her shoulder at him. "It's ancient history. Gone. Over." Damn the man to hell and back. She'd shoved it away, into a private vault and he'd opened the door and dusted all the fucking cobwebs of doubt and suspicion.

"You bought your own ship after your husband's death?"

"Yes."

"That's quite an expense. I assume you could have taken over your husband's ship?"

Oh, leave me alone. "It wasn't his ship. Having my own ship gives me flexibility. I can take a job or not depending on circumstances."

"You can refuse work?" She heard the disbelief in his voice. She looked over her shoulder at him, sitting relaxed, arms folded, in the opposite corner of the cabin. Still only polite interest, so she would give him a polite answer.

"I have to work but I try to fit around Tenna. It's a mother thing."

"I see."

"No you don't. You're not a mother." She turned her body away from him a bit further. He said nothing more. At least he had the sense to take a hint.

The road map of lights below the vehicle surprised Jess. Orham City already. *Time flies when you're having fun.* The big limo landed smoothly on the landing pad at her apartment.

"Thanks so much for dinner," Jess said. "I enjoyed it." She slid out of the seat.

Hudson joined her to walk beside her to the door. "So did I. Very much."

Before she had time to think he brushed his fingers down the side of her face, lifted her chin and brushed her lips with his. She stepped away before he could take the matter any further, the taste of him tingling on her lips. Wine and musk and sex. He had to be joking. Some men were so up themselves they didn't realize the lights had gone out.

"Goodnight, Admiral." She turned away.

"I'll call you. Personally. Soon," he said as the security door slid aside.

The door clicked closed. Jess took off her shoes to walk the short distance to her apartment. He'd call her himself, would he? Huh. Handsome, charming, intelligent and far too fucking interested in things that were none of his business. He could find somebody else for his bedtime entertainment. He wouldn't find *that* difficult.

Jess tossed her shoes in a corner, hung up her dress and stepped into the shower, where she dispensed gel into her hand and scrubbed the make-up from her face. Troy. She'd had to move on, for Tenna's sake but now Hudson had resurrected the memory and with it, questions; questions she'd dismissed, answers she'd accepted because it was the easiest way. Why would Troy, always so careful and cool, have pulled a gun during a search? Had there been something on *Kimberley*? It wasn't impossible, by a long shot. She and Troy had always sailed close to the legal wind, but not drugs. Never drugs. Surely.

She rinsed and switched on the drying cycle, turning in the warm air. Bed beckoned. She slipped between the sheets. "Shut down, Jeeves."

"*Goodnight, Jess.*"

The room darkened. Jess stared at the ceiling. She could ask Tanaka if she could see the files. But she didn't much like the merchant and she didn't want to involve him. *Kimberley* was in dock, had been for a few days having its annual overhaul. Maybe she should do a clandestine visit. But to do that, she'd need some authorization or something. A break-in at Tanaka's might be on the cards. But first she needed to see him anyway, to report on her impressions of Hudson.

Chapter Six

Hudson paced along the line of troopers drawn up in ceremonial splendor for the traditional inspection of the guard, Admiral Horatio Longford at his side. The local militia's dress uniforms were certainly colorful, blue trousers with red jackets. And if Longford had any more gold braid he'd disappear behind the stuff.

One final, full parade salute and the pleasantries, at least, were over. He'd have to tread carefully. Except in time of war Hudson, as a Fleet admiral, had no real authority here.

"As you can see, Admiral, we run a tight operation here," Longford said, leading him toward the officer's mess on the edge of the parade ground. "My people are always immaculately turned out."

"They certainly look magnificent," Hudson said. Not the most important thing in his list of must-haves. Still, the Volcron M-3 rifles the troops carried were state-of-the-art. He hoped the soldiers were as well-trained in their use of weapons as they seemed to be at polishing their boots.

Longford ushered Hudson into a carpeted hall where he introduced the admiral to his senior officers. Waiters brought tea and morsels of food served on silver trays while Hudson smiled and chatted about the current political situation with the Ptorix and about the battle of Forenisi. Someone asked about joint exercises for the troopers on his flagship.

"Good idea," Hudson said. "I expect we'll be here for a time and it does get boring, especially for the troopers."

"We're glad to have your help with our smugglers, too, Admiral," Longford said. "We do our best but these people are damnably clever." He shook his head. "They buy equipment from the backblocks of Kentor to evade detection. We don't have state-of-the-art InfoDroids at our disposal."

"You've had some success, though. You must be pleased with finding that haul of endangered species last month." Hudson threw a virtual salute to Mann. It was always good to have a real compliment in the diplomatic arsenal.

The man swelled. "Oh, we have our little triumphs. It's what keeps us going."

The other officers smiled and nodded, pleased at the praise. A little more small talk and Hudson said, "I wonder if we could have a private word, Admiral?"

The man's eyes narrowed for an instant. Suspicious. "Of course. Come this way."

Longford led Hudson into his own private office. The room reflected the man. Everything was positioned at right angles; the desk, the chairs, the pictures on the walls. You could have measured the angles with a set square. Longford walked around his desk and sat in the chair, upright and erect, directing Hudson to sit with a gesture.

Hudson pulled out one of the two visitors chairs and settled himself down. Longford still had the sword of honor he'd won at military college mounted on the wall behind him, its curved blade glinting in the light. A sword, for the spirit's sake.

"How can I help?" Longford asked.

"I'm interested in your raid on the *Kimberley*. The one when captain Grimani was killed."

Longford's lips pursed. "Not your jurisdiction, Admiral, if I may say."

"True. Idle curiosity, that's all. I had dinner with Jess Sondijk last evening and the matter came up in conversation. I believe you had an investigation?"

Longford hesitated, apparently debating with himself. Then he almost sneered. "Troy Bertrand Grimani. A rogue and a villain if ever there was one. He got what he deserved, no mistake."

"Why do you say that?"

"I suppose she tried to spin you a tale. Drugs were found on Grimani's ship. He was killed trying to stop the officer from finding the cache. Besides, have a look at his record. It's pages long." He spoke to his IS. "Display Grimani's record."

The data appeared on a sheet, which he handed to Hudson.

Break and enter. Affray. Possession of illicit goods. He'd been a kid. Hudson had known a few like that. "Hmmm. Minor offences that go back quite a few years. But nothing for the past twelve, except this two-kilo drug haul."

"All that means is he got smarter after he got married. Learned how to avoid getting caught. Him and his lovely wife. She bought her own ship after he died and named it *Saintly Maid*. Huh. One more example of her twisted sense of humor."

The man's eyes glittered, his lips twisted. He didn't like either of them. Interesting.

"She's a very attractive woman."

"To look at, oh, yes. Very nice, I'll grant you. But I wouldn't trust her as far as I could throw her."

Neither would he. But keeping her nice and close might be an alternative. His evening with her hadn't turned out as he'd expected. "Why did you stop *Kimberley*?"

"A tip-off the ship was carrying drugs."

"Anonymous?"

Longford frowned. "Yes, anonymous. A message left at the customs office on Tabora. They contacted our patrol ship immediately and we acted, of course. You think that wrong?"

Was Longford overly defensive? "Isn't it more usual to carry drugs from Nordheim to Tabora?"

The fellow rubbed his nose. "Yes, but even so. It may have been a ploy to avoid detection. Take the stuff to Tabora from Kentor, say, and back down to Nordheim. Nervana isn't the only drug in the Galaxy."

"But it *was* Nervana. Why bring it back?"

Longford shrugged, frowning. "How should I know? They're criminals. Perhaps it was a return for non-payment or something." He tossed the words out, as if he didn't care.

"Quite. I've read the report on the shooting. You have no qualms?"

If anything, Longford's spine became even more rigid. "Qualms? Sergeant Ellwood is a highly experienced, competent man. He served ten years in the Confederacy Fleet before he joined the Nordheim Military Forces. I'd say he knew exactly what he was doing. Grimani pulled a weapon on him in the cargo hold. Ellwood acted in self-defense. Grimani's weapon was set to maximum power." He leaned forward, palms flat on the desk. "Ellwood's was not."

"Half power is quite enough to kill at close range." Longford knew that, so would Ellwood. A cover-up?

"He followed our protocol in these matters exactly. I can ask no more."

"You saw no need for a further investigation?"

"None whatsoever." Longford ticked off the points on his fingers "Grimani was a known felon. He drew a weapon on an official carrying out an authorized search. The sergeant followed standard boarding procedure to the letter and acted in self-defense."

"Grimani had a wife and child."

"D'you think I don't know that? It was unfortunate the man died but I have no intention of hauling my people through the mire for following orders. D'you have any idea what that does to morale? To discipline? In the end they won't do anything for fear of getting into trouble."

"Forgive me, Admiral. You're right, of course. You must do what you feel is correct." But it wasn't how he ran his own operations. Particularly with boarding parties, personnel were instructed to use their initiative to a certain extent.

Longford glowered but seemed to accept his statement. He tilted his head to the side. "May I offer you a word of advice?"

Advice, huh? From this martinet? "Of course."

"Jestinia Sondijk is a beautiful woman. But she is clever, resourceful and about as trustworthy as a failing shift drive. I'd advise you to tread carefully."

"I'm always careful with beautiful women, Admiral," Hudson said, hoisting himself to his feet. "Thank you for your time. I must get on."

They exchanged a salute. The jurisdiction might be different but Hudson was still the senior of the two. He didn't think it important, but Longford clearly did, and that, of course, gave him an advantage.

***

Hudson made the trip back to his battle cruiser deep in thought. The whole business bothered him. One man bashed, the other killed after an anonymous tip-off. Would he have done the same as Longford, accepted that procedures had been followed? Maybe. Jess had her doubts about the weapon Grimani was supposed to have waved, and the drugs they were supposed to have seized.

He still had regrets about the abortive dinner date. He'd expected it would be a double seduction, him seducing her, her seducing him. He'd bet a year's pay she wanted to sound him out about why the Fleet was here, and he'd given her the answer she wanted to hear. Then he ruined his chances for a romantic interlude by playing on her emotions. He shook his head. He hadn't played that very well at all. A pity, in a way. But if Grimani's ship was actually carrying starhearts then he had good reason to look into the matter. As for the lovely Jess… he smiled. He may have lost the battle, but he hadn't lost the war.

"Have Commander Mann report to my office," he said as soon as he set foot on *Defender's* decks.

Mann arrived before Hudson, waiting for him in the reception area of the admiral's office. Hudson beckoned him through.

"I want you to do some investigation into the life and times of Troy Bertrand Grimani. Particularly his last trip up to Tabora. He was killed on the way back from there. What happened? Who did he meet? Find out about his first officer, too. And a woman named Vera Quattro. She's spacer crew, a navigator available for freelance work."

Mann saluted and left.

Chapter Seven

Jess jumped out of the cab at Tanaka's warehouse a few minutes early. This would give her time to look around, 'case the joint'. The building's façade didn't give much away. The ground floor was quite literally the shop front, huge picture windows made of armorglas where Tanaka displayed luxury goods available for sale. She'd checked the rating; you'd need a military-grade laser canon to get through that stuff. During the day the sensors in the entrance were set to allow people through, although, of course, images were recorded. Tanaka conducted his real business from the two windowless levels above the ground floor showroom. Behind the building, transport vehicles of various sizes stood in ordered rows, protected by smart-wire fences.

She strolled into the foyer, smiling at the two uniformed thugs standing beside the lift. They returned the smile. "Can I help you, ma'am?" one asked.

"I have an appointment with Mister Tanaka."

"Of course." He stepped into the lift with her, keying security to allow access to Tanaka's floor.

She'd been in the building many times before, but this time she took mental notes. If she'd not been mistaken, there had been another exit in the foyer, toward the back.

The lift door slid silently aside on the second floor. Her guard at her elbow, Jess strode down the corridor to Tanaka's office. Her sensor locator, hidden inside her jacket, plotted the devices as she walked.

Her escort left her in reception under the watchful glare of Tanaka's secretary who eventually ushered her into his presence.

She dropped into a visitor's chair and stretched her legs. "You wanted a report on Hudson," she said. "This is about the Ptorix, waving the Confederacy flag to let them know the Fleet's here."

Tanaka scratched at his close-cropped scalp. At length he nodded. "It makes sense. But we still need to be careful."

"Oh, yes, I agree. The man's no fool. He'd done his homework, too. He asked me a few questions about Troy's death."

Tanaka tensed. If she hadn't been looking for the slight jerk of his eyelids, she wouldn't have seen it. "And?"

She shrugged. "It's over. I didn't want to talk about it."

"But what did he ask?"

"How he died, what happened. I told him. Then we talked about ... other stuff." She deliberately glanced away.

Tanaka's lips curved in a salacious smile. "Does he snore?"

She rested her cheek on her fist. Grubby creep. Next he'd be asking for descriptions. "None of your business."

He laughed, an ugly, snorting sound. "Keep an eye on him for me, won't you? It's always good to be one move ahead of the military."

***

"We were lucky," Commander Mann said when he returned to Hudson's office some hours later. "The mining company stores old sensor data from the Tabora platform here on Nordheim. Regulations, in case of insurance claims and the like. I thought you might like to see this footage we turned up." He directed his words to the IS. "Run the file from where I marked it."

The holovid on Hudson's desk lit up, displaying the interior of the 'Star Struck' tavern on Tabora station. Bars like this abounded in Confederacy space, generic stops where spacers went for food, booze and to make contact with their own. Booths fitted with central tables and bench seats lined the walls, and round tables seating four or more dotted the rest of the floor. The place buzzed with conversation punctuated with clinking glasses and laughter. Two well-stacked girls stood behind the bar pouring drinks for a line of patrons, some standing, some perched on stools. Another two women in skimpy skirts and skimpier tops wove their way amongst the tables, giving the patrons something to look at while they served the drinks.

"This is where Grimani comes in, Sir," Commander Mann said, pointing at the flat screen in Hudson's office. "That's him there."

Troy Grimani had his back to the sensor. He walked into the room, glanced around in nonchalant fashion as if looking for somebody and ambled over to lean on the bar. He raised a finger to attract the barmaid and ordered a drink. She came back carrying a tall glass of what looked like ale.

He'd hardly swallowed more than a mouthful when his head rose. Something had attracted his attention, to his left. He picked up his glass and maneuvered his way along the bar next to another man, who looked up at him, eyebrows lifted, surprised.

The background din disappeared, edited out by the software.

"Rocket," Troy said. "How're you doin', mate?"

"Troy. What're you doing here? Thought you worked the Kentor run?" The new man swayed slightly.

"I do Kentor a fair bit but I do a run from Nordheim to here quite often," Grimani said. "I thought you were working out of Chollarc?"

"Nah. Dint like that job," the other man said, his voice slurred. He gulped down the last of whatever was in his glass and set it back on the benchtop.

"Why? What was wrong with it? Paid pretty well, didn't it?"

"Sure. Yeah. Wanted to be closer to home." He belched.

"Fast forward, please," Commander Mann said. "They move to a table. The conversation is lost. My techs can't do anything more with the signal. We pick up the action a bit later."

The footage sped up into comical action, showing the two men scampering to claim a nearby table when the patrons left. A girl scurried over to serve them another round of drinks, flashing her cleavage at the customers with a smile. She probably earned more from extra services than for serving beer.

The speed returned to normal.

"Gotta get outta this, Troy. Gotta get another job. 'S wrong."

Grimani leant over the table toward his friend. "Why? What's the problem?"

Rocket sagged, cradling his beer. "Don' like workin' with Toe Rags. Blue fuckin' bastards."

"Toe Rags? What're you talking about."

"Ship 'em out, hand 'em over to them." He shook his head. "T'ain't right."

"What do you mean? Hand what over?"

Rocket swayed in his chair. "Alfons. Alfons was there," he mumbled.

"Stev Alfons?" Grimani said. "But he was working up here, on Tabora."

"Sure as I'm sittin' here. Tip 've 'is finger missin'." The other man lifted his left hand and tried to unfold his ring finger. "Don' like it, Troy."

Grimani's body tensed, his hand clenching and unclenching on his glass.

"Captain Grimani. I think your friend's had enough, don't you?"

Grimani raised his head. A third man, stiff and out of place in his maroon business suit, had approached the table where the two sat.

"Do we know who this is?" Hudson asked.

"His name is Orlando. He's an under-manager on the station," Mann said.

"Has something happened to Stev Alfons?" Grimani said.

Orlando shrugged. "He terminated his contract here, left weeks ago. It happens all the time."

Rocket swayed, lifted a hand to point a wavering finger at Orlando, his lips working to form words.

The manager forestalled him, pulling the man to his feet. "He's drunk. Look, I'll get him to his bed. Why don't you come by my office and we'll discuss the next shipment? I have some equipment I need to get to Nordheim for repair."

"Sure." Grimani's expression lightened, smiling at someone Hudson couldn't see. "I'll catch you later."

Orlando slipped an arm around Rocket's shoulders and led him away between the tables.

Grimani came toward the camera and shared an embrace with another man.

"That's Grimani's first officer, Santhias Dekstra," Mann said. He turned the display off. "Rocket's real name is Rodney Rawlings. He had a fall from the balcony of his room not long after he left here. Fell three levels and got himself impaled on an antennae. Not nice. They found a smashed bottle of rum beside his body."

"Who is this Alfons person?"

"A miner called Stev Alfons worked on Tabora some time ago. He broke the contract and left early. It's not uncommon, the place loses workers hand over fist."

Hudson drummed his fingers on his armrest. A drunken accident, a bashing and a military boarding. Each incident explained, the association coincidental. None of it merited his attention if it was all true. And yet. Rawlings worked for the Ptorix? Handing what over to them? In exchange for what?

"Should we share this with the Militia, Sir?" Mann asked.

"No. I expect they already know as much of this as they want. Did they investigate Dekstra's bashing? Or the death of this other fellow, Rawlings?"

"The case on Dekstra has been closed. Insufficient evidence, no chance of finding the culprits. Rawlings' death was declared accidental."

"What if they were carrying something for the Ptorix, though? Something like starhearts."

The intelligence officer's eyes widened. "Now that would be a prize worth killing for."

"Yes indeed. Admiral Gordon told me one stone sold for… five million, I think he said, not long ago." Hudson fingered his chin. "The Ptorix prize them, too. It's hard to imagine what they would exchange for starhearts."

"Weapons? Intelligence?"

Hudson lifted his shoulder. "Who knows? See what you can find out. And while you're at it, find out what you can about the relationship between Grimani and Dekstra."

Mann grinned. "You noticed it, too?"

"Very good friends, hmmm?"

The smile still on his face, Mann stood, saluted, and left Hudson's office.

Hudson asked the IS to find the article about the sale of the starheart Gordon had mentioned. Yes, five million. A picture of the stone accompanied the article about the sale. From what he knew, this stone wasn't even a particularly good example, the fire blazing in the stone's red heart more like embers than flames. Yet he gazed at the holographic image, turning it from one side to another, for far too long. It was almost an effort to banish the thing from his desk.

Starhearts. As far as Hudson knew, no-one had found a deposit in any human systems. The Ptorix kept their sources to themselves but there weren't very many. He'd seen a picture of the one in the *Khophir's* crown, a jewel they called the dragon's eye. No Ptorix would give up a starheart lightly. They were worth more than enough without having to trade with humans. Even so, central intel recently mentioned reports of starhearts appearing in odd places.

Hudson rubbed his face. He was getting ahead of himself. This could have nothing at all to do with starhearts, it probably didn't. He'd have to arrange a further chat with Jess Sondijk. If she knew this Rawlings fellow, perhaps she would have some more revelations for him. Besides, he'd promised to call her. That could be fun. Longford was right. She was a very beautiful woman. And a challenge.

Chapter Eight

Jess pulled Troy's special bag down from the back of the closet. He used to call it his smuggler's toolkit, a collection of tools, devices and gadgets that a smuggler or a burglar might find handy in case of emergency. He'd been a wild lad before they married; until they had Tenna. She threw Troy's 'invisible' suit, neatly packed in a protective bag, onto the bed and rummaged through a set of universal keys, suction caps for wall climbs, slender rope, special night glasses to detect a much wider range of radiation. Ah. This was what she wanted, a black, nail-shaped object.

The snooper stick; a data stick with a special connection that fitted ID scanner slots. They'd paid a lot of money for this on Kentor. She checked through the identities Troy had stolen. Her nerves tingled when she found Tanaka's was there. She'd hoped it would be but the confirmation felt odd. Why would Troy have pulled Tanaka's ID? She shrugged the thought away as something to consider later. Right now, unless Tanaka had changed his code, this should get her into his building and into his files.

The device lay in her palm, anonymous and innocent. Maybe Troy had left some other useful bits and pieces on that data stick. She connected via her implant and checked through the folders. Stuff she'd expect; one for Kentor, one for the Tabora platform, one for Renala where they made occasional deliveries. And one marked 'Other'. He'd put a password on it.

Damn and blast.

Birthdays? She tried his, hers, Tenna's. Hang on. Fool. She knew how to work out his passwords for *Kimberley*. What had it been? Month and year through the scrambler with the next word of the ship's procedures manual with eight letters or more, providing the key. Eighteen months ago it had been 'activate'. Or had it been 'stationary'? She ran the calculation on her comlink and keyed the letters in. Right the first time. The layout for Tanaka's warehouse appeared on her comlink's screen. This was starting to look more and more suspicious. What had Troy needed this for?

Whatever. This could get her into the warehouse. Not the front door, though, surely? There had to be a side entrance. She peered at the layout, concentrating on the foyer. Yes. Back of the foyer, around a corner and into the alley beside the building. She thought she'd seen an 'exit' sign when she visited earlier. An emergency exit which connected to a stairwell. However high-tech your building was, there still had to be a manual escape route.

She took a deep breath, sucking air into her lungs. Years had passed since she'd done a break-and-enter, retrieving stolen goods from a crooked dealer. They'd been fun, then. Dangerous, adrenalin-rush fun. Would she still have the necessary skills? Let the games begin.

The 'invisible' suit, set to standard black, shrunk to fit her form, molding to her body like a second skin. Jess caught the lift down to the basement and fired up Troy's in-line skimmer. Looking at the machine brought back memories. They'd ridden klicks on this thing, him driving, her behind, zooming along the back tracks of the mountains back in the days before Tenna was born. They'd gone away for weekends in the woods, camping up near Lake Maribou. She hadn't thrown a leg over since he died.

Settled in the seat she activated the sensor to open the basement door. It clicked and rose into the ceiling, allowing access to the street. Jess overrode the skimmer's auto-drive function. No point in sneaking out at night and leaving the evidence of where she'd been on the machine's system.

She pushed the throttle on. The nose lifted, flinging her back in the saddle. Shit. Too fast. She throttled back, only just avoiding a scrape along the wall. *Relax, let yourself remember.* She juggled the balance until she had it right, then let the skimmer glide up the ramp into the road, the door dropping into place behind her. At this time of night residential Orham City slept, at least for the most part. An automated cleaner bot rounded a corner up ahead but the road was free of traffic. Jess drove easily, enjoying the throb of the beast beneath her. She had clipped the sensor detection pen on her shirt and her Calvin C40 light laser pistol sat in its holster at her hip.

Tanaka's floodlit warehouse stood silent. She parked the in-line in the darkness under a tree in a nearby park and ambled up the street toward the building, hoping nobody was about. She'd activated the camouflage capability of the 'invisible' suit but she wasn't invisible to the naked eye even if it did change color to match its surroundings. After a quick glance around she strode down the alley looking for the side door. She found the entrance closer to the back of the building than the front, set into a recess in the wall.

The 'invisible' suit deflected any radiation, so the sensor at the door ignored her presence. She pushed Troy's data stick, set to Tanaka's ID, into the port at the entrance and held her breath. Sliding the door aside the IS said '*welcome, Mister Tanaka*'.

Jess put on Troy's night glasses and slipped through the door. Tanaka was like most people; if the InfoDroid said the system was secure, it must be. But every IS had to have some sort of override in case of mechanical failure. No doubt about it, Tanaka was a wheeler, not a burglar.

She tiptoed up the emergency stairs, aware of every soft shoe-scrape on the hard risers, slipped into the admin section on the second floor and hurried along the carpeted corridors to Tanaka's office. *Take it easy, now.* Reception wasn't too difficult, the single sensor ignored her. The man's inner office would be a different matter. Her heart hammering, she activated the door. It slid aside. Three narrow beams of red light danced in the doorway, infrared detector beams, moving at random, changing angles to prevent anyone jumping over them. They would have recognized Tanaka's implant and switched off but she didn't have his implant and she didn't have an override.

These things were activated when the beam was broken. If she could turn them off for long enough to get through, then turn them on again, that might be okay. She licked her lips. She'd have to be fast. Troy's warehouse map showed where the beams came from. Using the spy detector she toggled the switch. Off, leap through, on. She waited in the darkness, holding her breath. No alarms, no reaction. So far, so good, but she'd better hurry.

She slid a data stick into the port, looking through the menu system for forms and procedures. Ah. Authorizations. Permission to Enter. She found one already completed for *Kimberley* for Tanaka's chief engineer, Serg Jankovich, and downloaded a copy of the form. The clever little program on that ruinously expensive data stick allowed her to make the few changes to add her ID and tomorrow's date. That should get her on board her husband's old ship, no questions asked.

She paused, scanning her surroundings and sensors. Still quiet.

With the output directed to her comlink she entered 'Troy Bertrand Grimani' into the file system's search function. A list of contracts appeared in date order; jobs he'd done for Tanaka. They might be worth a better look later on. She saved them.

Lights flared outside. Her heart raced. Headlights. A flying vehicle, coming this way, fast. Oh, fuck. Back through the infrared beam, off, jump, on. She raced along the corridor and clattered down the stairs two at a time. Thrusters hissing, the vehicle landed outside the front of the building. Jess darted through the side door into the alley and scurried, bent double, around the back of the building. Muffled thuds and running feet. They'd gone in the front door but the copter idled, its engine thrumming in the night. She edged around a row of heavy vehicles standing side by side in the back lot, heading for the opposite side of the warehouse. Lights came on inside the building, flooding the ground floor show room. They'd be upstairs by now. A figure appeared at the corner of the alley. She froze against the side of a heavy lifter while a beam swept around and prayed the camouflage would be enough.

The figure disappeared. She breathed in deeply through her nose, aware of the artery throbbing in her neck. The lights went out. The copter took off, circled a few times and flew away. Jess waited.

The noise of the engines died away. Still she waited. One second ... two.

The copter roared back, swept around in a low arc, bright lights sweeping the ground. The suit registered a pass from an infrared detector, deflected. The machine swept around once, twice, three times, low and slow. God, any lower and they'd hear the thunder of her heart. At last, it banked away, the sound of the engine receding into silence.

Weak-kneed, Jess leaned against the heavy lifter. That was close. Hopefully they'd think they attended a false alarm, a glitch with the beam in Tanaka's office. She shoved herself away from the vehicle and loped back down the alley to recover the in-line. She'd need to get a bit of sleep to prepare for the next adventure tomorrow.

Chapter Nine

"The elevator has arrived at the space station. Please make sure you have all your belongings with you. We wish you a safe journey to your destination."

Buckles clicked along the row of seats. Passengers stood, snapped lockers open to drag out belongings and carried bags down the aisle to the exit. Stretching her shoulders, Jess followed the other people into reception.

Cynthia sat behind her desk, checking in the new arrivals. Her eyebrows lifted in surprise when she saw Jess. "Back already?"

Damn. The last thing she needed was to attract attention to herself.

"Not for long. I forgot some things. Must have been too excited about coming home. I'll be back for the next trip down, I imagine. Look, I'll need to hire an exo-suit. I don't want to air the whole ship up just for a quick visit."

"Sure." Cynthia pressed a few keys. "You'll have to pay for half a day?"

Jess shrugged. Whatever.

"You pick up the suit down at the main stores. You know where."

"Thanks."

She checked in and rode the transit, then the pedolator out to the docking bays on the station's rim. The fellow at the store handed her an exo-suit and pointed out a change room. She dressed in the silver suit and carried the helmet. No point in wasting air in here.

A short trip on the pedolator took her to the corridor leading to maintenance bay F-3, where *Kimberley* hung at her station, the airlock in place beyond a locked gate.

Jess waved the data stick with its forged credentials at the gate sensor. After a moment's delay while the processor checked, the gate unlatched with an audible click. Inside the airlock, Jess put on her helmet and pressed the button to revert to vacuum.

"*Are you sure?*" The station's IS spoke the words at the same time as they flashed on a screen.

"Yes. I have breathing apparatus."

She walked down the passage to the ship's entrance and waited for pressure to equalize. The warning light still flashed VACUUM VACUUM but the hatch slid open. Jess stepped inside the ship and floated.

46

"Hello, Mister Jankovich. Should I activate systems?" the IS said.

"No, I won't be here long."

She turned on the suit's headlamp and pulled herself along the corridor, using the handholds put in place for just this purpose.

She reached the hatch to the cargo hold, opened it and drifted inside. *Kimberley's* hold was much larger than *Saintly Maid's*. She did a slow somersault, just because she could. Weightlessness was fun. For a while. She floated, moving slowly so she could illuminate the corners and wondered why she'd bothered. Nothing to see apart from rows of empty racking waiting to be filled. If there had been anything here, it would be long gone now.

She spun around, scrambled back up to the bridge and into the captain's seat, hooking her feet under the console to keep herself in place.

"Show me the logs. Anything for Captain Grimani's last flight from Tabora."

"Searching..."

The IS displayed 2D images taken from sensors on the bridge and in the hold. At first the images were boringly routine, Troy in the captain's chair, the Vera woman, Troy again, going through the in-flight checks. Until the ship was boarded, not long after she left the jump gate at Nordheim. Vera had been in the captain's chair.

"We're going to be boarded, Grimani," she said. "I don't like this; I don't like this one bit."

"Relax, Vera. There's nothing on board for them to get their knickers in a knot about. You stay there. I'll deal with them."

Vera looked as though she'd sucked on a sour fruit. All she had to do was tell the IS to heave to and sit still. Silly bitch.

"What's happening at the airlock?" Jess asked the IS. "In fact for now, show me Troy, nobody else. I want to see what happens with him."

"Just a moment," the IS said. *"I'll sort the data."*

Troy stood at the airlock, waiting for the boarding party. The hatch slid aside and four people appeared, three men and a woman, armed and wearing the battle armor of the local Militia.

"G'day, folks. What can I do for you?" *Troy looked a little bit tense, but he would, wouldn't he?*

"We'll be doing a search of your cargo hold," said one of the men. "Acker, you and Dax go up to the bridge, check their manifests and so on and keep an eye on the duty officer. Zet, you stay here. Let's see your cargo hold, Grimani."

"Sure."

Troy led him along the passage through the common room, out of the hatch and into the hold. He opened the lockers one by one. Nothing to see.

At least, Jess assumed so. Those bays were for smaller, specialized items. Troy slapped a panel to open the hatch into the main hold and stepped inside, the trooper behind him. The hold's sensor took over.

Troy stood, his hands lifted, palms up. "Here you are. Not a thing." He folded his arms.

The sensor followed the soldier moving around the bay, checking corners, running his hands over panels. Troy disappeared when the man moved in front of the single sensor. She saw the soldier's face clearly for a fraction of a second as he glanced up at the camera. Then he spun around.

"Hey. What the fuck do you think you're doing?" the trooper said. A blast of energy flared at almost the same time the words were spoken, accompanied by the hiss-zip of an M3.

Jess winced, closing her eyes. This was the moment Troy had died. They'd never shown her this footage but she'd never asked to see it.

When she opened her eyes again the soldier had bent over Troy, who lay spread-eagled on his back.

Running footsteps rang in the corridor.

"Sarge?"

The trooper bending over Troy straightened and turned to face the new arrival.

"I'm okay. Bastard pulled a gun on me. See?" He pointed at a pistol lying near Troy's hand.

"Shit. Is he ... is he dead?"

"Yeah. I'll have to write a report."

"Hang on," Jess said. "Play it again from where they went into the bay."

Troy stood, the sensor followed the trooper, who moved between Troy and the sensor. The trooper turned, yelled his warning, then fired. She wished she could see more, but the system in the hold wasn't designed for surveillance. It collected information about air quality, temperature, shifts of cargo and took visuals because it could.

The trooper's bulk had obscured Troy but that could have been coincidence. Troy did carry a weapon in his flight suit. They said the gun fell from his hand. But it didn't make sense. Why would he pull a gun?

Something was wrong. What? One more time through the sequence. She saw the trooper's face, then he whirled and fired. Would he have had time to see Troy reach for a gun? Troy hadn't made a sound. She enhanced the volume, stepped through the sequence to be sure she hadn't missed anything. No. She'd be willing to stake anything that the sergeant had deliberately placed his body between the sensor and Troy before he shot him.

In which case Troy had been, quite deliberately, shot dead. He'd been murdered.

Murdered.

The word sawed around her head, a screech that set her teeth on edge. Jess tried to run a hand back through her hair and hit the helmet. She started to drift upwards. Shit. Hooking her feet back in place, she tried to slow her racing heart. A botched accident was one thing. Murder; that was something else again. Why? Was Troy carrying something on the ship? A cache of Nervana, but back from Tabora? But he wouldn't carry drugs, they never had. Fine wine, material, even jewelry but never drugs. She'd always thought the Militia had planted the drugs to cover up the botched raid. But if that wasn't the reason, why?

Jess played the images again. It was half a minute before the other soldier appeared in the bay. By which time the sergeant was bent over Troy, his back to the camera, checking for a pulse or something. Though how he'd have a pulse with a hole blasted in his chest... She couldn't see what he was doing. What if he'd pulled out Troy's gun, dropped it beside the body? He must have done. From what she could remember of the hearing the man said he'd found the drugs after he'd shot Troy, in a nearby compartment. She could hardly tell them he'd never hide anything in the cargo hold. She might have had to tell them where.

"Shut it down," she said.

Outside the ship a river of stars shone diamond bright amongst the litter of gases and debris that made up the spiral arm. In a way it was a perception, an illusion. Some of those stars no longer existed, blown into smithereens long before their last light arrived in the back of her retina. Maybe what she saw on these log files was a sleight of hand, much more than a none-too-subtle cover-up of a botched boarding.

She needed an ally. Santh.

Jess unhooked her toes and pushed away from the console toward the exit to the common room, and down to the external hatch. She stepped carefully into the access tunnel, knowing her feet would slam onto the floor when the artificial gravity took hold. Back on the station she took off her helmet and shook out her hair. By the time she got the exo-suit back to the store she had missed the next car down the elevator to the planet's surface. Never mind. There was always kaff in the boarding lounge and she had plenty to think about.

The vending machine on the station-side wall of the lounge hissed steam as it frothed the contents of the cup. Jess slid the kaff out of the slot and found a table close to the view screen. She never tired of watching the world turn below her. Cloud was gathering over the northern parts of the planet. They'd get snow falls in the mountains pretty soon, she'd reckon. By contrast much of the equator basked in sunshine.

"Jess. What brings you here?"

She gazed up at the man smiling down at her, kaff in hand. Ron Bates, one of the station's engineers. She grinned back.

"Ron. Take a seat."

He sank onto a chair and placed his cup on the table between them.

"They overheat these things, don't you think?" he said, shaking his fingers to cool them.

"Certainly do. You'd think they'd provide cups with better insulation."

"I'm surprised to see you up here. You've only been in port a few days."

"Yes, true," Jess said. "I wouldn't normally be back. But I forgot something. You know how it is. Stupid."

"So you've been on the *Maid*?"

Apprehension tied a knot in her belly. She'd have to be careful. He'd know she had no need to visit *Kimberley*. Besides, she hadn't used her own ID.

"Stupid. I had to come back for some clothes I forgot."

"Is that so? When was this?"

Oh, shit. If he'd been working on *Saintly Maid*, he'd know she hadn't been there. Her heart thudded painfully in her chest. "Have you been working on her? I must have missed you. Just in and out, you know?"

"I finished a half hour ago." He sipped at his coffee. "She's good to go. You look after her, not like some of the other spacejocks."

"Must have just missed you," she said.

"Must have done. Well, there you go."

Jess covered the relief with a smile. Phew. That was close.

Chapter Ten

Jess said goodbye to Ron at the spaceport and caught an autocab home, where she kicked off her shoes and dropped onto the couch. So what had she learnt? To be honest, not much. Not proof, anyway. Troy had been murdered. Okay, she'd accept that. Why?

She pulled the data stick out of her pocket and waved it at Jeeves's data ports.

"Have a rummage through Troy's trips for Tanaka, will you, Jeeves? Put them up in date order and tell me if there's anything odd about any of them."

"*Certainly, Jess.*"

She lay back and closed her eyes while Jeeves sucked the data in and carried out its analysis.

"*This one seems unusual.*"

Her eyes snapped open. "In what respect?"

"*The* Kimberley *carried bodies.*"

Jess shot up, eyes wide open. "What?" Bodies ... but they could be vehicle bodies, something like that. Couldn't they?

"*Yes. Twenty bodies instead of the usual cargoes of perishable goods for Tabora or trade goods for Kentor.*"

"What sort of bodies?"

"*The record doesn't say.*"

Information Systems weren't quite as smart as people thought they were. Great at sorting, great at math but the inference engines could only get so far.

"Show me."

Jeeves displayed what little data existed. Tabora to Kentor, about two weeks before Troy was killed. Human bodies. The names were listed in alphabetical order by family name and the manifesto recorded delivery was to be made to a crematorium on Bylgara Island on Kentor. Why would *Kimberley* have been used for that?

Time to talk to Santh.

***

"What? Who's this?" Santh sounded half asleep.

"It's Jess, Santh. Let me in. Open your basement, I've come on Troy's in-line."

"Jess? Bloody hell, give a man a break. Just a minute."

The connection went dead. Jess waited outside the basement door of Santh's apartment block. Machinery whirring, the doors slid apart. Jess parked the in-line before catching the lift up to Santh's floor. He'd opened the doors for her and stood in the sitting room, bleary eyed and tousled, in jeans and bare feet.

"What have you been doing?" she said. "You look a mess."

"Had a few drinks with some mates last night, didn't I. Didn't get back till lunchtime."

"How about some kaff? Looks like we could both use some."

He straggled off to the kitchen while she sagged into a modern, angular chair that proved to be remarkably comfortable. That was Santh. Modern, contemporary, bright colors. Not her taste at all. The smell of the brewing kaff filled the room. Oh, she was looking forward to this. If not to the conversation.

Santh put a bright green, square cup down in front of her and sat opposite her. "So where have you been?"

"Last night I broke into Tanaka's place."

His eyes widened, cup halfway to his lips. "You did what?"

"Only just got out, too. He had an infrared beam across his office door. I switched it off for long enough to get in and switched it back on again, you know, like a power blink. But that, or something else, summoned some off-site security people. I managed to hide around the back while they poked around, then skedaddled."

Santh gulped down some kaff and gazed at her over the cup's rim. "You gonna tell me why you broke into Tanaka's?"

"I went to Tanaka's to forge an authorization so I could get on the *Kimberley* to see her logs."

Santh sagged in the chair, his mouth open. "What the fuck for?"

"The night before, I went to dinner at the Mountain View with Admiral Hudson—"

"The Mountain View, huh? Did he expect you to pay for dinner?" He waggled his eyebrows.

"Pay? No." No, that's not what he meant. "Oh, you blokes are all the same. No, no sex. Dinner. May I go on, please?"

"Did you have a lovers' spat?"

"Don't interrupt. We talked about Troy."

Santh put his cup down, the grin gone. "And?"

"Hudson said a few things that got me thinking. Like what really happened that day? You know—different crew because you were bashed. Drugs going from Tabora to Nordheim, not the other way around. How it looked like a cover-up, which he agreed. And he asked me if I wanted another investigation."

He snorted. "What's the point? I saw the original one."

"That's what I said. But... I dunno. He seemed to think it was odd."

"And?"

"That's what I did today. I went and downloaded the footage from *Kimberley's* security systems for that day. It's inconclusive. It doesn't show Troy being shot. At least, you can't *see* him being shot because the trooper is between him and the sensor."

"Well, shit, eh? He's dead, though, and the Militia said they shot him. I don't get it, Jess. You've said for ages they bumped Troy off by accident and they've been covering their asses ever since. What's different?"

"What's different is I'm starting to think he was killed deliberately."

Santh's brow wrinkled.

"I played that footage a few times. I don't see how the guy could've seen Troy pull a gun. He was facing the wrong way. And he can't have heard anything, either. So it wasn't a botched boarding. He was stopped so they could murder him."

He bowed his head, rubbing his hand up and down his thigh. She waited while he dealt with it, sipping her kaff until the cup was empty.

"You're sure?" he said.

"No. But that's how it looks to me."

The silence between them grew. At last Santh said, "Why? Why would they kill him?"

"I don't know. And I can't be certain. That's why I'm here. If it's true it must have something to do with what was on the ship or something."

"It could have been drugs."

"We've been through that. Troy wouldn't carry drugs. You know that."

"Not knowingly but maybe Vera did."

"She's a whining pain in the butt but she's not a drug courier. I still say the Militia brought it on the raid with them. So if it wasn't drugs, what?"

Santh scratched a hand back through his hair. "He'd been a bit edgy before we took that last trip up to Tabora. I figured he was worried about Tenna."

"What did you take? What was the shipment?"

"The usual. Perishables, spare parts. Nothing special."

"Nothing ... extra?"

"Smuggled stuff?" He shook his head. "We never took extras to Tabora. That was always just Kentor."

"Um ... one odd thing ... a couple of months before Troy died you carried bodies?"

Santh nodded. "Uh-huh. We were taking them to Kentor. Usually *Beaconsfield* had that job but she was in dock for five months for repair."

"Oh." She'd expected a bit more of a reaction from him.

"It's the guys who die up there whose bodies aren't claimed. Their families can't afford to bring them home, they don't have families or whatever. They get taken to be disposed of." He scratched his ear. "I don't think I want to know what happens before they go into the fire."

"What do you mean? You stick a body in a bag and shove it in an airless cargo hold, don't you?"

"You could, but they don't, otherwise they'd desiccate. That's one of the reasons I'd rather not know what happens to them. The bodies are stored in special, aired-up cylinders that are kept just above freezing, like a meat store. I wondered if they took organs and sold them on or something, you know?"

"Yuck."

He shrugged. "They're dead; they wouldn't know. I guess it could help somebody, somewhere. Anyway, at Kentor guys came and picked them up, took them away in sleds. Troy and I didn't even talk about it."

No, she'd bet on that. Lots of other, unsavory, ideas came to mind, many concerning food. Her stomach roiled. Okay, scratch that one. "Let's move on. Tell me everything you can remember about that last trip."

Santh relaxed into his chair. For a moment he didn't say anything, staring at something only he could see.

"It was a normal trip. We carried perishables; fruit, veg, meat, eggs. I checked the cargo on, made sure the temperature was correct in the sealed units. Troy was irritable, as though he had something on his mind. I asked but he nearly bit my head off. He apologized, said he was worried about Tenna."

"He probably was. She was on life-support." While she, Jess, hoped and prayed the nanobots would do their job and bring her back undamaged. God, what a horrible time it had been.

"Anyway, when we got to Tabora, he went off to register, as normal. I had a wander around, checking out the shops and later I went to meet Troy in the 'Star Struck'."

He frowned. "Now I come to think of it, Troy was talking with two guys at a table when I first walked in. It was no happy chat. You know how he used to drum his fingers when he was upset?" Santh demonstrated the movement, the fingers of his left hand thrumming on his thigh.

Jess had seen the same often enough, a sign of suppressed nerves. "So who were these guys?"

Santh shook his head. "Don't know. I wasn't looking. Troy saw me and gave me a smile and a wave. The other fellows left."

"What? Walked out?"

"Um... I think maybe the guy Troy had been talking with helped the guy at the table. I didn't take much notice. Troy and I had a bite to eat and a drink. Oh, yes. I'd forgotten. I asked him what the business in the pub was about and he said the man at the table reckoned he'd seen Alfons. Remember him? Mid height, had a piece missing from a finger?"

Jess searched her mind. No match. "Not really. But what about him?"

"To be honest, I don't know." He pulled at his lip for a moment. "Troy and I spent some time with Alfons here and there. We knew him pretty well. I even worked with him for a while before I met you two. You know how it is with spacers. He owned his own ship, a contract freighter, but it was pretty decrepit. He told us in a pub on Kentor that he'd taken a job at Tabora to earn some quick money so he could afford repairs."

"So what?"

"Yeah, good question. Alfons left before the contract expired but that happens all the time. It seemed to bother Troy, though." Santh lifted a shoulder. "Anyway, we went off for a meal. We didn't talk about it anymore."

Santh frowned, rubbed at his nose. "Troy said he had to meet somebody. I wanted to go with him but he said no, he'd meet me at the ship. So I decided to go back to the pub."

He stared at his hands for a moment. Jess waited. This must be difficult for him. The attack had left him a mess. He'd been lucky the doctors had been able to recover his good looks.

"You know what Tabora's like; rough and tough and ugly and when the miners come in from the job they head straight for the boozer to drink the place out of their systems. Well, two guys lurched out of the 'Star Struck', both drunk as galahs. One bumps into me and accuses me of trying to grope him. I back off, sorry, sorry." Santh raised his hands, illustrating as he spoke. "Then he goes berserk, accusing me of being a poofter ass-licker, slamming into me with a fist like a ham. That's the last I remember."

He leaned forward in his chair, his eyes hooded. "It does sound a bit cozy. Troy talks to somebody, I'm bashed, then Troy dies."

Santh stared outside where the light glowed with the yellowish tinge of late afternoon. Shaking his head, he turned back to her.

"Still, Jess. You can't bring Troy back and if they're happy to kill him, what would they do to you, or Tenna?" He laid a hand on her arm. "Let it go, Jess-babe. You can't change the past."

Jess didn't miss the look in his eyes, far away, pained, haunted.

Chapter Eleven

Jess stood on the balcony staring at the clouds on the horizon. She'd had an awful night. Damn Hudson. She'd put Troy's death out of her mind and now he'd opened up old wounds, raised questions she couldn't answer. Somehow, she'd have to persuade Santh to help her find answers, otherwise she'd never rest easy.

"*You have a visitor, Jess,*" Jeeves said.

She wandered inside, a half-empty cup in her hand. Santh? No, Jeeves would've said. Anyway, it was too early. "Who is it?"

"*A gentleman from the Militia.*" Jeeves showed her the figure at the door, dressed in everyday Nordheim Militia blue. A sergeant.

"Ask him what he wants. Oh, hang on. I'll do it myself."

Jeeves turned on the intercom, no visuals.

"What can I do for you, Sergeant?" Jess said.

He spun around to face the door. "I'm to escort you to Headquarters, ma'am."

"Is that so? On whose orders and what for?"

"Admiral Hudson's, ma'am and I don't know."

Hudson. Alarm bells rang. She hadn't expected to hear from him so soon, and certainly not like this. Now what would he be wanting? Surely they hadn't found out about Tanaka's? Or *Kimberley*? She could refuse, but that would be suspicious.

"All right. But you'll have to wait. I'm not dressed."

She selected a conservative, navy-blue suit and sensible shoes, put on some lipstick, pulled a comb through her hair and made sure no cleavage was on display. This was going to be a business meeting whether he liked it or not.

The sergeant waited outside the door, hands clasped behind his back. "If you'll come this way, ma'am."

He led her to a waiting skimmer, black, low and unmarked. The backdoor slid aside and she climbed in. Another figure already sat there, pulling at his lower lip with his teeth.

"Santh. Hello."

He managed a grin. "Do you know what this is about?"

"No." She raised her hands, palms up. *"Can't be much,"* she said via his implant. *"Have you done anything they might find interesting?"*

"No."

And if they picked up that conversation, good luck to them. Why would Hudson want to see them? The break-in at Tanaka's was a police problem, not Militia, and certainly not Star Fleet. And the visit to *Kimberley* was above board. Mainly. If she could settle down the throbbing of her pulse, she could maybe even convince herself.

***

Hudson rose from his chair when Jess and Dekstra entered the sitting room he'd appropriated in Nordheim Militia's administrative building. "Good day to you, Captain and to you, Mister Dekstra." He nodded at the escort. "You may go."

She folded her arms. Not impressed, not impressed at all, but also a hint of caution in those stormy grey eyes. Dekstra's eyes darted around. Nervous, twitchy.

"What have I done now?" she said. "This had better not be another strip-search."

Dekstra started to giggle. She skewered him with a glare and he cleared his throat. Hudson rubbed his hand over his mouth to smother the smile. Not the right time to consider that sort of thing.

"I had a few questions to ask. I was here, you were nearby. I won't keep you long." He gestured at the comfortable chairs grouped around the table.

She plonked herself in an armchair, legs crossed, while Dekstra perched on the edge of a second. "Well?"

"What can you tell me about Rodney Rawlings?"

They exchanged a look of surprise. "Rocket Rawlings?" Jess said. "He's a freighter captain. I might have met him once or twice."

"He was an acquaintance," Dekstra said.

"Not a friend?"

Dekstra shook his head. "No. He worked some of the same routes we did. Owned his own freighter that had seen better times. We came across him a few times in bars."

"What can you tell me about him?" Hudson asked.

"Not much." Dekstra fingered his chin. "He liked a drink, gambled a bit."

"Captain Sondijk?"

She shook her head slowly. "I don't recall the guy. Obviously not a stand-out."

No suspicious response. They were careful, a little bit nervous—especially Dekstra—but he'd expect that. "When did you see him last?"

"Oh, gee, it must be three years ago. On a trip to Kentor." Dekstra said. "He said something about moving his operation to Chollarc."

"Ah. So you never saw him on Tabora?"

"Tabora?" Dekstra put his fingers to his lips while the wheels turned in his head. His eyes widened as the lights came on. He shot a glance at Jess, then back to Hudson. "Yeah. Last trip, just before Troy was killed. We saw him in the pub."

She didn't react to the information, simply frowned. "What's this got to do with us?"

"His name was mentioned in connection with starhearts. You can only get them from the Ptorix and there are no official channels."

Jess almost rolled her eyes. "Oh, so we're back to smuggling. I've never even *seen* a real starheart." She turned to Dekstra. "You?"

"I've seen 'em, yeah. But that's all." Dekstra picked at the edge of the seat he sat on.

"Why are you asking us about Rawlings?" she said.

"He's dead. It seems he had an accident after talking to your husband at Tabora."

They looked at each other. No, he'd check with surveillance but he'd bet that was genuine surprise, followed by concern. Why should they be concerned?

She straightened. "You're not suggesting Troy had anything—"

He raised his voice. "The death is described as accidental, with excessive alcohol a major contributing factor. He fell over a balcony while drunk." She subsided again, deflating into the chair.

"Gee." Dekstra swallowed. "I didn't know that, Sir."

"It appears so." He'd done enough to impress Dekstra, but not the lovely Jess.

"Look, why are *you* asking these questions? You have investigators, don't you?" she said.

He grinned. "Why should they have all the fun? Dekstra, wait outside."

She glowered at him, but Dekstra obediently struggled to his feet and headed for the door.

"Wait for me, Santh," she said as he left the room.

Hudson waited until the door closed behind her first officer. She met his gaze, assessing, evaluating. She wasn't particularly nervous but she was cautious.

"I wanted to ask you to dinner, lovely lady. Our previous meeting was far too brief. I'm told Aristide's is good."

She didn't answer immediately. He could almost see the cogs whirring. "When?"

"The sixth."

She shook her head. "Nope. I'll be away for a couple of weeks. School holidays with Tenna."

"No leave pass for a night out?"

Brushing a stray lock of hair away from her face she smiled that wonderful smile. "Not a chance. This is Tenna's two weeks."

A pity, such a pity. Ah well. He could wait for two weeks. Meanwhile, surveillance would keep an eye on her. "When will you be back?"

"She's back at school on the thirteenth."

And he was booked for two days at Ottenshaw's country estate on the fifteenth and sixteenth. "The evening of the fourteenth?"

She fingered her lower lip. "The fourteenth..." Her eyes tilted while she accessed her implant, then she shrugged. "Why not? I've got nothing better planned."

Oh, she was delicious. He laughed. "The fourteenth, Captain. I look forward to it." Enormously. Meanwhile, Delia Marati could provide a passable substitute. He supposed.

"That's it? I can go?"

"You may. I apologize for any inconvenience."

She stood and flashed him that wonderful, cheeky smile. "Yes, I'll bet you do. Until the fourteenth, Admiral."

A hint of perfume lingered when she left.

He steepled his hands on the arms of the chair. They'd reacted to the news about Rawlings, both of them. He'd be interested to see where this took them.

***

Jess grabbed Santh and headed out of the militia offices past the blue-clad guards at the entrance gates. She hailed a cab and had it take them to La Placa beach. Neither of them spoke a word until they'd parked themselves on a bench overlooking the sea. The fresh, salt-laden breeze that whipped up the whitecaps flicked Jess' hair back from her face.

"Well, wasn't that interesting?" she said. "So now we know, courtesy of Admiral Hudson, that Rocket Rawlings died after talking to Troy about Stev Alfons, you were bashed and Troy was killed. And that there's some connection with starhearts."

"It starts to make sense in a way," Santh murmured. "A lot of people would kill for starhearts."

"Maybe that's why Hudson asked me about Kentor and the Ptorix there."

Santh nodded, staring at the horizon. "I think I need to go visit Tabora. Maybe I should get me a job working in the mines for a while."

Jess jolted upright. "What for?"

He slung an arm around her shoulders and squeezed. "Jess, it's about Tabora. You won't get any answers here."

"Yet yesterday you were telling me to leave it."

"I've had some time to think. Troy, me, Alfons. And now Rawlings. Who else?"

Jess' spirits soared. Santh would help. "I'd say Tanaka's involved, too, but right now, I don't see how."

For a moment Santh seemed to disappear into his own thoughts, deeply sad. "I guess if Troy was murdered, I'd like to know who and why."

So did she. He was right, everything seemed to come back to Tabora. Sure, Hudson was manipulating them for some purpose of his own. Why else would he have told them about Rawlings? But what the hell, it was their purpose, too.

"But what are you going to say to get a job? You're a first officer on freighters."

"Doesn't pay as much as the miners get. It'd be just like Alfons. They get plenty of people wanting to make money fast. Don't worry about me."

"You'll keep in touch, though?"

He hugged her. "'Course I will. This is you 'n me finding out what happened to Troy."

They sat in silence for a moment while gulls circled in the sky above.

"What did he want you for? On your own?" Santh said, startling her.

"Who? Hudson?" He nodded. She grinned. "A quickie on the sofa."

Santh's eyes widened. "Aw, what? You're not serious?"

She could see Hudson in her mind, see his smile, those blue eyes. If she'd offered he wouldn't have said no. "No, I'm not. He's willing to work for it. He wants to take me to Aristide's."

"Aristide's, huh? Not sparing expense, is he?" He tapped the side of his nose. "Sweet surrender?"

She grinned. "Oh, getting a leg over is probably on his agenda. And I'll admit I could think of worse potential partners."

"Be careful, Jess," Santh said, putting a hand on her arm. "If he's looking for smugglers working out of Kentor, sex isn't the only thing on his mind."

"I'll see how I feel. It won't be till I get back from Paradise Cove. And I appreciate your concern, but Hudson could be useful to us, too. He has access to information we can't get."

"True." Santh hesitated, chewing his lip. "Do you like him?"

Like him? He was good looking, charming, good company. True, some of their date had been like an inquisition, but at least he'd apologized. Jess could imagine herself falling for a man like Hudson. He had that same easy, sexy charm that had attracted her to Troy. Only Hudson wasn't a devil-may-care adventurer, he was a very powerful man. An admiral. "Like is such a naff word, Santh. I quite fancy him as a man. And he's smart. But he's also a bit dangerous."

He sighed. "Yeah. But it's time you got yourself somebody. Tenna needs a father."

"And you think a handsome womanizer like Hudson fits the bill, do you? No thanks, all the same. She's exceedingly fond of her Uncle Santh, though."

"And I'm exceedingly fond of her," he replied, his smile wide.

It was a bit of banter. Santh was a great friend, someone she could rely on. His sexuality was not, never had been, an issue. "Look, are you sure about getting a job on Tabora?" Jess asked.

"Yes. Gotta start somewhere."

"Yes, but up there, after what they did to you."

"Got a better suggestion?"

She hadn't. He was right but the whole thing reeked of danger. "Okay. But I want you to go along to Yasser Siemens and have your ID altered. I'll pay."

His jaw dropped. "That costs ... that's expensive."

"I'm a bit keen on the idea of you being safe. Seems to me quite a few people associated with Troy ended up dead."

"Jess, can you afford that? What with Tenna?"

"We do all right, don't we? And I got a huge pay-out when Troy died." A lot of which she'd used to buy *Saintly Maid*. But still.

"Yeah, well, thanks. I'll admit I'd rather not be that poofter Dekstra."

Chapter Twelve

Santh shouldered his pack and joined the line of brand new miners waiting to disembark onto the Tabora mining platform. He scratched at his hair, now ridiculously short and almost black. They could have hung him upside down and used him for a sander. He'd never forgive Brian. He'd said short but he'd been cut so close he was almost bald.

The line shuffled along, ten men aiming to earn a fortune and go home rich. The fellow in front of him stood a whole head taller than him with shoulders to match, while the one behind, about his height, was stick thin. All types, from all over, all after a fortune. Once in the airlock, the pace picked up.

He stepped out of the hatch and onto the platform, so like any other space station. Their boots clanging on the floor, the men were herded out of the docking area and into the platform itself, most gazing around them. He was probably one of the few who'd actually been to this gods forsaken joint before, drab utilitarian form-work disappearing into the distance above and below, covered with bad paintings of various landscapes to hide the shabbiness.

A man dressed in maroon Company uniform waited for the new arrivals.

"Are we all here?" he said, smiling when they'd gathered around him.

Well, he should know, shouldn't he? He went through the names, ticking them off on a sheet. Santh almost forgot his adopted name was Jim Jonson.

"Welcome to Tabora. My name's Mister Orlando," said smiling boy in the maroon suit. "I'll show you your accommodation first, then I'll take you on an orientation tour."

Santh tramped along behind Orlando, who led them to a lift. The man was quite cute, nice butt, but he had one of those smiles with too many teeth. The car zoomed up eight levels, where they straggled out again into the accommodation block.

At least they each had their own room. If you could call it that. Santh dumped his pack on the bed. Standing here if he held out an arm and stretched a little he could touch the wall on the other side of the bed and the other way he could touch the closet door with his elbow bent. The shared ablutions block was down a fenced-off walkway. They'd built the accommodation around one of the utility cores, lots of vacant space punctuated with walkways and aerials. If you peered, you could just pick the gray matt floor bottom maybe two hundred meters down. Not a great place for anybody afraid of heights.

A man emerged from the next cell, grimacing. "Not exactly the comforts of home."

"Just somewhere to sleep, I guess." Santh held out his hand. "I'm Jim. Jim Jonson."

Dark eyes lit up in a pale face. Santh's hand was grasped like a lifebuoy. "Ace. Ace Connor. You been here before?"

"No," Santh said, easing his hand away. "You?"

"Me neither."

Orlando ordered everyone back into the lift and took them to an observation platform. Eerie light flooded the room. The entire far wall appeared to be transparent, giving an uninterrupted view of the gas giant Tabora. Rivers of red, orange, brown and grey drifted together in whorls and swirls like oil on water. It was almost romantic, a silent, perpetual dance, slow and stately.

"Looks peaceful, doesn't it?" Orlando said. "The winds down there blow at quarter of a million klicks per hour. But don't worry. If you ever get buffeted by the wind, you'll have already been crushed to a pulp by the gravity, so you won't notice."

He'd made his point. Quite a few people sucked in an audible breath.

"For any of you who didn't realize, this isn't a real window, by the way. It's a giant screen showing you sensor data. Now, if you'll look carefully here," he pointed at a dark, ragged line barely visible against the planet's light. "You'll see a ring. That's what we mine. Go out there, break up the asteroids, bring them back in the hopper of your vehicle. They are fully shielded, tough little buses specially designed for this environment so you'll be quite safe if you follow the rules."

They were taken down to see the hoppers, tough, one-man craft with strengthened shields and triple thickness duracarb exteriors. The mining claws folded underneath the vehicle in flight.

"It looks a bit like a beetle, doesn't it?" Ace muttered.

"It does. If it's as tough as a beetle, I'll be happy," Santh said.

"I've set up a schedule for you to practice on the simulators. You'll be deployed in two-man teams sharing the one hopper. If any of you want to work together, now's the time to say so." Orlando gazed around at them.

"You and me?" Ace said to Santh.

The guy wasn't much more than a kid, a bit on the skinny side with those big, dark eyes dominating his face. Oh, what the hell.

"Yes, okay." Santh raised a hand. "Ace 'n me'll team."

"Okay, that'll do, gents," Orlando announced after several hours of practice and instruction. "You'll find your rosters in the mess hall. We work around the clock, fifteen hours on, fifteen off."

"Hey, you're pretty good." Santh clapped a hand on Ace's shoulder on the way to the mess hall.

The kid beamed. "I drove in the mines on Inchcliffe. Easier, safer, but not with this kind of money."

Santh snaffled a tray and joined the queue for dinner. The line already must have numbered twenty-five, but they moved smoothly past the self-serve piles of food. The smells were enough to make his mouth water. They served plain food—meat, vegetables, thick soup, crusty bread. None of it would make the grade at Aristides but it would sure fill your stomach.

"Inchcliffe, huh? That's the operation on Black Range, right? They mined the last of the copper there, didn't they?" Santh said.

"S'right."

Their turn. Santh ladled soup into a bowl, slices of meat and vegetables onto his plate. Ace piled his plate even higher. Wow. The kid must have hollow legs.

They danced their way between crowded tables and grabbed one when the occupants stood to leave.

"Black Range is mined out," Ace said between mouthfuls of food. "Don't think there are enough minerals left on Nordheim to fill a cruiser. At least, nothing close enough to the surface to be economical."

"So why're you doing this?" Santh said. "Just for a job?"

Ace chewed his meat and swallowed. "I want to save enough to buy a farm. Do something different. Maybe get married, have some kids. What about you?"

Santh had thought about that and had his answer off-pat. "I owe some people some money. Got a debt to pay off."

Ace stared at him, round-eyed. "Yeah?"

"Yeah. I don't want to talk about it."

"Sure. Um ... right."

After dinner they hit the bar, the 'Star Struck', complete with dim, atmospheric lighting, scantily clad women and background 'music'. Ace's eyes swiveled from side to side. He grinned.

"They did this at Black Range, too. You sweat for your money, then you piss it up against a urinal or hand it over to some floozy for your turn at sticking your dick into her. Huh. I settled for the virtual sex programs on the IS."

Smart lad. Santh could keep his advice to himself. Some of the others could have used a few words of wisdom. The floozy behind the bar poured two glasses, the froth cascading down the sides. She handed them over, thrusting her tits at him, her nipples pushing against the white material of her top. A chord of music warbled in a pause in conversation. Why they even bothered with music was beyond him.

Santh handed Ace his beer and wiped his fingers on his trousers. Droplets of water had condensed on the glass and wet his hand. Icy cold, strong and bitter. Good stuff.

Surveying the room, he sipped. Drinking seemed to be a favored pastime here. Quite a few of the men were absolutely wasted, slumped over their tables. He didn't recognize anybody. The drunken tough who'd started beating him up all those months ago wasn't here but he wouldn't have expected him to be. People didn't last on Tabora.

In a corner a fight started over one of the hostesses. The two idiots, both high as starshine, swung ludicrous, roundhouse punches at each other. Men gathered around them in a loose circle, egging them on until the local security patrol broke it up with nerve whips.

"Best clear off," Santh said. "I'm on shift in seven hours. Look after yourself."

He strolled back through the walkways and tunnels to the lift and to his cell.

***

Tabora, garish and brilliant, dominated space. Its vast bulk eclipsed the starscape and only a few of the most brilliant stars were visible beyond the influence of its eerie light. Santh eased the hopper out of its airlock and headed for the ring of asteroids, barely visible to the naked eye but a row of slowly tumbling rocks on the system-enhanced navigation graphic.

No artificial gravity or climate conditioning here. A harness held him in his seat, the heavy articulated suit he wore provided life support. He sucked in water from the straw inside the helmet. Funny how a planet like Tabora made you feel thirsty.

The heads-up display of the navigation system inside his helmet zeroed in on a rock, pinged and flashed. *That one's mine.* A brief burst of power sent the hopper at an angle. A few more corrections and the little machine skimmed the asteroid's surface. This was why you needed pilots. The IS could fly the hopper but they hadn't worked out how to select the best place to mine; not economically, anyway. Santh stopped at a cliff face and deployed the claws from beneath the vehicle's belly. They arced up and over the hopper's back, while he landed and anchored. Using the levers he sliced the claws down, one after another, to break up the rock and suck it into the covered bay that took up most of the space beyond the tiny cockpit.

Tabora leered at him, a growing presence in his mind.

He was glad to hear the beeping in the suit and the flashing signal to 'come in now' toward the end of the shift. At least this part was pretty well automated. He pressed the 'End of Shift' button on the console and let the IS take over, rotating the hopper to face the platform and setting course for the ore bins. The little ship idled along third in line, waiting for a turn at the chute that sucked the ore out of the bay behind him. He never heard a thing but he felt the ship shudder under the suction. Empty, the hopper set course for the airlocks. Shut down, out through the hatch, out of the suit and into the shower.

Water streaming over his body, Santh looked at his shaking hands. Even in the power-assisted suit he hadn't had to do so much physical labor in a long time. If he closed his eyes he could still see Tabora emblazoned on his mind.

He handed over to Ace and went to find a drink. Beer, ice-cold, water from the glass condensing on his hand. He leant on the bar looking for somebody to talk to, someone who'd been here for a while. One fellow came in, bought a drink and sat at a nearby table. Santh ambled over to him and pointed at the vacant chair.

"G'day. This seat free?"

"Sure, buddy," the man said. "Just come off shift?"

"Yeah," Santh said, sagging into the chair. The other guy looked frazzled, too. "Name's Jim Jonson."

"Keki Vilmarin. New?"

"S'right." Santh gulped at his beer, feeling the cold of the liquid running down his gullet and into his stomach.

"It gets a bit better after a time," Keki said, a hint of a smile on his lips. "You can see this great swirling wheel in your brain, can't you?"

"Yeah. Feel like I've spent ten hours in a gym, too."

"That gets better. Tabora doesn't. It hangs there in your brain, you watch the patterns swirl in your sleep."

He poured whatever he was drinking down his throat. His Adam's apple bobbed as he swallowed.

"Is that why people don't stay long, d'you reckon?"

Keki shrugged. "Some people turn to Nervana to help them sleep. You can get it pretty cheap here."

Nervana. Takes you to heaven, keeps you going, but it enslaves you. Or so he'd been told. He wasn't touching that stuff, no way.

"See him?" Keki said, pointing at a nearby table. "He's taking it."

Santh looked over at the miner. The man sat upright in his chair, rock steady. That man was on Nervana?

"See how stiff he looks?" Keki said. "Like he's frozen in place? And his eyes are blank. Like he's looking at nothin'. He'll go to bed and he'll sleep well. Or so they say."

"And sometimes they don't wake up, yeah?" Santh said.

"Yup. Seen a couple go that way in my time here. And two die in stupid accidents."

Keki waved a hand at a lurking attendant, who approached, flashing her tits as usual. "What'll you have, love?" she said.

"Another double blaster for me... what about you?"

"Beer," Santh said.

The woman winked at him, turned a coquettish hip and went back to the bar to fetch the order.

"Nice knockers, that one," Keki said, leering. "Might put myself to sleep with a bit of her later."

Whatever turns you on. "How long have you been here?" Santh said.

"Nearly finished my half year. Twenty-nine days left to go. But who's counting?"

Fuck. Double fuck. In not even half a year this man had seen four men turn up their toes. No wonder the money was so good. "Has it been hard?"

"Fuck, yeah. But I'm tough, see? Most of 'em don't last. Bugger off before they've done fifty days. Scores of 'em. It's like a revolving door up here." He belched.

"Any mates of yours die?" Santh said, leaning over the table so his voice could be heard above the din.

"Not mates, no. Guys I knew."

"Any names?"

Keki swallowed another mouthful of blaster and wiped his mouth with his sleeve. His eyes narrowed. "Why d'you want to know?"

"Oh, nothin'. Just curious."

"You don't remember names up here. Revolving door, they come, they go."

Santh finished his beer and pushed his way out of the tavern. He walked past the gym to the row of comm booths and found one empty. He went in, closed the door behind him, activated the personal privacy screen Jess had given him and raised a real-time, multi-dim call to Nordheim.

Jess, swathed in a robe, blonde hair hanging around her shoulders, answered almost straight away. He must have woken her up. Shit.

"What's the time there?" Santh asked.

"Early. It's okay. How's it going?"

"I've only been here a day and I can see why guys go nuts. Tabora gets to you."

She raised an eyebrow.

"It's there while you're working. The planet, that is. This looming presence, eerie light and weird, slow patterns." He shivered at the thought. "That's why they drink and take Nervana. I got to thinking."

"Uh-huh."

"Can you find out how many men died up here, and how? Names, that sort of thing?"

She screwed up her face. "I'd have to ask the company that."

"You could ask Hudson. He could find out."

"Don't be daft, Santh. It's unbecoming."

He laughed. "Not open to a bit of seduction?"

She gave him one of those weary, give-me-a-break smiles. "No."

"You could do another break-in."

"Leave it with me. I'll think of something."

He rang off and sighed. She was such a beautiful woman. One day he'd tell her about him and Troy. He'd felt like a cheat, a marriage-wrecker. He loved Troy but he didn't want to hurt Jess. He'd tell her. But not right now. If he could find out who killed Troy, he'd tell her. For sure.

Chapter Thirteen

Jess sucked in a deep breath. Staring at the horizon wasn't getting her anywhere. She'd try this, if it didn't work, she could collect what she needed for yet another break-in. She eased her shoulders back, had the shirt gape a little more. If you've got it, use it.

"Get me Sullivan MacIntyre at Tabora Mining Company, will you, Jeeves. Tell them it's Captain Sondijk."

MacIntyre appeared before she'd had time to blink, all slicked-back hair and glittering teeth.

"Jestinia. How lovely to see you. How can I help?"

"I was wondering if I could take you to lunch, Sullivan?"

He flushed, a tide of red rising into his face from his neck. She almost backed away. Poor bastard didn't stand a chance and she was going to use him up and spit him out.

"Lunch? You and me? Alone?"

"Um, yes. It's a business lunch, you understand. I'm a free-lancer and I want to catch up on what's happening in your part of the world."

"Sure. When?"

"Today? Meet you at the Beach House? Noon?"

His eyes widened, his mouth formed an O. "Yes. Yes, great. Terrific."

Jess closed the call. It was pathetic. Sullivan had been chasing her for months. If he hadn't been the logistics manager at Tabora Mining she would have told him to fuck off. But that wasn't a great way of keeping your clients.

A walk down the beach would be good, give her a chance to stretch her legs, blow away the cobwebs.

***

MacIntyre loitered in the restaurant's foyer, swaying nervously from foot to foot, hands behind his back, when she came in.

"Sullivan, how are you?" Jess planted a fleeting kiss on his cheek and he beamed.

"Jestinia. You look beautiful, as always." He'd gone red again.

The waiter led them to a table on the deck, where the water slapped at the pylons and the breeze held a trace of ozone tang.

"You usually work through Tanaka, don't you?" Sullivan said after they'd ordered the lunch special.

"For Kentor trips, yes. But I like doing the runs to Tabora because it means I don't have to be away from my daughter so long."

She refused the waiter's offer of wine and settled for iced water. MacIntyre ordered beer.

"We tend to use bigger ships for the supply runs."

"Mm, like *Kimberley*, I know. But I'd appreciate it if you could bear me in mind. The *Maid* has modern, aired-up refrigeration for delicate cargoes that dehydrate in vacuum, for example. We'd do a great job of carrying drugs."

His jaw dropped. The waiter delivered his beer and departed.

"Drugs?"

"Oh, Sullivan, I don't mean Nervana. I mean medicinal drugs." She leaned toward him, finger raised. "I would never, ever carry something like Nervana. It's dreadful stuff, so I've heard."

"Sorry, of course." He sipped at his glass.

"How many people has that stuff killed on the platform in the past year?"

"Nervana? Oh, that's a personnel thing but it would have to be getting close to ten." He shook his head. "They mix it with alcohol, the idiots."

The food arrived, bowls of steaming chowder served with crusty bread. It smelled divine and tasted even better, thick and chunky with pieces of fish.

"We knew someone who took a job at the mine. This was before Troy died. I've lost contact with him. Any chance you could have a look to see if he made it down again?"

"That I can do. I can't access personal details, mind, so I couldn't give you an address."

"That's fine, I understand. Can you access remotely?"

"Yes, but I can send it to your house."

She waved a hand. "It's just that I'm having kaff with a friend this afternoon. She knew Alfons, too. I'd like to be able to tell her. But if it's not possible..."

"Of course it is." He took out his comlink and entered a code. "What was the fellow's name?"

"Alfons, Stev Alfons." She spelled the surname for him.

"Yes, here it is." He lifted his head to gaze at her sorrowfully. "It's so common out there. He could only handle two months, it seems."

"Is he dead?"

"Oh, no, no, no. He took his pay and moved on." He shook his head slowly from side to side. "So many of them do. It must be rough out there."

"Oh." Jess mashed her lips, let her head droop. "And no forwarding address?"

"I'm sorry." MacIntyre reached across to touch her hand. "Even if I could tell you, there's nothing recorded. Was he a close friend?"

"No, more a friend of Troy's." She heaved a sigh. "Such a pity. But let's not talk about sad things. Have you seen that new drama with Olivia Leddbetter?"

His eyes lit up. "*The Farthest Shore*? Certainly have. Disappointing, I have to say. I hate the way they play with historical facts, you know? There was no happy ending in real life."

"Wasn't there?" She rested her elbows on the table and supported her chin on her linked hands. History and drama were MacIntyre's passion. She'd probably learn something if she listened. And he'd have a wonderful time.

Meanwhile, the eavesdropper concealed in her brooch had recorded a detailed image of his retina, the code he'd used to access the data and the connection signature.

A cup of kaff later Jess said, "It's been fascinating, Sullivan, but I must go. I have another appointment."

"Oh. Yes, of course." He pushed the chair back and rose to his feet. "Dinner? On the weekend?"

"Thanks, but no. I'm taking Tenna away for the holidays."

"After that?"

He was so hopeful, like a puppy asking to go for a walk. So eminently not sexy. "I'll get back to you, Sullivan. Thanks for coming. I enjoyed myself."

The wind had picked up, whipping crests off the waves. Jess fastened her jacket and called an autocab for the trip home.

She waited until evening to check out Tabora's personnel system. The data she'd collected with the eavesdropper created a new record on her comlink. She entered the code MacIntyre had used and waited while the software neatly inserted the image of his retina in response to the request.

She asked for a list of the names of personnel killed on Tabora in the last two years, with cause of death. The list appeared in date order, ten names. Four were related to 'drugs and alcohol', the rest were industrial accidents.

Wait a minute. Seven deaths. How many bodies had been on Kimberley? She checked back. Twenty. But that was ridiculous. *Beaconsfield* usually had the job of transporting bodies so according to these records there wouldn't have been twenty bodies.

Something odd appeared to be happening up there.

She changed the search criteria. How many people had left early, cashed up and gone elsewhere?

Sixty-seven. She scrolled through the names. Only a handful had a forwarding address.

Santh called later that evening, on schedule. She relayed the data to him.

"Strewth. Ten in two years. That's not many."

"No, it's not; not for a site like Tabora. And bear in mind there were twenty bodies on *Kimberley*. Were they all supposed to be from Tabora?"

"Yep. That's where we loaded." He'd picked up on it, too. He frowned, the familiar tightening between the eyes.

"If there weren't bodies in those cylinders, I wonder what was?"

He nodded. "Contraband of some sort. Those tubes could carry anything."

"Yeah, but you'd have to fool the system into believing it really was bodies."

"Could be done."

Yes, it could. The shady workshops in the backblocks of Sal Menoa, Kentor's capital, could produce little features to fool anything but the most sophisticated InfoDroids.

"Be careful, Santh," Jess said. "Whoever's running this show is dangerous."

"Yep. Been there, done that. Talk to you soon." But the glib words didn't match his expression. He cut the call.

Chapter Fourteen

Orham Girl's College appeared below the coptercab, beautiful old brick buildings and playing fields set amongst landscaped gardens within a security fence. Jess had to get special permission to land within the grounds to return Tenna and Sufi to school.

"I don't want to go back, Mum," Tenna said, gazing out of the window.

Sufi frowned at her. "You should appreciate it more, Tenna."

"S'pose. Holidays was great though, wasn't it?"

"Yes, it was. I..." Sufi bowed her head.

The kid was embarrassed. Jess hugged her shoulders. "It was wonderful having you along with us. I think Tenna might even have learnt a few things through you being there to tell her about oliphaunts and things."

Tenna grinned. "Yeah, Mum, that's really going to help me in life, isn't it? But it was great fun riding them."

The coptercab slowed and commenced its landing descent, aiming for the circular pad next to the main building. It dropped past stone walls covered in the flaming red leaves of a creeper preparing for winter hibernation, and settled. The door slid aside as the engines reduced to idle.

"Wait," Jess said to its IS.

She clambered out and helped Tenna and Sufi with their luggage.

"Okay, babe, you behave yourself and work hard, you hear?"

Tenna rolled her eyes and grinned, her dark eyes dancing. "You called me babe again, Mum."

"Sorry, love." Jess grabbed her daughter in a huge hug. "I promise to break the habit." She tilted her forehead so that it met Tenna's. They stood together, head to head, for a long moment, blonde hair entangling with blonde hair.

"Thanks for the great holiday. It was terrific."

Jess turned to Sufi and hugged her, too, laughing at the delighted surprise. "Make sure Tenna does her homework, honey. Off you go, the pair of you. I'll call you in a day or two."

Tenna enveloped her in a final hug and a kiss. The pair of them ambled off up the pathway to the school's entrance, Sufi dragging her suitcase, Tenna's more upmarket hovercase floating behind. A fellow who'd been tending the borders nearby helped Sufi get her case through the door. One last wave and they were gone.

Jess swung back into the coptercab and entered the address for home. Ah well. After two weeks with Tenna in sunlight and sand, late Fall in Orham was depressing and lonely. She should at least have a message from Santh, and she had an evening at Aristide's with Admiral Hudson to look forward to.

"Hi, Jeeves. Everything quiet?" she said to the IS as she walked along the corridor to her apartment.

"*Yes, Jess. Three calls from Sullivan MacIntyre. Two from Santh.*"

She took a quick look at Sullivan's messages, all sheep's eyes and longing, thanks for the great lunch, what about dinner?

"Play me the ones from Santh."

He looked drawn, the lines etched into his face. "This is a helluva job, Jess. So glad I won't be staying long. After a while that bloody planet haunts you. No wonder nobody stays long. I heard some fellows talking in the tavern, something about supplying girls. One of them was Oper Suleiman. Remember him? Did quite a few deals with the GPR on Kentor? He said not even the girls in the brothels up here hang around and they'd be able to earn a packet. Anyhow, hope you're having a great time with Tenna. Give her my love. Catch you."

"When was this one, Jeeves?"

"Ten days ago."

No luck so far. She hoped he was still okay.

"Let's see the next one."

Santh looked ill and positively furtive, glancing over his shoulder from the booth. She straightened, nerves twanging.

"Two things; I found out Rawlings was cargo master on *Beaconsfield* for one tour. And, another guy has 'disappeared'." He hooked his fingers around the last two words. "His name's Ace Connor, supposed to have left for Nordheim. *Beaconsfield* is here now, to pick up bodies. It'll be interesting to see if my mate Ace turns up in *Beaconsfield's* corpse tubes." He glanced over his shoulder again. "Gotta go. I'm on my way to find those body tubes. Sorry I missed you."

He disappeared.

"When was this?"

"*Two days ago.*"

Two days and he hadn't called back. Surely he would have called. "Jeeves, can you connect me to Tabora? Real time?"

"*Of course. Their administration?*"

"Yes."

She fidgeted while she waited. What had he called himself, again? Jonson, that was it. Jim Jonson. No, wait. She had a better idea. "Belay that call, Jeeves." If anything was happening up there, the last thing she wanted was to warn them. She might still have access to Tabora's data through MacIntyre. "See if we can still get into Tabora's personnel data."

"*The code was accepted. But with a message that it should be changed.*"

She was almost sure Jeeves had a mischievous streak.

"Let's see what we've got. Rerun that query I did last time, for deaths." She hesitated before she spoke the word. Deaths. A shiver slipped down her spine.

Eleven names. Not ten. And the last was Jim Jonson. She crumpled, her forehead on her knees, her eyes squeezed shut. No. Not Santh, too. Not dead. He couldn't be. *Think, Jess, think.* She sat back on the couch and ran her hands back through her hair. He was up there snooping around. Maybe he found something out? Maybe they'd killed him. Or maybe they'd shoved him into a body tube and were taking him ... somewhere.

Damn it, she felt so bloody helpless. She slammed her fist down on the armrest. She had to do something; anything. This was a repeat of the business with Troy. The police? They had no jurisdiction off Nordheim and she wouldn't ask that clown Longford the time of day. Once *Beaconsfield* left Tabora, the trail would go cold. She stood. Right. She'd go herself, see what she could find out.

"I'm heading for Tabora, Jeeves. Redirect calls to the *Maid*. If they're important."

Jess booked a departure slot on the way to the space port. Three hours ahead, plenty of time to get up to the station and prepare. That hole in the pit of her stomach sat there but at least she was doing something. She shuddered at the thought, trapped in one of those body tubes; like being buried alive. Not her best friend; not Santh.

She went straight to the check-in counter outside the elevator, put her bag on the scanner and handed her data stick to the attendant, William. She didn't like him much but if she had to flirt, she would.

"Hmmm," he said, frowning. "You don't have a first officer."

"Yeah. It's a short trip, the ship's on auto most of the time."

"But even so, regulations state that every ship must carry two licensed personnel."

"I know, William. But it's only enforced for trips outside the system. I could give you a heap of examples."

Still frowning, he shook his head. "I could get into trouble."

She looked around her, then leaned toward him. "Tell you what, I won't tell if you don't. Oh, please, William? For me? As a huge favor?" She widened her eyes, pleading.

He flushed. "All right. Go on, get out of here."

She beamed at him, blew him a kiss and sped off to the pedolator before he could change his mind. She'd forgotten something. What? Halfway to the ship she remembered. Damn and blast, she had a date with Hudson. Oh, well. She wouldn't have enjoyed herself anyway, not with Santh missing. She'd better call him, though.

She raised a call to *Defender* from the *Maid's* bridge and was transferred to the admiral's adjutant, Senior Commander Tomas. "I'm sorry, ma'am, Admiral Hudson is in a meeting. Can I give him a message?"

Good. At least she wouldn't have to explain herself.

"Yes, we were to meet this evening. Something urgent has come up and I won't be able to make it. Tell him I'm sorry."

She ended the call and had the IS carry out the pre-departure checks while she changed into her usual grey ship suit.

"*All clear, Jess.*"

She slipped into the familiar captain's chair. "Fine. Locked in with the station's departure slot?"

"*Yes. The route to the gate is set.*"

"Have the station withdraw services."

The airlock tunnel withdrew into its housing on the pier. Service hoses disengaged and retracted.

"*Saintly Maid you are good to go. Repeat, you are good to go.*"

"Thanks, Nordheim Station. *Saintly Maid* backing out," Jess said.

The IS fired a short, low-power burst from the forward thrusters, enough to start the *Maid* sliding out of her bay. Nordheim appeared, a sliver of daylight giving way to the advancing night. Another short burst on the starboard thrusters turned the ship.

"*Setting course for the jump gate.*"

Jess' harness rose from its bay in the chair to slip over her shoulders and snap across her legs. "Acknowledge."

Saintly Maid's main engines eased to full power, thrusting her back into the seat. *Defender*, defined by its running lights, hung between the space station and the jump gate. At this distance the massive ship looked small but it grew steadily in the view screen. She'd pass the vessel by at a distance of four point five klicks. Almost a close shave. No-one would call the ship pretty; she wasn't much more than a long, deep triangle with a smaller triangle on top. Still, in space you didn't need streamlining.

"Saintly Maid, *this is Confederacy battle cruiser* Defender. *You are to shut down your drives.*"

Jess' heart thumped. What the fuck? Not again?

"*Defender*, this is *Saintly Maid*. What's the problem?"

"*No problem. Shut down your drives.*"

"*They're locking on with a gravity beam, Jess. If we accelerate now, we could outrun it.*" The IS said the words as if it was as commonplace as docking with a space station.

Outrun it, head for the gate? She grinned. Wouldn't that upset Hudson?

"*They've launched fighters*," the IS said, displaying two arrow-shaped vessels approaching fast.

"*One last chance,* Saintly Maid. *Shut down now or you will be disabled.*"

Military speak for 'we'll shoot up your engines.' Fuck fuck fuck. Damn them to every hell in every fucking galaxy in the whole fucking universe.

"Shut down."

Jess sat back in the chair and pinched the bridge of her nose. *Defender's* towering side wall loomed, a green light flashing above the allocated airlock. *Maid* slipped between the walls into a bay large enough to contain two of her and settled to the deck. The hatch closed. And meanwhile, Santh was somewhere on Tabora, maybe alive in a body tube. The thought made her shudder. Damn it. She carried nothing, not even a cargo. Of all days to stop her, why now?

Somebody was going to pay for this.

Seething, Jess watched the gauge change color as the airlock came to equal pressure. At last. The light flashed green and the lock clicked. She slammed the hatch aside and vaulted through onto *Defender's* deck.

"What the fuck is this about?" she demanded, thrusting her face at the officer waiting for her.

He blinked but his expression didn't change. "You will come with me, ma'am." He reached out to grasp her arm but she jerked away.

"What for and where are we going?"

"You'll be told in due course."

She marched between the troopers, at the pace they set, into a lift car. A short journey up, then along a familiar corridor marked 4D. This was where they'd taken her last time, for interrogation. And a body search. Her skin crawled at the memory.

The officer stopped in front of a door, which slid aside, revealing a table with two chairs at the back, one at the front, none occupied.

"Ma'am."

Oh, bloody hell. Her heart hammering, Jess stepped into the room. The door closed behind her.

Chapter Fifteen

Hudson raised a hand in the meeting to cut off the speaker. "Forgive me, Mister President. My adjutant wants a word."

Ottenshaw and his ministers stared at him across the table. Tomas' voice spoke via his implant. "*A message from Jess Sondijk, Sir. She's cancelled dinner with you this evening and I thought you might like to know she's on her way to Tabora in her ship.*"

"*Is that so. Any idea why?*"

"*No, Sir.*"

It could be perfectly legitimate, he supposed. "*Anything from Tabora to explain this sudden departure?*"

"*No, nothing.*"

The last thing he needed was somebody blundering around up there. Perhaps it was time to take Captain Sondijk in hand, find out a little more forcefully what was going through her brain. And find out what happened to Dekstra, who seemed to have vanished.

"*Take her ship. And send a shuttle down to the President's Palace to pick me up. I'm coming back.*"

"Something important has come up, Mister President. I'll have to leave you. I think we were about finished anyway, weren't we?" Except for the self-important speech Ottenshaw hadn't finished. Even his ministerial colleagues looked bored.

"Yes, of course, Admiral. Anything further can be discussed at my lodge. You'll still be attending the house party?"

"I will be. We do have a few moments before my shuttle arrives if you require my input?" The sooner the better.

***

The shuttle pilot didn't even switch off the engines, running on idle while Hudson climbed on board. The ship lifted and banked over the palace gardens and Orham City, veering away from the space elevator tower for the power burst out of the planet's gravity well.

Tomas was waiting for him when he disembarked. "Where is she?"

"In an interrogation cell, Sir." His adjutant's eyes twinkled. "The same one the Militia used last time she was here."

Hudson grinned. How would she have reacted to that? "Have her brought to my office."

"Sir."

He hardly had time to make himself comfortable in his chair when his clerk said via his implant, *"Captain Sondijk is here, Sir."*

He sat back in his seat, watching the door when she entered. Her grey ship suit was unzipped at the front and the scoop-necked white shirt she wore underneath revealed a tantalizing expanse of breast. The last time she'd been brought aboard she'd dressed for the occasion but this time she probably didn't even realize. Her eyes blazed with fury as she barged into his office, flanked by a lieutenant and two troopers. No, intimidation didn't work on Jess Sondijk.

"What in blazes is this about? Annoyed I stood you up?"

"Thank you, Lieutenant, you may go," Hudson said.

He waited until the door closed behind the troopers. "I admit, I'm not accustomed to being stood up."

She slammed both her palms on his desk and leaned towards him, affording him a lovely view of her cleavage. "You are not the fucking centre of the universe."

His gaze slid down to admire the swell of her breasts. Nice. Exquisite. Two delicious handfuls. His mouth watered. The prospect of a close and personal encounter with that body was enough to give a man a hard-on.

She pushed herself upright. "Oh, for fuck's sake. Do you ever think about anything but your cock?"

He leaned back, grinning. "If you flaunt your assets, my dear, you can hardly blame me for looking."

Scowling, she zipped up her suit.

"Very good. Now sit." He pointed at the visitor's chair beside her.

"Go to hell. You have no reason, no right to stop me and impound my ship. I've done nothing wrong and I've other things to do apart from some … some sort of verbal foreplay with you." She folded her arms, staring down at him.

"You're supposed to be having dinner with me at Aristides in a few hours' time. Instead, you've careered off Nordheim as if all the demons in hell were after you. Where are you going and why?"

"None of your business."

He held her gaze. "We can continue with this for as long as you like. But you will not be moving out of this office, let alone off this ship, unless you can give me a good reason."

She looked away for a few heartbeats, then raised her head to stare at him. "I'm going to Tabora platform. Which you would already know from my travel plans. Is there anything wrong with that?"

"Without a first officer, which isn't quite according to regulation. I would also like to know what has happened to Mister Dekstra, but that's another story. Why are going to Tabora?" Dekstra. Her eyes had flickered when he said the name.

"That's what I do. I quite often transport goods out to the platform and back. *Saintly Maid's* a freighter, remember?"

"You have no cargo. Or so the controllers at the space station tell me. I can have my people search, of course."

She snorted. "I'd expect they'd be finished by now."

"I'll ask you again. Why are you going to Tabora?"

She moistened her lips. "I'm picking something up. Or at least, I'm hoping to. I'm going out there to ask the manager for work. Drumming up business."

"Leaving aside your prior engagement with me, do you always fly an empty ship for that purpose?"

She summoned up some anger. "Look, it's not illegal is it? It's my fuel, my expense. We can make another date, for when I get back. If you want."

He waited. She sucked in a breath, looked away, blinking rapidly. She was about to crack.

"Hudson, Santh Dekstra is missing." She slumped onto a chair, her eyes glistening, clenching and unclenching her left hand. "They're saying he's dead but I'm not sure I believe that. If it is true I," she mashed her lips. "I need to see the body. He's my best friend in the world."

He hadn't expected this. No wonder she was distraught. He even felt a niggle of guilt. "Who is 'they'?"

Her nostrils flared. "If I knew who 'they' were I wouldn't be going to Tabora." Her head tilted so he could only see her hair.

"Why was he on Tabora? He's your first officer."

The look she gave him would have melted metal.

"Jess, help me. Help me and I'll help you. Is this to do with Rawlings or Alfons?"

She dithered, biting her lip, not looking him in the eye. After a few moments she sat up a little straighter. "No. At least, I don't think so. Maybe." Her shoulders drooped. "Santh and I are trying to find out why Troy was murdered."

"Murdered."

"Yes, we think so."

"Why?"

"I went and looked at the footage of the incident on *Kimberley*, when he was shot."

"I've seen it."

"The fellow Ellwood deliberately got between the sensor and Troy."

"That's open to interpretation."

She ground her teeth. "Yes, I know. But look at the rest. Troy talks to someone on Tabora, who dies accidentally, then Santh is bashed, Troy is boarded and killed. Santh told me Rawlings said that he'd seen Stev Alfons and somehow that freaked him. Alfons is recorded in the Tabora personnel system as having 'moved on'." She added the quotes with her fingers.

"That's hardly strange."

"Rawlings worked for one tour on *Beaconsfield*."

"Yes. So?"

"They use *Beaconsfield* to transport bodies from Tabora to Kentor. And they're transported in low temperature cylinders that are kept aired up. So they could transport almost anything in those things, including people."

Hudson leaned forward. This was getting interesting. "Are you sure? That's not in the Tabora records or in their procedures manuals."

"*Beaconsfield* was out for refit so they used *Kimberley* for one trip. Santh and Troy saw the things. I only heard about it from Santh recently, when we started wondering about Troy's death."

"What you're suggesting is a cryogenic cylinder."

"Yep. You could transport anything in those things."

She'd been almost eager but now she withdrew into herself. He waited. She had more to say in her own time. She chewed her lips, took a deep breath and said, "Something else you should know. We did some digging. It looks like they've shipped out a lot more bodies from Tabora platform than actually died."

"Is that so?" Hudson slumped back in his chair. This was becoming decidedly interesting. "How did you know about this ... anomaly in the statistics, Captain?"

She dithered again.

"Let me help you. You went and looked at the records?"

She tossed her head, glowering. "Yes, I fucking did. Nobody else was. Only a handful of people died on Tabora in a couple of years. But *Kimberley* carried twenty bodies and that was a one-off trip. *Beaconsfield*, which usually carried bodies, made other trips in that same period. *Beaconsfield* is docked up there now."

What was it Rawlings had said? *Alfons. Alfons was there. Hand 'em over.* And he didn't like dealing with Ptorix. Whatever he'd said may well have been enough to get him killed.

What to do? He had no jurisdiction on Tabora and causing a ruckus with the local planetary administration would not look good, given the need to show a united front to the Ptorix. Besides, it wasn't enough. He had to know what happened to whatever was transported in those cylinders. And was it enough to trade for starhearts? Best to have Mann inform his people of this new development, let the game play out and follow where it led. He couldn't tell her that, though. All she cared about was her friend.

"Thank you. I'll have my people do some digging."

"What are you going to do? Chuck me in the brig?"

"No. I'm taking you into protective custody. For your own good and for the good of an operation I'm conducting on Tabora at the moment. I don't want you up there getting in the way. You will accompany me for a hunting party at President Ottenshaw's country residence."

She sagged back against the chair, her jaw dropped. "You have got to be joking."

"You owe me a date."

"My best friend is missing."

"You cannot do anything but get in the way. You said it yourself. I have trained operatives on Tabora. It will do you good to be out of it. And your presence will help to insulate me from Delia Marati."

She snorted, her lip lifted in a sardonic grin. "Not impressed with La Delia? She was all over you at the reception. You could have had your wicked way with her in a back room, the balcony, a broom closet…"

"Once was enough." Although he'd availed himself a few times. Delia was beautiful enough but she didn't have the spark that Jess had. He leaned toward her. "The food and wine will be excellent. If any intelligence comes from Tabora, you'll be informed." She still looked rebellious, her nostrils flared, her chin jutting. "Of course, if you find the notion objectionable, I can have you locked in the cells?"

Her eyes widened, she stared at him. He returned her gaze. She blinked first. "If you think I'm going to sleep with you after this, you can think again."

He'd won that skirmish. He repressed the smile. "Sleeping is another issue. But you're under no obligation and I'm sure the suite will have a couch."

***

Jess sat beside Hudson in the back of the big limo staring out of the window the whole way to Ottenshaw's villa, ignoring him. He'd made her get some sleep on *Defender*, aligning her body clock to where they were going. They'd stopped briefly at her apartment to pick up clothes, including her red dress at his insistence. Although the way she made his blood race, he suspected she'd look good in anything. And even better in nothing. Dinner was going to be an irritation before the main course.

The mountains appeared below, rugged ravines and soaring cliffs, somber in the purple and green of late fall. Although the plains still basked in the sun's warmth, winter wasn't too far off at these latitudes. The westering sun tinged the snow that clung permanently to some of the higher peaks, with a golden light.

"So what's the drill, Sir?" she said.

"You can call me Ullric. What do you mean?"

"It's nearly sunset. Off hunting in the dark?"

"Dinner this evening and a trip into the foothills tomorrow."

She turned toward him, her gaze traveling over his body. He wriggled a little in the seat, easing the strain on his pants. He couldn't remember wanting a woman so much since Sylvie.

"So why the uniform?"

"To make a point, lovely lady. I don't want them to forget what I am."

"I suppose you're playing some subtle game with Ottenshaw and his cronies, as well."

"Always. We're supposed to be on the same side but matters can become ... territorial."

The limo shaped to land then touched down on the paved landing ground beside Ottenshaw's villa. Several other guests had already arrived; Delia Marati's elegant blue machine was parked next to industrialist Lex Cambric's flamboyant red vehicle. The more sedate deep blue limo belonged to Tanaka.

Attendants jumped forward to handle the luggage as the engines wound down. Hudson held his hand out to Jess but she curled a lip and stood of her own volition.

"Try to at least pretend you're here to enjoy yourself," he said. "The food should be good. And the wine."

Ottenshaw advanced to meet him, hand outstretched, with only a sideways glance at Jess. "Admiral. So good of you to join us." They shook hands, while Jess turned her back. "Lovely to see you, too, Miss Sondijk."

"Yes, likewise. I'm sure it'll be simply smashing." She smiled, one of those brittle I'm-doing-my-best smiles.

Hudson hid his irritation behind a smile. "We'll settle in and meet you ... where?"

"Yes, of course. Drinks on the terrace to watch the sunset. Shall we say half an hour?"

Hudson took Jess' arm and led her away toward the tall doors into the main building. She was still keeping her distance, not quite pouting, but certainly not happy. "Come on, Jess, relax. My people are doing their job. You'll be informed if anything comes up."

She looked up at him, keeping step with him. He was sure the tension in her body had eased a fraction. "Okay. Stop cutting off the blood circulation in my arm. Please. Sir."

He released his grip and she slipped her arm around his waist, nestled against his side. It felt good. "How's that?" She gazed up at him, a twinkle in her eyes. "I can tell you La Delia isn't impressed." She tilted her head a little to where Minister Marati stood with three other people, just inside the foyer.

Hudson put an arm around her shoulders and pulled her against his side even closer as he continued to walk. "Very good, Captain. Much better." Very much better. His hopes had flagged for a moment. This might well be a very pleasant evening; very pleasant indeed.

Reluctantly he released her to greet the group, exchange handshakes and introductions. But when he tried to take her arm to lead her into the transit with his two security guards, she tugged away from him. A pity. But the sun hadn't set. There was time yet to win her over. He always enjoyed a challenge.

He had been allocated a suite on the first floor. A servant opened the door for them, bowed and left. No-one spoke. The guard entered the room and turned on his detection equipment. Jess watched, a slight smile on her face.

"All clear, Sir," the guard said. "They had sensors here and in the bedroom."

"Thank you, Sergeant."

The man saluted and left, closing the door quietly behind him.

"Are you sure you wouldn't prefer to spend your time with La Delia? I do declare she's planning to boil me in oil and have you for dinner," Jess said.

Oh, she tried so hard to rile him. "Whereas I would prefer to have you for dinner. We don't have to be on the terrace for … oh … long enough."

She raised an eyebrow. "You're right. There's a sofa." She dropped onto the cushions. "Comfy. I'm sure I'll be happy here. Meanwhile, I'd better get changed. I'll have the washroom. Makeup, you understand?"

She pulled a large case from her bag, went through the bedroom to the washroom and closed the door behind her.

Chapter Sixteen

Jess leaned against the washroom door and closed her eyes. Bastard. Here she was at a fancy party she didn't want to go to and Santh was up there. Somewhere. Anger boiled but she forced it down. *Steady, Jess. There's nothing you can do about it. So let's get the best from a bad situation.* Her body went to automatic as she started to undress, while her brain kept whirling. Hudson said he had people up at Tabora, and Ottenshaw, Marati, Longford and Tanaka were all here. She might even find something out. Meanwhile, she could pay back His High Admiralness. So he thought he was the great seducer, did he? She chuckled as she stepped into the shower.

Jess kept him waiting until she heard his voice through the closed bedroom door. "Are you ready, yet, woman? By the time we get there, the sun will have set."

Time to go. She pressed the panel and the door slid open, as if at his command. Mmm mmm. He stood with his legs slightly apart, his hands behind his back. A self-centered prick he may be, but he was an attractive man. Oh, yes indeed. The ornate high collar at his throat and the gold rank insignia on his shoulders set off his white dress uniform and the ice blue of his eyes. Campaign ribbons lent color to his right breast. His gaze swept over her body. Her groin tingled. She almost regretted the game she was intending to play. Almost.

She closed the distance between them and ran two fingers over the ornate gold collar of his dress uniform. "Ooh, all sparkly. You do look nice, Admiral. Shall we go?"

She wasn't the only one feeling hot. It was like standing next to a furnace.

He flexed his fingers on the bare skin of her back and propelled her gently to the door. "The sooner we get there, the sooner we'll get back."

She smiled at him, doing her best bedroom eyes look, and didn't miss the gleam of lust in the returning smile. Ah, he was nothing if not confident.

Most of the other guests were already out on the terrace enjoying the display as the sun slid toward the horizon. At the moment its light shone through a broken band of dark cloud, painting the edge in brilliant red outline while rays as vivid as spotlights blazed through rents. The view could only be classed as spectacular.

"Just in time, Admiral," Ottenshaw said.

Like most of the other men he wore a glistening black evening suit with a high-collared white shirt. His wife's lips pinched together, oozing disapproval as she looked Jess over. Jess swallowed the smile. Madam Ottenshaw wore the currently fashionable extravaganza of overlapping material flowing down her body like lava. But Jess did like her earrings. As vivid and startling as the setting sun, they seemed to glow of their own accord.

Ottenshaw beckoned a waiter who offered drinks from a silver tray. Hudson selected two glasses of sparkling wine and handed one to her, being sure to brush her fingers with his. He took her closer to the balcony, not far from where La Delia held court with a number of others.

La Delia wasn't impressed, by the sour look on her face. Jess made sure she kept in contact with Hudson, who didn't seem to mind in the least. The scent of his cologne filled her nostrils.

"Do you like the bauble around Minister Marati's neck?" he said, leaning close to her ear.

Oh wow, a blue diamond. The light seemed to be trapped inside its facets, blinking and gleaming with every move she made.

"It's beautiful."

"What about Madam Ottenshaw's earrings?"

"Oh, yes, they are amazing. I've never seen anything like them." Her heart jolted. Oh, shit. She leaned back against Hudson, the back of her head touching his chest. "They're starhearts, aren't they?"

"Yes. Not especially large but it's vanishingly rare to see a matching pair." She felt his breath on her cheek.

"Huh. Seems it's not only boys who play at mine's bigger than yours," she murmured.

Hudson chuckled.

Ottenshaw himself came over to them, Longford in tow. The admiral's red and blue costume would have done a doorman proud. Especially with those cords across his chest. Lemony Longford. How delightful.

"You've met Admiral Longford, of course, Admiral Hudson?" Ottenshaw said.

"Yes. And I believe you have met Captain Jestinia Sondijk?" Hudson said.

Longford looked down his nose and offered her a brief nod. "Captain."

Stuffy prick. Jess beamed at him. "So nice to see you again, Admiral. Lovely costume, by the way. Are you angling for a job at the Palace Hotel?"

He glowered. Hudson's fist pushed against her back in wordless disapproval. Too bad.

"I believe your exercises with my troopers were a success?" Hudson said.

Longford's face lit up. "Yes, wonderful stuff, wonderful. My men get so few chances to face a real enemy, even a feigned one. The new exercise where your troops practice on the ground is going to be happening quite near here in these very mountains."

"Here?" Hudson said.

Longford smirked. "No, not here as such. On the other side of the range, a good hundred klicks beyond the peaks."

"Excellent," Hudson said. "It should challenge them. The troopers, in particular, can suffer from extreme boredom during these enforced periods of inactivity."

Exercises in these mountains would be challenging, indeed. Jess recalled the nights she'd spent out here with her father and Troy years ago, around Mount Egmont. The weather could change between one blink and the next. If you weren't prepared, didn't have your wits about you, you'd end up as one more plaque on Egmont's list of victims. Still, the troopers would have combat armor and provisions and comms equipment. Lucky them

Longford and Hudson moved on to discussing ships and armaments.

Jess gazed to the west where the sky show ended and the last of the light was fading. Darkness seemed to flood across the sky from the East, as though the sun pulled a cape behind it, a cape decorated with a spangle of stars. She gazed up, playing join the dots as she had with Tenna and Troy, connecting pinpoints of light billions of klicks away into imaginary animals; here an ambling bear, there a ship. Kites and snakes weren't allowed—too easy. You'd tell the others what you'd found—a bear or a ship—and they had to work out which stars you'd picked. Then you blinked and did it all over again. Happy days, long gone.

Ottenshaw's voice boomed. "Dinner is about to be served. If you would make your way to the dining room."

His hand on her back, Hudson guided her into the house. Jess' eyes swiveled, taking in the soaring ceilings, the furniture, the decorations. This place was quite something. Lush carpets lay against dark green walls which formed a backdrop for paintings and holographic displays. Anywhere else the opulence would have been garish and loud but here the feeling was one of elegance. Green and gold tableware had been set out on a long table covered with a red cloth. Light glinted from glasses and polished cutlery. Jess sat with Hudson on her right and Ottenshaw on her left in the centre of one side of the table. La Delia sat opposite Ottenshaw, with Longford beside her.

The blue diamond drew her eye, a beautiful bauble. But it was no match for Madam Ottenshaw's earrings which sucked Jess' attention to their writhing, seething centers. No wonder the jewel was so highly prized. It dazzled, out-shining the illumination in the room. Jess could take a pretty confident guess that Delia was every shade of envy.

"The diamond is magnificent, Delia," Hudson said. "The blue is so rare. A gift?"

The woman's smile held a tinge of sadness. Or it was supposed to. She placed a hand briefly on the rock on her breast. "Yes. From my late husband. I rarely wear it but I felt it should be publicly visible, at least occasionally."

How very kind of her to share.

"It's a generous gift," Hudson said.

Delia simpered. "My husband was a generous man."

"You're also a generous man, President Ottenshaw," Hudson said. "Your wife's earrings are extraordinary. I believe it's difficult to get a matching set."

Ottenshaw smiled, eyes hooded. "It is, yes. I bought them in Kentor a year or two ago."

The food arrived. Conversation was replaced by the scrape of fork on plate, clink of knives. Between courses Ottenshaw talked about tomorrow's trip to the foothills of Mount Egmont.

"I'll have a copter take us up to a likely spot. We'll have picnic hampers and we can spend the day however we wish. We'll be collected in the evening."

"Sounds good," Hudson said.

"Captain Sondijk, the ladies have generally elected to stay here—"

Stay here with this lot of boring biddies? She might get a chance to absent herself. And do... something. No, she didn't know what.

Hudson took her hand and squeezed it gently. "Miss Sondijk and I have discussed the matter. She'll come with me. Won't you, my dear?"

She directed an adoring smile at him. "I do so love to spend time in the countryside. So peaceful."

He chuckled. He would have read the sarcasm, damn his handsome hide. La Delia positively glowered.

After the main course Marati left the table, presumably to go to the ladies' room.

"Seems like a good idea," Jess murmured to Hudson as she stood.

He shook his head. "Why must women hunt in packs?"

She leaned over him, her hand on his shoulder covering the gold bars. "She's got her own pack and I'm not in it."

Outside the dining room she looked around, searching for some sort of indication of where to go. Voices, pitched low and private, brought her up short. Out on the terrace two figures stood close together.

Delia Marati and Tanaka, heads close together.

"Relax, I'll have it attended to," he said. "I have contacts—"

"Ah, Madam, can I be of any help?"

Damn, blast and be buggered. Jess turned to the approaching servant. "The ladies room?"

"Yes, Madam, up the stairs and to your right." He pointed to a staircase nearby.

"Thank you so much."

She gazed around, back at the terrace but they had both disappeared. What was that about? La Delia was a politician, though. And Tanaka had a finger in just about every pie on the planet. Whatever. Maybe they were setting up for an after-dinner assignation? Now that *would* be funny.

Ablutions done, Jess checked her makeup, ran a comb through her hair and returned to the table. La Delia was already back, in gracious conversation with Longford. The woman spared Jess hardly a glance.

"I'll be heading for Kentor in the next few days, Horatio," La Delia said. "I'll be sure to pass on your concerns to the Government there."

Jess refused dessert and another glass of wine.

At last Hudson leaned across to her and whispered, "Time we left, my dear. We have an early start tomorrow." His furnace-hot gaze swept down to her breasts. No prizes for guessing his intentions. Jess smiled at him, sending positive signals while her mind murmured 'dream on'.

Others said their goodnights, too. Hudson slid a possessive arm around her waist, and paced up the stairs with her, an overwhelming presence at her side. Jess felt her resolve wavering, and steeled her heart. He was not going to win.

As soon as the door closed behind them, she whirled out of his grip.

"Jess, enough games." He took a step toward her, a half smile tugging at his lips.

She grabbed her bag and pulled out a nightgown.

He stared. "You won't need that."

"Yes I will." She dodged past him into the washroom and locked the door behind her, stifling a laugh. The look on his face was priceless. He'd been so certain she'd fall into his arms or tear his clothes off. Or both. She stripped off the dress and pulled the night gown over her head. She caught a glimpse of herself in the mirror and stopped for a longer look. Maybe this one wasn't the best choice. It didn't cling but it was semi-transparent. Too late now. She'd have to hope the gesture itself was enough to make the point.

When she emerged he'd stripped to the waist, except for a chain hanging around his neck. She hesitated, feeling her resolve turn to water. What a body. Six pack, wide shoulders, sculpted muscles. She hadn't expected that. He must work out. He unfolded his arms and came a step closer, grinning. "Well, if you must wear a nightgown, this one will do."

He put his hands on her waist. No. She locked her palms on his upper arms and willed her pulse to slow down, difficult to do with the hard muscle of his biceps filling her hands. "No. I said I was going to sleep on the couch and I meant it."

He sighed, closed his eyes in a slow, exasperated blink. "You don't mean that. You're beautiful. I want you. And I don't believe you don't want me."

She twisted around him and dragged a pillow and a blanket off the bed.

"Jess." He snapped out her name, almost like an order.

She escaped to the living room, dropped the pillow on the couch and herself on that. He'd followed her. His eyes burned like a giant blue star, furnace hot, furious. This was one extremely angry man. A quiver of fear arced through her.

"I will have you." He snarled the words through twisted lips but he didn't try to touch her.

Her heart hammered. If he insisted, she was no match for him physically.

"Not with my permission, you won't. Any other way, they call it rape. And I wouldn't have picked you for a rapist."

She pulled the blanket over her shoulder, closed her eyes and held her breath.

Chapter Seventeen

Hudson awoke before the building's IS announced the time. Grey light filtered between the slats of the blinds covering the windows. He swung his legs out of the bed, stood and went to the washroom with barely a glance at the closed bedroom door. God, what a night. It had been hours before he'd fallen asleep. If he could rewind and start again, he would. Shame had heat rising to his face. How could he have stooped to that? Would she ever forgive him? She seemed to bring out the worst in him. First his interrogation at dinner, and now this. She'd led him on, and he was sure quite deliberately, but even so.

He showered and dressed in his ground combat uniform, dark green until he turned on the camouflage sensors. He flung the jacket onto a chair and went to wake her before the IS did. She slept on the couch, lying on her side with her back pressed against the backrest, eyelashes brushing her cheeks, her hair in disarray. The couch was long enough, but he doubted if she would have been too comfortable. Serve her right. God, she was lovely. And smart. And feisty.

Jerking the blanket off her, he said, "Get yourself up, we're going off to the countryside."

She raised herself on her elbow, the semi-transparent material of the night gown hanging open, revealing a luscious view of breast. "Good morning, Admiral."

He allowed himself a long, lingering look that set off a familiar tingle in his groin. "Get dressed, Captain. The washroom is free."

He turned away and went to lock out the window. Clouds hung on the peaks to the East. With the sun rising behind them, the foothills lay in shadow, dark forest lapping the steeper slopes.

While she was away he contacted Commander Mann. No further news from Tabora.

Jess appeared, dressed in jeans and a grayish-blue shirt. She carried a black jacket and she'd tied back her hair. She looked tired.

"Did you sleep well?" he said.

"No. I spent a lot of time thinking about Santh. Any news from Tabora?"

She gazed up at him, waiting. "No, nothing." She nodded sadly and turned away. He reached out to touch but thought better of it. "Look. Jess. I'm sorry about last night. I was out of line. It won't happen again."

The look she gave him would have penetrated armor. "You're right. It won't."

Damn it. Another battle lost. But not the war, never the war. "Let's go. Breakfast, then off out there."

***

Ottenshaw had organized three copters. Hudson, Jess and Longford climbed into the third with their local guide. The compartment held six, three seats on each side of a central aisle. He and Jess sat side-by-side in the last row, Longford and the guide in front of them.

The three machines lifted off into a sparkling, cloudless sky and headed toward the mountains. The highest peaks wore dazzling snow crowns, while lower down the bare rockfaces glistened with moisture. They flew a short distance over cultivated fields before trackless forests took over.

The guide stirred in his seat. "You're an experienced hunter, Sir?" he said to Longford.

"That's right. Why?"

"Well, Sir, we've been told to head for the hills below Egmont, where we can look for stikhorns in the high meadows."

"This late in the season? Not much chance, eh?"

"Not much," the guide said. "They've started moving down but the forests can be dangerous, so Master Ottenshaw thought it best to be safe."

"What are you saying? That there won't be any game?" Hudson said.

"Precisely. The stikhorns migrate down from the high peaks for the winter and the bears follow them to fill up before the deep sleep," Longford said. "The meadows are fine if you want to admire the view but if you actually want to hunt…" He shrugged.

"Well, Sir, seeing as how you're an experienced hunter and I'm sure Admiral Hudson is, too, mebbe you'd like to go lower? Some place you stand a better chance?" The guide looked between the two men, ignoring Jess, who gazed out the window.

"Show me what you have in mind," Longford said.

The guide swiveled in his seat so his legs were in the aisle, pulled out a map sheet so Hudson and Longford could both see it and pointed as he talked. "If we go over this spur, and cross to where Lake Maribou is, we can land here and try our luck in the forest here."

Longford grunted. "I'm happy with that. What about you, Hudson?"

"I'm easy," Hudson said. "Jess?"

She turned slowly, a slight smile on her face. "Is that a fact, Admiral?" She smirked. "I don't care where we hunt."

Hudson grinned. At least she hadn't lost her sharp sense of humor. Longford didn't even try to hide the sneer. Why was he so against Jess?

The guide clambered into the cockpit to talk to the pilot. When he came back, the machine veered off to port, leaving the other two copters behind. The wind-swept meadows led into open woodland giving way to thick, dark forest. Hudson couldn't see anything but treetops. Ahead, a towering buttress of bare rock angled out of the mountain side. On the other side, a valley opened up with a lake fed by a waterfall at its centre. The forest hugged the water's edge. The pilot turned the machine toward a bare area rising out of the forest like a bald pate and slowed for a descent. The thrusters flattened the sparse grass as the copter settled onto its landing pads.

Hudson followed Longford and the guide down the ramp, Jess right behind him. The blades slowed, the whirr becoming a thrum. The guide walked around to the luggage compartment and pulled out picnic hampers and two guns, which he handed to Hudson and Longford.

"Where's mine?" Jess said. She wasn't pleased, eyes narrowed as she spoke.

"Oh. Sure, miss," the guide said. He pulled out another gun and held it out to her. "Um ... do you know how to use this?"

She took the weapon in both hands and stared down at it. "Rysal laser rifle with adjustable power control. I think I'll be able to work it out." She checked the settings, flicked off the safety and extended the sights. "Let's see now ... see the nut hanging from that branch?" She pointed at a tree on the opposite side of the clearing. The gun zapped.

She grinned. "Eh. I missed. But the gun works."

She hadn't missed the target by much. Hudson wondered how hard she'd tried. He finished checking his weapon. Fully powered up, ready to go.

Longford sneered, raised his gun and shattered the nut with a single blast. The look of triumph on his face was almost obscene. Jess said nothing but her eyes twinkled.

"So, where do we start?" Longford asked the guide.

"Down thata ways, I'd suggest," the man said, indicating a narrow opening between the trees. "The pilot picked up some heat signatures, half a dozen bodies down there."

"Lead on," Longford said.

"Pick yourselves up some water and food you want to carry," the fellow said. "We won't be back afore late afternoon."

Water bottles filled, wrapped lunch packets stowed in pockets, they started off away from the copter. His gun's strap looped over his shoulder, the guide strode off the knoll into the forest. The gap he'd picked must have been an animal trail, well-trodden but narrow, winding between tree trunks and bushes. Longford came next, followed by Jess and Hudson. Hudson peered around him, trying to get a sense of the forest. The foliage was typical of leaves in a harsh climate; needle-thin and oily. He broke off a leaf; a sharp and astringent smell filled his nostrils. Fallen leaves covered the ground in a deep carpet, while the light struggled to find any breaks in the thick canopy. Even in the mid-morning of a bright day only the occasional ray of sunshine broke through into the gloom to add a fleeting hint of brightness to the beards of lichen hanging from the branches. The only color came from horn-like growths protruding from some of the trees, cones of coiled yellow and blue. A few harsh calls filled the air and he caught a glimpse of dark wings before they were lost.

"Kurrwans," the guide said. "They don't see people much." He trudged on, his footfalls no more than a rustle.

Longford followed his every step, the caricature of a hunter. Jess seemed to pick her own trail, almost as silent as the guide. Several times she veered off course and he wondered why, until he stumbled over the hidden obstacle she'd avoided. After that, he followed her lead. She was a local, after all. He wondered how well she knew this forest.

Once, the guide stopped and crouched down beside a pile of droppings. "Stikhorns," he said. "A few hours old, I'd say."

They continued on for another half hour before he called a halt where a fallen tree had ripped a hole in the forest. Already, saplings vied for the light. The guide sat on a trunk green with lichen and moss. Longford pulled out some food and walked away on his own.

"You seem very comfortable here," Hudson said to Jess.

She unwrapped a chunk of filled pastry and bit into it. "Mm. I came here with my father when I was in my teens and later Troy and I camped out. Not here, so much, but around Lake Maribou."

"You've never mentioned it."

She grinned, eyes twinkling. "We've got a guide, haven't we? And Lord High Admiral Longford, haven't we? What could a poor, dumb schmuck like me offer them?"

Lord High Admiral, huh? What did she call him behind his back? "Did you try to hit that nut?"

"Not terribly hard. I knew Longford wouldn't be able to resist. And he *is* a good shot."

Hudson glanced around. He couldn't see Longford but he could hear him out between the trees not far away. "Why doesn't he like you?"

The twinkle died from her eyes. "He's certain I'm a smuggler but he can't prove it. Besides, women shouldn't own starships. And I won't go to bed with him."

"Ah." He wasn't surprised. A man like Longford wouldn't handle contempt well. And the lovely Jess would make sure he knew.

Longford's voice cut through the silence, asking the guide about the animals they were tracking. Hudson unhooked the water bottle on his belt and drank a few mouthfuls.

Jess grasped his arm. "I forgot. Something happened last night."

He looked away, the guilt sharp as a needle.

"Not you. I heard La Delia talking to Tanaka. He said something like 'relax, I'll deal with it' and mentioned contacts. I didn't catch the last part. They were out on the patio in private conversation. Any notion what that might be about?"

Delia Marati with the owner of Tabora Mining. "I don't know. But I'll certainly give it some thought when I get a chance. Thank you for telling me."

"Come along, you two. We can't sit around here all day," Longford boomed.

Hudson traded a sharp glance with Jess as he rose to his feet. She'd been startled, too. The fellow had sneaked up on them.

They set off again. The trail narrowed, winding through the trees. Hudson flexed his fingers on his rifle to ward off the chill. Time to put on gloves. The temperature had certainly dropped .

Ahead, the guide stopped. "I think we should be getting back." He peered up, trying to see through the canopy. "The weather's changed. Wouldn't be surprised if we got snow."

"Rubbish. A little bit further, man. We've come this far," Longford said.

Hudson noticed Jess' slight shake of the head. "We have a guide, Longford. We should trust him," he said.

Longford glared at him and the hackles rose on the back of his neck. *Don't try that with me.* He'd stared down presidents, grand admirals. Longford's eyes flickered. "If you say so. For you and the woman."

"Thanks so much, Admiral Longford. I'd hate to be caught out in a storm with you," Jess said.

Hudson swallowed the smirk. Her rapier wit was delightful. The more time he spent with her, the more attractive he found her. Longford's scowl showed he hadn't missed the barb.

The guide led them back the way they'd come, climbing up the path between the trees. Something rustled to the left. He gazed in the direction of the sound but the trees crammed close together. Claustrophobic was the best word he could find. You had so much more room in space. He was relieved to see the dim glow of daylight as they approached the bald patch of hill where the copter was parked.

Longford had taken the lead, striding along. Jess followed with Hudson behind her as before. The guide slowed down, dropping back for some reason.

The copter's engine started, a dissident murmur in these pristine woods. The blades thrummed, idling. The pilot must be in a hurry to get out of here. Longford burst out of the forest, powering toward the machine. The copter rose.

"What the fuck are you doing?" Longford shouted. He stood, legs akimbo, the rifle still dangling from his shoulder.

Hudson cleared the trees as the machine lifted and tilted its nose. Fuck. Oh, fuck. He dived, collecting Jess in the shoulder. The grass and rock exploded into shrapnel behind him, splattering his back. Jess scampered away from him, heading for the trees. He scrambled after her, the hum of the copter loud in his ears. She'd turned, slipped the gun off her shoulder and raised it. The muzzle glared at him, a black, malevolent nothingness. His heart thundered.

Chapter Eighteen

The gun spat blue-white lightning. The bolt streaked past him. He heard a grunt.

"Get down here, Hudson." Jess' voice was sharp, urgent.

He leapt forward to where she crouched behind the tree and knelt beside her. Beyond where he'd stood the guide lay spread-eagled on the ground. She hadn't missed. And damn it, his rifle lay out there, too.

"Come on, we've got to skedaddle," she said, easing into the undergrowth.

"Longford?"

"Didn't stand a chance."

Gunfire spat from the hovering machine, shattering the leaves and twigs above them. She left the gun and slithered down a slope and under a bush. He followed her lead.

Maybe he could reach *Defender*? The implant placed into every Confederacy citizen's skull at an early age provided a powerful communication facility. He opened the channel with a thought. Nothing but static.

"Nordheim doesn't have enough satellites," Jess whispered. "Reception's crummy out here at the best of times, worse if the weather closes in. It only works at the lodge because Ottenshaw has a tower and a booster."

Damn. He shifted one receptor to short range. "Open a connection to your implant. At least we'll be able to communicate skull-to-skull."

"*Done*," she said in his head. She kept moving deeper into the forest.

He activated the camouflage function on his suit and flipped the hood over his head. "*You left the gun.*"

"*Yes. Useless. Lucky I got him. It's now out of charge. Rigged, I'd say.*" She scurried on.

Of course. The whole trip had been a setup. But who had set them up? Ottenshaw? One of Longford's people? Delia Marati, perhaps? The guide had been in on it. While he and Longford and Jess were away in the woods they'd swapped the simple copter used to ferry them here for a Militia gunship. He could think about that later. "*They'll have heat detection.*"

"*Guess so. What'll they do, d'you reckon?*"

"*If it was me I'd find us and put a missile down here.*"

"*Missile? Have they?*" Crouching, she skirted around a bush.

"*Oh, yes. This is one of the Militia copters. Keep moving, Jess. They might delay because they can't find me.*"

"*Ah. Invisible suit.*"

"*Yes. Come here. There's room for two. At least for a little while.*"

She didn't argue. He opened the jacket, facing away from the sound of the ship in the sky. She stood with her back to him and he wrapped the cloth and himself around her as best he could. "*We have to keep moving. Sideways. Fast.*"

The air rang as the missile howled past and struck ahead of where they'd been. A tree exploded. Debris splattered around them; mud, leaves, pebbles, twigs. He strained to listen. The sound of the copter's engines had changed.

"*They're landing,*" he said. "*They'll send in searchers.*"

"*But only the pilot stayed behind.*"

"*They've had plenty of time to pick up extras.*"

He pushed her, heading for the densest parts of the forest. "*Where to? Any ideas?*"

"*I don't know this part of the world. We need to get to Lake Maribou. Have you got a compass?*"

"*Yes. Comes with the suit.*"

"*We want East. And down.*"

Judging by the absence of noise, the copter had landed. Hudson wished he had brought the suit's helmet with him so he'd have increased surveillance capability but he hadn't expected to be the hunted in this expedition. They'd probably take off again, keep searching beyond the missile strike. Yes. The thrum of the blades became a whirr, the engines thrust down.

"*East is that way. Find the thickest forest you can,*" he said.

She moved carefully, making sure they stayed close together. How long could they keep this up and stay away from unencumbered hunters? Every time he heard a sound his nerves jolted.

The copter approached, invisible above the foliage. He urged her deeper under the trees.

"*Drop,*" Hudson said.

She dropped, face down, arms close to her sides. He covered her. Even if their infra-red cut down this far, the suit would deflect the sensors. The machine didn't even slow down, cruising overhead in a searching pattern. He waited.

Jess stirred beneath him. "*There's bugs down here.*"

"*There's death up there.*"

She sniffed.

The sound of the copter receded. They'd have to risk it. Searchers on foot could be closing in. He clambered to his feet. She followed, brushing off dirt and clinging leaves as best she could. She pulled a face and picked off a slithering, slimy creature which had attached itself to her pants. But no complaints. His admiration for her grew.

The trees crowded close but at least their footsteps were almost silent in the thick leaf litter covering the ground. Visibility was certainly limited and the shadows under the trees seemed to have deepened. He checked the compass, corrected their direction a little. She'd found a path, narrow, overgrown and winding but at least a path. They moved faster, still close together. He'd have to hope the searchers were looking for two people but surely they would have known he wore a camouflage suit? The skin prickled between his shoulder blades.

"*I think it's going to snow,*" Jess said. "*I can smell it.*"

"*I'll take your word for it.*" What does snow smell like? All he could smell was earth and trees and damp.

A sharp report sent the adrenalin screaming down his spine. Jess had stopped, too. That way, coming along the path behind them. It could be anything; a bear, a falling branch, a hunter.

Something fell on his cheek, feather soft, and disappeared. Snow.

"*That way. Quick.*" Jess half turned him, shielding her body with his and left the path. She slid around a bush, behind a tree and pulled her way up a bank. Good idea. They rolled over the top of the ridge and lay together. She had her arms around him, pulled close against his chest, the top of her head at his throat. He felt the pounding of her heart against his ribs. The irony made him smile.

A soft murmur filled the air, with an occasional plop that set his heart racing until he saw an overloaded leaf release its burden. This could be a blessing in disguise. Come to think of it, he hadn't heard the copter for a time, now. More snowflakes drifted past the foliage. He strained his ears, listening. Was that a footstep? A muffled scrape; the sound of fabric moving over fabric. A jingle; a clink. Two people, walking slowly. The footsteps stopped. He held his breath.

The snow thickened, tickling his eyelashes, settling on her hair. A trickle of melt water dribbled toward his chin.

"Fuck it. The signal's disappeared again. All I'm getting is snow," a male voice muttered.

"It wasn't much of a signal, anyway. I told you it was going to snow. And now it's getting heavier. We're not dressed for this." A female, querulous.

"Neither are they." A snort. "They'll freeze to death if they stay out."

"It's not they. There's only one, broken up signal. We might be following her, or him. Or maybe a bear or a stikhorn. And anyway, we won't achieve anything freezing to death." Feet stamped, thudding on the soft ground.

"We might be able to take this pair out," Hudson said. *"They're bickering and they don't know what they're chasing. If we can separate them, we stand a chance."*

"They might go away."

"Yes. But I'd like a weapon, wouldn't you?"

"I suppose so. What've you got in mind?"

"You run for it so they pick up your heat signature. If you head into the forest they won't get a clear shot. They'll have to cross over the ridge to shoot." She stirred against his chest. *"Not now. If they split up, so much the better. I'll tell you when."*

"Ah, you're probably right. Forecast says it'll get worse."

"Which means he or she won't survive the night out here, anyway. I'm going back to the others. You can stay if you want."

Footsteps thudded dully, retreating back the way they'd come. For a few heartbeats the other person didn't move. A muttered 'oh, bugger'.

"Now," Hudson said.

Jess pushed herself away from his chest, leapt to her feet and ran deeper into the trees. He gathered himself.

A gasping intake of air. "Fuck." A body crashed up the other side of the slope towards him, the rustles and bangs betraying somebody unslinging a rifle on the run. He'd have to be quick; the other one was coming back, running. The man rose above the ridge, rifle first. Hudson grabbed his arm, spun around, took the man's weight on his shoulder and pivoted him into the ground. The fellow rolled. Hudson dived for his gun at the same time he did. They snarled at each other over the barrel. Thrusting himself forward, Hudson caught his opponent square in the nose with his forehead. The trooper grunted, loosened his grip but didn't let go. Hudson tugged at the gun, but the other man was strong.

"Hold onto him, Tom," A female voice yelled from the ridge top. "Turn him a bit."

Chapter Nineteen

His opponent grinned, despite the blood trickling from a broken nose. Straining, he turned Hudson into the line of fire. Hudson's flesh crawled. He could almost feel the crosshairs lining up. Shit. He heaved with all his strength, pivoting Tom just as the other trooper fired. The beam hit the fellow in the side and blasted him sideways down the slope. If he wasn't dead he'd be out of it.

"Fuck it," the woman snarled. She fired again but Hudson dived away, feeling the heat as the beam seared into the ground. He'd have to take her out. But how? Tom's rifle lay out of reach. If he went for it, she'd have him.

He half turned, in time to see Jess slam into the woman's side, sending her staggering, off balance. Jess snatched the gun, but not before the trooper had fired a bolt that scorched through the canopy, scattering leaves. The two women struggled, crashing in the bushes, grunting. Jess was lighter than the other woman. Her opponent swung Jess around and slammed her against a tree trunk. Hudson dived for the fallen rifle, swung it up and shot the woman in the back.

Jess' mouth contorted in disgust as the body collapsed into her arms. "Uggh." She let go, allowing the corpse to slump into a heap on the ground, a blackened hole in its back.

Hudson ran up the ridge. "Are you okay?"

She nodded, her throat muscles working.

He rolled the body over. The trooper's eyes were open, her expression fixed in a grimace of astonishment. No pulse. He closed her eyes with two fingers.

"What about the other one?" Jess said.

"Wait. I'll check."

He scrambled down the slope to where the fellow lay in a tangle of limbs. Snow was beginning to settle on his body. Not much doubt but Hudson checked, anyway. Dead. He searched the man's pockets and removed his water bottle. They'd need it more than he would. He scooped up the fallen gun. No messing about. They had their weapons set to maximum power; shoot to kill.

Jess rubbed a hand over her mouth. "What'll we do with them?"

"Nothing we *can* do. There are others out there. This'll buy us some time but not much. Take her water and let's get moving."

"Yeah." Muscles twitched in her cheeks as she gazed at the bodies.

Hudson put a hand on her shoulder. "They would have killed us."

"Yeah."

He shook her lightly. He'd have to snap her out of this. "He was right when he said we'd freeze. Any ideas?"

"Only the one I had before. We head for the lake. There are emergency shelters I know of. We're still tracking right for that?"

"East and downhill. Yes."

"Well, then, Admiral. Shall we go?" She forced a grin, waiting for an answer. Dirt-streaked and damp, she was still delectable.

"Carry on, Captain."

She scrambled down the bank and back onto the path. Snow dusted the leaf litter, lighting up the path sufficiently to differentiate it from the surrounding forest where the gloom gathered under the trees. He checked his chrono; sunset should be in an hour and a half or thereabouts.

"Back to implants, I think," he said, slinging the rifle at his hip. "*The less noise, the better.*"

Jess gathered up the woman's rifle from the ground, hung it over her shoulder and set off, following the path between the trees in the deepening darkness. Bushes stirred as she brushed against them but the snow burden was heavy enough to prevent any rustling. They trudged on, close together but unencumbered. Snow filtered down around them. His boots sank a little deeper into the leaf litter with each step.

"*Why do they want you dead?*" Jess asked. "*You and Longford?*"

"*Good question. Maybe they want you dead, too.*"

"*Me?*"

"*Well, you saw Marati and Tanaka chatting. Did they see you?*"

Her soft footfalls filled the silence before she answered. "*Yes, they did and they disappeared real quick.*" She walked on a few steps. "*But why not get the guide to shoot us here?*"

"*Yes, I've been thinking about that. Maybe we were supposed to be killed in an accident.*"

She slowed down so fast he almost walked into her. "*What?*"

"*The joint exercises are close by. Maybe that's why they brought us here. Collateral damage. So sad.*"

"*Well, that gives us both something to think about.*"

Jess slithered down a short slope. A flat expanse lay ahead, presumably Lake Maribou. The water's surface seemed to absorb the light, a deeper, flatter darkness surrounded by white-encrusted vegetation. The lake would freeze, but not tonight. Moonlight appeared, a brief glow through a hole in the clouds, illuminating tree trunks leaning out from the shore. Nearby, a fallen tree lay half-submerged, its roots sticking up among the litter of logs and branches on the bank.

"*What now?*" Hudson said.

"*We'll head around the edge of the lake that way.*" She pointed. "*There's an emergency shelter in a cave in the cliffs.*"

"*Won't they know about it?*"

"*Yes. I'm hoping it's the last place they'll think to look. Especially in a snow storm.*"

True enough.

She followed the water's edge, finding a path around the tree trunks and undergrowth, the lake on her right. They were lucky she knew this place; very lucky.

Jess' foot slipped on a wet log, she teetered, staggered and fell backwards into the dark water. The sound of the splash was swallowed in the falling snow. Drenched, she rose to her feet. Ripples circled away from where she stood, knee-deep. Hudson grabbed her and dragged her out. Her teeth were already chattering; the dunking wouldn't have helped.

"*Okay?*"

"*Yeah. Not much further. I hope.*"

He hoped, too. She led him on a scramble up a rocky slope where the snow had not yet lodged, then followed a track he could barely see. The lake disappeared, somewhere down there to his right beyond the falling snow. She hesitated, unsure for a moment, standing with one hand against a rock face.

"*The place I'm heading for is more for people in boats. We have to go down. Take it easy.*"

She climbed carefully down rocks that formed a natural, if uneven, stair. The air burned in his lungs. He no longer felt his nose and cheeks and he flexed and unflexed his fingers to keep the circulation going. She had to be freezing.

"*Here.*"

She took his hand, tugged him forward under an overhang too low for him to stand upright. A few staggered steps and he sensed rather than saw the expanse of space.

"*Wait.*"

Wood scraped on stone. Light pierced his eyes and he shut them, waiting for ten seconds before opening them again.

He stood in a water-formed cave. Two lamps had been strung up on opposite sides, forming conjoined pools of soft illumination. Beyond the rings of light deep shadows congregated in unknown corners. Stalagmites hung from the ceiling, the parts inside the dome of light glowing in bands of browns and yellows. A folded blanket lay on a camp bed, and a table and two chairs stood against a wall.

Jess crouched beside a panel, fiddling with controls, a puddle forming around her.

"What's that?" he said, aloud.

"A-a h-heater. If I can get my fingers to turn it on." He barely understood the words, forced out between chattering teeth.

When she spoke with her own voice he could hear the shiver, the tiredness. The cold had etched into her face, accentuating her cheekbones. She could have been carved from porcelain. A click, she grunted and sucked a finger. Hudson removed his gloves and took over. One twist and the panel began to glow. He knelt beside her, warming his hands. The heat hurt.

"We have to get our clothes dry," he said. "Take them off. You're using your body heat."

She nodded, fought with her jacket, trying to pull her arms out of the sleeves. He helped her, dragged the chairs over and draped the coat over the back of one. Water dripped onto the floor. She struggled with her trousers. He tugged them off for her. She was shivering, her body icy.

"We'll have to share body heat. It's the easiest way of warming you up."

"Yes, I know," she managed through chattering teeth.

He stripped down to his undershorts and hung his clothes close to the heat. Steam had already begun to rise from the garments but the warmth hadn't reached the rest of the cave.

She was down to her knickers. "My n-nipples are so t-tight they hurt."

He doubted if she'd be impressed with his equipment at the moment. But looking at her was enough to stir his blood. She was everything he'd imagined and more. Cream skin, lovely breasts, their chocolate nipples currently tight as nails, a slim, athletic body. But she was exhausted, shivering with cold.

When she was down to her panties he guided her over to the camp bed and helped her lie down. He eased himself down beside her, pulled the blanket over them and put his arms around her. She trembled against his chest, her nipples hard and cold as studs. The thought of sex was enough to have his blood flowing again. His cock swelled and pressed against his undershorts, rigid and ready. Her nipples softened and he ached to take them in his mouth. No. She was barely conscious. It would amount to rape and he'd seen that far too many times in his career. Besides, her words echoed. *Not with my permission you won't.*

He ran his hand down her back to cup her buttock. His thumb found the edge of her panties, lifted. *Don't go there.* She stirred, moved her head, searching. He raised his head to look down at her, wondering what was wrong. She wound an arm around his neck and kissed him, her tongue probing politely between his lips. No. It wasn't right. He twisted his head away.

"S'all right," she murmured. "You've earned it." She found his lips again.

Oh, yes. He drank her in, tasted her, sucked at her lower lip while his hand fondled a nipple. He dragged his mouth from hers and nibbled on her breast, flicking the nipple with his tongue. She wriggled, moaned her pleasure as he slipped his hand into the warmth between her thighs. The panties were in the way. He pushed them down, impatient, and she curled up to flick them off and kick them aside while he shoved his undershorts down to his thighs. She parted her legs so he could explore and caress, pressing her hips up against his hand. He shifted his body over hers and guided himself into her. Warm and wet, smooth as honey. Oh, yes. She moved beneath him, matching his strokes, her knees drawn up. He arched over her, kissing as he fucked her, her fingers at the back of his neck.

He came too soon, pressing into her as deep as he could. Stupid. He should have controlled himself, throttled back. God, this woman made him feel like an idiot again.

"I'm sorry," he mumbled against her hair.

He felt her smile. "No worries. We're both warm now. And we should both get some sleep. We have to be out of here before dawn."

Chapter Twenty

Another day at Tabora. Santh closed his eyes as his hopper soared away from the latest asteroid, a full load of ore locked inside. Even with his eyes closed Tabora's rippling clouds streamed across his brain, interlocking streaks of red and brown and grey. The pattern could have been etched into his sub-conscious. No wonder people left before their contracts were up. Except for Ace. The kid didn't seem to have an imagination. Tabora didn't bother him; or so he said. It seemed to be true, too. He didn't have that pinched look around the eyes like so many of the other miners. Like himself.

He jolted in his seat as the hopper joined the tipping queue, fourth in line, firing its forward thrusters to slow down. He could sure use a drink. After he'd had a shower.

Santh eased himself out of the airlock and released his helmet seals. Ah. The station air sure tasted better than the recycled stuff in the suit after a day out there. No sign of Ace. He was probably suiting up. Santh shuffled into the change room and clambered out of his suit; it stank of sweat. He hung it away, where the systems would empty out the shit bags and clean the inside.

"Hello. Are you Jim Jonson?"

This guy was new, no doubt about it. Clean and scrubbed, bright eyed and ready to go. "Yeah?"

"I'm your new partner. Phin Lamb." He held out a hand.

"Huh? New partner? Where's Ace?" Santh ignored the hand.

Lamb's hand dropped, his gaze faltering. "I don't know anything about any Ace. I was told to come down here to start my shift."

Was Ace sick? Could be, although he seemed strong as a bull.

"Look, I need the tags." Lamb glanced at him, wary and edgy.

"Uh ... yeah." Santh picked up the pair of tags that gained access to the hopper's cockpit from where he'd dropped them on the change room seat and thrust them at the other man. "Here you go. Keep safe."

He spun around and strode off to the shower, ignoring the man's thanks. Hot water, turned on hard, pummeled his body, working out the sweat and the stink of the suit. He washed his hair, too, as he did every day. What happened to Ace? First things first; check his room.

Dried and dressed, he hurried along the walkways to the room next to his. Locked. The strip on the door said 'Anderson'. Shit. Chewing at his lip, he tried Ace's number on his comlink. He listened to the first few words of the message. *'Cheers, whoever you are. I'll get back to you'.*

He stared down at the comlink in his hand. It didn't make sense. The guy had to be sick or something. He'd better ask at admin. He strode along the walkway to the transit and punched in the destination.

The lift opened in reception. A girl sat at a desk directly opposite. She ran an admiring glance over his body and smiled. "Can I help you?"

Sometimes it helped to be the smooth hetero. Santh put on his best sultry 'you-turn-me-on' look as he approached the desk. "Yes, darling. I'm wondering what's happened to my partner? He didn't show up for his shift." He rested a buttock on her desk.

She leant her chin on her fist and batted her eyelashes at him. "What's his name?"

"Ace. Ace Connor." He made a show of admiring her cleavage.

She turned to her systems. "Record for Ace Connor." The data appeared. "He's gone," she said. "Shipped out."

Santh's heart lurched. "Are you sure?"

"Sure I'm sure. Here." She directed the display onto the wall so he could see. "And you can see here, his signature as well as an electronic ID."

That's what it said. Ace had terminated his contract and shipped out on a delivery vessel that docked yesterday and headed back to Nordheim three hours ago. Shit.

"I'll be off duty in an hour," the girl said, curling a lock of her hair coquettishly around her finger.

Santh jerked out of his reverie. She had blue eyes and her lips curved in a hopeful smile. "Uh, sorry, sweetheart, I'd love to but I've already got a date for tonight. Another time, yeah?"

She pouted. "Okay. Well, you know where to find me."

"Yeah. I'll be sure to. Soon. Thanks." He headed back to the transit.

As he stood in the lift the door to the manager's office opened. Santh caught a glimpse of two men standing together, talking. Orlando. He sprinted out of the car and into Orlando's office, almost pushing the departing man aside. "Got a minute, Mister Orlando?"

The other fellow stared at him, jaw dropped, then looked back at Orlando.

"I'll be with you in a moment, Captain," Orlando said. "I'm sure this won't take long. If you'll wait outside?"

The man nodded and walked out.

"Well?" Orlando faced him, legs apart, arms folded.

"Ace Connor. He's left," Santh said.

Orlando lifted a shoulder. "Happens all the time. He shipped out on *Trader Horn*."

Santh shook his head. "He wasn't the type. Did he leave a forwarding address? Have you informed his family?"

"Look, Jonson, he isn't dead, he isn't sick. He left of his own accord whether you like it or not. So no, I haven't informed his family and wouldn't have even if he had given us a contact address which he didn't. And no, he didn't leave a forwarding address. Will that be all? Captain Zhan and I are going for a drink."

He shifted his hands to his hips, a long-suffering manager putting up with a cantankerous idiot. Santh wasn't going to get anywhere with him.

"Sure." He walked out, past Captain Zhan and into the lift.

The two men stood in the foyer, exchanging some remarks. As the doors closed, something zinged in Santh's brain, a memory. He'd seen that posture before. What had he seen? He shook his head. It didn't matter right now.

The mechanism hummed as the lift descended. No way known would Ace have broken his contract. The guy was cool as dried ice. He knew what he wanted; credits to buy a farm. He hadn't been a drinker, wouldn't have taken Nervana, didn't mess with the girls; at least, as far as he knew from spending two days off together. He could be wrong, he supposed. But he didn't think so.

After the lift doors swished aside he walked to the 'Star Struck' on automatic. The sound blasted as he approached, music interlaced with raucous laughter, the din of conversation. He fronted up to the bar and ordered a beer from Tracey, the floozy in residence. He'd been here long enough now to know all their names.

"How was your day, Jim?" Tracey said, placing a brimming glass in front of him. Froth flowed down the side onto the sodden beer mat.

"Yeah, good. Listen, Tracey, did you see Ace yesterday? Ace Connor? He's my partner."

Tracey grinned. "Sure. He was in here yesterday, had a couple of beers." She giggled. "The new girl, Annie, tried to latch on to him. I tried to tell her not to bother. It was pretty funny."

"Anything different about him?"

"No. Same as usual. Why? Is something the matter?"

"No." He tried a grin. "Just wondered. He left on his own?"

"Yeah. Like he always does." She turned away to serve another customer.

Santh downed his beer. Shit. He banged his glass down on the counter. Orlando in his office, talking to somebody. The memory slotted into place. Troy talking to somebody here in this bar. Orlando; he'd been talking to

Orlando. After that, Orlando had helped Troy's companion—Rawlings—out of the tavern. It might mean nothing. The man was a manager. Why shouldn't he talk to the staff?

"Another beer, Jim?" Tracey said.

"Huh? Yeah, why not."

She filled his glass. He leaned on his elbow against the bar and lifted the glass to his lips. A jolt in the back lurched him forward. Beer spilled over the counter, ran down his face into his shirt. "Fuck."

"Sorry, buddy. Really sorry."

Santh looked up at a man in a ship suit, red-faced and apologetic. He had to shout above the din. "Somebody barged into me. The place is so crowded. Let me get you another one."

"Yeah. No problem," Santh said, wiping ineffectually at his shirt. Tracey had hurried over, mopping at the spilled beer. She replaced the beer mat and put a new glass in front of Santh.

"Sheesh I should know better. It's always like this," the new man said. He leaned close to be heard over the noise.

"Yes. Been here before?" Santh read his name from the label on his ship suit. Trent. The ship insignia on the other side of his suit read *Beaconsfield*. A shiver of something—alarm, dread—trickled down his spine.

Trent nodded. "Sure. Several times."

"When are you out?"

"Let's see ... ten hours, local time."

"What's your cargo?" Santh said.

"This 'n that."

"Bodies?"

Trent glanced around him. "You know about that, do you? Oh, well, they're dead, aren't they?"

Bodies. Yes, but were they all dead? His heart jolted. He hadn't thought about that before. "Yeah, guess so. Did you bring up the body tubes?"

Trent frowned. "You know a lot about it."

Shit. "A friend of mine told me about it. Bloke called Rawlings."

"Him?" Trent sneered, lip curled. "He did one tour, then he disappeared."

Santh tightened his grip on his glass. Rawlings had slipped out, the first name that came to mind. So he'd served on *Beaconsfield*.

"Wanker," Trent said. "It's no big deal. We collect the tubes and take 'em to Kentor. Nothing spooky about it."

"No, guess not." So those blasted tubes were here somewhere, loaded with something. Santh drained his beer. "Thanks, pal. Gotta go. Have a good flight."

He waved goodbye and headed for the comms booth. Jess and Tenna should be back from Paradise Cove by now.

Jeeves answered. Yes, she was home but she'd gone out. Fuck it. He couldn't wait. He left her a message.

First stop, the morgue.

He stopped the lift at the floor for the med centre.

Frowning and clutching at his forehead, he shambled up to the desk. "Can I see the doctor?" he asked the male attendant.

The fellow glowered at him. "What's the problem?"

"Migraine. Severe. Medication isn't helping."

"Sit down. Doctor Berger won't be long."

Berger called him into a treatment room. Santh took a moment to admire soft brown eyes and sculpted lips. Pity he hadn't met *him* earlier. He'd bet a month's pay the fellow was homo; you could always tell.

"Migraine, huh?" the doctor said.

"Yeah. I'm stressed. That planet, you know? You can't get the damn thing out of your head."

They exchanged a smile. "Yes, it certainly gets into people's brains. Sit down here, will you?"

Santh subsided into a chair. Berger dragged over a diagnostic unit and attached the connection to Santh's ear lobe.

"A man's tempted to try Nervana."

Berger stiffened, looked up. "I wouldn't recommend it."

"No. I heard it can be lethal. Has anybody died of an overdose lately?"

"Yes, one, about twelve days ago."

"I heard somebody died earlier today," Santh said.

"No," Berger said, still studying the lines on the screen. "We've only got the two bodies."

"Two?"

Berger shot a glance at him. "Yes. The other one died of an accident a month or so ago."

Okay, scrub that one. Maybe Ace really had just left.

"Your brain functions are fairly normal," Berger said, switching off the diagnostic unit. He removed the connection and selected a phial from a shelf. "Here's an anti-depressant. It'll help you to get rid of that planetary wheel before your eyes. Take one before bed."

"Thanks, doc." Santh made sure his hand made contact with the doctor's. They shared a smile that said they'd like to know each other better. "Listen, I'm a bit worried about my partner, Ace Connor. Has he been to see you?"

Berger's lips quirked. "Let me check." His eyes took on that faraway look as he accessed his implant. "No, I haven't seen anyone of that name."

"Okay. Thanks."

"Come and let me know how you get on, huh?" Berger said.

"I'd love to. Soon."

He smiled to himself as he walked back to the transit. Well, an unexpected glimmer of light in the darkness, something to look forward to. They'd have to be careful but that was okay.

Back in his dogbox of a room he called up the graphic display of the Tabora platform. Where would those tubes be? They stored the ore out in space, ready for the big transports. Of course. Bodies were packed into tubes and they didn't need air, they had their own supply. Why waste a precious commodity? "Show me the warehouses."

The display moved to the warehouses near the docks. Santh zoomed in on an area colored red. A warning message flashed VACUUM. It made sense. He'd bet a month's pay that was the right place. If he wanted to have a look in there, he'd need an exo-suit. He could go and fetch his suit from the change rooms. He checked the chart. Maintenance here, change room here with hopper docks this side, ship docks that side. He'd have no need to be there, no excuse if they asked him why he was in the warehouse or, for that matter, where he was going with a suit?

He could say he was a maintenance tech. Their suits would be the same as a hopper jock's, surely. Yes, carrying out maintenance in the store. Checking the airtight seals. Sure. He could do that.

Santh strolled back down to the change rooms. At least between shifts no one was around. He pulled on his suit, still warm from the cleansing and tucked the helmet under his arm. The system hadn't finished replenishing the air supply but there'd be enough. His heart hammered so fast he could have set double time for a marching display. *Look like you belong, look like you've got somewhere to go.*

He walked out of the change rooms and resisting the temptation to look around, turned right, off past the freighter docks. The first was empty. Tabora didn't take much traffic and this bay was for smaller ships like *Saintly Maid*. *Beaconsfield* was parked at the next bay. They'd already fitted the hoses to replenish air and water, and a couple of maintenance people stood with heads together over a diagnostic. They were still unloading, running low loaders carrying containers to the stores. Santh waited for one to pass and dodged in behind another to follow it into the store room.

The robot low loader trundled over to a stack of containers, where a crane made ready to transfer its cargo to the pile. Santh hurried past. According to the graphic, a shielded door opened into an airlock for the vacuum area. They'd painted the door red.

"Hey, you. What're you doing?" A strident woman's voice cut across the hum of the machinery.

Fuck. Santh's heart raced. He turned to face the person striding towards him, frown in place, clip in hand. "Is there a problem?"

"That's a vacuum in there." She glared at him.

"Yes. I'm from *Beaconsfield*. I'm here to check the … er cargo. Know what I mean?" His exo-suit didn't have name patches, wasn't distinguishable from any other exo-suit. He crossed virtual fingers.

Her eyes narrowed. "They didn't say."

"It's just routine. We like to know what we're dealing with."

The frown lifted. "Huh. Body tubes." She shrugged. "Fair enough. There's nothing valuable in there, anyway."

Santh schooled his expression and punched the touch pad to open the door. Inside the airlock, he donned his helmet. He'd have to be quick; only half an hour's worth of air. He watched the familiar color graduation on the gauge fade from red to green. Blinking green. The door opened and lights flickered on.

Santh stepped into a long, relatively narrow room. He gave the containers stacked to the ceiling on one side a cursory glance. On the other side cylinders longer than a tall man lay on semi-circular battens, four lines of five. A shiver ran up his spine. He'd felt like that when he checked them onto *Kimberley*, rows of dead guys. Maybe. He paced along one row, then another, checking names. The first few he didn't recognize; then Dunblain, Arthur. He stopped short. Artie Dunblain. He'd been part of his intake, short guy with muscles. He'd left after a week, he was sure he'd heard. Dead? Nobody had said dead, he was certain. His stride lengthening, he searched for Ace's name. The one down the end, the last one; Ace Connor. He stared down at the name plate, the letters burning into his brain.

The door to the airlock hissed open. He whirled, his heart pounding. Two figures approached, anonymous in exo-suits. Santh backed away, trying to get a tube between him and his assailants. That's what they were; assailants. One of them raised a laser rifle.

"Come along quietly, Jonson, and you won't be hurt."

Santh hesitated, gloved hands on the corpse tube between him and the man with the gun.

"Or I can kill you where you stand."

The words were casual, ice-cold. Santh shivered. He meant what he said. "Okay. Don't shoot."

They shepherded him to the airlock door and inside the chamber. He watched the gauge change color, his heart thudding against his ribs. Green.

"Helmet off." One man kept his gun trained while the other man took off his own helmet.

Santh complied. What else to do? Maybe he was just going to get a telling off. He hoped. The chamber door opened. One of his guards pushed him out, a hand in the small of his back.

Out in the warehouse the woman he'd spoken to grinned at him. And here came Orlando, thrusting through the warehouse entrance, a nasty smirk on his face. "Did you find your friend, Jonson?"

"Uh, no. No sign of him."

Orlando snorted. "You know, I don't believe you. Ah well, I'm sure there's room for one more. Take him out, boys."

Chapter Twenty-one

Jess blinked her eyelashes. They felt sticky, gummed up. Memories came crashing back; shooting the guide, Longford torn apart in a hail of fire from the copter, she and Hudson hurrying through the forest. And having sex. He lay beside her, his arm a weight across her body, eyelashes draped on his cheek, mouth loose and relaxed in sleep. If he was like any other man she'd come across, he'd wake up randy, wanting sex but, nice as it undoubtedly would be, they needed to get out of here. She checked the chrono on her implant. Going for seven. Dawn should be an hour or so away. They'd left the lights on. The stalagmites hung down, the bands of color shining softly, deep shadows beyond them. The air was warmer than it had been but she wouldn't call it warm. Her breath still misted in front of her face.

She put her hand on his shoulder, the 'not now' speech ready in her head. "Hudson."

His eyes opened, alert, aware, ready. "Something wrong?" He moved his weight, sitting up as he spoke.

"No. Dawn's maybe an hour away. We need to get out of here."

His mouth quirked in a wry smile as he flicked the blanket away, revealing a massive ridge inside his undershorts. "A pity, but you're right."

She grinned. She'd have to learn to never underestimate this man. "I'll make it up to you later."

He caught her eye and smiled. "Well, well; things have changed."

"They have a bit, haven't they? We seem to be on the same side. For now, anyway." She hesitated. Things had changed. And she'd played him for a fool at Ottenshaw's. "Look, what happened at the villa." He stared at her, his eyes unreadable. "I was angry at being dragged off from what I was doing."

She couldn't bring herself to say the 's' word. To hide the rising blush she fumbled on the ground for her discarded panties. A shower would have been good.

The incident had passed. Hudson retrieved his trousers from the chairs where they'd hung their clothes to dry and pulled them on. The round disc he wore on a chain around his neck swung as he moved. She wondered what it was. A military ID thing?

Her pants were almost dry. Oh well, it couldn't be helped. She stepped into them, squirming at the damp, cold contact. Her body heat would dry them out some more.

"Is there any food here?" Hudson said.

"There should be some hard rations." Jess searched the boxes stacked in the corner and found some vacuum packed snack bars. "This'll have to do."

"As long as it's food." He unwrapped a bar and bit into it.

Jess followed suit, chewing on dried fruit and nuts. "Where to, Admiral?" she said when she could.

"My troops are supposed to be conducting exercises near here. They might even be searching if the word's out we're missing. We look for them."

"We can trust them?"

"I have no reason not to. Longford's Militia ... I'm not so sure."

"No, neither am I. First Troy and now us."

"It wouldn't be the first time troopers or police were on the take. It's certainly not impossible." Hudson found two glasses and filled them with water.

She took the glass and drank. "If they're on the take, you'd expect it would be through Tanaka."

"Maybe. Or people who work for him."

She drained the glass. "I know Tanaka. He's sly, devious and not above bumping off anybody in his way."

Hudson finished his water and she rinsed the glasses, ready for the next visitors. "We have a lot to talk about, but not now."

He gathered up the rifle from where he'd leant it against a wall, eased the shelter door open and peered outside. Jess retrieved the other weapon, slung it on her shoulder and accompanied him out into still darkness. Stars shone steady, diamond bright in a space-cold sky. Any parts of the landscape not covered by snow stood out dark and ominous. Below, the wide, black expanse was Lake Maribou, not yet frozen. The cold seeped in, insidious fingers feeling a way into the cloth. Her breath misted before her face.

"*Good in a way, bad in another,*" he said to her implant. "*We can't avoid leaving footprints.*"

She nodded. What more was there to say?

"*Which way?*"

"*Up. Back up the path we came and around the mountain.*"

"*You lead.*"

She passed around him and headed up the slope, footsteps crunching in fresh snow. "*Careful. The rocks will be slippery.*" She picked her way over ice-slicked stone, using handholds to help where she could. Hudson's breathing sounded loud in the still air. The noise of their passing would be audible for klicks, however quiet they tried to be.

She stopped at the top of the ridge, breathing hard. Dawn couldn't be far off. Grey light hovered on the Eastern horizon. The bulk of Mount Egmont rose on their right as they climbed, but now the path dipped down, disappearing under the snow mantle.

Hudson came up beside her. "*Do you know where you're going?*"

"*Yes. Up ahead the path reappears, going up the ridge. See?*" If she squinted, concentrated, she could see the dark line against the snow, skirting a rock face.

"*Carry on.*"

"*Yes, Sir, Admiral, Sir.*"

She started forward into ankle-deep snow; one step, lift, then the other, prancing, like the Stikhorn sheep native to these mountains. Hard work. The muscles in her calves started to burn. She slipped on a rock under the snow but Hudson caught her, his grip sure and firm. They plodded on, toiling through the drift. How much further? And what if she'd been wrong and they'd turned aside from the path? The snow seemed to be deeper. She stopped, sucking air into her lungs, looking for landmarks.

"*It's fine,*" he said. "*This is the deepest part. We go up from here.*"

He was right. She heaved a silent sigh of relief; the path lay dead ahead, curving around the mountain. A last scramble and they were through the drift.

"*It's one way of keeping warm.*" He didn't say the rest, that he'd preferred the other, but the words hung between them. She felt that sexy shimmy again. She would have to be very, very careful with this man.

One hand trailing on the rock face, she walked around the path. This was 'one slip and you're dead' territory. She glanced at the edge, not a meter away. Beyond, the ground fell away, into a shadow-filled valley where a rocky river fed Lake Maribou. A sudden bright light flared on the mountain peaks to the left; dawn glowed rosy on the snow, beautiful and treacherous. She risked a glance over her shoulder; Hudson strode close behind, his breath a mist.

He afforded her a ghost of a smile. "*Pretty.*"

He called a halt when they'd finished their ascent and offered her a water bottle. She drank gratefully, feeling the water drain down her gullet into her stomach.

"*A good hour's work.*" Jess handed the bottle back. "*Mostly downhill now, to the other valley. But I don't know much about that part of the world.*"

A wavering howl drifted through the air at the edge of hearing. "Oh, shit." She said the words aloud, heart thudding.

"*What was that?*" He gazed down at her, eyes narrowed.

"*A sniffert. We're in trouble.*" She started to move, clambering along the path.

"*A what?*" Hudson followed her, his feet sliding a little.

"*Sniffert. A tracker. A kind of lizard trained to follow scent.*"

"*How fast are they?*"

"*They'll have handlers. They won't be able to travel any faster than us but if they catch our scent, the handlers can—*"

"*—call up aerial support.*"

"*Yes.*" Her foot slipped on a rock. Fuck, going down was worse than going up. "*What chance of contacting one of your units?*"

"*We have to be close enough for them to pick up a signal from my implant.*"

Great. Fantastic. But the trackers would have to get to the cave to pick up a scent. So maybe they could reach Hudson's people first. She brushed against an icicle hanging down over a rim. It broke off and shattered on the rocks, strewing glittering fragments over the path. The sun was higher now, slanting rays of light slicing into the valley ahead. Trees swathed the lower slopes, their reddish-green foliage bare of the snow that carpeted the flatter areas. Mountains towered on three sides although none, Jess knew, topped Egmont.

She shifted the rifle she carried to her other shoulder and trudged on. Amazing how something so apparently light could get so damned heavy. Another distant howl set her teeth on edge. "*Uh-oh.*"

"*They have our scent?*" Hudson said.

"*Yes.*"

The path disappeared into another snowdrift. She shoved her way through, her leg muscles grumbling with each step. Her pants were wet to her thighs; she couldn't feel her skin anymore. No chance of stopping, though. The air burned in her lungs. So tired.

"Make for the trees," Hudson said aloud, "As fast as you can."

Another half a klick and the serious tree cover started. She shambled along, faster than a walk, not quite a jog, Hudson's footfall a reassuring counter-point. Another howl, exultant and eager, scraped over her nerves. And beyond that, a different sound, a low, mechanical hum.

"They've called in the air support," Hudson said. "We'll have to run."

Down here the path had widened enough for him to move alongside her. Holding the gun at his side, he gripped her arm with his free hand and almost pushed her along. The forest beckoned, a deep canopy covering a dusting of snow. The hum grew louder with each stride.

"*We can do it, Jess, keep moving.*" He'd gone back to implant to conserve air. He was panting almost as much as she was.

The skin tingled between her shoulder blades. But it wouldn't be like that; they'd do what they did to Longford, shred them both with their cannon or maybe even fire a missile. She lurched in the snow as her foot drove through into a hole. Hudson dragged her back up. A few strides more. She stretched out a hand to touch rough bark. Thank the spirit. But he forced her on, away at an angle.

The attacker soared over the forest, engines set to dead low, searching.

Jess sucked air into her lungs. This wasn't the same as working out in a gym. She hadn't run so far, oh, ever. Hudson wasn't much better, his chest heaving with the effort.

"*Back inside my jacket, sweet heart,*" he said. "*They'll be using sensors. Let's try and move on before the ground support arrives.*"

He'd flipped up his hood, unfastened the jacket. She rested her back against his chest and let him fold the material around her, a warm, reassuring presence. Slowly, carefully, they walked forward, their backs to the hovering machine. The sound of it thundered in Jess' ears, even muffled as it was by the thick canopy. If they fired a missile in the right place… The sound changed.

"*They're landing,*" Hudson said.

A howl reverberated in the air. Jess' nerves jangled. "*They've brought the sniffert up.*"

He released her from his jacket, urged her forward. "*We need somewhere with shelter where we can fire back at them.*"

Aching muscles complained with every jolting step. "*I don't know this place.*"

They could hear the beast now; eager, whiffling grunts albeit still distant. Shit shit shit. They couldn't keep up this pace and the people following were fresh.

Hudson grabbed her arm, dragged her to the left. A rocky outcrop rose out of the snow, a few boulders littered around the base. He surged forward, unslinging the rifle as he ran. She could hear them behind her, the deep crunch of the men's boots. The exultant growl sent the adrenalin screeching through her body. The beast had sighted them. She leapt after Hudson, behind the shelter of a boulder. A laser bolt screamed past, splattering on the rock. Hudson already had his weapon raised, blazing answering fire.

Jess turned in time to see the handler trying to back up, restraining the lunging sniffert. It thrust forward against its harness, its black tongue tasting the air, the claws of four splayed legs digging into the dirt. Hudson ducked back. She fell to her knees on the other side of their shelter and aimed for the creature's scaly head.

The blast hit the sniffert on the muzzle. It reared, whimpering, before the men fired back. Hudson fired. One of the attackers grunted, clutching at his arm. The others fell back, into the trees, while the handler knelt beside his injured beast. At the other side of the forest the copter rose above the trees.

"*We may be able to damage it if we both hit it together,*" Hudson said. "*Wait till I give the word. Go for the thruster jets underneath.*"

Her heart beat too fast. *Breathe in... breathe out.* She brought the rifle up to her shoulder. The copter's nose angled down. *Here it comes...* Her finger rested on the firing button.

Chapter Twenty-two

Hudson sprayed fire at the ground troops to keep them in place. The copter rushed across the treetops, the thrum of the engines booming around the peaks.

Jess set up the target and stared down the sights of her rifle. Closer, a little closer. The thruster grew in her mind, dominated her vision. It disappeared. She lifted her head from the gun sight. What the hell? The copter soared into the air, swept around in a banking turn then raced away toward Mount Egmont. Jess exchanged a glance with Hudson; he seemed as surprised as she was. The ground troops had disappeared, too, including the man with the injured sniffert. Scuffed snow and a greenish stain marked the place where it had been.

"*They're going,*" she said. A different sound echoed around the hills, heavier, deeper. "*What's that?*" Oh, shit no. Another aircraft, larger by the sound. She spun around, searching for a target.

Hudson laughed and looked over his shoulder at two sleek shapes barely visible against the bright sky. "That's a pair of mine. T14 Hunters."

He pulled her into his arms, swung her around and kissed her. What started off as a gesture of delight quickly evolved into rather more. Jess wound her arms around his neck while one of his hands slid down to her buttocks. Tongues wrestled briefly. He pushed her away and cleared his throat.

"This will have to wait until later." His voice was husky and his eyes held a fading spark.

Jess said nothing. The last couple of days had seen a change in him, no longer the arrogant asshole she'd first seen on *Defender*. Maybe His Admiralship was starting to shed his shell.

Hudson gazed up at the approaching craft, contacting them, she presumed, via his implant. One of them sped up, following the same track as the copter, while the other slowed and settled beyond a belt of trees.

Jess slung the rifle. It felt like a hawser cutting into her shoulder, and her feet were blocks of ice. Oh, for a warm shower, clean clothes and some food. Hudson strode through the snow into the woods toward the machine a few hundred meters away. Troops came running, weapons poised. He stopped and allowed them to approach. One of them stepped forward, sweeping up the visor of his helmet. His name patch said Tully.

"Good to have you back."

"Good to be back."

Hudson slipped an arm around Jess' shoulders and walked up the ramp into the vehicle. She collapsed onto the nearest seat, an acceleration chair against a bulkhead.

The officer who'd met them saluted, a fist struck against his chest. "We've been searching since they told us you didn't come back from your trip. We ... hoped we weren't looking for bodies."

A trooper poured tea into mugs and handed them over. Jess cradled hers in her hands, grateful for the warmth and the aroma. The liquid slipped down her throat, sweet and strong. So good.

"When were you told?"

"Late last night. We flew the area for a few hours but the weather made it very difficult."

"Did you find Longford?" Hudson said between sips of tea.

"The Militia did." Tully shook his head. "Splattered. Huh. They were trying to suggest it was one of our gunships."

"Wrong side of the mountain, surely, Commander?"

"No, Sir. They found the body down here." Tully jerked his head at the graphic display on a screen at the front of the cabin, the exercise area outlined in blue.

Frowning, Hudson examined the spot Tully indicated. "The body was moved. He was shot here." He pointed. "When was he found?"

"This morning, half-buried in snow. They found the guide, as well, also hit from the air."

"Huh," Hudson said. "Do you think you killed him, Jess?"

"No. That was the last dregs of power in the rifle's pack. I wonder how much they paid him."

"Nothing, by the looks," Hudson said.

"I even feel sorry for him, in a way. He did his job and they slaughtered him. You were right; setting up for collateral damage." She emptied her mug. "Is there any more tea?"

Tully flicked an eyebrow at a trooper who hurried forward to refill Jess' cup.

"There are a few operatives in the forest here. See if you can find them. One has an injured tracker beast, a thing called a sniffert. Have any captives brought to the ship," Hudson said.

"Sir." Tully went off to give orders. He was back in a moment. "If you'll strap in, Sir, ma'am, we're ready for departure."

The seats shifted into a more central position in the cabin and swiveled to face forward.

"Set course for Miss Sondijk's apartment, Commander. I'll have a shuttle sent there," Hudson said as the harness snapped over his shoulders. "If that's suitable?"

Jess grinned at him. It had been an afterthought. "If you've already given the orders, it had better be."

The gunship rose swiftly, pushing her down in the seat. She watched the red dot that represented the vehicle cross the terrain on the holograph. Pretty as a picture, sparkling white snow and reddish-green trees. Nice to look at from a distance.

"Apart from anything else, I'll have the troops check your apartment. As soon as we're in range have your IS open it to the troops."

Gee, she hadn't thought about that. "I suppose you're right."

He put a hand, warm and familiar, on her knee. "I think it's time we pooled our knowledge, Jess."

"It probably is." She told him what she knew; the visit to Tanaka's office, and to *Kimberley*.

He stroked his chin with a thumb. "Well, let's see what we've got. On Tabora, your husband talks to a man called Rawlings. He exchanges words with Orlando. Rawlings dies in an accident, Dekstra is bashed and your husband is killed in a boarding. It has to do, we think, with this man called Alfons. But you see, take a step back and look at the bigger picture. Madam Ottenshaw owns a pair of starhearts."

The gunship slowed and swiveled to land on her apartment's platform. Jess contacted Jeeves.

"*You have a message*," the IS said.

"Never mind now. I'll be in soon. Allow any visitors in, okay?"

She turned back to Hudson. "Madam Ottenshaw owns starheart earrings. So what?"

"Starhearts have only been found on Ptorix worlds. The Ptorix prize them; the translation of the Ptorix name is something like 'windows of the soul' because they resemble Ptorix eyes. I would very much like to know where the starhearts came from; if from the Ptorix, what goods or services were sufficient to buy them?"

"Ah. Starhearts instead of drugs."

He nodded. "Nordheim is hardly a democracy. Ottenshaw is almost a dictator."

"He *is* a dictator," Jess said. "The elections are a farce. But so what?"

Hudson smiled. "It means he isn't controlled by an opposition. He can do what he likes."

"You mean he could have some kind of arrangement with the Ptorix? Surely not. And what would that have to do with Troy and Tabora?"

"Even if he has absolute power, he wouldn't want to be obvious, trading with the Ptorix. Perhaps someone hid starhearts on his ship for the Militia to collect? But that's just one possibility."

The gunship's forward movement halted. Jess watched the display as, shuddering, the ship settled on the platform. A ramp thudded down. Troopers charged out, weapons poised.

"Sensors show there's nobody there," Hudson said. "But they'll search for anything else."

Jess hoped that didn't include Troy's burglar bag.

"All clear, Admiral," a voice announced. The harnesses clicked open and slid back into the seat.

Hudson stood and waved a hand at the exit. She waited for him at the base of the ramp as he exchanged words and salutes with Tully. His arms behind his back, he walked beside her down the passage to her apartment. The gunship soared away but two troopers remained behind.

"Were you looking for starhearts when you searched my ship? And me?" she asked.

He grinned. "No. We did as Longford asked; conducted a search using InfoDroids."

Not a very good one, though. She kept that thought to herself.

"So *are* you a smuggler?"

She looked into his amused eyes. Should she lie through her teeth? Or could she trust him with the truth? What the hell? She'd never felt there had been much wrong with what she did. "A fair exchange of goods isn't smuggling. Not really. But I've never carried drugs or starhearts." She suddenly wondered if Troy had.

"Your husband?"

They'd reached the front door. Hudson waited, his gaze fixed on her. Her expression must have betrayed her.

She sighed. "I don't know. I just don't know. I'm beginning to think it has something to do with those body tubes they carried on *Kimberley*. What was in them?"

She pirouetted, hands out, in her living room. "Here we are, home. What's the message, Jeeves?"

"*You had a call from Miss Somers of Orham Girl's College, Jess. She asked that you make contact as soon as you returned. She said it was urgent.*"

Whatever for? She exchanged a look with Hudson, who shrugged.

"I'll be out here talking to the ship." He went out to the balcony and leaned on the rail.

"Make the call, Jeeves." She hoped it was something stupid like wagging classes or something. She'd met the principal when Tenna had enrolled two years ago, a brisk, efficient woman with a no-nonsense manner. She wasn't really dressed for a parent-teacher discussion. But what the hell, the woman would have to accept her in her mud-caked glory.

Miss Somers appeared sitting behind a desk, dark hair piled high, her expression serious. Judging by the shadows on her face the window was to her right.

"Miss Somers," Jess said. "This is unexpected."

"I wondered if there was a problem, Miss Sondijk?"

Jess frowned. Problem? "About what?"

"Tenna should have arrived by now." The principal's manner was almost accusatory.

Ice trickled down Jess' spine. "Tenna *is* there. What are you saying?"

"Her class mistress has advised me Tenna hasn't returned to school."

"Let's get this straight, shall we? I brought her and Sufi back to school myself, in a coptercab, got permission to land in the school grounds. She's back there, got that? I saw her walk in the doors with Sufi Wickram." *No. No. There has to be a mistake. This isn't happening; it can't be happening.*

Somers blinked, mouth agape. "Are you certain?"

"Certain? Of course I'm fucking certain. I dropped them off two days ago." *You stupid, up yourself bitch.* Fury and anxiety waged a war in her gut.

The principal pursed her lips. "There is no need to be coarse, Miss Sondijk."

Stupid bitch. "What about Sufi? Is she there?"

"Er ... no. She isn't here, either. I wasn't aware she and Tenna were together."

Jess stood. "You go and check you haven't made some sort of mistake and do it quickly. If you haven't made a mistake, call the police. I'll be there in person as soon as I can get there so you can tell me what the fuck is going on at your school."

Chapter Twenty-three

"Jeeves, call me a coptercab."

Hudson stepped inside from the balcony. "There's no need. A shuttle will be here in a few minutes. We'll take that."

She whirled. "This isn't your problem. Go back to your ship."

He shook his head. "This may be related. They haven't killed you, so they kidnapped your daughter."

Her heart had been thundering; now it almost stopped. Oh, God. "We have to find her."

He put a hand on her shoulder. "Calm down. It might be nothing. Let's hope she's played truant."

"Tenna wouldn't—"

"Of course not." He gazed around him. "You've got ten minutes. Go and shower." He gave her a little shake. "Go on, you'll feel better."

He was probably right. She shucked of her filthy clothes and stepped into the shower, letting the warm water sluice down her body. She pumped gel into her hand and massaged her skin and hair. God. Troy, then Santh and now Tenna. Her whole world was falling apart. What had she ever done to deserve this? *Steady, Jess. This isn't helping*. After she'd rinsed she moved the control to the dry cycle, turning in the air current.

She stepped into her bedroom. Hudson leaned against a wall, his arms folded. Surely he didn't... No. She admonished herself for even thinking he'd want sex. He hadn't moved, just cast a quick glance over her.

"That's better," he said. "Get dressed. The shuttle's shaping to land."

"What about you?" she said, pulling on casual pants and a tee shirt.

"I'm a soldier. Soldiers are allowed to be muddy. I'll clean up on *Defender*. Let's go."

Jess scooped up a jacket and followed him to the platform, where a shuttle idled. Armed troops stood at the ramp.

"We'll keep an eye on the apartment while you're gone," Hudson said.

No sooner had they settled into the seats when the shuttle lifted and banked. Jess stared out of the machine's window down onto every street, behind every tree, peering at every person. If Tenna was missing somebody was going to pay. And if she'd snuck off to meet some boy, Tenna would be paying herself; after Jess had finished hugging her within an inch of her life.

Somehow she couldn't imagine Sufi playing truant. She *wanted* to go back to school. Why would they have disappeared?

What must have been an age later the shuttle descended onto the same landing pad she'd been at the day before yesterday, saying goodbye to her smiling, lovely daughter and her best friend. Only last time, there hadn't been a police copter sitting to one side. Shit. Not looking good. Apprehension tearing at her throat, Jess bounded out of the vehicle and strode up the path to the admin centre, hardly aware of Hudson pacing beside her.

The woman at reception must have been warned to expect her. She came out from behind her protective counter, doing her best to smile. "Miss Sondijk? This way, please."

Jess followed her to the principal's office. The woman leaned in and said, "Miss Sondijk," then ducked away out of Jess' path.

Miss Somers sat behind her desk, the same as she had in this morning's hologram, a row of antique books displayed in a shelf behind her. The window out to the garden took up most of the wall to her right. The hands folded on the desk before her looked calm but her fingers flexed. "Miss Sondijk." She looked down her nose at Hudson. "This is a private matter, Sir. If you would wait outside."

"Admiral Hudson's here at my request. Can we get on, please," Jess said.

Her eyes narrowed, Somers looked Hudson up and down. The camouflage suit had shed the dirt but carried no rank insignia.

"This might help," Hudson said. The wide admiral's bars appeared on his shoulders. "We tend not to advertise rank out in the field."

That got her attention. Her mouth forming an O, she batted her eyelashes and patted her hair. It was all Jess could do not to vomit.

"Of course." Somers positively beamed. "Do sit down. This is Inspector Davignon, from the local police."

Hudson pulled out a chair and sat while Jess glowered at the fellow who'd risen from his seat when she'd entered. "Have you started an investigation?"

Somers cleared her throat. "They might be playing trua—"

"Don't give me that." Jess hooked a chair leg with a booted foot and sat down. "He's not here to look for a kid wagging school."

Davignon sagged back onto his chair. "On the contrary, ma'am. That would be a wonderful result."

"What, they've both gone off to seek their fortunes in a brothel? Run off with a pair of brothers?" Jess said. "Tenna doesn't come from Burkesville, and Sufi doesn't come from that kind of home. Her mother will be as worried sick as I am."

Hudson put a hand on her arm. "*Settle, Jess. This isn't getting us anywhere.*" He was right, of course he was.

"You brought them back from holiday and dropped them both back here?" Davignon said.

"That's right. I waited till they'd gone inside and then I went home."

"Why didn't you take Sufi home?" The policeman's gaze bored into her.

"I did. Haven't you spoken to Miss Wickram?"

"We will but I'd like to hear it from you."

"We went to Sufi's house first, so the girls could show off their holiday pictures, share their time with her."

The holiday had meant as much to the mother as it had to the daughter. Sufi looked so much brighter, tanned and healthy. The girls showed off their pictures of them splashing in the warm sea, cavorting under a waterfall, sharing a ride on an oliphaunt's broad back. Sufi had brought back a souvenir, a Paradise Cove cup and saucer for her mother. The woman had almost burst into tears. The Wickrams might not have much, but their daughter was loved; more than some of the others at this snooty girl's school could say.

"How long were you there?"

"A few hours. We had lunch." Jess had brought a picnic, far too much so she could leave some behind.

"After which you took them both back to school?"

"Yes. The girls had things to do before classes started. We agreed it was easier to drop them off together." Something about his expression didn't sit right, polite, enquiring but something more. "What are you getting at?"

He scratched at his ear. "No one saw them except you. There's no sign of them in the dormitory wing, they don't appear to have gone to their room."

"What about their suitcases?"

Davignon and Somers shared a look.

"Tenna had one of those follow-along ones that floats behind you with a tag but Sufi had to physically drag hers along. Some fellow, a gardener, I think, helped Sufi into the building with it."

Another exchanged look.

"What time was this?" Somers asked.

Oh for fuck's sake. "You'll have that in your records. I got permission to land out there."

"Yes, we've looked," Davignon said. "A number of vehicles came in at that time, ferrying girls back to school. Yours landed at eighteen twenty-three. You say a man helped Sufi with the bag?"

"That's right."

"What did he look like?" the inspector said.

"I don't know. I didn't really look. Just some man." She searched her memory, but nothing stood out. Just a fellow in brown workman's clothes.

"I can show you pictures of every gardener and maintenance person we have," Somers said. She gave the IS the instruction and handed Jess a sheet of images, face shots, rotating body shots.

Not one of them looked familiar. But she'd been so far away and who'd look, anyway? Damn it. She shook her head. "I don't know."

"We'll talk to them," Davignon's face went blank as if he was using his implant. "You're sure, Miss Sondijk, that your daughter and her friend didn't act in any way unusually?"

"Absolutely sure. Sufi loved the holiday but she was looking forward to the new term. Sufi had goals which involved high academic achievement. She wants to be a medical practitioner. I wish Tenna had more of an aim."

"If you could give me a few minutes alone with Miss Sondijk, Miss Somers?" Davignon said.

"Of course." Somers rose to her feet, a picture of dignity and straight back, and left the room, not without a sideways look at Hudson on the way past. He gave her a brief smile.

Davignon opened his mouth to say something to Hudson, who hadn't moved.

"I stay," Hudson said.

Jess shot a look at him. This was the face his troops would see, the one that said 'I'm in command'. He hadn't raised his voice, hadn't altered his body language. Just sat there and said 'I stay'.

The inspector nodded. "Did your daughter have a boyfriend?"

"Not that I know of." The Mad Hatter had certainly been a venue for the girls and boys but they were kids. "She's just a kid. Barely fourteen. I expect you'll go talk to Sufi's mother but I'll tell you in advance she didn't have a boyfriend. At Paradise Cove they giggled over a couple of lads but they were much more interested in the holovid stars."

"I'll have somebody ask some questions at Paradise Cove. You realize there are perverts out there who fancy younger girls?"

"Yes. I'm a freighter captain. You see all sorts of things." Underage kids working in brothels. It was sickening but it happened everywhere.

"This isn't the first time girls have gone missing, is it?" Hudson said. She'd almost forgotten he was there.

Davignon blinked. "Perhaps not."

"What d'you mean, perhaps?" Jess said.

"Girls have gone missing from places like Burkesville; pretty young girls. Most of them have turned up in brothels or they ran away with some young fellow. One or two have been found dead in a ditch. There's a tendency to dismiss these cases because of where the girls come from. We always have a list of unsolved cases and I wouldn't have made a connection but there does seem to be a pattern with a few more cases over the past year. Pretty girls from slums. Your daughter is an exception. Maybe she was collateral damage."

"You can't mean that. Grab Sufi and take Tenna along because she's there? Wouldn't it have been easier to grab Sufi in Burkesville? Have you been there?"

"A good question. It may have been a crime of opportunity."

"No. You don't think that." Jess found herself kneading her knee and stopped.

"Can you think of any reason why anyone should target your daughter?" Davignon glanced at Hudson.

"Perhaps," Hudson said. "Someone attempted to kill us recently. We don't know who and we don't know why. We can't even be certain if the target was me, Jess or both of us."

The officer frowned. "Ah. Not good. Revenge?"

Tanaka? Maybe he'd worked out she'd visited his warehouse or *Kimberley*? "If that's the case, I'd get a note or something, wouldn't I?"

He nodded. "I'd expect so. If you do, come to me directly, won't you?"

Hudson stirred in his chair. "If it's revenge they might kill the girls and leave them somewhere for you to find. They might draw the process out by trying ransom to give you hope for a time."

Jess tasted blood in her mouth. God, she'd bitten her lip.

Davignon scowled at Hudson. "That's the extreme. We'd hope for better."

Hudson leaned toward him. "And what is 'better', Inspector?"

The policeman sighed. "That we find them alive."

"If it's ransom I would've had something by now, wouldn't I?" Jess said. "It's been nearly two days. Wouldn't they have made sure I knew she was missing straight away? And said stuff about not talking to the police?"

"That's the normal modus operandi, yes, but anything's possible. I suggest you take her home, Admiral. There's nothing you can do except try to remember every little detail you can, people, things said inadvertently." Davignon smiled, a look of compassion. "I'm a father. I can imagine how hard this is for you. I promise we'll do what we can."

"Yeah. Thanks." A lump of lead sat in Jess's stomach.

"These girls who have disappeared, Inspector," Hudson said. "Do you have any theories?"

Davignon, looked away, frowning, then passed a fist across his mouth. "There's nothing to say."

"But you have an idea, however silly it might sound. Try me."

The policeman hesitated, the argument with himself playing across his face. "I wondered if they'd been taken off-planet." He raised his hands. "But that's extreme speculation on my part."

Hudson's lips jerked. "Understood. Have you perhaps raised that idea with Admiral Longford's people?"

"Longford isn't … wasn't taken with that argument." The answer was stiff, the man's face rigid.

"Thank you for your time, Inspector. If you're finished?" Hudson said.

Davignon nodded. "For now."

Hudson took Jess' arm and guided her to the door. She almost stumbled into the reception area. Somers sat in a chair, elegant legs crossed. She rose to her feet with 'finally' plastered over her face.

"Are you going to tell the parents?" Jess said.

"I don't wish to alarm people," Somers said, her tone prim and standoffish.

"No warnings to be aware of odd workmen at the school?"

"Miss Sondijk," Davignon put in, "It's best you go home. Rest assured we'll keep you informed."

"*Time to go, Jess.*" Hudson's voice was gentle, the pull on her arm insistent.

Ah, he was probably right. She turned against his pressure. "Oh, if you're checking the brothels, don't forget 'Tender Delights' here in Orham City. They have a special section for underage kids."

Somers's face drew down; eyebrows, forehead, lips.

"Fact," Jess said. "There are perverts out there." Let her think on that as she stared at her ceiling at night. Hudson dragged her out.

Chapter Twenty-four

"Let the man do his job," Hudson said, marching her along. "He seems competent and caring."

"What am I going to do? Sit at home and stare at the walls? I can't, Hudson. I won't." She climbed up the ramp into the shuttle. "Damn it, I can't get Tabora out of my head. The place is beginning to haunt me."

"We may well have some additional information about Tabora. Let's see what my people have to say."

The shuttle rose, heading for space. Santh. Tabora. Jess gasped and clutched at Hudson's arm. "Santh said something in his last broadcast. He heard some fellows talking in the tavern, something about supplying girls. He mentioned a name."

She had his attention, his blue eyes alert. "The name?"

"Sullivan. No, Suleiman. Oper Suleiman. Does deals with the GPR on Kentor."

"All right. I'll have it checked."

Tears threatened. She brushed them away. "What do you think, Hudson? Do you think she's dead?"

He ran a hand down her cheek, his expression softened. "When you're planning strategy, consider every possible outcome. There's no point pretending it couldn't happen but no, I don't think she's dead. The attack on us has muddied the water. I'm not sure what it means."

"What you asked the inspector. Do you think they've been taken off-planet?"

"It's possible, yes. I think that's what he was implying. And if he was being honest, he would have said Longford wasn't interested in what happened to a few kids from the slums. It wasn't in his job description."

"Right. That settles it. I have to go to Tabora."

"Steady." He took her shoulders in his hands, strong but gentle. "You're panicking, overreacting."

Defender's bulk loomed ahead of the slowing shuttle. The ship slid into the airlock, the walls crowding close.

"If they've taken them there ... I need to know. I need to find them."

"Jess, who are 'they' and why would they take the girls to Tabora?" He kept a hand on her shoulder, leaning close.

"If I knew who 'they' were I'd carve their balls off with a rusty hacksaw. And I'm thinking they might be there because I'm running out of ideas." Her eyes glittered. "There's a brothel on the platform..." Her voice trailed off. The thought of her girls being forced into sex with those animals on Tabora made her blood boil.

Hudson remained an island of calm. "You're kneejerk-reacting to nothing. I'll have my people check the brothels and look for this Suleiman person. I have no authority in police matters on Nordheim but I have ways of obtaining information." He rose from his seat. "We have some planning to do. About the girls and Dekstra. And I don't know about you, but I'm hungry."

She almost had to run to keep up with him as he swept through the ship to his own office. An officer stood when Hudson entered the reception area and followed the admiral and Jess into an office smaller than she might have expected, fitted with banks of view screens. A tray of pastries and sandwiches sat on the side of his desk.

"Come in. Sit down." He waved a hand at the other officer. "This is Commander Mann, in charge of intelligence. He already knows what you told me about *Kimberley*. Report." He directed the last word at Mann as he selected a pastry from the tray.

"Our agent is missing, Sir. We're told he broke his contract and left. He's recorded as having left Tabora on a transport."

"Another man missing," Jess said.

"Correct," Mann said. "It seems he and Jonson were friends. They shared shifts on the same hopper. His name up there was Ace Connor. Did Dekstra mention him?"

A discordant tremor jolted through her nerves. "Connor? Santh left me a message before I headed for Tabora and you stopped me. He said that name, Connor; that he'd disappeared. Santh was off to check the body tubes on *Beaconsfield*."

"And *Beaconsfield* is now on its way to Kentor."

Jess clenched her hands on the desk. *Beaconsfield*. Body tubes. To Tabora and from there, where else? "Tanaka gets the girls to Tabora. Then somebody takes them to Kentor as sex slaves or something. Maybe they're in those body tubes, drugged and in suspension or something. Troy worked it out, what they were doing. So they killed him." She leapt to her feet. "I'm going to Tabora."

Frowning, Hudson shook his head. "Sit down. No, you're not."

"Oh, yes I fucking am. I'm going to follow *Beaconsfield*, see what's really on that ship." *Don't try to stop me; don't you dare.*

"How are you going to do that?"

He spoke softly, without any expression, asking a question she couldn't answer. Damn him. "I don't know. I'll work it out." She was right; she had to be. It all made sense.

"Don't be silly. We have agents—"

Anger rose, bitter as bile in her mouth. "They haven't got you very far, have they? Look, I don't expect you to understand. I can't sit here and twiddle my thumbs. Those assholes have got my daughter." She leaned over the desk at him, her finger jabbing. "You wouldn't have a clue what that feels like; not a fucking clue, so don't pontificate at me about what I can and cannot do. I'll do anything for my kid."

Hudson's face had hardened into a mask. Only the glitter in his eyes betrayed his fury. Jess shoved down the 'uh-oh'. She wasn't one of his crew and he couldn't order her around.

"Commander Mann, if you would wait outside for a moment, please?" Ice coated every word.

Mann complied instantly, silently. The door swished closed behind him.

Hudson held her stare, unblinking. He reached down inside the collar of his jacket, pulled out the chain he wore around his neck and unfastened it. He opened the locket the chain held and placed it on the desk top between them.

A hologram rose, displaying an image of a lovely, laughing young woman. Her dark hair billowed around her head and her hand rested on her swollen belly.

Jess' heart sank. "Your daughter?"

"No, my wife."

His demeanor had softened from glacial fury to sadness. "In this image Sylvie was twenty-two. She was the love of my life. I had been promoted to commander and she decided to take a cruise liner to join me at my new posting, so she could visit her parents on the way. She was pregnant. She decided for whatever reason to go the old-fashioned way and carry the child herself instead of using an incubator. Said she wanted a natural birth, in spite of the danger and the pain."

He licked his lips. She could have sworn his eyes glistened. "Pirates hijacked the liner. It disappeared for two years but we caught them; eventually. They'd converted it to a slave ship. Some of the crew had been on the original raid. They remembered the pregnant woman, two for the price of one. They were taking her to the slave markets but the baby came early and they both died. Or so they told me. They jettisoned the bodies."

What could she say? She felt numb. Stupid. Tears gathered in her eyes.

He snapped the locket closed. "So you see, I might have some idea about how you feel. And that, incidentally, is why I have a reputation for my harsh dealings with pirates."

"I'm sorry. I'm so terribly sorry." *Idiot, selfish idiot.*

He shook himself, back out of the past and into the present. "I'm not saying your summation is wrong, but we don't have all the facts we need. Neither do we have time. So..." He took a deep breath. "I'll allow you to go to Kentor in your own ship. But not alone."

"Are you going to come?"

He sighed. "I wish I could. But I can't. My job is here. I'll organize for you to have appropriate assistance and we'll fit your ship with some extra equipment. A moment. I'll call Mann back in."

"How many people can your ship sustain?" Hudson said as soon as Mann had returned.

"With additional air and water, four easily." Jess was amazed how he could turn off the emotion, like a tap. But it still had to be there, pent up, behind the admiral's façade. "More at a pinch but we'd be pushing safety if we're talking Kentor."

"Commander, select a good scan tech and two other special forces men. And have Captain Sondijk's ship fitted with extra surveillance capability. Have the ship provisioned for four."

He waited while Mann's eyes glassed over, giving orders via his implant.

"So, in summary, we have an unknown number of men, maybe forty, maybe more, missing. See if you can find any of them. Do background checks on each of them and look for patterns."

Mann nodded. "Anything else?"

"There are also two attractive young girls missing."

Hudson waved a hand at Jess. She fished out her comlink and showed Mann the image of Sufi and Tenna.

"Davignon, the police officer in charge, said there are other unexplained disappearances, pretty young girls from slums." Jess looked down at her hands, resting on the desk. "What puzzles me is why they took such a risk with Tenna. Sufi ... a kid from a slum disappears. That's a common occurrence. But a daughter from a good home, a reasonably well-off home..." She shook her head. "The police aren't going to ignore that. They didn't."

Mann cleared his throat. "I'd say you're correct, ma'am, in thinking they're not on Nordheim. Blondes are highly prized by GPR men."

She felt ill. "Oh, fuck. Some disgusting brothel on Kentor or something."

"I'm sorry, ma'am," Mann said.

"If they *are* there, we can find them, don't worry," Hudson said. "Carry on, Commander. We need to move quickly."

Mann saluted and left.

Jess stared at the bulkhead. The only sound in the office was the barely heard whisper of the climate conditioning. She felt drained, empty, useless. *Tenna. Where are you sweetheart? What have those bastards done to you?*

Hudson's chair creaked. He walked around his desk to where she sat and drew her gently to her feet.

"Jess, I know how hard this is, believe me. We'll find them." He put his arms around her and pulled her close. "I'd love to make love to you but I know that's not what you want right now." He lifted her chin with his fingertips and brushed her lips with his.

She kissed him back, a gentle kiss full of promise. He was right; sex was far from her mind. She could so easily fall for this man.

She withdrew, inhaling the scent of his uniform, savoring the taste of his lips. "We'll get it together next time, I promise." She heaved a deep breath. "And I'll tell you something else for free. If some bastard has raped my little girl, I'll cut off his cock with a meat cleaver and shove it down his throat."

Chapter Twenty-five

Jess poked her head carefully around the trunk of the forest giant, one hand on the rough bark, the other hefting her Valray blaster pistol. One clear shot at him and she'd have won. He was coming. He thought he was quiet but occasionally he'd snap a twig or crunch some leaves. She leant back. Come on, a few meters more...

"I'm sorry to interrupt," *Saintly Maid's* IS said. "*We're coming up on the Kentor jump gate, Jess.*"

The forest of Denarion disappeared. Jess took off the simulator helmet and grinned at the three men seated around the table in the freighter's common room, also peeling off helmets.

"Just when I was winning, too. Come on, Mayfield, time to show our faces in the bridge. Strap in, guys." One step closer to finding out what had happened to Tenna.

"Can we save the game first?" Cartwright said. "You might think you're wining but I reckon I can outmaneuver you."

"Oh, good luck. Save the game, *Maid*." She pushed herself to her feet and followed Lieutenant Mayfield through the hatch into the bridge, leaving Cartwright and Burgess to settle into the couches that folded out from the holding sections in the deck.

The swirling, multi-colored blur of shift space filled the view screen but the navigation graphic showed their destination, two flashing points of light, one red, one green. The harness deployed as soon as she'd settled in the chair. Ten minutes later *Maid* shot out into clear space, shift drive disengaged, forward thrusters at full power to slow her down. Kentor lay one hundred thousand klicks away, a brown and white bauble scattered with blue. The larger of the planet's two space stations rotated slowly four thousand clicks to starboard, geostationary over Kentor's capital city, Sal Menoa. It sprawled, a vast, teeming metropolis ablaze with light for a few hours yet.

Mayfield pointed. "Is that the jump gate exit queue over there, where that liner is?"

She checked the planet's space graphic. "Yes, that's it."

He adjusted the scanner newly fitted into the bridge array. This was his job; hot-shot scantech able to manipulate the military gadgets fitted to her ship.

"The liner is the *Imperial Queen*, the new flagship of the Imperial Line."

Mention of a liner reminded her of Hudson. Not that she needed much reminding; he filled her thoughts and her dreams. She'd promised to make it up to him and she would, with pleasure, as soon as she could, as soon as she'd found Tenna. The revelation about his wife had shaken her, rocked her view of him as a carefree womanizer. He'd taken up his own special niche in her heart, alongside Tenna. In comparison, Troy had become a ghost, a shadow.

"We're not in the space station's control area yet. Can you take the *Maid* alongside, as if you were a sightseer?" Mayfield asked.

"Sure. *Maid*, take us for a look-see, but not too close."

"*Acknowledge*."

Maid altered course, skimming past the liner at a respectable distance. It had a fancy paint job, a glittering show of curves and color designed to wow the paying passengers, but when you came down to it, the ship was a box that presumably housed the guest rooms and public spaces, with a smaller, plainer rectangle jutting out of the end for the engines.

"What are you after?" she said.

"I want to check for any body tubes in the cargo manifesto."

That made sense. Transfer the cargo at the station and have it taken off somewhere on the liner's route.

A stream of data appeared on the unit's small screen. The *Maid's* IS translated. Luggage, foodstuffs, cleaning supplies, linen; things you'd expect in what was actually a space-worthy, top-class, hideously expensive, hotel. She'd seen the glossy brochures of the ballrooms, dining halls, palatial suites, swimming pools hidden behind that unattractive exterior.

"Looks okay," Mayfield said. "At least the scanner gear's working well."

"Take us in, *Maid*."

The space station filled the screen, slowly rotating stacked wheels, the rear ends of ships protruding from the docking bays around the perimeters. They'd be allocated a berth higher up, with the rest of the smaller ships. Sure enough; B4.

Mayfield sucked data from the station while Jess spoke with the customs people. No, she didn't have a cargo, only passengers and maybe she'd have a pick-up if she could find work. She transmitted the three men's forged IDs along with her own.

"Where is *Beaconsfield*?" she asked Mayfield.

"Second tier from the bottom, E6. She arrived half a day ago. Strange; I would have expected her to reach here well ahead of us. Cargo manifest confirmed; bodies for a crematorium." He jerked in his seat and frowned. "There's only two bodies checked for the crematorium."

Jess stared at him. "Two? What happened to the other eighteen?"

"Don't know. Can we take a look at *Beaconsfield* from out here?"

"Yep. Take us in slowly, please, *Maid*, sort of at an angle so we can see *Beaconsfield*."

"*Acknowledge*."

The station was busy, as usual, with most bays occupied. What an odd collection of ships from everywhere. The battered engine units of an elderly GPR ship stuck out from a central bay beside the sleek lines of what looked like a private yacht. An ugly ore transport hung out of one of the lower levels and two slots down the curls and curves of a Ptorix ship provided a colorful red and gold contrast to the drab grays and browns of the utility vessels. She counted. From here she could see four Ptorix ships and two GPR vessels. *Beaconsfield* jutted out of her docking bay like a tick embedded in a host, the four engine cowls staring blankly into space.

Mayfield checked his data. "There are a couple of people on board. I've sent the message from Exelcraft. We're not going to have long to take a look at that ship, though. She's locked in for departure in three hours."

Jess nodded.

They'd already agreed on a course of action. Mann and his people had forged a priority message from Exelcraft, the company which manufactured the body tubes, reporting a possible fault and advising that maintenance technicians would be coming on board at Kentor to check the units. Mayfield would go on board *Beaconsfield* and find out what they contained, while Jess had a look around the station and Burgess and Cartwright waited to follow the bodies when they were taken away.

"Acknowledgement from *Beaconsfield* for a visit from a tech." Mayfield shook his head, frowning. "The ship should have beaten us in by a full day at least."

Jess met his gaze. That didn't sound right. "Can you pull their nav data?"

"I'll give it a go." Mayfield sent a string of commands, responded to prompts, entered stolen passwords. After a pause the data stream commenced, row after row of meaningless symbols.

"*Maid*, tell us what their track was."

"*The ship left Tabora on schedule, headed for the Kentor gate. After departure she changed destination to these coordinates.*" The graphic display shifted, zooming in on the location in space. Empty.

"What's the nearest star?"

"*Mancor, a red dwarf with no planets.*" The IS backed off the graphic to show the star and a billion klicks away, the stopping point.

"Okay, what?"

"*The ship recalculated its route and headed for Kentor.*"

"How long was she at Mancor?" Mayfield said.

"*Eight point three seven standard hours.*"

Jess exchanged a look with Mayfield. "They were transferred." Blast and damn. They'd been out-maneuvered.

"Yeah. Is there anything to indicate a rendezvous?"

"*Searching…*"

They waited, gazing at a swirling display that Jess always thought of as 'thinking colors'.

"*I have a visual from the port sensor array.*"

The IS had enhanced the image so they could see the details, an old-fashioned, much-patched GPR ship, shipping ID GPR-87, name *Cordoba*. She hung in space, not twenty klicks away from *Beaconsfield*.

Good. At least they had a starting point. "Anything in the station's database for this ship?"

Mayfield entered more commands, danced with the security. "Not recently. It's an ordinary trader by the looks of things. I'll send on the data to Commander Mann. He might be able to find out something more."

Beside her, Mayfield set up for the shielded transmission to *Defender*. Hudson and his people would have to know that *Beaconsfield* had made a stop-off. Damn it, she felt so useless, frustrated.

"Maybe we should go back to the rendezvous point and see what we can find? Trawl for transmissions?"

"No. They are better equipped for that than this ship is. Besides, I still want to go on board *Beaconsfield*. I might learn something from the two remaining tubes and Cartwright and Burgess will follow up on what happens to whatever is in them."

He didn't need to be right, damn him. "I suppose. I'll need to replenish for the trip back, too."

Jess let the IS take the ship in while her thoughts turned to Tenna and Sufi. Would they have been on *Beaconsfield*? It was possible, she supposed but if they were they'd most likely been taken off somewhere else. No, Mayfield was right; leave *Beaconsfield* to Hudson. She knew a couple of the traders who had done business with *Cordoba*. Maybe she could find out something from them.

Cartwright and Burgess had already left to nose around the docks while Mayfield, fitted out in his Exelcraft uniform, went off to *Beaconsfield*.

Jess did the things she always did in any port; organized replenishment, paid docking fees. Her tasks done, Jess bought herself a cup of take away kaff and waited for Mayfield outside Station Admin. The kaff tasted like reheated dishwater but it was wet. She'd finished most of it and thrown the cup into the recycler when Mayfield turned up, back in ordinary spacer gray.

"Anything?" she asked.

"No. The tubes were minimally aired up. What they contain is dead bodies. No vital signs. I scanned for drugs or any sign of serious contraband but nothing showed up. Cartwright and Burgess will follow when they're picked up and taken wherever they're going. Nothing else interesting in the hold."

"Who was in the tubes?"

"The name tags said Inkerman and Low. I suppose it doesn't mean much but it does match Tabora's data. Low died of Nervana overdose, the other man died in an accident."

Which didn't, of course, mean that the eighteen other tubes held nothing of interest; probably quite the reverse. Tenna, Sufi, Ace and Santh were possibilities. *Don't think about it. Leave it to Hudson.*

She checked the station's index for Hucksberry's, last known listed supplier to do business with *Cordoba*. Not one of the classier establishments, down on deck D-3, deepest of the three levels associated with the level D docking bays, and down the corridor out toward the station's hub. She locked the location into her comlink and set off, following the route planned for her, Mayfield by her side.

"Been here before?" The way his head swiveled from side to side, she probably hadn't needed to ask.

"No."

She led him into a transit car. "This space station is a bit like Sal Menoa the city; a glittering, squeaky-clean façade until you scratch the surface."

Up here, you scratched the surface as soon as you moved into the deeper levels and away from the station's core. The transit pinged softly as it stopped at level D-3. She adjusted the blaster pistol in its holster on her hip and stepped out into a reasonably busy corridor. Mayfield was armed, too, but he kept his weapon hidden in his jacket. To each his own; in places like this it didn't hurt to advertize.

The same sorts of shops clustered down here that you found in the higher levels; souvenirs, mid-range clothing, leather goods, gadgets, shoes, music, but not the expensive designer items you could buy on level A. You could buy some very convincing copies, though, at a fraction of the price. Bright lights flashed, inviting custom. People looked in windows, bought take-away food from stalls, sat at tables in the central arena. Food smells competed with kaff; schmaltzy music fought with the buzz of conversation.

She stopped and glanced around, scanning the usual types of people you saw at the station, some busy, some aimless; freighter jocks from the fringe planets, quite a few from the Confederacy, even a few Ptorix; strange, conical shapes in floor-length robes gliding along walkways or looking in windows. Nobody she recognized. Corridor nine was across the way, through the food court. She went the long way, skirting the tables.

"This is where it gets a little bit edgy," she said.

The mix of shops changed gradually, became a little less inviting, a little less cheerful. Here a weapons shop, there second-hand equipment and over there a place with shuttered windows which may or may not have been closed. The lights weren't as bright, the passers-by seemed furtive. Her heart beat a little faster, her nerves strained to hear, to process. Mayfield's soft-soled boots tramped beside her.

At last; Hucksberry's Emporium, purveyors of strange and wonderful foodstuffs from across the Galaxy. Together they checked the window display. Many of the goods you could buy in the better class of store on Nordheim, but they certainly stocked some strange items with labels written in local languages she didn't understand, which was universally understood to mean 'non-locals will find this yucky'.

A cacophony of aromas hit her as soon as she went inside the shop. Shelves groaned with boxes, packets and jars. Dried items hung in bunches. She recognized a number of herbs but what that scaly thing was, could be anybody's guess. Clear containers held colored objects that could have been fruit and might not be. The sharp smell of herbs vied with something altogether more unpleasant. She fronted up to the counter while Mayfield browsed, wide-eyed.

A woman appeared from behind a curtain, Jess would guess GPR judging by the wrinkles and colored hair. The smile was warm and genuine. "Can I help you?"

"Could be. I have a friend who comes from Chollarc. I want to buy him a birthday present. Got anything special to that area?"

"Yes, a few." The woman came around the counter and pointed out items, at least food Jess could recognize.

Mayfield turned to concentrate on the higher shelves toward the curtain. Ah. He must be getting some sort of signal. Jess asked questions to buy him time. He stirred and lifted his shoulder, lips down-turned. Not much luck, then. Jess selected a jar of pickled hoffra fruits and paid in the local currency.

"Thanks for your help, that was fascinating. I own a freighter. If you ever have any larger jobs, I might be able to help."

"Oh, we don't have much call for large jobs."

"Oh. A friend told me you had a consignment on *Cordoba* recently?"

She shook her head. "No. We provided provisions for their next trip. The captain at the time had some interesting tastes." She chuckled, deep laughter lines gouged around sparkling dark eyes.

"Well, thanks."

"My pleasure. It was nice chatting. Call again, won't you?"

Outside, Jess exchanged a look with Mayfield. "Might as well head back. Did you get anything?"

"Not much. Their tech is so bad it took a minute for the scanners to cope. But it's an ordinary shop with an accounting system. They might have some illegal bits and pieces but nothing we'd be interested in."

They passed a sex shop advertising the best in virtual entertainment and no risk of disease.

The brighter lights beckoned. "Let's stop for a kaff, at least," she said. "I could use something."

Mayfield needed no encouragement. Jess claimed a table in the food court while he bought kaff from one of the vendors. The place had cleared since they'd passed through before. A few people still sat at scattered tables while a cleanerbot nosed around the floor. Laughter erupted nearby where a group of unkempt freighter jocks sat around a large table littered with food packets. Something clattered on the hard floor. The laughter stopped.

"What the fuck d'yew think yew're doin'?"

Funny how raucous laughter can so easily become a snarl of rage. She wasn't the only one to turn to watch the burly spacer towering, fists clenched, over the non-descript fellow with his hands raised in apology.

"Stay cool, friend. No problem. Can I buy you another beer?"

The spacer settled. Jess frowned. Something ... something familiar. The smaller man returned from a vendor with beer and placed the bottles on the table. Light glinted from a blue stone on a ring on his little finger. Jess' heart bounded. That was him, the fellow from Burkesville who'd saved her and Tenna from the teenage louts. What the fuck was he doing here? He headed off down a corridor.

Mayfield put a tray on the table.

"No time," she said, grabbing his arm. "Come on."

She towed him along. "*The fellow in gray, dead ahead. Can you get anything?*" She used her implant.

"*Uh. No implant. Has a comlink. Just a sec.*"

The man slowed, looking around him. Jess took Mayfield's arm and towed him to a shop window. He stiffened. "*I don't want him to see me. He might recognize me.*" She nestled against his chest, aware of his discomfort.

"*Oh.*" Even in his head he sounded relieved. She could guess where that came from; the admiral's girlfriend. Hudson's blue eyes smiled in her mind. It was sort of true, she guessed. For now, anyway.

"*What's on his comlink?*"

"*Well, well. His most recent call was to Delia Marati, no more than twenty minutes ago.*"

Her heart thumped louder. Marati. "*Show me the call.*"

The first voice was male, her mate with the ring. '*Rossmoyne is delighted. He wants to move immediately.*'

Followed by La Delia's dulcet tones. '*Excellent. Get back here as soon as you can. I'll have the captain schedule a departure slot.*'

The name Rossmoyne meant nothing to Jess but Marati must be here. "*Can you find out which ship?*"

Mayfield was ahead of her. *Dreamweaver* was docked at B-14. Marati's name was on the passenger list.

"*What about this Rossmoyne person?*"

He shook his head. "*Nothing on the station database.*"

The fellow with the ring had disappeared but at least they knew where he was going.

"*When's Delia's ship scheduled out?*"

"*One hour.*"

She sped up. "*We're going to follow.*"

Mayfield lengthened his stride to keep up. "*What about Cartwright and Burgess?*"

Damn. She'd forgotten about them. "*If they're back, fine, if not I'm sure they'll be okay.*"

"*Look, Jess, you can't just charge off like that.*"

"*You know what? I can. That fellow works for Marati, and he's seen Tenna and Sufi. He even said stuff about beautiful blondes in Burkesville.*"

He'd slowed down, reverting to voice. "*You're guessing. It could be anything.*"

Of course she was guessing. But it felt right. No, he wouldn't understand. She stopped so suddenly he nearly bumped into her. "*You don't have to come. It's kind of an instinct.*"

He almost rolled his eyes. "*I can't let you go on your own.*"

She stuck her hands on her hips. "*Orders?*"

He looked sheepish, not meeting her eyes. "*I would've anyway.*"

"*Your choice.*"

She strode away, back to the transit and docking level B. They rode the short journey in the lift in silence, jammed in with four other people. Two of them also exited at level B. She and Mayfield threaded their way through an ambling crowd of tourists and down the corridor to the docking bay where *Saintly Maid* drifted with the station.

"Call traffic control, *Maid*," Jess said as soon as her feet hit the deck. "I want a departure slot as soon after *Dreamweaver* as I can get. Tell them destination is Nordheim."

"*Acknowledge.*"

"Are we loaded up and ready to go?"

"*Yes, Jess.*"

"Jess, you're knee-jerk reacting." Mayfield held out a hand, fingers splayed. "Let me contact *Defender*."

"Sure. But first find out where Marati is headed."

He grimaced but he complied. "Luciana."

"Luciana? Where's that?"

"It's GPR. Jess, you can't do this." Mayfield shook his head, a picture of misery. "Admiral Hudson's going to be furious."

"Too bad." She pictured his face, those blue eyes cold as ice chips. *Sorry, Your Admiralship. Some things have to happen.* "Are we in line, *Maid*?"

"*I have slotted us in a quarter of an hour after* Dreamweaver, *Jess. Shall I conduct checks?*"

"Yes."

Chapter Twenty-six

Santh kept his eyes closed. His head spun and he felt ill and hungry at the same time. What the hell. The last he remembered was Orlando's smirking face. He'd thought he was dead. Seemed not. He forced his eyelids open a crack. Light filtered in, artificial, not strong. The place smelled a little like antiseptic. Maybe he was in Tabora's medical centre. That wouldn't be so bad; perhaps Doctor Berger would be around.

"How are you feeling?"

A male voice, not someone he knew. He opened his eyes a little more. The world was a blur.

"Your eyes will adjust. You're coming out of suspension. Drink some water. There's a tube near your mouth."

Suspension? He flexed his arms and encountered some sort of stiff padding. He lay in a cocoon of some type. He shifted his head, found a tube with his lips and sucked. Cool water flowed down his throat into his stomach. He could almost feel the liquid spreading through his veins. That was better. He tried opening his eyes again, blinking his eyelashes. At least he could see a little more than fuzzy light. The man's face swam into view, dark eyed, dispassionate. His glance flicked between Santh and a monitor.

"You'll be fine. Get out when you're ready. You'll find some light food."

Santh heard the door swish closed. He was on a space ship, no doubt about it. The air had that recycled taste and the life support systems whispered in the background. You never had perfect silence on a space ship. At least his stomach had settled with the water. He sat up slowly, hands grasping the sides of the contraption in which he lay. His stomach lurched; water rushed up to his mouth and he forced it down. He was in a corpse tube.

They'd slid half the top back so he could sit up but his legs were still down there, under the shell and he wasn't ready to try to get them out yet. He gazed around a closet of a room, with barely enough space for the tube, the monitoring equipment and a table and chair. As the man had said, a tray of food sat on the table, a bowl with a spoon sticking out of it, and a drink. So. He'd been sedated, shoved in a corpse tube and sent off. With anybody else? He'd expect so. Who else? He wished the fog in his brain would lift.

Ace. Yes, that was the name. Ace Connor. Would he be here? Wherever here was.

Gods he felt weak. But his legs seemed to be doing as they were told now. He dragged himself backwards until he could raise his knees and clamber out of the tube. His legs almost collapsed under him. He hung onto the tube, panting, until they stopped trembling and flung himself into the chair. He lifted the spoon from the bowl and tasted. Porridge or something, sweet and sticky; just what he needed. He ate slowly, feeling the stuff stick to his ribs. Now what?

His heart hammered when the door opened. The same fellow who had awakened him stood in the frame, looking him up and down.

"On your feet. Time to go."

Santh stood, aware of the nerve whip in the man's hand. "Where am I going?"

"Move along. You'll find out soon enough." Standing aside, the man jerked the whip in an impatient gesture.

Sounds filtered through from outside, feet shuffling past. At least he wasn't alone. His muscles creaking, he passed through into a corridor and joined a line of other men, all as slow and diffident in their movements as he was.

"Come on, you fellows, get a move on," somebody barked up ahead.

Six men, including himself, stumbled along between two armed men into an airlock where a shuttle waited. One by one, they climbed through the hatch. Santh sat down on a torn seat and squinted around at men who looked as bad as he felt. Hey, that looked like Ace over there.

"Ace?" He croaked the word.

The man ahead stiffened and started to turn. "Jim?"

Fire crackled through Santh's nerves, spreading from his shoulder where the guard's whip had struck him. He groaned through gritted teeth, clutching at the spot. Ace, hunched over, had suffered the same treatment.

"No talking," the guard barked.

The shuttle lurched and started to move. Where to? He'd hardly had time to try to put his thoughts together when the journey ended. Ship transfer? He stayed in his seat, waiting for orders, hardly daring to look at his companions.

The hatch opened. "All right, get out, move it." The fellow brandished a pistol, a nerve whip at his belt.

Santh scrambled out with the others and followed them down a narrow corridor, its bulkheads scuffed and grubby. Somewhere a light flickered. Another stone-faced guard directed them into a cell fitted with six bunk beds and a toilet stinking of shit.

"Talk about the Ritz," one of the men muttered.

The guard chuckled. "You might think of it like that later. Get some shut-eye."

He slammed the door behind them. Santh dropped onto a bunk, wondering why he was suddenly so exhausted.

A klaxon blasted in Santh's brain. He jerked upright and smashed his head into the flat surface above him. Fuck. Oh yes. A bunk. Around him the other men stirred. Legs appeared over the edge of the bed above him.

"Where are we?"

The hatch to their prison opened and a guard poked his head inside. "Out. Move."

Move to where? They shuffled along the same dimly-remembered corridor they'd come down however long ago. Back to the airlock? They were herded like sheep into a lander, seated in three rows of two. Santh settled in his seat as the harness pushed down over his shoulders. Ace sat beside him, his face drawn and gray. But maybe his face looked that way, too. His heart thundered in his ribs. Any thoughts he had about what may happen next entailed pain; or maybe death. Not straight away, though. They'd been kept alive for something.

His cranial implant asked if he wanted to be connected to the caller, Ace Connor. Wow. How had he done that? Santh hadn't given anyone his headline. "*Ace?*"

"*Yes. You okay?*"

"*As okay as you.*"

"*Any idea where we are?*"

The shuttle lurched. Pressure pushed him into his seat. Launch. The lander shot out into space.

"*No idea. Except they transferred us off* Beaconsfield." Santh wriggled in his seat, easing his muscles.

"*Yeah. Some old crate.*"

He wished they had visuals so at least they could see where they were being taken. Creaks and groans filled the cabin. Santh peered around, looking for faults. Wouldn't it be ironic if the thing crashed? Engines roared as they were flung forward into their harnesses. The ship eased to a halt and descended to the hiss of thrusters. Silence. Except for the sound of breathing. Frightened, gray-faced men looked at each other for support.

"Anybody know where we are?" somebody muttered.

Muffled clangs reverberated through the cabin. The door opened to the usual sighing hiss of mingling gases. A guard stomped in.

"Out, all of you. Make it fast. No talking, no dawdling." He tapped his nerve whip against his booted leg.

Santh clambered out into an airlock passage. He felt light, as if the gravity was less, which could well be true, and the air tasted stale, as if the climate conditioners needed maintenance. The whole place was artificial, like Tabora but with less space. The guards drove them along a passage and into a hall. Twelve other people sat, stood or leant against bare walls, all eyeing each other. Four of them were women, huddled together in a corner. Santh recognized Anthea, who had tried to seduce him in the first few nights on Tabora. He didn't know the others.

He traded a look with Ace. "*At least we're still alive.*"

Ace's lips twitched in a parody of a smile "*Gotta look at the positives.*"

"On your feet. Look lively." The guard pointed to a spot near his feet. "Females over here. The rest of you form two lines."

Santh moved. These guards were the usual types of bullies, little men with little dicks who relished the power to dictate. Any excuse would be sufficient. One fellow seated with his back against the wall didn't get up fast enough and felt the fury of the nerve whip. He howled his agony through clenched teeth.

The four girls sidled over to the guard, who looked them over with the sort of leer that made Santh want to punch his lights out. It was pretty obvious what they were here for. Sure, that's what they did on Tabora but there, they'd had a choice.

Another man strolled into the room, hands clasped loosely behind his back. This guy had to be GPR. Nobody in the Confederacy would have a gut like that hanging over his belt. Two others followed him, armed flunkies by the looks.

"Ah, the new women. Excellent." He smiled, sending his jowls quivering. "Take them along to the seraglio, would you?"

Santh watched them leave, heads bowed, shoulders slumped. Poor kids. The head honcho approached the two lines of men, casting an assessing eye along the ranks.

"Okay, straighten up." The fellows with the nerve whips strutted along in attendance, lips curled in a permanent sneer.

"Welcome to Orroyex, gentlemen," the man said. "You will call me Master. You are here to do a job, namely to mine starhearts. You're miners; used to the lure of riches. Work hard, don't complain and you will be able to earn certain concessions, such as a night with a woman, alcohol. Find something really worthwhile and you may win your freedom. Please don't bother trying to escape. There's nowhere to go. Orroyex is a moon of a gas giant in a Ptorix system. This is the only settlement. We'll give you some time to recover from suspension, then you'll eat and be taken to your work place." He waved a hand.

A Ptorix planet. Santh slid his eyes toward Ace, standing beside him. "*Shit.*"

"*Shit is right.*"

***

Hudson rocked back in his chair and steepled his hands. So *Beaconsfield* had stopped, had it? Transferred most of its body tubes. "So what do you think we have, Mann?"

The commander lifted a shoulder. "Either some sort of contraband or some sort of slavery. Those tubes could be used to keep a body in suspension for quite some time."

"Mmm. Yes, that's what I thought." Husdon gazed at the hologram where Mancor's malevolent red light took centre stage. "Any significance in that location?"

Mann asked the IS to display political boundaries like a 3-D Venn diagram, overlapping arcs of red, blue and yellow.

"Mancor isn't in anybody's territory. You can see it's pretty close to our border, to the GPR's border and the Ptorix border, sort of a no-man's land. It's a great place to stop if you're on your way to Kentor. Hardly a diversion."

The display changed to show the picture of the ship *Saintly Maid* had purloined from *Beaconsfield's* database.

"*Cordoba* is a GPR ship, Sir, but apart from the registration, there isn't much. As far as I can find out she hasn't been to any of our ports and not to either Chollarc or Kentor, either. There are other, independent stations we don't have access to, but those two would be the most likely for a GPR ship."

"No clues as to where the cargo might have been taken?"

Mann shook his head. "There's nothing obvious. My guess would be one of the GPR planets but what for, I don't know. Unless they're going to sell them in a slave market on one of the edge planets."

Hudson pushed his fingers past his lips and his nose. What to do? He was supposed to be here, showing off Confederacy power to Governor Anxhou. But if those tubes did contain people, that was a straight act of piracy. And what if Sufi and Tenna had been stashed in one of them? Other girls were missing, too. The thought of Tenna brought him back to Jess. He'd hated having to let her go to Kentor. But he couldn't go himself and she had every excuse, the perfect cover. She'd be fine; she had to be.

"We're going a bit closer to this encounter to see what we can see. Get your scan techs ready. I'll want to know where that ship went."

Mann saluted and departed.

Hudson called his adjutant. "Get me Admiral Saahren on a code five, Tomas." Code five; urgent, private, using real-time, multi-dim comms. He didn't think Saahren would mind but the protocol had to be followed.

Saahren's hologram appeared, dark skinned, dark haired, seated in his office chair on his flagship. "Hudson. All's well at Nordheim?"

"So well it's boring. I have a situation, a potential case of piracy, Sir. The GPR may be taking our people as slaves."

Saahren's eyes glittered; he was known to be as hard on pirates as Hudson was. "Explain."

Hudson set out the facts as he knew them. "I want permission to chase, Sir, find out where they were taken and bring them back if I can."

"Agreed. Deal with it as you see appropriate." Saahren raised a finger. "But be careful not to stray into Ptorix space. Anxhou is itching for an excuse to cause a fight, especially where it comes to the edge planets. I'll want a report."

Hudson grinned. "Of course."

Saahren's image disappeared.

He called Captain Sundra and issued his orders, then he called Ottenshaw. The President wasn't happy but that was too bad.

Chapter Twenty-seven

Maid backed out of her dock and turned around. *Dreamweaver* was invisible against the starscape but her track could be seen on the nav display, a yellow dot approaching the exit queue for the jump gate. Even now, a heavy transport accelerated to departure speed. Jess threw on the power.

"Keep a track on *Dreamweaver*, *Maid*. Mayfield, pull her nav when we're close enough. Make sure nothing changes."

Four ships were lined up, holding position. The IS fired the forward thrusters to bring *Maid* into the queue, two behind *Dreamweaver*.

"Okay, that's close enough." Mayfield fiddled with the settings on his equipment. "Hang at this range. Any closer and they'll think you're stalking them."

"Have you got their precise coordinates?"

"Yes."

"Feed them through to the IS. *Maid*, I want to go to these coordinates but I want you to make the change at the last moment, okay?"

"*Acknowledge.*"

Mayfield looked at her sideways, eyebrows arched. "What's that about?"

"I don't trust Kentor control. If they think I'm going home, that suits me."

Jess fidgeted. She always did when she was ready to move. Displacement behavior, Troy had said. He used to laugh and poke fun at her for rubbing her hands up and down her thighs or picking at a seam in her suit. Up ahead, engines glowed brightly as the ship before *Dreamweaver* shot toward the jump gate.

"Get me what you have on Luciana, Maid."

"*We have little information, Jess. It is a Galactic People's Republic planet, therefore I assume low tech.*" The planet appeared in the display, the usual blue and white marble streaked with green and brown. "*It has one space station, four moons and a single jump gate. Approach is restricted.*"

"Restricted? Why is that?"

"*A visa is required to dock at the space station.*"

"Is that usual?"

"It would be for a Confederacy ship," Mayfield said. "They don't like us, remember." His fingers flew over keys.

"Which makes it even more intriguing why a minister from a Confederacy planetary Government would be going there, don't you think?"

Dreamweaver's engines flared from yellow to blue. The ship streaked off, reached the jump gate and vanished. *Maid's* turn.

Mayfield scowled and pressed keys. "I'm telling *Defender*."

"Sounds like a good idea to me."

Kentor Control broke in almost immediately. "*Saintly Maid, you are cleared to go. Say again, you are cleared to go. Safe journey.*"

Maid acknowledged. Acceleration pushed Jess back into her chair. "Change the destination, *Maid*."

"*Acknowledge*."

The gate's running lights brightened as the distance decreased, red to port, green to starboard. Nobody had ever been able to explain why those colors. On the nav display the destination changed.

"We're cutting it fine," Mayfield muttered.

"It should be okay. The gate will have the data from *Dreamweaver*." She hoped. This was one of those times you had to trust the technology. It wasn't that you needed a jump gate; you didn't. Gates made transits easier to control, especially in crowded space lanes like those for Kentor. The gates could slingshot a ship in the right direction, too, saving energy.

Space disappeared.

Mayfield shrugged out of his harness as soon as the fasteners clicked open. "Right, so what now, Captain? We don't have a visa and you're going to arrive at the space station right after somebody who knows you."

"Marati doesn't know anything about my ship except the name. So we'll change her registration. We'll dock under the name *Hesperus*, registered on Kentor."

"I haven't got anything to do that."

Yes, well. It was a bit late to be coy now. "I have."

He lifted a lip in a knowing sneer. "Goes with that hidden compartment in the shift drive, I guess."

"Oh." Shit. They must've done a proper inspection when they fitted the surveillance devices. Hudson would have to know. Her heart sank. Damn it, it was never going to be anything but a bit of fun. Probably best not to start.

"It comes with being an independent freighter captain. My husband and I had to make a few deliveries where the recipient wasn't to know we were Confederacy, so we had some extra ship identities made up."

His lip curled. "Smuggling."

"Cutting out usurious planetary taxes. Providing a cheaper service." She held his gaze for a moment. "We were younger. And it was fun."

She stood. "I'll go and change *Maid's* ID. I'll be Susan Oakley and you'll be Alan Davis. I already have Kentor id's for them. We'll have to change the pictures on the ID cards, though."

"And then what?"

"We follow them. Find out where they go."

He scowled.

"C'mon, Mayfield. You're not going to try to tell me you haven't got one of those things to keep track of somebody's implant?"

One look at his face was enough to confirm it. "La Delia's going to be one of the few with one of those, isn't she?"

"They only work up to a certain distance."

True. She'd learnt that during her unintended camping expedition with Hudson. "You could get a fix on her, surely? Via the satellites?"

"Nope. Not their satellites."

Damn. "We'll play it by ear, then."

At last. *Saintly Maid*, alias *Hesperus*, shot out of the jump gate at Luciana, thrusters blasting to slow her down. The space station, in accordance with best practice, lay five thousand klicks away.

"No sign of *Dreamweaver*," Jess said, scanning the visuals. "Perhaps they've already docked."

"Could be." Mayfield hunched over his work station. "I'll see if I can pick up the space station's control."

The planet sported the usual characteristics of most habitable planets; oceans, clouds, continents. Lights sprinkled the darkness of the night side but nowhere near the multitude you'd see even on Nordheim. If Tenna and Sufi were there, she'd find them; that was a promise. She'd get them out, too.

"Strange." Mayfield straightened up. "She hasn't docked."

Maid lurched, flinging Jess sideways almost out of her chair. Adrenalin raced through her body, sending her nerves tingling. "We're under attack. Raise shields, Maid." She dragged herself upright. "Take evasive action, seal the blast doors."

She lurched again, the other way, thrown when *Maid* dodged. Red lights flashed on the consoles. The ship shuddered and jibed. White-knuckled, Jess hung on to her chair. Mayfield bent over his equipment, face set. He'd know the *Maid* had no weapons. Another hit had the ship shuddering. Rear shields down to fifty-seven percent.

"That's *Dreamweaver* behind us," Mayfield said.

The vessel appeared to dance in the view screen as *Maid* ducked and dived. Underneath *Dreamweaver's* blunt bow two blank ports resembling nostrils had to be missile tubes. They both appeared to blink. Jess' heart hammered. Oh fuck. Two tracking missiles. They didn't stand a chance.

A blast rocked the ship. A klaxon blared. Warning lights flashed red in a dozen places around the bridge. Jess dragged a fire extinguisher out of a compartment in the bulkhead and aimed the stream at a smoldering electrical fire. The stink floated in the air.

"The main engines have been destroyed, Jess. I don't think I can maintain the integrity of the hull." The IS spoke the words in a tone it might have used to welcome them on board, wishing them a nice day. Another alarm began to ping; air pressure falling.

"Grab an exo-suit." Jess dragged hers out of the emergency compartment next to her chair and pulled it on over her ship suit. She'd leave the helmet in the housing for the longest possible time.

Mayfield geared up with practiced speed and headed aft toward the crew capsule, fending off the bulkheads with his fingertips as he slipped and swayed. Smoke drifted past. *Maid* was finished; nothing could withstand this. She'd die with her ship, she'd never know what happened to her daughter. *Oh, Tenna, I'm so sorry.*

Snap out of it, woman. You're not finished yet. The voice spoke in her mind. Hudson? Troy? Both of them? She pushed it aside. "Mayfield, let's launch the crew capsule, empty. If they take that out and think we're finished, we might think of something else."

"Right."

They staggered through the cargo hold. The capsule stood ready. You crawled in the rear compartment, sealed the hatch and launched straight out into space. It had enough air to keep up to four alive for three days. Which might be worth something if you were near a planet.

Balancing herself against another jolt, Jess sealed her helmet and latched the suit's line onto a hook in the floor. Mayfield did, too. When the capsule launched, the hold would lose its air.

"Maid, launch the capsule."

No answer. Fuck, even the IS was shut down. Jess staggered over a buckling deck to a manual launch lever. She pulled. If this were real, she'd have twenty seconds to get into the capsule. She found a hand hold well away from the capsule and fixed herself. Even so, the air blasting out after the capsule ejected dragged at her. Broken pieces of equipment, wires, the empty extinguisher all sucked out into space.

The artificial gravity generators had been destroyed in the last explosions. She let herself float in the vacuum of the cargo hold. Where was Mayfield? Sucked out of the hold? He must have been; she couldn't see him anywhere.

What now? At least the firing had stopped. *Maid* rolled, settling into a rhythm. If she could only see what was happening. She dragged herself along the corridor to the computer's machine room. There might not be any operational peripherals but the computer itself was housed deep inside the ship and protected by armor plate. If the sensors still worked, Jess could at least see. She used the override lever to set the computer system to manual. That worked, at least. The monitor burst into life, 2-D and pretty basic but much better than nothing. The sensor arrays aft were gone; hardly surprising; but one on the bow and two to starboard produced a fuzzy, wavering picture, changing with the roll of the ship. Even so, *Dreamweaver* was in view often enough; a rapidly receding object heading for the space station. The escape capsule had disappeared.

Where was Mayfield? He would have tumbled out with the rest of the junk, heading away from the ship and behind its current heading. Oh, fuck. She'd loused this up big-time. Worse. Mayfield was going to die out there because of her. Stupid, knee-jerk, idiot. She imagined Hudson standing there with his arms folded, shaking his head. And what good was this doing for Tenna and Sufi? She put her helmeted head in her gloved hands and let the tears flow.

Chapter Twenty-eight

The guards shoved the prisoners along another corridor where the tramp of boots seemed to be swallowed into the climate conditioning. The smell of food sent Santh's mouth watering. How long had it been since he'd eaten a proper meal? He didn't know. They must have used intravenous nutrients in the body tubes; he was sure they'd been in them for a few days at least. Some of these men, even longer. The file of men turned left through a door and into a mess hall.

"Line up. Take a bowl and put it under the dispenser. You sit at this table." The guard barked the instructions, his voice loud above the background hum of machinery.

Each man took a bowl and stood in line along the service bench. The food slopped out of dispensers and splattered into the bowl, some sort of dark brown stew dotted with bits of orange and green. He wrinkled his nose and followed Ace to a couple of spare stools on the long table the guard had indicated. The place was obviously set up to cater for many more than their party of a dozen men; six tables filled the mess hall, enough for maybe sixty. Except for the clatter of spoons the room was strangely silent. A soft voice raised in conversation seemed strange, out of place.

Santh put down his spoon. He'd eaten the lot and he'd have to admit it didn't taste too bad. Nobody else seemed to have left much, either, except for the fellow down the end, who looked like he had a hangover.

"Okay, on yer feet."

They were herded out again, around a corner along yet another anonymous corridor. Sliding doors on each side carried labels, simple letters of the alphabet; A, B, C... Santh and Ace were ordered to door D. When they hesitated too long, the guard shoved them inside a room stinking of unwashed bodies. Four double bunk beds were crowded too close together. Two pairs of eyes stared at them, two men sitting on the front lower bunks. The other guys lay on their beds.

"The top two at the back," the nearest man said. His voice sounded gravelly.

"Thanks." It made sense. Last in gets the crummiest bunk. Santh glanced at Ace. "I'll take the left one."

"Sure." The metal groaning, Ace swung himself up to the right top bunk.

"Umm ... what's the drill?" Santh asked the man who had spoken. "My name's Jim, by the way." He stuck out a hand.

"Names don't matter here." The fellow's eyes were sunken into his head as though he'd seen too much horror, a bit like the long-time miners up at Tabora.

"Are you from Tabora?"

"Aren't we all?" The man swiveled and lay down on his bunk, his arm over his eyes.

Santh wiped his hand on his trousers and climbed up to his bunk. Up here the air was even staler, far from the vents above the door. Hot air rises.

A clamoring bell startled Santh out of a doze. He sat up too fast and hit his head on the ceiling. Shit. He clambered down to the floor and shared a look with Ace. The other men were already on their way out of the door. Showers first, in a great open room with a row of nozzles on the wall. He stripped off and cleaned himself up as well as he could in the timed interval. No long, hot showers here, it seemed.

A new guard, short and bad-tempered, drove them to a locker room. Bright green exo-suits hung from a rail behind a line of benches. They looked stiffer than the usual ones, as if they were constructed of reinforced carbon fiber.

"You. Don't stand there like a Nancy. Get into a suit."

Santh took a step forward before the whip connected properly. It delivered a tingle rather than the usual jolt. The guard grinned, eyes twinkling with malice. "Don't make me use full power."

Santh stripped off and climbed into a suit, which adjusted itself automatically to fit correctly. He flexed his fingers in surprisingly malleable gloves. Although, looking at the fingers, they'd done some hard work. He could swear they'd been subjected to a lot of heat. He slid the airpack onto his back, three cylinders each holding two hours' supply and a fourth cylinder holding water that would feed to a tube in the helmet. A set of tongs and a pouch lay on the bench. He glanced around. Everybody else had those items hanging from the belt, so he clipped them on. Ace, already suited up, his helmet in his hand, stood in line waiting to go into the airlock for outside. Santh pulled the helmet down from the rack and joined the line behind the others. Into what? His nerves tightened. Shit, he didn't know anything about this place except it was a moon.

"*Steady, pal,*" Ace said. "*They want us to work. We're not gonna die if we're smart.*"

Cheers. So why was his pulse hammering like a freight train while he watched the gauge on the hatch change color?

He stepped outside into darkness. Star-filled space extended around him. To his left one star blazed much brighter than the rest, a discernible disk; Orroyex's distant sun. A few of the other, larger, objects were probably other moons.

"This way." The voice sounded in his helmet, tinny and metallic.

He joined the other men from dorms C and D in a battered, topless vehicle that raised itself on thrusters and took them over rocky terrain, the details hidden by darkness. Orroyex rose before them, at first a gleam in the sky becoming an arc glowing with the reflected light of its sun thrown back from the cloud tops that whipped around its hidden core. A little like Tabora. In fact, a lot like Tabora.

"*A bit of volcanic activity here*," Ace said. He inclined his head at a cone surrounded with debris. Now he'd mentioned it, Santh noticed a heap more. And yet the outside temperature was so far below freezing that a few minutes outside would freeze a man to death.

The vehicle stopped within sight of one of the vents and stopped. The shift leader's voice echoed through Santh's helmet.

"What we're waiting for is an eruption. This one is pretty regular."

Nice to know. Santh shot a look at Ace but all he could see was Orroyex's eerie light reflected from the darkened visor. Seconds went by. The clouds on the gas giant's surface swirled. The vehicle shook. Santh grabbed the bars of his seat, his heart thundering. "Shit."

"It'll pass," the shift boss said.

The opening of the vent glowed red, brightening to brilliant white-yellow. A tower of molten rock spewed high into the air and splattered across the surface, the whole performance taking place in total silence. Bloody hell. And it did this regularly? The gobbets of rock still glowed like coals, despite the cold.

"Everybody out. New men stay here, the rest, get on with it."

Santh and Ace and one guy they didn't know hung around while the rest strode off toward the debris around the vent. Black and yellow dust drifted up with each footfall but settled quickly.

"Right, you three, what happens is, we wait for an eruption, then we get there before the rock freezes again. Come with me and I'll show you what we're after."

He led them over to some of the rocks and began to pick them over with tongs he removed from his belt. Most he discarded but a few he checked more carefully, bouncing them around on his gloved hand. So that's what damaged the gloves. He'd examined three before he retained one.

"See?" he said, holding the chunk up in the tongs. "There's a life form down there. Don't ask me how. Sometimes a piece gets trapped in the molten rock. That's what forms the starhearts. You can only see it when the rock is hot but whatever's inside disintegrates if it gets too cold, which it does lying on the surface."

Deep in the cooling heart of the stone a bright light blazed. Within moments the display faded to black.

"That's what you want. Collect them in your sack. You have a quota to meet if you want to stay alive. If you're useless, they'll turf you out without a suit."

"Shit." The third man, the one Santh didn't know, choked the word out.

"Has anybody ever escaped from here?" Santh asked. "Earned their way out?"

"Not that I know of. Enough talking. Start looking. And when I say back to the cart, move your asses because that's when the vent will blow again, every half hour or so."

Santh unclipped his tongs. He'd wondered what they were for. He picked up a rock and turned it. Not a glimmer. One more, then another. Ah. A bright gleam in the darkness. Better be sure. He turned his back on the roiling planet half-filling the sky. No, not a good move. He knelt, the weight of the tanks pressing down on his back but at least the rock couldn't reflect anything but its own gleam. He dropped the stone into his hand and turned it. Yes. The light flickered, not a dull glow like you'd get from a dying coal. He straightened and dropped his find into the collection pouch at his waist.

They searched the spewed stone furthest from the vent first, working up the mound toward the pit, a black hole into the core of the moon. Santh would have liked to take a look down into it but the shift boss kept them working. Sheesh. You'd think he was getting the benefit. Then again, perhaps he did. There had to be some perks to lording it over your fellow slaves. He felt the shiver in the rocks before he heard the call.

"Move. Back to the cart."

He bounded rather than ran in this lower gravity, even with the rocks hanging from his belt. Ace, who had been sent over to the other side of the vent to work, beat him in; so did the other new guy. The old hands probably weren't so nervous. The ground shook, the geyser sprayed. They spread out in a circle around the mouth and worked their way in again. Santh found a few more rocks and dropped them into his pouch.

Each time back to the cart was harder. If he'd thought Tabora was difficult, this was so much worse. His arms and legs ached. Even with the tongs he had to bend too often. His stomach gnawed at him, too. He'd had nothing since he'd arrived here. He settled into his seat on the cart, muscles weak with relief when the shift boss finally called a halt.

They drove back around the way they'd come, into the darkness on the far side of the moon.

"*This moon must be pretty much synced with the planet,*" Ace said. "*The view didn't change all day.*"

True enough. Santh peered ahead at the surface revealed in the cart's headlights. Apart from some evidence of meteor impacts, there didn't appear to be the same evidence of volcanism over here. So you live over here and get some poor schmucks to go to the side that's torn apart by the planet's gravitational force and let them face the dangers.

The base hove into view, a collection of dust-covered, domed pre-fabs sunken into the ground to take advantage of the thermal protection. The cart drove into an airlock, which sealed behind them.

"You new guys come in last, just before me, got that?" the shift boss said as the bay aired up. "You hand over your collection pouches and they're assessed. Never let anybody else handle your pouch. Folks have been known to cheat. And for you new guys, if you've set up a cranial connection, be warned if they even suspect you're doing it, they'll come down hard." He glared at Ace and Santh.

"*Fancy that,*" Ace said. "*Some folks cheat. Guess we'd better shut up, eh?*"

They lined up and stumbled through into a corridor, dragging their helmets off. Santh ran a hand through hair damp with sweat and glanced along the line where an assessor sat at a desk checking the contents of the shift boss's pouch. His heart lurched. Fuck. A Ptorix.

Chapter Twenty-nine

The trouble with crying in your helmet is you couldn't blow your nose, couldn't wipe your eyes. When was the last time crying fixed anything? She must have been about five, when bursting into tears got her an ice cream. She blinked the last droplets from her eyelashes and treated herself to a mighty sniff.

Right. A space ship that wasn't going anywhere except round and around until the orbit decayed and it plunged into the atmosphere. That was one way of going out in a blaze of glory. Maybe something had survived, the forward thrusters. Yes, sure, not much chance but she'd never know if she didn't look. She eased herself out of the cramped machine room and floated down the corridor back through the cargo hold, eerie and strange in the light of the helmet's headlamp.

She stopped, her heart pounding. Something there, where the escape capsule had ejected. Something moving. The light bounced off it, a many-fingered ... Mayfield? She pushed her legs against the bulkhead to gain momentum, landed on the opposite wall and eased herself along. Yes, a hand. She hoped it was connected to a body.

"Mayfield?" she said via the helmet mike.

"Yeah." He sounded exhausted. His fingers flexed on the ship's hull.

Safely latched onto a section of the hold, Jess grabbed his hand, dragged him into the cargo hold and choked back the tears of relief. It might not help to have somebody else here but at least it wouldn't be so lonely when she died. "You okay?"

"Yeah. The thing I latched to tore away. I was outside before I knew it but I was lucky. The line tangled with the hull. I've only just managed to pull myself back to the escape hatch. They blew the capsule away, did you know?"

"No. But it's what I expected. That's good."

Mayfield managed a laugh. "Sure. What now?"

"I was going to check the engine room, see if I can do anything."

"Don't bother."

As bad as that, huh? Still. "What else can we do? I'm too young to die and I need to find my daughter. If we stay here, we're going to become a spectacular shooting star before we know it."

"Standard practice for a lot of places is that if a ship is damaged, it's salvaged. They don't want bits of ship splattering their planet. Besides, there'll be worthwhile pieces on board, especially for a GPR planet where they don't get any of the best tech."

"You mean they'd use it? Our tech? I thought they despised us."

"They do. But it doesn't mean they won't take advantage—some of 'em, anyway. The dyed-in-the-wool fundamentalists won't, but that's not who you get at a space station."

Hope raised a diffident hand. "So somebody's going to come out here and check it out? Or drag it in?"

"Yes. That's my guess, anyway."

Jess shifted, the helmet light casting weird shadows in the once-familiar hold. "We've got a few sensors. Come on down to the machine room and we'll see what we can see."

Without being able to steady the ship, the view rolled but the space station became visible often enough. At least at this proximity the computer would recognize commands from her implant. She couldn't have used the keyboard that came with every machine room, not in these gloves.

"Anything approaching?"

Letters marched across the screen, the best the computer could do. 'Sensor data is confused. The ship is not on my database but appears to have the configuration of a tug.'

"Woohoo." Mayfield punched the air, pushing himself backwards into the bulkhead. "That means they're coming to fetch us."

"Yeah. But I don't want to be captured or killed."

"No problem. They'll attach a tow, most likely to the bow and take *Maid* down to the shipyards. If we hide outside we can go along for the ride and drift free when we want to."

"Why outside? Why not wait it out here?"

"They may board to check for anything too dangerous to bring to the yards."

"Fair enough. Where'll we hide?"

"I reckon amongst the wreckage. If we can find a big enough breach in the hull, we can skulk around there and slip outside if we have to."

"Good. But I'm going to disable the computer. I'm not going to let those bastards have a state of the art nav system."

Jess caught a distorted smile through Mayfield's face plate. "Great. I was going to ask you to do that."

The system had a self-destruct. Jess stared at the flickering, wavering monitor. In a way the IS was almost a living thing. *Saintly Maid*, her friend since Troy had died. *Goodbye, my friend. Best you die by my hand than become a slave for somebody who doesn't love you.* Tears pricked. She pushed a button. Nothing appeared to happen but deep inside, the data cleared, the circuits scrambled. In moments the computer was junk, worthless.

Wishing she had a hanky, Jess pushed away. "You've got one pistol in your suit but we could take an extra."

"Sure. I'll see what I can salvage of my surveillance gear, too."

Together, they pulled their way up to the bridge. The familiar consoles still flashed their warning lights. A few globs of liquid drifted in the air along with a discarded light pen and a mug. The chairs swung with the ship. Jess opened the weapons locker and took out two rifles and extra power packs while Mayfield hung suspended over his workstation looking for gadgets he could use. She made her way to her quarters, pulled out the secret drawer where she kept her snooper devices and shoved the items into her pockets.

Back at the bridge, Mayfield was bent over his station. "How did you go?" she asked.

"Screen with functions. I was set up for Kentor and GPR so I should be able to get into most of their systems. GPR security is crap, no match for InfoDroid tech like this. And I've got a tracker unit and a couple of tags."

"Yeah? What does that mean?"

"That if we each attach a tag, high-powered tracker units can find us. Anyway, enough jawing, let's get in position. There's a big hole in the hull forward of the living quarters."

She let him go first, the knot in her stomach tightening as she moved through the once-familiar spaces. *Maid* had been her refuge, her home, her job; not anymore. She bit on her lip to stop it trembling.

Mayfield stopped next to a gaping, jagged gap where the common room used to be and secured his line to a piece of hull. She followed suit. They both turned off their helmet lamps. The galaxy glowed outside, teetering, drunken lights against the blackness.

"Can you see the tug?" she asked.

"Not yet. We stay here until the last moment."

We detach at the space station, find our way on there somehow and find Delia Marati. She still had that feeling in her gut that the woman had something to do with Tenna and Sufi. *Maid's* destruction had enhanced her belief. Why else destroy the ship? On that basis, she'd obviously been the target at Nordheim, too. Which meant Longford had been collateral damage and Hudson would have been, too. Something dangerous must be going on here. Where was *Defender*? Hudson would know *Maid* had left; Mayfield had passed that back with, no doubt, the real intended destination. It didn't do her any good, though. He couldn't enter GPR territory. No, whichever way she looked at it, she was on her own.

"Incoming." Mayfield's voice startled her out of her thoughts.

A shadow eclipsed the stars, passing the gap in the hull. She wished she could hear them. Her nerves were as tight as hawsers. Minutes passed. The shadow passed again.

"That was a guy on a scooter, doing a visual and scanning for radiation, I reckon," Mayfield said.

The ship's roll changed. Jess grabbed the hull section to alter her balance. Mayfield did the same. They must be stabilizing the vessel. Yes. The Galaxy firmed, held stationary. Her body began to move toward the back of the ship. So they were moving forward, under tow.

"Look, I owe you an apology," Mayfield said.

"You what?"

"You've got to be right. Something's important enough to kill you."

She cringed. He was apologizing to her? "I almost got you killed."

"Yeah, well, you didn't. Let's assume we get to the station without being caught. How do we find Marati?"

"I've been thinking about that. That conversation Marati had with our friend with the blue stone. She mentioned a name; Rossmoyne. We look for him. He's probably involved in this."

"What's 'this'?"

What a very good question. "I wish I knew. But I guess it has to be something to do with Tabora and those missing men. And I hope, I desperately hope, it has something to do with the missing girls."

After what felt like hours of unchanging tedium Jess drifted forward. "They're slowing her down. We must be nearly here."

Mayfield shifted so he could peer outside and ahead between the shards of the hole. Jess did the same. Sure enough, the space station rose in front of them, towering scaffolds. They were approaching the ship yards, situated at the bottom of the station, the bay blazing with light. Above them, three ships were attached to simple docks, their airlocks umbilical cords to the central cylinder. *Maid* lurched. Jess fought to hold her grip. Either the ship had been picked up by a grav beam or a tug was nosing them in from behind. A girder appeared, then a cross bar, both open to space. A ceiling blocked the view far above.

"Next upright. Give me your line." Mayfield detached his line and set himself up at the hole in the hull, his boot against a solid piece. Jess handed the end of her line to him.

Launch. Jess followed him, hoping she wouldn't have to use the suit's jets to direct herself the right way. For a change it worked out well. Mayfield grabbed the girder and fixed himself. Jess jolted to a halt, her line taut. He hauled her in, like a fish, while *Maid* moved inexorably on. From out here, she had a better view of the damage, the gaping hole in the common room, breaches in the hull near the crew quarters. They'd targeted the humans on board, without a doubt. The shattered engine cowls came into view. Nearly past.

"Let's go before they finish docking her." Mayfield pulled himself along a cross beam between the girders, away from the light.

Jess gave *Maid* one final look. Her ship; hers. Dead. Shrugging aside her heavy heart, she followed the trooper up through the maze of gantries and platforms. "Do you know what you're doing?"

"No," he said, "but there has to be some sort of exit or work hatch down here. There has been in any other dock I've seen. We look for the utility towers; the lifts and services. They should be lit up and somewhere in the middle."

He pulled himself along, hand over hand, aiming for the columns up ahead. Jess followed. Pull, let go, float. Under different circumstances it might be fun. A ceiling appeared over their heads. After a quick upward scramble they stood on the ceiling, which turned out to be a platform in front of a lift. Mayfield took out a card and slid it into the card slot. The lift opened.

"One of your useful little gadgets, huh?" Jess said, pulling herself inside. Her feet smacked to the floor. It hurt. "Shit. Careful. There's AG in here."

"So I noticed." He followed more carefully.

"Where to?"

Mayfield's comlink was obviously a little more than a comlink. "We're here," he said, showing her the screen. "Two levels up we can exit an airlock and dump the suits. Then we can see if we can find this Rossmoyne person and Marati."

"Sounds good." Jess pressed the button herself. They'd been made extra-large, designed for somebody dressed in gloves. The lift rose smoothly. A light flashed when it reached their destination. They walked into an airlock and waited, impatient, until the hatch unsealed. Jess withdrew her helmet and sucked in air. It might have been filtered space station air but it tasted so good after the metallic tank air. They stood in a utility room, dingy and bare, a row of massive waste containers along the back wall.

Mayfield was already pulling off his gloves. "Hurry, get rid of the suit. It marks you as coming from the Confederacy."

The things you learn. Jess shucked out of the exo-suit and threw it into the nearest waste bin. Her pale-gray ship suit should be suitably anonymous. An exit sign hung over the door into the main station.

"Can you tell if Marati's ship is still here?" Jess asked.

Nodding, Mayfield took out his screen and concentrated, issuing instructions via his implant. After a few seconds a list appeared.

"Yes. Or at least, the ship's still docked. Wait while I get into the traffic control database." Jess gazed around her inhaling the smells from the waste containers. Something was definitely rotten in there. And something clattered, too.

"Got it. She's scheduled to leave next week."

Jess' heart flipped. "Next week? What's the passenger list?"

Mayfield gazed up at her, brows drawn together. "Marati ... two other females. They're shown going in—but not going out."

Jess' heart bounded. "My girls." So they been brought here. What now? Where would they have been taken? What for? "Is Marati on board?"

"I can't tell from here. We'd have to get closer."

She dragged his arm. "Let's get closer."

"Easy, Jess, easy. We walk out there without any ID, the first security guard who stops us will grab us."

"We've got ID."

"For Kentor. How did we get here?"

Good point. She hated to admit it, but he was right. She rummaged in the pocket of her jacket and fished out her ID card. "We'll need money, too."

"I'll need to have a look around but I reckon I can create a bank account. Unless you have one?"

"Not here. But I have a card."

She gave him a credit card blank. "Set us up with these. The card will assume whatever appearance you need. Or it used to, a few years back."

He afforded her an admiring look.

"You'd be amazed what independent freighter captains find useful."

Mayfield grinned. "I must say, I've never had to use any of these. In a way, it's fun." He bent over the screen, presumably issuing instructions.

Fun. Yes, it was in a way—an adrenalin rush. Right now, though, she wanted Tenna and Sufi. But how was she going to find them? The clatter in the climate conditioner insinuated itself in her mind, a soft click click click. Once, she thought she heard footsteps. She gripped Mayfield's shoulder.

"*Let go*," he said. "*It's nothing.*"

She wished he'd hurry.

At last he straightened up. "All right, done. We have money and ID's. I listed us as crew on a Kentor ship that just docked. And this is the only place on this planet where I can get a multi-dim transmission to *Defender*."

"Yeah? Why's that?"

"They had to buy it from us—the Confederacy. So we built in some backdoor functions." He winked. "Anything an independent freighter captain can do, the Fleet can do better. Anyway, the admiral knows we're here." He pushed a large button next to the exit door, which slid aside.

They strode through into a corridor, acting as if they belonged.

The place seemed clean enough, but the grey walls were scuffed and the utility carpet they walked on had seen many years. At least the decorators had chosen sensible colors, an amorphous pattern of green and red and purple, visible here and there in the less well-trodden areas. This was a thoroughfare, nothing more. In Kentor's space station shops would have lined the corridors; not here. There was a food court, though, up closer to the hub. People sat around tables surrounding a central kiosk.

"Might be a good place to stop for something to eat."

Mayfield picked one of the many vacant tables while Jess took the card to the kiosk. The woman behind the counter waved it in front of a reader without even glancing at it. Phew. Jess brought back watery kaff and rolls on a tray.

"Where will Marati be? If she's here officially, it should be recorded somewhere." Jess gulped a mouthful of kaff, luxuriating in the feel of liquid sliding down her parched throat.

He shook his head, his mouth full. "Can't find her," he said when he'd swallowed. "She's not on the arrival list."

Jess gulped a mouthful of kaff. "She has to be here. An assumed name?"

"Maybe, but what?"

"I don't know. Rossmoyne?"

Mayfield made a show of rubbing his forehead with his fingers, elbow resting on the table to hide his accessing his implant. "There's a few listed. Main one is a doctor with interests in genetics. He's got a research place on an island somewhere."

Jess chewed on a surprisingly good roll stuffed with cheese and crisp salad. "Genetics, huh? I thought that was a no-no in the GPR?"

"Genetic engineering is, so are implants and other enhancements. This looks more like breeding. Yeah, this guy's background is animal husbandry. Doesn't help us much." Mayfield slurped some more kaff.

"Let's see." He went back to the arrivals list. "A Miss Fortescue has arrived from Kentor at about the right time. It says she's booked a room at the La Plaza Hotel. Oh-ho. She's booked two rooms; one for herself and one for her two daughters."

Nerves zinged down Jess' spine. "Any other info?"

He shook his head, slurping at his kaff. "No. That's it."

"I think we'd better go and take a look, don't you?"

Chapter Thirty

The Ptorix wasn't sitting; they couldn't, with four legs. It stood next to the desk, its lower arms hanging loosely, tentacles twitching, while the top two examined the contents of the pouch. Santh had seen Ptorix before on Kentor and other edge worlds but he'd never taken such detailed notice. Two of the alien's three eyes were visible underneath its helmet, both swirling orangey-yellow. That meant it was happy; he thought. Yes, violet meant anger. He'd heard something about the color of the fur, too, but he wasn't sure. One of the guards stood beside it, his fingers hooked into his belt, his nerve whip hanging next to his hand. Two more guards lounged on each side of the door they'd come through, their guns in their hands.

The tentacles on the ends of the Ptorix's arms gripped each rock, rotating, inspecting until it was satisfied and placed the stone into one of four trays. Grading them, he guessed. When the last rock had been sorted it said something in their strange, hissing language. The guard nodded.

"Satisfactory. You can go."

The man picked up his empty pouch, bowed to the Ptorix and made off into the change room. Santh could almost feel the radiated relief from here.

Everybody moved along a few steps. Santh caught the glint of light from the guard's earpiece. He must be wearing a translator. The rocks from the next man's pouch clattered on the desk top. Tentacles quivering, the Ptorix lifted the largest stone. Weird beings. No nose, that proboscis thing was its eating mouth, he'd heard, and that slit lower down on its head the speaking mouth. Short blue fur covered the visible skin surface but not the muscular arms. Yuck. They looked like snakes; snakes with multiple heads.

The next man stepped forward. Tentacles engulfed a rock, then lifted it. The Ptorix eyes glowed green-gold and settled. Santh held his breath. What did that mean? A high pitched, hissing stream of syllables, while the guard frowned, concentrating, listening to the translation. The climate conditioning hummed. The guard grinned.

"Lord Carrex likes this one. You've earned yourself a night with the girls, my lad. How's that?"

Santh wasn't the only one who sighed. You could almost cut the relief with a knife. The man at the desk straightened his shoulders and bowed deeply from the waist. "Thank you, Lord Carrex."

The Ptorix still held the prized rock, twirling it lightly in those infinitely flexible tentacles as the man left the room.

Seven men had submitted their haul and been dismissed. But this one was different. The Ptorix's eyes swirled blue and the tentacles of its free arms swished. Not happy. The guard bent forward, listening to the sibilant sounds from the slit mouth.

"Not good enough. Half your rock contains nothing." The guard frowned, hands on hips. That pleased glitter in his eyes didn't bode well.

The man spread his arms, hands to the front. "I could see color. He's gotta be wrong. Why would I bring back rock with nothing?"

"If he says there's nothing there, there's nothing there. This is your last warning." The guard flicked the nerve whip from his belt and fired a blast.

The air zinged. Howling in agony the victim collapsed to the floor, writhing. Nobody did anything. They stood there, watching while the victim's howls subsided to sobs. Santh's heart hammered in his chest. A bit more and the energy could have killed that guy. Fuck. He made to move but Ace grabbed his arm.

"You and you." The guard pointed at the two closest men. "Get him through."

They stepped forward, took hold of an armpit each, and dragged the stricken man through to the change room. They were back in a moment, white-faced, expressionless, to resume their places in the queue.

Well, he'd learnt something. Don't bother adding empty rocks to your stash. And no wonder some people cheated.

Soon enough he took the few paces forward and stood before the Ptorix behind the desk. Sweat gathered around his hairline. You could hardly tell what the thing was thinking, only by the color of the eyes and the way the tentacles moved. Lazy at the moment, like weed in a backwater. So far, so good. It lifted the largest rock, inspected, sorted. The eyes swirling a little redder, it placed the second rock in the high grade pile. The next was a discard. The Ptorix said something. Santh swallowed, eyeing the guard's nerve whip.

"You're new," the guard said. "Take more care next time."

"Yes. Thank you." He bobbed his head.

The process seemed to take forever, even if it was only a couple of minutes.

"Okay, you can go." The guard jerked his head at the door. Santh snatched up the empty pouch, sketched a bow and turned.

The guard stepped in front of him, the nerve whip in his hand. "Properly. Bow properly."

Santh stared at him, gazing into eyes that blazed vindictive contempt. He faced the Ptorix and bowed from the waist. *And one of these days I'll spit in your eye, you alien abortion.*

The collection pouch in his hand, he went to change out of his suit. The man who'd been hit with the nerve whip was gone, no doubt helped by his colleagues. Santh had finished hanging up his suit when Ace appeared.

"Okay?" he asked.

Ace pushed his helmet onto the shelf and began to unfasten the seals on the suit. "Yes, I passed."

Ace was pulling off his boots when the shift boss appeared. He leant with his back against the door for a moment, breathing deeply. A nerve twitched in his cheek. He pushed himself upright and almost staggered to the bench.

"You didn't do bad, either of you. Make sure you don't confuse color in the rock with heat or sun flare."

"What'll happen to that guy? The one who was whipped?" Ace said.

The shift boss snapped the seals, pulled off his boots. "If he does it again, he's dead." For a moment he looked Santh right in the eye, then he looked away.

Fuck. He'd never seen such pits of despair, of total, resigned hopelessness. This man never expected to get out of here. Santh had wondered why anybody would be a shift boss for these GPR shit kickers; what would a guy do to live a little longer? Steal from his fellow-workers in this hell-hole? Drive them? Sure, why not?

"*Coming?*" Ace waited by the door.

He hurried into the corridor. "*Can we talk?*" Santh said, matching Ace's stride.

"*Yes. GPR pricks. Anything to hit us machine men.*"

"*I thought they despised the Ptorix even more than us?*"

"*They do.*" He huffed a sigh. "*All I can think of is they get extremely well paid, like with starhearts.*"

They rounded a corner, approaching the mess hall. This time the place was busier. A murmur of conversation filled the air, competing with the clatter of cutlery. Santh's stomach growled. He and Ace grabbed a tray each and joined the line approaching the dispensers. If the rest of these hopeless fellows were anything to go by, he was going to die here, work until he couldn't see straight or he made a mistake. Fuck. There had to be some way out, surely. Maybe Jess would work out where he was. He stifled the groan. She didn't know where he was. She didn't even know he was on *Beaconsfield*. He wasn't even sure of that himself. Fuck fuck fuck.

The dispensers glooped brown stew into his bowl. Santh spied a couple of seats at a table, nudged Ace and headed in that direction. At least there was plenty of food. He expected he was going to get sick of it real fast.

"Why don't the Ptorix mine the place themselves?"

"Couldn't tell you. Seems like a labor-intensive business. You could maybe build a machine but what the hell? Give the GPR a few second-rate baubles and use free Confederacy labor. Why not?"

Santh scooped up another spoonful of brown stuff. *"I don't want to die here."*

"Neither do I."

"Any ideas?"

The mess hall drone wavered. A guard walked along a table in front of them. Heads rose, shoulders stiffened as he passed.

"Bastard," Ace said. "See the look on his face? He's amusing himself with the victims. I'd like to..." His hand clenched into a fist.

The guard wheeled around and walked behind them. He slammed a palm down on the table between them. Santh jumped. Heads turned. Conversation stopped.

"You two aren't doing that talking in the head thing, are you? Wouldn't like to hear that. That's machine man stuff." He took his hand away, a looming presence behind them.

Santh's shoulder blades itched. The energy blast seared through his body. He moaned, clenching his teeth as fire burned through his nerves.

"You're new so I'll take it easy on you."

Somebody chuckled. Santh peered up through pain-filled eyes. The other guards, standing against the walls, gloated. The prisoners—the slaves—turned away, eyes expressionless.

Chapter Thirty-one

Jess handed over her card so the woman at the shuttle desk could scan it. These people were so pedestrian in the way they did things. She wasn't too impressed with the fashion, either. Her hair itched under the headscarf but her blonde hair was too obvious. They'd gone into a clothing store to buy appropriate clothing, in her case a shapeless robe and the appalling headscarf. At least Mayfield got to wear relatively comfortable trousers, shirt and jacket.

"*Try and look a bit more relaxed*," he said in her head. "*You look like you're about to bite somebody's head off.*"

"*If I have to wear this rubbish for too long, I probably will.*"

The woman ran suspicious eyes over Jess. "You're from Kentor?"

"That's right." She forced a smile.

"When are you leaving?"

"We'll be heading home on the *Toro* next week."

The woman didn't smile but she handed them back their cards. "Enjoy your stay."

The shuttle to the planet left ten minutes after they booked their tickets. Thank goodness for that; they only departed once every two hours and hanging around this depressing space station would have been a nightmare.

Jess heaved a sigh of relief once they stood on the pavement outside the space port. Everywhere you went, narrowed-eyed guards seemed to be looking you over. A fresh breeze blew down the street, bringing with it a whiff of something sweet. A cab drove up beside them, a vehicle with wheels and a driver, like something out of a historical holovid.

She slid into the back seat, cursing the heavy, uncomfortable robe, let alone the two pistols hidden against her thighs. Why women put up with this crap was beyond her. Mayfield joined her, carrying the bag that held their normal clothes.

"La Plaza hotel, please."

The cab deposited them at the front entrance of a grand building in a style Jess had never seen before; bricks and arches, a tiled roof. Potted plants framed the entrance doors under a portico. A doorman in a flamboyant red coat hurried down to greet them. She swallowed a smile. They must have pinched the uniform design from Longford's Militia.

Mayfield had already booked rooms on the third floor, directly below Miss Fortescue's, from a data port on the space station.

"*Wow.*" Jess gazed around the hotel room. "*It's like something out of a museum.*" Deep, multi-colored carpets, over-stuffed sofa and chairs, tasteful 2-D prints on the walls. She pulled off the headscarf while Mayfield checked for surveillance.

"Nothing here," he said aloud.

"Glad to hear it." She raised her skirts and removed the pistols. "Damned uncomfortable, these things." She dropped the weapons on the sofa next to her, laughing at Mayfield's apparent embarrassment. "See what you can find out about Marati's 'daughters'." Tenna and Sufi.

She brought up the picture from her comlink and stared at her lovely, smiling, fresh-faced daughter and her equally lovely friend. Like chalk and cheese, these two; Tenna with her bubbling laugh and fun personality, Sufi so much more focused, serious and steady. She'd got to know Sufi while they were on holiday; a nice, self-effacing kid who couldn't help showing how smart she was, how interested she was in the world. What her mother was going through didn't bear thinking about.

"There's nothing on the system, Jess. We'd have to go and look to see if it's them," Mayfield said.

Damn. "Any ideas how we do that?"

"I have, yes." He pulled a flat box out of his coat pocket and extracted a microdot. "Get this in there and we have a spy camera."

"I say again…"

He grinned. "These things get themselves in. I give it a location and set it on the floor outside the room. I'll go and set it up."

He was back in a moment, the corners of his mouth drawn down. "There's a guard outside the door. That tells us something, I suppose."

"It sure does. Now what?" If they'd been hurt, someone was going to pay dearly.

Mayfield raised his hands, pushed the palms downward in a damping motion. "Stay calm. You're not going to help anybody by over-reacting. We're not even sure if it's them."

True enough. She settled back into the chair. "What?"

"There's always the window." Mayfield went onto the balcony outside the double glass doors and set the device on the stone wall. Jess had to peer to pick it up, a tiny dot on the white surface. The sensor took a moment to grab before moving as Mayfield directed with commands from his screen.

"It'll find a way in. Give it a minute to stick to the wall and we're done."

Jess sat beside him, eyes fixed on Mayfield's screen. It seemed to take an age before an image appeared. Somebody crossed in front of the sensor, stopped, sat down. The tiny camera focused. She sucked in a breath, her heart thudding. Tenna and Sufi, sitting close together on a sofa. They didn't look hurt or harmed but the body language spoke volumes. They were scared, supporting each other through simple body warmth. What she'd give to gather up the pair of them and hug them till they squealed.

"It's them. We have to get them out."

"Hang on, Jess. And do what? The room's guarded, we don't have a ship, we can't expect that Marati's going to let you take them without a fight. We don't even know why they're here."

Jess leapt to her feet and paced, three strides this way, three strides that. "Of course we know why they're here. Some sordid fucking brothel. These GPR creeps like blondes."

"They don't look like they've been hurt. A bit scared, maybe."

She spun on her heel to face him. "I'm not leaving those kids there. Marati's got a ship; we'll steal that."

He frowned, shaking his head. "You don't think they might've left guards?"

"Guards, shmards. We have weapons. C'mon, Mayfield; a hit and run. We get the girls out ... no, I get the girls out, you wait below with a cab."

"Jess, you're crazy."

"Only one guard at the door?"

He nodded.

"I'll take him out." She picked up a pistol from the sofa, checked the charge and set power to minimum, enough to stun but not kill. Hudson frowned at her in her mind. Sorry, Admiral. There were some things a mother had to do. He wouldn't be able to do anything, anyway, she knew that. This was GPR space, beyond the Confederacy's jurisdiction.

"Will this card get me into that room?" she asked, holding up the object in question.

"Yes. Look, this is not a good idea."

"Got a better one?"

Mayfield hadn't. "At least wait until dark. And make sure your daughter has something to cover her hair."

***

"*Ready to go?*" Jess said outside the room.

Mayfield gave her a resigned nod. They climbed the stairs up to the fourth floor, Jess holding the front of her robe lifted so she wouldn't trip on the hem. The guard stood alone in the passage, next to the door where the girls were, arms behind his back. She paced past, eyes downcast. He didn't even shift his feet. She drew the pistol out of the wide sleeve and slowed her steps. Any second now. A clatter from the stairwell, the agreed signal.

She spun around and shot the guard. He pitched forward onto his face with little more than a grunt.

Jess shoved the card into the door. It clicked open. Mayfield dragged the guard inside. The two girls were on their feet, side by side, their mouths Os of surprise. Jess' heart soared.

"Mum." Tenna darted across the room and flung her arms around her. It was all Jess could do to stay on her feet. "Mum, we've been so scared."

"I'm sure you have, honey. No time now. We have to get out of here. We're not safe."

Mayfield secured the guard lying on his face, his arms and feet trussed up with his belt. "Stay here. I'll go find a cab. Give me five, all right?" He didn't wait for her nod, just hurried out.

"You've not been harmed, either of you?" Jess glanced between the two girls, an arm around each waist.

"No, we've been well treated but we were kept prisoner," Sufi said. "We guessed we weren't in the Confederacy anymore."

"No. This is GPR. Have you two got dresses like I'm wearing? Good. Go put them on over your trousers."

They ran off to their bedroom and returned covered up. Sufi had put on the headscarf; Tenna's dangled from her hand.

"Tenna, put that on and don't pout. You must keep your hair covered, understand? Blondes are unusual here. And you do what I say, when I say, both of you. No discussion. Got it?"

They both nodded, eyes wide.

"What are we going to do, Mum?" Tenna wrapped the headscarf around her head. It actually looked rather nice, better than Jess' did.

"We're going to go and steal Marati's space ship." She even got a giggle from them for that. "Remember, only talk through your implants. Ready?"

More nods. Jess stuck her head out the door. No one around. She slipped into the passage and led the girls to the lift. *"Look natural, like we belong. Don't run, don't hurry."*

The lift sank to the ground floor. The doors parted with a soft ping.

"Remember, don't hurry." Taking small steps, eyes down, Jess walked out of the lift, the girls by her side. She directed a nod at the attendant at reception. He didn't notice, busy with a customer. So far so good. The pistol nestled in her hand, covered within the sleeve. She shot a glance at the girls. They looked nervous; Tenna was biting at her lip.

"Give me a smile, kids, and stop with the lip biting."

A few more steps across the foyer. The front doors swept open.

"Well done, girls. Keep calm." She swept down the steps to the street, kicking the hem away to keep from tripping. A cab approached. Mayfield?

"Stay close to me. We're waiting for someone."

The cab rolled to a halt. Her heartbeat rose to a crescendo; her hand tightened on the pistol's grip. The door opened. She breathed a sigh of relief. Mayfield.

"In you go, girls," she said aloud.

They slid into the back seat, one at a time, holding up the horrible robes. Jess followed.

"The space port, please," Mayfield said.

"*This is Mister Mayfield. He's here to help us. Do as he says.*"

Jess gazed out of the window as they drove through tree-lined streets. Light glowed in windows half-hidden by gardens. There wasn't a lot of traffic around; a few other cabs, the occasional private vehicle. The blare of a siren cut through the night. Jess stiffened, so did the girls but the skimmer careered past them, hurrying the other way. It seemed not everyone was stuck with wheels.

"Space port," the driver said, steering his vehicle to the kerb next to a brightly-lit building.

Jess followed Tenna and Sufi onto the pavement and waited while Mayfield paid the man. A few bored security guards stood outside but she'd expect that; they weren't taking much notice of them.

"*Hurry up, Mayfield.*"

As the cab drove away a car roared up to the pavement where it had stood. Men leapt out, running toward them.

"Run, girls."

They obeyed, wide skirts flapping but the guards advanced on them from the space port. Trapped.

"Can I offer you a lift somewhere?" A woman stepped out of the vehicle, her voice oozing condescension.

Jess whirled, pulling out the pistol. Marati.

Behind her, Tenna's scream was stifled. "Mum."

A hard hand grabbed her from behind, pushing her arm down. "Drop it," a male voice snarled.

Not on your life. Jess ducked, pulled him down with her then launched a surge upwards. The man groaned, jerked backwards from her skull connecting with his face. They had the girls. If she could get Marati… She lunged forward. Marati's eyes widened, fear glittering.

Pain blossomed. Jess pitched into the pavement.

Chapter Thirty-two

Ace slung an arm around Santh to help him back to the dormitory. Each step was agony, fire shooting through his nerves. He held onto the bunk's upright, waiting for the pain to ease enough so he could climb up to his bed.

"You okay?" Ace asked.

"Guess I'll have to be."

The others filed in, blank-eyed. "That's what you get for being smart," one muttered as he pushed past.

The shift boss strode in, lips curled in a snarl. "Listen, pal, you do as you're told. This isn't just about you."

Santh managed a grin. "It isn't? Nobody told my nervous system."

The shift boss glowered, his thumbs in his belt. "Smart mouth. If you can't work, we all suffer."

"What? What d'you mean?"

"We got away with it today. We had enough color to cover what the man who was short didn't collect. If we hadn't, the whole shift would've been on short rations. Or worse."

Santh gazed around the room at angry, hopeless faces. "So you're all willing to die here?"

"Huh. Listen to you. Get this through your skull, dickhead. There's nowhere to go, nothing we can do." Bitterness dripped from the speaker's lips.

"We could fight," Santh said.

"Fight and do what? They've got weapons, we haven't. Just means we die faster."

"We could contact the Fleet." Ace spoke softly.

"Yeah? How're you going to manage that? Magic?" Willis, owner of the lower bunk under Santh, rippled his fingers in the air. "Brought a magic wand?"

"If I can get into the comms room I can send a message out via multi-dim." Ace leaned against the support for his bunk, staring around the group.

The climate conditioner rattled in the silence as all eyes turned to him. Santh leant his head back. He had to be joking.

"You'd need fleet relay coordinates," another man said. But the sneer was gone. He'd shifted from lying down to sitting on the edge of his bunk, hands clutching the edge.

"I've got them. I'm from Fleet Intel," Ace said.

Santh swallowed his astonishment. A Fleet plant, an agent, checking out Tabora. Maybe Admiral Hudson had something to do with it. Around him, eyes narrowed, hands went to chins, somebody passed a tongue across his lips. Ace had them listening, all of them.

"You're not being funny?"

"No," Ace said. "If I can get to that comms room, Fleet will know we're here."

"Yes, but it doesn't mean they'll come for us. This is Ptorix territory." That was the shift boss's mate, next in line for the top job, his voice querulous.

"I think they'll do something. It'll be Hudson's fleet. He has a reputation when it comes to pirates and slavers," Ace said.

Santh straightened. The tingles were lessening, the spasms less painful. "Come on, guys, it's a chance. I'm prepared to take a risk if I might get out of here."

The atmosphere had changed. Hopelessness had given way to wary interest. They all looked at Ace. "Who wants to put up a fight?" he said.

"I will." Santh banged his hand on his chest.

"If we lose, they'll kill us," muttered the shift boss's mate.

"Huh. We'll die anyway," somebody else said. "Better to die fighting."

"We'll never get away with it. They'll kill us." The fellow's voice trembled with anxiety.

The shift boss spoke at last. "They'll kill us, anyway. I've had a gutful. I'm pretty sure another beating will be the end of me and I'd rather go down fighting. Especially if there's a chance of coming out alive. Raise your hand if you want to fight."

Yes. A wave of joy surged up Santh's spine. Five hands rose immediately, the other two a little slower.

The shift boss turned to Ace. "Okay, what have you got in mind?"

***

Santh rolled off his bunk onto the floor and trailed out of the dormitory with the rest. He flexed his shoulder, still stiff from the remains of the nerve whip's effects. Those things were dangerous, especially with a sadistic bastard on the other end. He ate with a wary eye on the resident bully-boy, memorizing the guard's features. If he had a chance, he'd give that one a bit of his own medicine.

They suited up in silence. Everybody seemed more somber than usual, covering up their new optimism. They'd agreed to go out as usual, do a day's work and start their revolt when they returned. This time, they'd be out there looking for souvenirs. The teams climbed into the cart and headed out.

Orroyex filled the sky, casting its sickly gleam over the blasted landscape. No trees, no green, no life except for the trapped threads vomited up from the deeps. The shift boss steered the cart to their usual vent, bumping and bucketing over the shattered surface. Grateful for a rest from the lurching, jarring motion, Santh sat waiting for the first eruption, the beginning of their last working day, while the twisting clouds careered around the gas giant that dominated the sky.

The ground shook. The geyser spurted its load into the sky. Rocks splattered silently to the surface and rolled down the slope away from the vent. The men dismounted and took up their positions, working inwards in a circle. Santh lifted a rock and checked for vibrancy. Nothing; nor in the next three. He'd stored two medium-grade stones in his pouch by the time they reached the vent and retreated to await the next load.

The eruption kept to schedule, coating everything in the ubiquitous dust. Santh headed out again and spied a large rock, still glowing with the heat of its exit from the depths. Oh, wow. This one was a starheart, all right. The filaments twisted and writhed in the cooling rock. He could certainly understand their lure, their fascination. He stuffed the rock into his pouch before the deathly cold penetrated deep enough to destroy its fire. All around him the other men were doing the same thing, discarding stones they usually would have kept. If this revolt didn't work out, they'd all be dead. A scary thought but better, surely, than this hell. *If there is an afterlife, I might be seeing you soon, Troy.*

The atmosphere in the cart on the way back to the base was different. Santh wasn't sure what it was, a lift in the shoulders, a sense of purpose. For himself it was simply grim determination, a chance to give those sniveling bully-boys what for. He wriggled his fingers inside his gloves. Bring it on. The men in the vehicle were connected now, linked together through their cranial implants, their machine-man modification. In a fight it would be a huge advantage.

The cart slid into the airlock and settled down. He swallowed. His heart rate had increased, the double thump pounding in his ears. They filed through the hatch into the change room. A guard stood at the door to the assessment room, one hand hooked in his belt, the other tapping his nerve whip idly on his leg. Tap... tap... tap. If he had a chance, Santh would be wiping that leering, anticipatory smile off the bastard's face any minute now.

Santh peeled off his helmet and shook his head. The guard strolled over, jutted his chin into Santh's face. "Well, well. Let's hope you picked real well, pal, because—"

Santh slammed the helmet into the man's face. Blood welling from his broken nose he tried to lift the nerve whip but two other men grabbed him while Ace dragged the weapon out of his hand. The man scrabbled, tried to yell but the shift boss locked his arm against the man's throat and squeezed him back against the exo-suit. The guard's face turned red. His eyes bulged. The sharp stink of urine and shit filled the air. A last jerk and the neck bones cracked. He slumped.

The shift boss dropped him, a crumpled, stinking mess. "One down."

A sigh of satisfaction went around the group, like a breeze through grass. A small victory but an important one.

Ace knelt and searched the body, retrieving pass cards, a comlink and a blaster. He kept the blaster, hefting it in his right hand. The shift boss took the nerve whip.

"Everybody ready?"

Nods, a few licks of lips.

Ace went first, the shift boss right behind him, Santh and the others at their heels. There were three armed men in that room. If they got an inkling of what was happening, they'd all be dead before they started. Ace slouched forward, ready to present his pick for the day, his pouch hiding the blaster.

"*Now.*" Every man heard the order in his head.

Ace fired. The guard next to the Ptorix staggered backwards and collapsed. Santh struck out, using all of his weight to shove the guard to the right of the door sideways. The man's mouth opened in surprise as he stumbled backwards, trying to lift his weapon. Another man came to Santh's aid, forcing the gun out of the guard's fingers. Lips bared, the miner shot the fellow in the chest at point-blank range. He fell, dead eyes wide open, the stench of burnt flash drifting. Fragments of white bone surrounded the blackened hole in his chest. The third guard, who had been on the opposite side of the doorway, also lay dead. Men collected weapons and nerve whips from the corpses. The shift boss blasted the Ptorix with the nerve whip, a continuous stream of pulsating energy. The creature howled, a high-pitched shriek like fingers on board. The howling reached a fever pitch and then stopped. The alien, still twitching, disappeared behind the assessor's desk.

A ragged cheer reverberated round the room, Santh's voice raised with the rest.

"Well done, everybody." Ace gazed around the group, smiling grimly. "But it isn't over yet. Make sure the weapons go to guys who can use them."

Santh clamped his fingers around the pistol's grip, checking for the position of the firing buttons and the power regulator. Sure. Easy. He pulled off his exo-suit and let it drop to the floor. Whatever else happened now, he wouldn't be needing it. All around him the other miners did the same, the only sound the rustle of fabric.

He exchanged glances with other men. Their eyes glittered with hope, maybe some fear, maybe some eagerness for revenge. They wouldn't all make it. This initial surge was planned to make enough noise to give Ace time to get a signal out. Santh's blood fizzed in his veins. He'd never been so nervous in his life.

"*Set?*" the shift boss asked.

Heads nodded.

The shift boss opened the door, peering from one side to the other, before he stepped out. A sizzling blast tore past and was immediately answered.

"Fuck." The shift boss ducked his head back in. "I missed the bastard. We're going to get company. Move it."

One after another they dodged through the door. Santh noticed Ace dart down a corridor and wished him all the luck under all the Galaxy's suns. A sawing siren brayed around them as they burst through into the mess hall. The men with the guns went first. Santh picked his target. The guard's body thudded against the wall before he'd pulled the gun out of his holster. Startled faces gaped at them from the tables where men sat over plates. Some fell to the floor, others tried to stand. A guard dodged behind some miners but they grabbed him. He screamed as the nerve whip struck, again and again. The sound scraped on Santh's nerves. He was glad when somebody shot the fellow.

Somebody blasted the door locks. The guards wouldn't be coming in that way, at least. The siren wailed on. A miner looked for the speaker and shot it down. The sound continued, but muffled, behind closed doors.

The shift boss jumped up on a table. "Listen up, guys. We're fighting back. We just need to hold out for a few days. The Fleet's on its way. Pretty soon we'll be able to go home."

Incredulous faces stared at him. A moment of silence ended in a cacophony of voices, asking questions.

Santh hoped Ace had made it.

"What if the guards call for help? Call in a Ptorix warship?" somebody called out.

"They might but I doubt it. They don't like the toe rags any more than we do. They're more likely to call their own people, the GPR. They're no match for our cruisers."

"Depends which one gets here first," a voice muttered.

"So what do we do?"

"We've got food and water here. We defend this place and we wait."

Santh gazed at the faces, some hopeful, some despondent, some resigned. "Yes, we wait and hope our guys get here first."

Chapter Thirty-three

Hudson gazed at the holovid displaying best guesses of where *Cordoba* might have been headed. Three options, none of them good and all deep into Ptorix territory. There were closer systems, to be sure, but none of them had habitable worlds for Ptorix or for humans. "Not much to go on."

"It's the best we can do, Sir. If they've pulled out of shift space somewhere and recalculated, we'd have no idea."

"True enough. I can't follow any of these, not on a guess." He rubbed his fist across his lips. "Do some more digging, Mann. There may be something else."

Mann saluted and left.

He might as well empty his inbox while he was waiting. He pulled up a report on the political situation between the Ptorix Khophirate and the Confederacy. Nothing new; ice-cold as ever. Governor Anxhou appeared to be stirring the masses, preaching about human encroachment on what should be Ptorix territory. He'd had some impact; there had been a spot of unrest on Kentor but the Government had slapped it down.

Speaking of Kentor, he'd heard nothing from Mayfield for an age. Another situation he couldn't alter. When he got his hands on her, he'd tan her hide. *Stop thinking about Jess. It only makes you horny.* Stupid, stupid girl. At least she had Mayfield with her.

"*We have two messages from Mayfield, Admiral,*" the IS said.

Hudson leaned back in his seat. Funny how that worked. Think about something, and the universe delivers. "Go ahead."

No visuals, just an encrypted message. '*Saintly Maid* following Marati to Luciana.'

Luciana? "Show me," Hudson said.

The holovid image shifted, focusing on a G class star, a habitable planet. Luciana system; GPR but on the fringes. The system didn't have a lot to say about the place. A sprinkling of cities scattered across the habitable regions, mainly agricultural, mining and a bit of manufacturing for the home market. A typical, low-tech GPR planet. Why would a Confederacy planet minister be going there?

"*I'm sorry to intrude, Admiral. A code five signal has arrived. Your adjutant thought you'd want to know.*"

"What is it?"

"A signal from Ace Carter."

The man on Tabora, who disappeared. "Get Commander Mann in here."

Mann must have been waiting at the door. The display shifted direction as soon as the officer entered. Stars appeared and disappeared from the side of the display until one star dominated. Inxora, another red dwarf. Closer and closer, centering on a gas giant with a myriad of moons.

"The signal came from here." Mann pointed at one of the larger moons. "He says sixty miners from Tabora are being kept here as slaves to mine for starhearts. It's run by GPR people but there are a few Ptorix there."

"Really? GPR purists rubbing shoulders with the Ptorix, eh? That's different."

What to do? Inxora was in Ptorix space; not deep in but to take a Confederacy battle cruiser into the systems could be seen as an act of aggression even if he did want to free Confederacy slaves. Saahren would have his balls on a spit. What about Jess? What was Delia Marati doing at a GPR planet on an unscheduled stop?

Chapter Thirty-four

Jess shook her head to clear her fuzzy vision. Somebody leant over her, somebody in a white coat. Memories spun a kaleidoscope of images; Hudson, Tenna, Sufi, Marati... She blinked, gazed steadily at a man beside the bed she lay on. Short, receding hair; a moustache covered his upper lip.

"How do you feel?" he asked.

"Okay. You gave me an antidote?" She directed a glance at the hypodermic lying on a tray next to the bed.

"Yes. The nurse will bring food and drink. Please sit up."

No dizziness, no aches and pains. She felt fine except that her stomach growled and her hair felt like string. She pulled herself upright, leaning against the pillows. Her armpits felt sticky; she probably didn't smell too good. A hospital room, with hard floors, green surfaces, bright lights and no windows. The man stood, arms folded, watching her, appraising.

"Where am I?"

"You'll be told more, presently."

A woman appeared, robed and wearing a headscarf, with a tray of food that emanated mouth-watering aromas. She rolled a table over to the bed and left, soft-footed. Jess ate hungrily, reveling in the taste of fresh vegetable soup and delicious, crusty bread. She mopped up the last of the soup with the bread. At least they weren't going to starve her to death.

"Where are the girls? Where am I? How long—"

The man held up a hand. "You will find a washroom through here and clothing in the wardrobe. Please dress yourself. Knock on the door when you're ready."

He walked out.

Clean and dry, Jess opened the wardrobe. Huh. Pretty, feminine, lacy underwear but the usual shapeless gown. At least this one was a nice mid-blue. No headscarf; she wouldn't have worn it, anyway. She finished the outfit with a pair of matching, soft slippers. Knock on the door, eh? She checked the handle. Locked. She knocked, two short raps.

The man opened the door, two armed guards behind him. "Come this way."

He led her along an anonymous passage and ushered her into an opulent apartment. The door clicked behind her. Good grief. Wall hangings and cushions, a huge bed, mirrors in the ceiling... Mirrors. Oh, fuck. This was a bordello, a brothel, a seraglio. Anger raced up her spine, flared her nostrils, curled her lips. And where were her girls? What had they done to Tenna and Sufi? Somebody was going to pay for this.

She sank down onto the bed, bedecked in shimmering cream silk. Where was Mayfield? Probably dead. Well, first things first; where was she and what was she here for, although the second one had to be a no-brainer. Weapons. She wandered around, opening drawers filled with sexy lingerie. She could throttle somebody with a bra, she supposed. A wardrobe held diaphanous gowns in gaudy colors, some patterned, some plain but all see-through. The washroom had a spa bath, a shower, lavish appointments but nothing she could use to attack anybody, unless she could drown them.

Two chairs stood next to a dining table in the corner. She pulled one out and sat. God, she'd messed this up. Stuck in GPR territory with her kids who-knew-where; she couldn't contact Hudson and even if she could, what could he do? Launch an offensive into GPR space? Despair drifted closer, a dark shroud ready to engulf. She recognized it; she'd seen it before, when Troy died leaving her with a barely recovered daughter and a battered best friend. Well, she'd waved depression away then and she'd wave it away now.

A key clicked in the lock. Marati and two guards. She didn't wear a shapeless sack. She wore tight black pants, a green shirt, high-heeled boots and a smile that would have curdled milk. *Stay calm, Jess. Stay cool.*

"I see you're recovered," Marati said, undulating over to the other chair.

"How long was I drugged?"

"Long enough to get you here."

"Which is?"

"You needn't know the details. It's an island, a lovely place."

"Where are Tenna and Sufi?"

"Here. Rest assured they'll be well looked after." She sniggered. "Oh yes indeed."

Jess seethed. "This is a brothel?"

The woman hooked an arm over the back of the chair and crossed her legs. "Not exactly, no."

Jess made a point of staring around the apartment. "Another name for the same thing?"

Marati chuckled. "It's a special center to enhance the human genome in the GPR."

What? "A medical center? I don't understand." She wished she could wipe that supercilious smile off the benighted woman's face. *Stay calm, Jess. You don't know enough yet.*

"Mister Rossmoyne has established this facility so that carefully selected, suitably physically qualified men can be put to young Confederacy women. The offspring are fostered out to good families."

Jess' stomach lurched. Bile rose. Stay calm. Marati's eyes glittered, cold and amused.

"It's a... a breeding farm. A stud."

Another chuckle. "If you like. They particularly favor rare human types, like blondes and redheads, so when you insisted on being so troublesome I decided I'd bring you along, too. You're still of child-bearing age."

She couldn't be serious; she couldn't be. This was a joke, a figment of her twisted sense of humor. "They could take eggs, artificially inseminate."

"Oh, no, no, no. Not in the GPR. That's unnatural. So, fertilization in the manner of all mammals followed by the normal gestation period."

"What? Natural childbirth?"

This couldn't be real. Pain, danger, they were in the past. Sure, some people liked the old way, as Hudson's wife had. But she and Troy had gone the normal, safe route. They'd taken an egg from her, sperm from Troy and developed Tenna in an incubator. No danger for mother or baby and they both got to watch her grow within the transparent walls.

Marati examined her red-varnished fingernails. "That's how they do it here."

"For pity's sake. They're kids, fourteen year old kids." Jess' fingers itched. One lunge and she'd have her hands around Marati's neck.

Marati sniffed. "Fourteen would have been old enough in earlier times. But not to worry, things have changed. They like to start the girls young, teach them their responsibilities before they're introduced to the male. It will be a little while before that happens, though. I believe sixteen is the legal age and the GPR is nothing if not meticulous about regulations."

She smirked. "Of course, with you, it's different. You can't imagine Rossmoyne's face when I told him I had you for him to play with. But never fear, you'll get to meet him soon enough."

Jess controlled the anger boiling in her gut. So this Rossmoyne fancied himself as a stud, did he? Or maybe a bit of rape was more to his taste. Well, if he thought she'd play nicely he had another thing coming.

Marati had risen to her feet and turned toward the door. "Please don't imagine Admiral Hudson cares where you are. He's quite the one for the women and I'm sure you amused him. But an admiral and a tramp freighter captain... Well, what would people think?"

A last tinkling laugh and she minced out of the door, her bully boys at her heels.

Chapter Thirty-five

"How much longer?" The miner swept a hand over his face, wiping away the sweat.

"As long as it takes." Santh rested his back against the wall, his pistol in his right hand.

"You don't fuckin' know, do you?" The fellow rose from his seat and took a step forward. "You know what? I'm beginnin' to believe all of this is shit. He didn't call the Fleet, did he? You're deluded." Another step forward. His fists clenched.

The shift boss stepped between them. "That's enough. The last thing we need is to fight amongst ourselves."

The wait was getting to them and to tell the truth, Santh was concerned. They had food for quite a while yet and water enough. Disease was the biggest risk, without access to toilets. After the first few hours, the guards had given up wasting their time on the reinforced door. They'd heard nothing and that, in itself, was a worry.

"Yeah?" A pulse beat in the big man's forehead. "You're 'is mate, ain't you? Did you see him make this call? Eh? Did you?"

"I couldn't, could I?" Santh said. "He risked his life to get to the comms room. For all I know, he's dead."

The shift boss, who Santh now knew as Gordon, said, "Even with multi-dim it takes time."

The miner stuck his hands on his hips. "We've been here for fuckin' days. Hardly any sleep. Now they've turned off the climate con."

"It won't be any easier for them. Sit down, Jimmy. You're just gettin' yoursel' hotter." Gordon took the fellow's arm, tried to tow him away.

Jimmy snatched his arm free, took one more stride and stood over Santh, who stared up at him. "You got anythin' to say?"

For fuck's sake, he didn't need this. Santh stood and put the gun into the holster at his belt. "You'd rather play with the GPR chappies? Is that what you're saying? You'd rather work till you drop, picking up their bloody rocks for them?" He wished he knew for certain if Ace had succeeded and if he'd survived. He didn't even want to think about what the commandant and his cronies would have done to the agent if they caught him.

"I say we charge 'em. Fight our way out and steal a ship. There's enough of us." His eyes glittering, Jimmy stared around the ring of miners encircling them.

"Easier to wait for the Fleet, Jimmy."

Jimmy turned to glare at the speaker. "If it comes at all. Come on, Ted. What're you doin' here? I'll tell you. You're sittin' here getting' ready to die in yer own shit."

"Cut it out, guys." Gordon stepped in. "This isn't helping."

"Shuddup, you guys." The man on door duty flung up a hand. "Something's happening."

They could all hear it now, muffled bangs and clanks from outside. Santh exchanged a look with Gordon, who had already pulled his gun out of its holster. He lifted one shoulder. Something hissed or sizzled.

"Shit. That's a laser beam," someone said.

"Hurry. Get more tables. Pile 'em up there," the shift boss yelled. "You four, get to work on that one, you four over there."

The room erupted as men hurried to obey the instruction, blasting the bolts that held the legs down, scraping the tables across the floor to pile them as barricades.

"Guys with weapons, take up position so you're out of direct line of fire," Gordon said.

Heat rose. The door glowed crimson. Crouching in a corner at an angle, Santh's heart hammered in his chest. He'd fight to the bitter end but if they brought in a laser unit strong enough to carve through the door that had to mean reinforcements had arrived. He eased his grip on the pistol in his hand. Well, if he was going down, he wouldn't be going alone.

The crimson glow brightened to cherry, to fiery yellow, then the beam seared across the mess hall to splatter on the far wall. Santh aimed at the gap. They'd need a lot more space if they were going to get through. The door's hardened metal ran like water, leaving a blinding, molten trail down the surface.

Something passed through the hole in the door and landed, clattering, on the floor. An explosion ripped through the room, booming in the confined space, tearing apart stools and the remaining tables. Six or seven men lay shrieking in pain; a few didn't move. Blood splattered the walls, ran down in ugly, red-brown streaks. Santh swallowed down the vomit.

"Withdraw, guys, into the pantry."

They ran, heading for the gap to get behind the serving counter, Santh and the other armed men last in case guards came through. They threw another bomb instead. Shrapnel flew, thudding into the walls and fittings. Some of the groans stopped. He ducked down. A few shots hissed. No more human noises from the floor. They must have finished off the wounded. Brown fluid dripped out of a hole in one of the dispensers. Shit. They wouldn't stand a chance, cooped up in the pantry.

Gordon appeared beside him, crouched below the servery. "*Stay with me. When they come through we can maybe take a couple out before we run again.*"

More clangs and bangs and then the sound of boots, stealthy and careful. Take a few out, huh? And chances of survival, zip. Santh felt calm about that. He'd given it his best.

"*D'you reckon Ace made it? The Fleet's coming?*" Gordon asked.

Santh wished he knew. But without hope, they had nothing. "*Let's believe he did and the Fleet's still coming,*" he said. "*Ready?*"

"Take this, yer sniveling bastards." Jimmy reared up from behind the counter, spraying fire in a wide arc. He ducked down again, grinning. "Got one, at least."

He must have done. They heard the slapping thud of a body hitting the floor, then scurrying. If they could see over the top, life would be easier. The polished metal edge of the splash tray on the back wall provided a distorted image. He pointed.

"*Good thinking.*" Gordon peered up. "*Two. Up against the wall, trying to outflank.*"

A phut. A projectile hit the wall, fell. Santh dived sideways, hand outstretched, grabbed the canister before it hit the ground and flung it back over the counter. Shrapnel battered the walls and ceiling. The splash tray, dented and scarred, wouldn't be any help any longer.

Jimmy's heavy breathing sounded loud in the silence.

More noise. Running feet, shouts. Gordon shifted position, easing his legs. "*Sounds like they're getting ready for an assault.*"

"Bring it on." Jimmy muttered the words through clenched teeth.

Santh waved a hand. "Shut up, everybody. This sounds different." Howls outside, tramping feet, not running. The clunking clatter of weapons. The fluttering hope died.

"Fuck. They're Ptorix troops."

Chapter Thirty-six

Hudson steepled his hands on his desk. Deliberate disobedience of an order from a superior warranted a court-martial. He'd been expressly forbidden from entering Ptorix space. But what was the option? Leave sixty or more men digging up starhearts? He knew enough about the jewels, a rare life form trapped in molten rock retained their luminescence even after they died, provided they didn't freeze first. The moon they worked on would be airless, frozen yet wracked by seismic events. No wonder the Ptorix didn't mine the crystals themselves. Could he take a risk? The agent said the GPR ran the base. Perhaps if he carried out a lightning raid the Ptorix wouldn't even notice. And if he didn't? If he didn't, he'd be ignoring every fiber of his morality.

Hudson straightened and contacted the bridge. "Set course for Inxora, Captain."

"What about Luciana, Sir?" Mann asked.

He'd forgotten. "What was Mayfield's second message?"

"Delia Marati's ship destroyed *Saintly Maid*. Jess has been captured and she and the girls are being held in a research facility owned by Rossmoyne."

Jess and the girls captured? For what? He could take a guess without trying too hard. Marati. Interesting. Was her visit political or was this a grubby, money-making scheme? With Rossmoyne involved, he'd suspect the latter. A muffled announcement echoed through the corridors outside, preparations for the jump to shift space. What the hell? His head was on the chopping block already.

"Send a signal to *Dark Knight*. Tell Captain Tamar to put on his camouflage suit and make for Luciana. He's to keep in contact with Mayfield and keep us informed."

A fast, light frigate fitted with top of the range stealth technology, *Dark Knight* could enter GPR space and he'd have a crack commando team available to throw into the mix if warranted.

Mann nodded, a twinkle in his deep-set eyes. He approved, anyway.

The sound of *Defender's* engines changed from the scarcely-heard rumble of cruise mode to the deep throb of powering up the shift drive. Whatever happened next, his career was on the line.

***

Hudson stood on the bridge next to Captain Sundra for the exit to real space. The techs bent over their equipment ready for the onslaught of data coming from the sensors scanning the area.

"*Real time in five seconds,*" the IS said. "*four... three... two... one...*"

He braced himself. So did Sundra. The bridge area was shielded to minimize the effects of re-entry and slow-down, but even so the change in speed caused him to lean forward. In the centre of the bridge the IS activated the graphic displaying the ship's position and surrounds. Sundra had brought the ship into real space twenty million klicks from the target planet and its herd of moons. A few micro-jumps would cover the distance in less than an hour.

"Report on target moon," Sundra said.

"*There is a vessel in orbit. The characteristics match* Cordoba." The IS displayed a distant visual of a battered freighter.

Sundra grunted. "At least we're in the right place."

Hudson nodded. And no sign of anything else. "Bring us in closer, Sundra. The edge of the planet's moon system."

"Aye, Sir."

Hudson sat in one of the acceleration chairs at the back of the bridge while Sundra gave his orders. Where was Jess? Last he'd heard from *Dark Knight*, Mayfield was in pursuit of Rossmoyne. Marati, it seemed, had remained on the planet. He'd love to know why. Still, he had the frigate's elite commando team at his disposal if anything happened.

He rose to his feet after the smaller impact of the return from a micro-jump. Oroyex dominated the central display, a sickly, orange-and-red ball like so many other gas giants in so many systems, surrounded by a flotilla of moons.

"*Ptorix warship.*" The IS showed a graphic of the vessel, a typical Ptorix frigate, slightly smaller than *Defender*. In the dim light from the system's red dwarf sun, the blue and purple curves of the hull design were barely visible.

"Red alert, all stations. Weapons ready," Sundra said.

Klaxons blared, blast doors sealed. The atmosphere in the bridge changed; people bent over stations, tense and ready.

Damn. This was the last thing he needed. The frigate matched *Defender* in size but not in fire power. He could blow it away. And then what? Trigger a war?

"She's seen us, Sir," Sundra said. "Shields up, weapons ready."

Hudson's heart thudded. "Okay. Cruise in slowly. Ask for a connection. I want to talk to the ship's captain." He schooled his expression. More than one of those techs had sneaked a glance at him, over their shoulders.

"Keep your eyes on your stations," an NCO barked.

Sundra eyed him without turning his head, his Adam's apple bobbed when he swallowed.

"*We have a connection, Admiral,*" said the IS, steadying an image of a blue-skinned alien wearing the pointed silver hat of a Khophirate Fleet captain. The creature's eyes held a hint of violet, the color of aggression and the tentacles at the end of its arms slashed. Not good.

The alien's speaking mouth moved but the voice issuing from the speaker was that of a translator in *Defender's* IS. "Confederacy ship you are in violation of Ptorix space. I demand you leave here."

"My apologies, Captain. I have no wish to cause trouble between the Khophirate and the Confederacy. We have intelligence that the Galactic People's Republic has invaded your space. Enslaved Confederacy citizens are being held on this moon base. I wish to liberate the slaves, then I will leave. You may deal with the Galactic People's Republic invaders however you wish."

He wondered how he'd come across on the Ptorix ship's visuals, how the alien vessel's translator would interpret his words. Had the eye color morphed to green? That would mean he'd given the alien something to think about.

"*Connor, Sir. He says the Ptorix have landed troops on the ground.*" Mann's words whispered in his implant.

"There are no slaves here, just human workers," the Ptorix captain said.

The voice, of course, was expressionless but Hudson was sure he'd seen hesitation. Slavery was illegal in the Khophirate, as it was in the Confederacy, but that didn't mean it didn't happen.

"Can you be sure?" Hudson said. "Men snatched from their families, forced to work in dreadful conditions without reward? If they work here of their own choice, I will leave."

Hudson counted the seconds, waiting for a response. Perhaps he'd struck a chord.

"May I have your permission to check for myself? Our intelligence was certain. You may have been tricked." *Except you weren't, you toe rag bastard.* Still, if he could avoid a fight, he would. If the Ptorix captain would save face and turn on the GPR scum they could both emerge from this relatively unscathed.

"You cannot land on a Ptorix planet." But judging by the amount of green in its eyes and the way its tentacles moved the alien wasn't convinced.

The Ptorix had a job to do, orders to follow. If it didn't follow them their equivalent of a court martial was the least of its worries. More likely, it would be executed. He would have to give the alien an honorable way out.

"It's a moon, not a planet. And I must insist." He turned to Sundra. "Captain, send an assault team to the base."

"You have no right. I will destroy any landing ship." The alien's eyes fairly burned a strange shade of green-blue-violet, its tentacles thrashing. Sundra relayed his orders to an assault team already on board a lander in the airlocks.

"*Lander launched*," the IS said. A new element in the central display illuminated, following the lander's course toward the base while the Ptorix vessel continued to fill the main display.

"I mean no harm to the Ptorix. You leave me no choice. If you attempt to leave orbit or if you fire on my landing ship, I will be forced to retaliate."

Hudson straightened into a caricature of steely resolve, feet apart, hands clenched behind his back, chin up, eyes hard and cold. He had to hope the Ptorix had been taught enough about human body language to interpret the gesture correctly. He was glad the Ptorix couldn't see his thundering heart. The alien captain would certainly know his ship was no match for *Defender*. But just to be sure, "If you do not comply, I will destroy your ship, Captain."

Hudson moistened his lips. If the Ptorix called his bluff a troop of commandos would perish. The Ptorix captain turned to someone off-camera. They'd turned off the audio. Hudson kept one eye on the lander, now slowing to finalize its descent.

The Ptorix captain faced him again. "Take your humans and go."

Hudson held his position, hoping his legs would continue to hold him. They trembled with relief. "You have been warned, Captain. Attempt to leave orbit or attack my troops or landers and I will fire on your vessel."

He ended the call and left the bridge. "What's the status down there?" he asked, as he sat behind his desk in his office. The monitors surrounding him showed everything he could see on the bridge.

The IS relayed the messages from troop commander Lieutenant Fry. The young man's voice boomed. "There are Ptorix troops down here, Sir, but it looks like they've been ordered to withdraw. I'm approaching the commander now."

Hudson rubbed a trickle of perspiration from the side of his face. The result hung in the balance.

Fry's voice returned. "We've been allowed to take any humans here. Do we take prisoners?"

"See how much room you've got. If there's space and you can take the weight, bring back the most senior people you can get. The slaves should be able to point out the worst of them."

"Aye, Sir."

On second thoughts, maybe he could do something else. He could herd the miserable GPR scum into their slave ship and make sure that justice was done.

"Captain Sundra, pick a team to take control of *Cordoba*. In the meantime, get another lander down there to collect the GPR rats and house them on their own ship."

"Sir." Sundra began issuing orders and Hudson learned that Ace Connor, the agent sent to Tabora, had presented himself to *Defender's* troopers. The first of the freed slaves were on their way.

***

Hudson went down to the hangar bay to watch them come on board, forty-eight filthy, stinking men with grinning, beaming faces, some with arms around each other, some assisting wounded colleagues. Four slight figures emerged in a group. God. Women. The bastards had even taken women here. But not to work as miners, he'd bet on that.

His troop commanders met them, assessing and directing. The injured were sent to the med centre, while the able-bodied would be billeted with the troopers. They could always find room for a few more men and women. His counselors would be kept busy if what the troop commander had told him about conditions down there was true.

One man caught his eye. "Dekstra."

Dekstra stopped, a wide grin plastered across his face. "Admiral. So glad to see you, Sir." He thrust out a hand, noticed the grime, the black fingernails and started to withdraw.

Hudson snatched the hand and shook it. "So glad to see you, too. They won't get away with this, I promise you. Go and get yourself cleaned up. I'll have someone fetch you later. You and I need to chat."

"Thank you." Dekstra caught up with a few other men, who had waited for him, and disappeared with the others down to the ship's troop levels.

"That's the lot, Sir." Fry stood beside him. "They've started bringing up the prisoners and loading them onto *Cordoba*. When that's finished, do you want the base destroyed?"

"No. It's Ptorix jurisdiction. They can clean up their own mess." Ah, this was satisfying. This was when he loved his job the most; to stand here seeing slaves turned free, their captors, prisoners. Yes, he'd done the right thing, whatever else might happen. In his mind he nodded to the memory of Sylvie and his unborn child.

"When he's had time to clean up, I want to see Santhias Dekstra." Hudson acknowledged the salute and returned to his office.

***

Dekstra, clean and dressed in a grey trooper's working outfit, sidled through the door into Hudson's office looking nervous. A handsome man, without a doubt, slim and athletic behind the weary, wary eyes.

"Sit." Hudson waved a hand at a chair.

"Admiral. Thanks for coming."

"My pleasure. My very great pleasure. You'll be debriefed by my people about your experience on this hell-hole. First I want to talk to you about Jess and her husband."

His face lit up. "You've seen her? Can you tell her I'm okay? She'll be worried about me."

"I haven't seen her and I'm not sure where she is. Tenna and her friend were kidnapped. Jess went after them into GPR space."

The man sank into the chair, the lines in his face deeper. "But she's okay? Jess and the girls?" His concern was deep and genuine.

"I don't know."

"Shit." Dekstra held his face in his hands, eyes closed. When he opened them again he said, "What are you going to do?"

"I've sent support. I need more information before I can do more. Now then, Jess and Grimani."

Dekstra blinked.

"Does Jess know about your relationship with him?"

The man's face crumpled as if he'd been struck. "We're friends. All good friends."

"You know, I can't imagine Jess in a threesome." Hudson put his elbow on the desk and leaned his chin on his fist.

Dekstra looked away, sighing. "No threesome. Troy and I were lovers. She doesn't know. I couldn't bring myself to tell her after Troy died. She had enough to worry about with Tenna being so ill, on top of the inquest into Troy's death. How did you know?"

"Military Intelligence is thorough." No threesome. Yes, he felt relief. He didn't like the idea of Jess with anybody else.

The man's Adam's apple bobbed. "Are you going to tell her?"

"I think you should do that, don't you?"

"I should, yes." He nodded. "But I'm afraid."

"Of what?"

Dekstra bent his head. "I'm afraid she'll hate me. I never wanted to hurt her. We kept it secret, then Troy was killed." He rested his cheek on his fist. "I wished it hadn't been that way. But what do you do? You can't help who you fall in love with."

Hudson sat back in his chair. Wasn't that the truth? He'd never thought he'd ever get over Sylvie. In a way he probably never would. Her memory was locked in his heart, a lovely, vibrant girl. Normally he didn't notice the locket hanging around his neck but now it felt hot against his skin.

He cleared his throat, deliberately becoming more formal. "Now, tell me what happened down there."

They'd talked for half an hour when his clerk interrupted. "Sorry to interrupt. You're to call Admiral Saahren, Sir."

Hudson nodded. "Thanks for your time, Dekstra. We'll talk again."

The man rose, smiling and almost bobbed a bow when he left the room.

His office sealed, Hudson waited for Saahren. The admiral appeared, seated in his office on his flagship, his eyes hard. "Where are you, Hudson?"

He probably knew by now. "Ptorix space, Sir. Slaves were being used to mine starhearts. I took it upon myself to take a chance to free them. It worked. I'd hoped to flit in and out without being detected. It didn't work."

Saahren frowned. Hudson counted the seconds. He'd take a guess, knowing the man he faced, that Saahren wasn't displeased with his actions, simply calculating the cost.

"Do the Ptorix know you're there?" Saahren said at last.

"Yes. There is a Ptorix frigate here, now. I discussed the situation with her captain and he agreed to allow me to take the humans here."

Saahren fingered his chin. "Have you fired on them?"

"No need. It's a frigate. It's no match for *Defender* and her captain knows it."

Saahren leaned forward a little. "Hudson, this is going to be trouble. Get out of Ptorix space. Grand Admiral Haskett is not going to be impressed with you or with me. If that idiot Bloom finds out, he'll be muttering rubbish about violating our neighbor's territory."

Bloom. He'd been promoted to minister almost as soon as he was elected to the parliament. "I still don't understand why anybody thinks an actor can make political decisions," Hudson said.

"I agree. But the man's a minister and Haskett will follow orders. To the letter. Not only will he inform Bloom, since he's Minister for Foreign Relations, he's likely to insist on a court martial."

Traditional, old school Haskett, soon to retire but with enough power to make a difference. He could have a man dismissed or sent to some obscure corner of the Galaxy if he wanted. "I had considered that. I couldn't leave these men out here. I'll pay the price." But his heart sank.

"I'll do my best, Hudson." Saahren sighed. "If I can get to President Jamiru, we might stand a chance. Keep your nose clean." He disappeared.

One more thing to have to worry about; upsetting the hierarchy. President Jamiru had the courage to stare the Ptorix down—if Saahren could bypass Haskett and get to him. Perhaps he could, given his reputation after the battle of Forenisi. But even so, this was it; he'd have to go home like a good boy. At least he'd be taking these men to freedom and their captors to judgment.

What he'd give to be able to gallop off into the GPR to see what was happening with Jess. Damn it, he didn't know enough. Last message he'd had she was on her way to Luciana. If he could be sure Jess was there, sure something had gone wrong: but he didn't. He wished he could. Her face haunted him, that delicious smile, those laughing eyes.

"*A message from* Dark Knight, *Admiral. I thought you'd want it straight away.*"

The IS presented the message on his monitor. The unencrypted words danced before his eyes. 'Marati's ship destroyed *Saintly Maid*. The girls were held captive on her ship. Marati's connection is certain but unclear. Jess and the girls are being held here.' They'd added a location on Luciana.

"Show me."

The display slewed, star systems appeared, then the vision speared in, focusing on Luciana's smallest ocean. An archipelago coalesced, a myriad of islands in shallow seas. A flashing point appeared on an island.

He sat back in his chair. A GPR planet visited by a senior Nordheim politician who had abducted two young girls. At least. She'd destroyed Jess' ship and taken her prisoner.

From his implant he produced an image of Jess Sondijk in her red dress. Could he argue the case that he had the right to invade a foreign government's space to rescue a handful of prisoners? Given that he'd already done exactly that with the slaves?

He unfastened his collar, drew the locket out and placed it on the desk. Sylvie appeared, laughing, pregnant, trapped in a moment of time. He hadn't been able to do anything to save her. The weight of that knowledge had hung around his neck all these years.

"You'll always be a part of me, Sylvie, but it's time I moved on."

What happened to Sylvie wasn't going to happen to Jess. He'd take the risk and pay the price. It wouldn't end in war with the GPR, even though Haskett may want to deliver his, Hudson's, sacrificial head. This whole situation—the girls, the slaves, a starheart mine, the GPR and the Ptorix—somehow they fitted together and he wanted to know how.

"Have *Dark Knight* send a detachment. Get them out of there. I'll be on my way immediately we've finished here."

He closed the locket and placed it in his pocket.

Chapter Thirty-seven

Jess gazed around the room, at the pastel colors, soft cushions and huge bed. It was enough to make her puke. Days and she was still no further on. Tenna and Sufi were here somewhere, probably in rooms identical to this one; she needed a chance, an opportunity to get out of here. She flexed her fingers. Nobody had come near her except to give her food.

A clink and scrape of a key. The door opened. She tensed. Maybe she'd get a chance now. The door slid aside.

"Hello again, Captain Sondijk."

Marati's tinkling laugh matched the dancing eyes, her lips curved in a mocking smile. The woman's elegant maroon business suit fitted her like a glove. Jess shifted but one of the guards with her grunted and raised his weapon. Two of them.

"You might be wondering why you've been left alone for so long. We've decided to auction your, er, services. We've had a number of interested bidders. I'm off home so I won't be able to introduce you to the lucky winner." She pouted for show. "Such a pity. I shall have to console Admiral Hudson as best I can."

Jess spat in her face.

A guard shoved her backwards onto the bed, while Marati, eyes blazing, wiped spittle from her cheek.

"Common slut," she hissed. "You'll be taught manners." She stopped, swallowed, a smirking smile spreading over her features. "Yes, you'll be taught manners."

Once again that hateful, tinkling, mocking giggle. "I'll be off."

She swung around on impractically high heels and minced out of the door, punctuating her final exit with a wave of her fingers and a last giggle. The sound of footsteps receded into silence.

Jess caught up one of the ornate cushions and flung it at the wall. The vase of flowers followed, shattering with a satisfying crack. Water spattered the wall, running down to the fallen flower stems.

The door rattled. Shit. Not again. Jess eased behind the sofa. Damn. She shouldn't have broken the vase. No time to find anything else.

The door opened, slower this time.

"Jess?"

Jess' legs turned to jelly. Mayfield. Mayfield with two Confederacy troopers.

"Mayfield. I thought you were dead."

He beamed at her. "Not yet. There's a warship in orbit. We've gotta get the girls and get out of here fast." He dragged her along. "This way."

"You know where they are?" she said, almost running down the corridor at his side.

"Sure. Pulled their data. There's a lot of women here but I matched Tenna and Sufi with their pictures."

They stopped outside a door. "This one's Tenna."

"Quickly ma'am," one trooper said.

Jess slid the door open to a room fitted out with frills and lace. Tenna sat on the sofa, her dark eyes round and frightened. Her expression melted into relief. "Mum."

That one little word turned Jess' knees to water. Her body shaking, she slipped inside and wrapped her arms around her daughter, hugging her tight. Tears started in her eyes. Not now; not now. She held the girl at arms' length, searching her face. "Are you all right? Have those bastards hurt you?"

Tenna shook her head. "No. What's this about, Mum? Do you know where Sufi is?"

"Later, babe. Let's collect Sufi. This is dangerous, okay? Do as I say, immediately."

"Yes, Mum." Tenna slid a tongue over her lips.

Mayfield hovered in the door. "Quick, Jess. Sufi's up a few doors."

Sounds of firing, short, staccato bursts. The troopers covered them, searching for pursuit. Tenna opened Sufi's door and rushed inside. The two girls hugged, shared a sob.

"Not now, kids. We have to be brave."

"This way to the lander," Mayfield said, taking hold of Jess' arm.

Jess leaned against his pressure. "What about the others?"

"What others?"

"This place is full of women snatched from the Confederacy to be used as breeding stock. We have to get them out of here." She planted her feet, held his gaze.

"Jess, we don't have time."

"Make time."

He tossed his head, grimacing. "God, you're a difficult woman." His eyes glazed over while he spoke via his implant. "Commander Tang is on the way."

A tall soldier, anonymous behind the camouflage suit, appeared a few moments later. The visor of the helmet retracted. Sharp female eyes looked Jess over. "What's the issue here?"

Jess explained, glossing over the details. "Some of these are girls kidnapped from Nordheim slums. They deserve a chance to go home if they want to."

Tang nodded, chewing at her lower lip. "Give me a minute while I clear it with the captain."

Tang's eyes went blank. Jess dithered. *Hurry up, woman.*

"How many?" Tang asked, refocusing.

"Twenty, if they all want to come."

Tang nodded. "We can manage that. But we'll have to be quick."

Marati. Marati was going home. Maybe she hadn't left yet. And if she had, they could at least seize her ship. "Look, tell your captain. There's a ship at the space station called *Salome* or *Dreamweaver*. If it leaves, stop it."

"Ma'am, I can pass on the request."

"It's carrying a suspect in this whole sordid business. Tell me, have you seen a woman wearing a maroon suit and ridiculous high heels?"

A nod. "We've detained all the staff in admin."

Savage glee roared through Jess' veins. Auction her off to the highest bidder, huh? "Right. You get the rest of the women out. I've got something to do." She turned to Sufi and Tenna. "Go with the soldiers, girls. I'll be there soon."

Jess ran. This was going to be satisfying.

Frightened people sat in a group under armed guard in the admin area. No Marati. Jess pulled the manager to his feet. "You. Where's Marati?"

"She... uh." The man turned pleading eyes on the guard.

Jess swung around. "Beautiful, maroon suit, high heels."

The man nodded. "She went to the washroom with an escort."

"Which way?"

The soldier pointed. Jess bolted down a corridor to the washroom. She glanced at the body of the soldier slumped on the tiles. Where was Marati? The corridor led to an emergency exit. She sprinted, her heart pumping, skidded around a corner and through the exit into a garden. There, running for a copter parked nearby. She'd taken off her high heels but Jess was younger, faster and angrier. She sped up, her feet flying over the ground.

Marati glanced over her shoulder, then turned and raised a pistol.

Fuck. Jess dived.

The bolt sizzled past her, searing into the grass. Jess rolled back to her feet, zig-zagging as the woman tried to find her aim. Another blast whizzed by, close enough to feel the wind. Jess dodged again. A few more meters.

Marati licked her lips, nervous, maybe even frightened. She took a step back, tripped and sprawled onto her back. The gun jerked out her hand. Jess sprinted, her heart singing. *I've got you now.* But Marati scrambled up and dived for the weapon. Her fingers around the grip, she rolled and tried to aim. Jess landed on top of her and grabbed her wrist with both hands. If she could bend Marati's fingers back, she'd have to let go. Marati snarled at her, lips bared like a wild animal, and snaked her body, trying to kick, while her left hand came around, fingernails raking at Jess' cheek.

With the last of her strength Jess twisted Marati's wrist, wrenched the gun from her grip, rolled and leapt to her feet. Snarling like an animal, Marati made one last despairing lunge which left her sprawled face down on the grass.

Jess stepped out of reach and aimed right between the smoldering, furious eyes. "On your feet, Minister."

Marati struggled to her feet, wincing. Her tousled hair hung around her shoulders. A twig stuck out at an angle.

"Don't know much about guns, do you? This is on low power." Deliberately, never taking her gaze from Marati's face, Jess flicked the weapon to maximum power. "Now it's not."

Her voice rang with contempt, but Jess would swear there was a glint of fear in those hard eyes. "You'll never get away with this."

Jess longed to plant a fist in the woman's face. "Don't push me. You sold my daughter and her friend to these animals. Didn't you ever hear what happened to the hunter who got between a mother bear and her cubs?"

That hit home. Marati was a politician. She wiped the fear off her face in a nanosecond but Jess had seen it. Perhaps she should just pull the trigger, blast the woman to hell? She could claim self-defense. But then there would be un-answered questions and she'd had enough of those. She gestured with the gun. "Get moving. And please don't delude yourself I wouldn't use this."

Marati shuffled past her, back toward the admin block.

Jess tensed at the muted roar of an engine. No more than one hundred meters away the copter took off, rising above the level of the trees. For a moment she thought it might turn for the attack but the pilot wasn't a hero. It banked right, out over the ocean.

Mayfield approached at the run. "We have to get out of here. We've collected the women who want to come."

"Fine. Keep this on her." Jess handed him the pistol, which he leveled at Marati.

"Hands up high, legs apart."

If looks could deliver poison, Jess was sure she'd be dead. She frisked the woman, making no attempt to be gentle. She drew a slim cylinder out of

Marati's pocket. "Nerve toxin. It's a syringe. That's how she brought down the guard."

Marati glared, lips pressed together. She had the sense to keep her mouth shut.

Dragging Marati along with them, Jess and Mayfield ran out to the camouflaged landing ship sitting on the grass, its engines idling. A group of women filed through the vessel's hatch, attendant soldiers keeping watch. A salt-laden breeze stirred their skirts, rustled through their hair. They pressed forward, faces glowing with eagerness and hope, even if some glanced around in fear. Tenna, fourth in line, saw her and made to run back. "Mum."

"Go, love. I'll be there in a moment."

An aircraft screamed through the air above them, so low Jess ducked.

Marati's eyes glittered, her lips curved in a mocking smile. "You're nearly finished, Sondijk. Rossmoyne's people will end this stupid uprising. You'll make a beautiful baby together, you and—"

Jess smashed a hand across the bitch's face. Marati staggered, blood oozing from the corner of her mouth. She lifted a hand to her lips. "You'll regret that."

"Don't count on it," Jess said, shaking her stinging hand. God, that felt good.

A soldier handcuffed Marati, then dragged her over to the lander and shoved her inside, Jess at her heels. Tenna and Sufi sat three rows up, heads craned to look for her. She gave them a grin, then pushed her prisoner into the last row, up against the bulkhead, and fastened the harness over her body, clicking the restraints into place.

"You won't get away with this," Marati muttered. She didn't sound quite so confident now.

"So you said." Jess wished the machine would take off. The engines thrummed. One trooper, then another, clambered through the hatch. Tang, only recognizable from the bars on the front of her tunic, came last. She'd hardly slipped into the seat on the opposite side of the aisle from Jess when the hatch hissed closed. The pitch of the engines deepened, the hull shuddered and the transport rose. Jess kept her eyes on the monitor on the fore bulkhead. Wow. The grounds were on a tiny island in the middle of a beautiful archipelago of green and yellow dots in a turquoise sea.

"Hang on people. We've got trouble." The pilot spoke, his voice clipped and harsh, through the compartment's speakers.

The ship lurched, flinging Jess against Marati's body. Somebody whimpered. Another lurch, the other way. This was worse than being a pilot. At least if you were in control, you could do something. In the display something hurtled past. Jess hoped it wasn't a missile.

Chapter Thirty-eight

"A message from Dark Knight, Admiral," the IS said when *Defender* returned to real space. *"The rescue mission is under way but the transport carrying the prisoners is under attack. Additional help is required."*

Hudson turned to Sundra. "Deploy a squadron of fighters when we've slowed down enough."

"Dark Knight *also advises that Delia Marati is set to leave the planet in a ship currently called* Salome. *There is a ship of that name at the space station now. Sensors bearing..."*

A glance at his status monitors showed Hudson the ship's braking maneuvers were almost complete. Sundra had come in close to the planet, ignoring the jump gate. To port and several hundred klicks closer to Luciana, *Dark Knight* was a dark shape silhouetted against the green and blue of the planet. The space station rotated a thousand klicks to starboard.

"Salome's *engines are hot, Admiral, suggesting the ship is preparing to leave."*

"Bring it on board and arrest the occupants." As the captain turned away, Hudson asked for visuals of the transport powering up through the atmosphere.

Sundra had launched his fighters through the big ship's stern bays. A full squadron of twenty shapes streaked down into atmosphere, leaving a trail in their wake. Below, the transport dodged and weaved its way upward, under attack from six GPR attack ships. They were no match for Confederacy fighters, but even so, the two ships from *Dark Knight* were hard pressed defending without actually shooting down the attackers. A bright yellow flare danced over the transport's shields, sending her lurching sideways. Judging by the color, the shields were starting to give. Any more and he'd have to order the Confederacy ships to destroy the GPR ships and he'd wanted to avoid that. *Defender's* fighters split, spreading around the fleeing transport. It was enough. The attacking group turned tail, heading back to port. Hudson grinned. What a difference impossible odds make.

"Message to *Dark Knight*," Hudson said. "We'll send a shuttle to transfer the women and any prisoners over here. And well done."

He turned to the display showing the space station. Marati's yacht had backed out, turned and started the approach to the jump gate. Sundra's squadron of fighters seemed to make a difference. *Salome* pivoted, heading off as fast as its engines could take it. But fast yacht though she was, she was no match for attack fighters. Surrounded, the ship's master shut down engines and turned, as instructed.

Any minute now, he'd get a call from the planetary President. Mayfield's data from the women's prison was being analyzed right now. In this paranoid, over-regulated society, he'd have to hope enough backside-covering had been going on to provide him with evidence.

Hudson rubbed his chin over his steepled hands. Bring it on. Then he could go home and face whatever was to come.

Commander Mann knocked on his door minutes later. He was smiling. "I thought you'd need these right away."

Hudson looked through the streamed images and grinned. "Thank you. Mayfield's done well. A commendation is in order, I feel."

"Not for this. He's an Intel officer. It's his job."

"Even so."

"*Excuse me, Admiral. The planetary president would like a word.*"

Hudson shooed Mann out of his office. This was going to be fun. "Of course. Put him through."

A mountain of a man dressed in the long, shapeless robe of a GPR fundamentalist shimmered into view on the 2-D panel. Red-faced and with jowls trembling, he jabbed a finger at Hudson. "How dare you? This is an act of aggression against a sovereign state. It's nothing short of piracy."

"Nice to meet you, President Goya. I'm Admiral Hudson. You *have* noticed I haven't actually done anything but defend my own ships from attack?"

"You have violated our atmosphere and attacked a private dwelling."

"And you have taken women from the Confederacy into slavery." Hudson didn't vary his delivery, said the words in a simple, matter-of-fact way. That always caught theatrical people like this man off-guard.

Goya's mouth dropped open. "What are you talking about?"

"Diamante, an island in the Necklace archipelago in your Southern Ocean, was maintained as a brothel, staffed by women stolen from the Confederacy."

Behind him, the IS pinpointed the spot, showing a graphic of the walled buildings so the President could see. Give the man his due, he recovered pretty well. His intelligence record indicated he was an astute politician in his own part of the Galaxy.

Frowning, he tossed a fat hand. "This is nonsense. Your women are anathema to us. Ungodly, altered abominations. It may be a brothel but the women are ours."

Hudson smiled. "The women are on my ship, so let's dispense with that nonsense for a start." A slight untruth, to be sure, but they would be here shortly. He paused for the count of three, still smiling. "Did you know the center filmed all visitors? Our people extracted the data from the memory banks in the computer system. Perhaps you'd like to see?"

Watching Goya's face as the images played out for him was a joy. The self-righteous indignation faded. He was too clever a politician to betray his dismay too overtly but Hudson noted the bob of the Adam's apple, the sudden fidgeting with the formal robe. Goya, Rossmoyne and Marati sharing a toast, interesting enough in a society where alcohol was banned. Then Goya with a girl, his fat rump bouncing on her slight body.

"Well, what of it? I had a drink with your Minister Marati and Doctor Rossmoyne. There's nothing underhanded about that. As for the girl." He shrugged. "You have quite a reputation yourself, Admiral Hudson."

"My reputation is not at issue here. This girl you're crushing is from the Confederacy. We have rescued her from your state-run brothel, Mister President."

Only the slightest pause. "I was not aware that the woman was from the Confederacy."

"Oh, I very much doubt that."

Goya sagged into a chair, fingers tapping on the arm rests.

"You have violated GPR space. If I were to complain to your president, I imagine you might very well face a court martial. In fact, I'm certain of it."

Hudson suppressed the grin. *So our fat friend thinks he's moved to check, does he?* "What are you proposing?"

"Destroy those images, leave this system and we will call the matter closed. A fair bargain, wouldn't you say? Why throw away your career on a civilian matter that is none of the Confederacy's business?"

Hudson held his chin in his hand. "Thanks, Mister President. I'll take my chances."

Goya leaned forward in his chair, fingers clawed over the armrests. His eyes glittered. "Your president will hear of my displeasure."

"A pity. I guess these," Hudson flicked his fingers at the graphic images of Goya heaving his bulk on the girl, "will become public in your systems as well as ours. It's up to you. Now, if you will excuse me." He rose from his chair and had the IS terminate the transmission.

A court martial hung in the balance but at least his conscience was clear. Time to meet his guests. Jess.

Chapter Thirty-nine

Jess held Marati back to let the others go first, filing down the corridor from the shuttle and into the airlock. Now she was here, actually on board *Defender*, her legs felt like jelly. Hudson would be there, waiting for her; she hoped. His face appeared in her mind, blue eyes glinting, that sexy smile curving his lips. The girls filed past, their gaze meeting hers. "I'll be there real soon, you two."

The last of the women passed her seat.

"Okay, let's go." Jess pulled Marati, bare-foot and disheveled, out of her seat and shoved her down the ramp in front of her. Finally, she stepped onto the battle cruiser's crowded deck. She looked around for the girls and saw them being looked after with the others. And there was Hudson, striding toward her, grim faced. To say she was pleased to see him was an understatement, but she hadn't rehearsed a speech.

"Welcome back, Captain," Hudson said. His gaze flicked over Marati, taking in the bare feet, the tousled hair, the torn suit.

Marati tilted her head. "Admiral Hudson, I want this woman arrested. I'm a member of the Nordheim Planetary Government and I don't take kindly to ridiculous accusations, let alone physical abuse." The tone was that of affront.

How dare she? Rage seared up Jess's spine. Hudson didn't believe the woman, did he? *"Don't say a thing,"* Hudson said in Jess' mind before she could open her mouth.

"Jess." She followed the direction of the shout; Santh, running down the deck toward her. She rushed to meet him. They grabbed each other in a bear hug and whirled around like kids. "Oh, man, I am so glad to see you safe," he said, grinning from ear to ear.

She beamed at him. "Hey, guy, you too. We were so worried about you." He looked a bit strained but otherwise fit and well in Fleet working clothes.

"Not Dekstra as well, Sondijk?" Marati sneered. "I thought your husband was more his type. Or did you have a threesome?"

Out of the corner of her eye Jess registered Santh's stricken face, his mouth an O of horror.

Hudson waved an imperious hand. "Remove the manacles, the escort Minister Marati to the detention cells, Sergeant. I'll talk to her later." Marati chuckled over her shoulder as she was led away.

Jess' hands clenched into fists. La fucking Delia. Bitch incarnate. What had she said? Oh, fuck. Her head spun. No. No she couldn't believe ... Santh gazed at her, pleading.

Jess' stomach lurched. Santh... and Troy. No. Oh no.

Hudson gripped her shoulder. "Go to the girls, Jess. They need you. Go. Now." Hudson pointed. "Over there, where the other women are. Commander Ditmar will look after you."

She felt numb. Santh and Troy.

"Jess?" Hudson tugged. Jess' feet moved automatically, letting him lead her. Somebody followed; one step, two.

"Dekstra." Hudson turned the name into a command. The footsteps stopped.

She glanced over her shoulder at Santh, standing ashen-faced.

"Leave it," Hudson's tone was stern. "The girls come first." He gave Jess a little shove to where Tenna and Sufi stood huddled together. Tenna stared at her, those dark eyes just like Troy's, round and worried.

Jess dredged up a smile. Hudson was right. She'd come for the girls. What had happened in the past would have to wait. "Tenna, Sufi." She draped an arm around each slender shoulder and fronted up to Commander Ditmar who turned out to be a formidable woman wearing the red cross of the med centre on her uniform. The last of the other women were being led away.

"You're to be housed in the executive section, ma'am. If you'll follow me." She guided them back across the hangar bay to the transit. The place had almost emptied out, apart from a few techs going about their business. Neither Hudson nor Santh were around, thank goodness. She'd need to address that hurdle by herself before she faced either of them again.

Ditmar activated a door panel for a room which wouldn't have been out of place in a swish hotel. Nice. Grey carpet, dark blue upholstery, cream table and wall unit, color-coordinated pictures on the walls. The bedroom held one double bed but they'd found an extra cot. The girls could share the bed; at least she wouldn't have to sleep on the couch.

"You'll find some clothes in the wardrobe, girls. It's not fashionable but it will be better than what you're wearing. Why don't you go and get changed?"

Tenna and Sufi exchanged a glance. They would have translated for themselves; go away and let me talk to your mother.

"We thought it best to keep you separated from the others," Ditmar said as soon as the door closed behind them. "Some of them were in that place for quite some time. We need to get those poor girls to talk and give each other support. It would only traumatize your two if they heard the stories from those who had been there longer."

Jess nodded. "Thank you."

Ditmar frowned, running her gaze over Jess' face. "You're hurt. There's blood on your face."

Jess lifted a hand and felt the ridges from where Marati's claws had raked her. The blood had dried. "Just scratches. The blood will wash off. A bit of antiseptic ointment?"

"You'll find some in the washroom."

Jess nodded again.

"Are you all right? You look a bit depressed. It's quite normal, you know. We have people who can help you."

"I'm fine." Jess smiled. "Honestly. Hungry, more than anything else."

Astute gray eyes assessed her. "Food will arrive in a moment. If you need help, someone to talk to, that's my job."

She radiated compassion, understanding. Jess fought the urge to throw herself onto the woman's neck and blubber. Tears threatened, a burning pressure behind the eyes. That was the last thing she needed. "Thanks, but I need to think a few things through. Look, don't let me keep you. I'm sure you're busy."

Ditmar put a hand on her shoulder and nodded. "Take care."

Jess sighed with relief when the door closed behind her. No sounds emanated from the bedroom. What she'd give for some giggles but it would take time for them to recover from their ordeal. She collapsed on the couch, her head in her hands.

Troy and Santh. She hugged herself. Judging by the look on Santh's face, it was true. Oh, Lord. *My husband left me for another man.* Wow. Only he hadn't left her, he'd had an affair on the side. Maybe Troy was going to tell her, divorce her. She'd never know. Unless Santh told her. He was her friend for fuck's sake. Her best friend. Or he used to be. Now? Now she didn't know anymore. Why hadn't Santh told her?

She squeezed her eyes shut, trapping the tears under the lids. She had to stay strong, for the girls' sakes. Strong. And Hudson; what would he think? Troy, Santh and her, writhing together in a bed.

"Mum?"

Jess' eyes snapped open. Tenna stared at her, two little furrows between her eyebrows. She wore the standard working dress for Fleet personnel, grey trousers and shirt.

"Can't say the color does much for you, darling. You, either, Sufi. But at least they're clean."

Tenna reached out a hand to touch her face.

"It's okay. Just scratches. But I won."

Tenna's lips sketched a smile.

Jess stood. "Commander Ditmar said food's coming. You two wait here while I change. I expect they've left me a uniform, too."

By the time she'd returned, dressed in military gray, the food had, indeed, arrived. The girls had set up the dining table in the corner, leaving the plates covered until she arrived. She lifted a cover, revealing large portions of vegetables and fish.

Jess picked, forced the food down her throat. She had to eat. The girls were as bad, pushing the food around the plate.

"I know you don't feel like it but you have to eat. Come on, eat a little more of the leafy green." She demonstrated by stuffing a forkful into her mouth.

A little bit more and Sufi pushed her plate away. "I've had enough."

"Me too." Tenna put her cutlery neatly on the plate, beside a heap of left-over food.

Admiral Hudson wishes to enter," the IS said.

"Of course."

Hudson came in with Ditmar at his heels. His blue eyes swept over them, lingered briefly on Jess. "Ladies. I trust dinner was satisfactory?"

The exchanged a glance and turned away from him.

"Excellent, thank you." Jess forced a grin. "I feel this overwhelming urge to salute. Must be the uniform."

His eyes twinkled, while Ditmar smothered a smile. "Yes, not up to your usual sartorial standard but the best we could do under the circumstances. Couldn't the logistics people find you a pair of shoes?" He looked pointedly at her bare feet.

"It feels good giving them an airing." She wiggled her toes.

"If that's your wish. You and I need to talk and Commander Ditmar would like to talk to Tenna and Sufi. She will remain here and you will come with me."

Jess directed a look at the two girls. Tenna chewed her lip and Sufi twirled her dark hair between her fingers. "You two behave yourselves, you hear?"

"Yes, Mum," from Tenna, "Yes, Jess," from Sufi.

She took a deep breath and followed Hudson into his quarters.

Chapter Forty

The door had hardly closed behind her. She threw herself against him, wound her arms around his neck and kissed him. He pulled her close, his hands sliding over her back, his tongue pushing into her mouth. He drank in the smell of her, his fingers in her hair, her breasts crushed against his chest.

But it didn't feel right. This wasn't passion he felt from her; it was despair. He lifted his head but she clung to him with desperate fingers. "Fuck me, Hudson. I want you to fuck me."

He loosened his grip on her, slid an arm under her knees, and carried her the two steps to the couch, where he sat with her in his lap. She felt like a coiled spring.

Tears filled her eyes. "What's the matter? Don't you want me ei—" *Either*. She bit the word off.

"Jess, darling, you must know that I want nothing more than to make love to you. But I'd rather not have the ghost of your husband leaning over my shoulder while I'm doing it."

Tears trickled down her cheeks. "I didn't know. I didn't know anything about it." She brushed the tears away. "There wasn't any threesome."

"Don't let it get to you, Jess. It doesn't matter."

She sat up straight, staring at him. "It does. Can you imagine how it feels? My husband was having an affair with another man. He couldn't even find some beautiful bimbo to have it off with. He fucked my best friend." Her eyebrows were clenched together, eyes half closed in pain.

"He didn't need a beautiful bimbo. He already had a beautiful, gorgeous, desirable woman. Believe me, I don't understand, not for a moment. If you were mine—" He broke off. "You know as well as I do that homosexual people can't help it; that's their genetic makeup. I would have absolutely no interest in having sex with another man but that's me."

She swallowed. "All those times in otherworld ports he'd go off by himself to do a deal, chase something up. Yes, chase up a lover, maybe even a boy." Her voice dripped bitterness.

"No. Don't imagine it's worse than it was. They never wanted you to know. You and your daughter meant too much to both of them."

"You knew?"

"My intelligence people are thorough. And I talked to Dekstra about it. He told me he and your husband resisted the temptation for a long time, until they were thrown together when you had to stay with Tenna."

Tears welled again. "He was my friend."

"He still is. Or wants to be. He said he was going to tell you but he was afraid you'd hate him."

She'd settled, leaning into his shoulder so the curves of her body pressed against his. She chewed at her lip.

"You can't choose who you fall in love with." He hesitated. "Tell me something; did you love Troy?"

He lifted her chin so she had to look at him.

She gazed up at him, her eyes wide. At last she said, "I guess I did, at first. Or maybe I thought I did. We had a bit in common, with the ships and adrenalin rushes and doing things on the shady side of the law. Then we had Tenna and, and..." Her words drained away. "And we were kind of stuck with it. For her."

She sighed. "No, I guess at the end I didn't love him. But it was comfortable. And we had Tenna."

She relaxed, fitting against him, an invitation. His mouth closed over hers, not a brutal, peremptory kiss but soft, gentle. Her tongue twined with his. Eyes closed, he memorized her; her touch, her smell, the way she ran her fingers through his hair, the taste of her lips.

He withdrew. He couldn't afford to mess this up now, not with what she'd gone through. "I would very much like to make love to you, Captain. With your permission."

She grinned, the sparkle back in those marvelous eyes. "Permission granted, Admiral."

He carried her to the bedroom and set her on her feet at the end of the bed. "Don't move. Not a muscle."

He kicked off his boots, shucked off his socks. He was pleased to see the lust darkening her eyes. She shifted.

He frowned. "You're moving. Don't."

Never taking his eyes off her, he unfastened his jacket, took it off and hung it over the chair. Now his undershirt. He could swear her mouth was watering. He pulled the undershirt up over his head. She squirmed. Her nipples appeared, tight little buds pushing against her shirt.

He stepped over to her and slowly, deliberately, unfastened the buttons on her shirt, peeled the garment from her shoulders and let it fall to the floor. His hands slid over her breasts, fondled her nipples. Her eyes closed, she murmured his name. "Hudson."

"Shhh." He sucked her lips while his hands brushed over her waist, her hips, down to her pants. They joined the shirt on the floor. He kissed her more deeply, his tongue moving around her mouth while his hands cupped her buttocks. Her whole body quivered. She raised her hands to his shoulders, clasped his neck. Disobedience. He lifted his head.

"You're such a naughty girl," he whispered.

He grasped her by the waist and laid her on the bed. This time, he'd show her what she meant to him, give her pleasure like she'd never had before.

He knelt over her, nuzzled her throat then slowly, tenderly, trailed kisses down her breastbone, her abdomen. She wriggled. Lower, even lower. Her scent invaded his brain. He longed to plunge into her but not yet. She shivered as he licked her skin, delved down into her. Her back arched, her fingers dug into his hair. "Oh, this is wonderful," she murmured.

She bucked against him as she came, gasping her pleasure until the spasms died away. She sighed. "Oh, man, that was incredible."

His turn. But carefully. He unbuckled his belt and eased his pants off while she watched. The point of her tongue poked out between her lips. She lay back, open to him, ready for whatever he wanted. He slid inside her easily, right up to the hilt. His body wanted to thrust. He closed his eyes. Control, ease back. She draped her arms around his shoulders, lifted her knees to grip his hips. Her skin was damp, tasting of sweat and sex.

He forced himself into a slow, even rhythm. His lips sought her breast, tickling the nipple with the tip of his tongue. She squirmed beneath him, her lips at his throat. Her fingers dug into his shoulders, clutching at them as if they were the only real thing in this world of passion, as tremors of pleasure surged through her. Her eyes closed, she moved in automatic harmony with him. The floodgates burst. She gasped his name in ecstatic release. Now he did hammer into her, a brief flurry that left him groaning, pressing deep inside her. "Jess. Oh, Jess."

He slumped on her body. She wiped away the little line of sweat that trickled down his hairline. "Oh, man, that was awesome, Admiral, Sir."

"Pleased to be of service, Captain." He raised his body on his elbows.

"No, stay there," she said. "I like you inside me."

He settled back down and nuzzled her neck. "I'm glad to hear it. I was intending to make a habit of it."

Her fingers trailed around his shoulders and neck. "You're not wearing the locket."

"No. I suppose I'm ready to let her go, let her rest in peace."

"Like I should with Troy?"

"Yes." This time he did move off her, shifting so he could see her face. "Maybe we should start again, hmm? A lot of things have changed between us."

She snorted. "I'll say. Santh. Tenna and Sufi. And the *Maid's* gone." She sighed, then wriggled around to look into his eyes. "I never, never expected to see you here in GPR space. Not for a moment."

No, he hadn't either. "I couldn't not, Jess. I lost Sylvie to slavers. It's cut me to the core that I couldn't save her. If I'd lost you the same way, I couldn't have lived with myself."

Jess' eyes clouded. "You didn't have permission." It was a statement.

"That's right." He stroked her arm, aware of her soft, smooth skin. "I disobeyed a direct order by entering Ptorix space to rescue Santh and the others and I violated GPR space without permission to rescue you. So I may not be an admiral for much longer." The idea hurt, to lose his commission. But he had no regrets.

"But surely they'd understand? That's slavery. It's wrong. Evil."

"The military doesn't see things in those terms, my dear. I disobeyed an order. I think my commanding officer is supportive but it's not his call. And brilliant as Saahren is, he's a strategist and tactician, not a diplomat."

"So you're going to lose your job because of Santh and me?"

"No. I make my own decisions. I couldn't live with myself if I'd walked away from either of those situations and if it costs me my commission, so be it. I'm sure I'll be able to find something else to do." He grinned, hoping lightness would fill the hollow in his soul. Life without the Fleet loomed like an abyss. "Maybe we could set up a freighter line together. Or there'll be a planetary militia somewhere that could use a good man."

"Nordheim." She frowned. "That bitch Marati thinks she'll get away with it."

He'd given some thought to that. The woman was a consummate politician, clever and slippery. Also rich. She would stoop at nothing to wriggle out of any accusations leveled at her. Just like President Goya, she would try bribery. Their type always did. But it wasn't going to work. "She won't."

"If she gets back to a court in Nordheim, that's what she's thinking, isn't it? Ottenshaw will get her off, or she'll serve a week's home detention or they'll make her do a day's community service or something."

He put a finger on her lips. "She won't get away with it. Trust me, darling. You have my word, whatever happens."

Brushing hair from her cheek, he paused. Ottenshaw. Would he be involved in this?

"What are you thinking?" Jess asked.

"Ottenshaw's wife's starheart earrings."

Her eyebrows arched. "You don't think he's involved as well?"

He settled himself on his back and pulled her against his side, her head on his shoulder. "Something to think about. Go to sleep, my lovely lady."

She snuggled against him, his arm holding her close. "Will the girls be okay?"

"Ditmar has orders to stay with them. You'll be called if you're needed. I'm rather hoping the only one needing you will be me. I want you fit and well and raring to go when you wake up."

Grinning, she slid a hand down to his groin. "I'm sure our friend here will be upstanding when the time comes."

"You can count on it."

Chapter Forty-one

Hudson went through to his office trying to wipe the smile off his face. He probably looked like a lad after his first time with a woman. Although, as he recalled, that first time lasted about two minutes and last night with Jess had been incredible. What a woman. Thinking about her was enough to get him hard, which he did not need right now.

He sifted through the new files until he found the interrogation report for Delia Marati. She'd denied doing anything wrong, of course. She claimed no knowledge of Tabora's illicit kidnapping of men. The destruction of *Saintly Maid* was an unfortunate accident, a case of mistaken identity, she had no idea the place was being used as a breeding centre, just giving some of the Nordheim girls a better chance in life. And if his suspicions were correct, taking her back to Nordheim for trial wouldn't achieve a great deal.

"Have Delia Marati brought to my private quarters, Tomas," he said to his adjutant. "I'll be waiting."

He went back to his sitting room and sat down in the chair facing the door. The staff had already reorganized the bed; there was no sign of Jess here. The lingering memory was seared into his brain, with the promise of more to come.

"Your guest has arrived, Admiral."

He rose to his feet when the guards brought Delia in.

"Oh. Ullric. How nice." Smiling, she undulated her way to the chair opposite his across the coffee table while he jerked his head to tell the guard to leave.

She was a beautiful woman without a doubt; auburn hair hung in waves around her shoulders, complimenting the cat-green eyes and pale skin. He'd allowed her to select clothing from her cabin on *Dreamweaver*, which still sat on *Defender's* decks. She wore black, clinging pants and she'd left the top button of her shirt undone. She lounged in the chair, arm over the back, legs crossed. He looked, as she intended he should, but she'd never make his heart race the way Jess could.

"What can I do for you, Admiral?" She purred, sexy and sultry with a decidedly unsexy, calculating glint in her eyes.

"I thought a private chat may be valuable. I've read the interrogation report." He smiled. "Let's talk about the girls you abducted."

"Abducted is such an ugly word."

"Yes. Akin to slavery, don't you think?"

She shook her head, tossing her hair around her shoulders, and leaned toward him. "Ullric, these women from the slums, they're stuck in a rut with nowhere to go. There's no work on Nordheim in general but in those dumps women have two choices; marriage to the nearest dimwit who'll have them, or prostitution. And the brothels..." she wrinkled her perfect nose. "The brothels are nothing more than doss houses. On Luciana they had their own apartments, lovely clothes, comfortable surroundings. Most were very grateful."

"You're saying they were willing?"

She nodded. "Oh, yes. For the most part, when they understood."

"You never tried to recruit them? Legally?"

"You have to understand. These are uneducated..." She poked her tongue between her lips, "...girls with no experience of their own world, let alone what might be beyond it. They would not have understood."

He wondered what word she had in her mouth before she said 'girls'. For the rest of it—prostitution on another planet didn't sound so hard to understand to him. He pushed down his growing anger. "We've interviewed them, you know."

"Yes, I expect you have. How many said it was bad?"

Not many, he had to admit. They'd been well treated, as you would any prized stud animals. A clever lawyer could twist the words, confuse these kids to say anything. "Not many."

"Let's face it, they weren't harmed." She curled a lock of hair around a finger, simpering at him.

Weren't harmed. *But you tried your best to kill Jess. More than once. And the women—used as breeding stock, raped, made pregnant, forced to bear a rapist's child in their bodies and have the child taken away. And she sits there and tells me that's okay.* Anger simmered. He had to keep it under control, she must not realize.

"True. But you must understand, Delia, on the facts I have, I'll be forced to take you to the Confederacy High Court on Malmos for trial."

She blinked. "Malmos? Why?"

"Because of the foreign affairs element of the whole business."

"But... surely this is a Nordheim civil matter?" He noted the bluster. He'd thrown her.

"No. You've handed over Confederacy citizens to another regime." He affected a sigh. "A pity. As you say, they weren't harmed. But the civil libertarians and the anti-GPR elements in the capital will have a party with this. I can't see you coming out of it well. Your name in the gossip sheets, discussed in the reviews." He shook his head.

He waited while she considered, eyes narrowed.

"Erm, is this a private conversation?" she asked, looking around the room at the sensors.

"Defender, security level five, please. That's top secret, no records," he told her.

"*Adjusting...*"

Marati was silent for a count of five. Then she leaned forward, making sure he could get a good view of her cleavage. "You're a sector admiral. What could you do to ensure that any trial takes place on Nordheim? Or suppress the whole episode?"

"I can't suppress it," he said slowly. "Perhaps if none of the girls is prepared to press charges... It shouldn't be too hard to manage that. We could say you were involved in rescuing them."

Her cat's eyes gleamed. "So you could have the report altered?"

He made a show of fingering his chin. "I could. If it was worth my while. Tampering with reports is illegal, you know."

"How much does an admiral earn? Quite a bit, I expect. But not as much as the officer in charge of Nordheim's Militia. The position's vacant, as you know. The president and I are looking for a top man and we're willing to pay. I'd say the job is overdue for a pay rise, too."

"Nordheim is impoverished."

She flipped her fingers. "I get paid in starhearts, Ullric. Starhearts that make those pathetic baubles Madam Ottenshaw was wearing look like trinkets. I can share that wealth with you."

He frowned. "I don't know..."

"This is a lucrative trade and what harm is there in it? The GPR has a chance to improve its genome and a bunch of women heading for a dead end get a better life. We're not talking security here."

She was trying to bribe him, just as he'd expected. "Did Ottenshaw get those earrings through you?"

That cat's smile; cruel, green eyes and a glint of teeth. "I did him a favor."

So that was it. If she went to trial on Nordheim, Ottenshaw would see her treated lightly at worst. And his legal experts had made it clear that the trial *would* be held on Nordheim.

"Tell me, how did you know that Grimani and Dekstra were lovers?"

"That?" She hesitated for a fraction of a second. The question had thrown her. "Tanaka must have mentioned it. I'd forgotten until I saw him again, with her." She grinned, eyes dancing with malice. "I bet they had threesomes."

"So you know Tanaka pretty well?"

She became more guarded, pushed her hair back with one hand. "We do business occasionally. His mine on Tabora has been of great benefit to Nordheim. Offered employment to many." She straightened, jaw clenched. "Of course, I was absolutely horrified to hear about the conditions those men were forced to work under at that other place. That was truly disgusting."

No sign of deceit there, even given her skills as a politician. But she was outraged at the conditions, not the slavery. He'd have to get her to admit it.

"Yet you prize starhearts."

She raised perfect eyebrows. "What woman doesn't?"

So Marati knew about Tanaka's slave trade. She might not have known about the conditions but she would have seen the traffic in men in exactly the same cold-blooded light as she did the women.

"What about Captain Sondijk and her daughter?"

She at least looked a little bit embarrassed. "It's the blonde hair. You don't get it in the slums and it's highly prized. I'd had a special request." She shrugged. "I did my best to keep the customer happy. Besides, the girl hasn't got a future with a mother like that."

She stopped, scrutinizing him. "I know she's beautiful. I expect you could have a rollicking good time with her. You probably already have. But face it, she's a common little tart, far beneath your status."

He remembered Jess at Ottenshaw's dinner. She'd held her own in that company easily, even when she didn't want to be there. Yes, she said 'fuck' when she got angry; so did he.

"And whatever she might have told you, what I said to the interrogator was true. She acted like a hostile so my captain had no choice but to defend his ship. It's not his fault that she dodged the wrong way and caught a missile. And she attacked us at our hotel."

You sold her as a slave, to be raped by the highest bidder. The anger bubbled higher. Calm; he had to stay calm. "Did you try to have her killed at Ottenshaw's villa?"

Alarm flared for a moment, suppressed so quickly he was impressed. "Not me. I have no say about what happens in the Militia. Look, I despise the woman. She doesn't like me, either. And yes, I scored those marks on her face. Haven't you ever hated anybody?" The anger had begun to rise, a bitter edge to her voice. Now she collected herself, calm and smiling, the polished politician. "What were we saying? Oh yes. Admiral of Nordheim Militia?"

Marati had no say in the Militia but Tanaka clearly had contacts. Hudson wondered what would have happened to Jess if she'd stayed at the villa instead of coming hunting with him. "These starhearts, you're willing to share?"

The gleam of triumph might have been brief but it was unmistakable. "I don't have any here. If you arrange for the report to be changed, I'm willing to cut you in at let's say twenty-five percent."

"Fifty."

She waved the figures away. "You're taking no risk. And I have people to pay."

"Like the procurers who brought you Tenna Sondijk?"

"Nothing you need to know. Thirty percent. That's it."

He pursed his lips. That should do. "I'll need a down-payment as soon as we get planetside on Nordheim."

She nodded. "I can do that."

"You'd better. I can change a report but I can unchange it just as fast." He didn't have to fake the glare of distrust.

"Defender, revert to normal security. Tell SenCom Tomas Miss Marati is to be returned to the cells."

"*Acknowledge...*"

"Thank you for your time, madam. It has been most interesting."

"It has, indeed, Admiral."

She simpered at him, a mocking glitter in her eyes. She'd think she had him both ways. He'd get her off the major charges and then she could blackmail him if he tried to turn on her.

"*The guard, Sir.*"

Hudson rose and guided her politely to the door. He even managed to smile down at her. As soon as the door closed behind her he collapsed into a chair. He could have throttled the woman. His hands were shaking, releasing the pent-up fury that he forced himself to contain. Breathe. In... out... He knew how to deal with this.

Chapter Forty-two

Jess took a deep breath before she went into the quarters she was supposed to share with the girls. This was going to be interesting. Commander Ditmar rose from the couch when the door opened. She'd have to know where Jess had spent the night but her face was expressionless.

"The girls are in their room," Ditmar said. "I started trying to get them to talk last night."

Jess bit her lip. "Sorry. I should have been here."

"No. You have your own demons, I don't doubt. And, I know you'll find this hard but the girls are more likely to open up to me, a stranger, than to you."

Jess dropped onto the couch and ran both hands back through her hair. "I feel so inadequate. What can I do to help them?"

"Make them feel safe and wanted. Don't expect too much, too soon."

"Okay."

"I can at least tell you they haven't been physically harmed. No one has molested them, which is a great relief."

Jess swiped the gathering tears from her eyes. Thank God; thank God for that.

Ditmar put a hand on her shoulder. "It's okay to cry. It'll do you good. Remember, I'm here for you. Just call." The hand squeezed gently, then drew away. "I'll come and talk to them again later."

Jess waited until the door had closed behind Ditmar, then went into the bedroom. They were awake, watching a vid, a comedy that neither seemed to find funny.

She exchanged looks with both of them. "How did you go with Commander Ditmar?"

"Good," Tenna said. Shields up, in defense mode. The bottom lip pouted.

Sufi shot a glance at her friend. "It helped a bit. Don't pout, Ten, it did. But it's going to be a long time before I feel safe again."

Yes, Jess expected that, after what happened to her. Sufi was such a smart, level-headed kid. She deserved so much more than the drop-kicks in Burkesville or the arrogant, ignorant bitches at Orham Girl's College.

"Turn that off and come and talk to me."

Tenna pouted some more but she switched off the program, then slouched off the bed to join Sufi. In their identical, too large pajamas, they looked younger than their fourteen years.

Jess stood. "Come on, over here." The girls followed her into the other room. Jess sat down on the floor and they sat side by side, arms intertwined, opposite her.

"Okay, time to talk. What happened to you after I left you at school?"

They exchanged a glance.

"I know it isn't easy but please, I need you to tell me." Her heart raced. She might not like what she heard but she had to know.

Tenna stared at the carpet. "A man came and helped Sufi with her bag. I recognized him. He was the man who helped us when we went to visit Sufi's house in Burkesville. Remember?"

"Yes, I remember."

"He was really nice, smiling and everything. He told us to bring the bags through a door. He'd helped us before, so I figured it was safe." She shot a look at Sufi when she said that. Jess met Sufi's eye.

"I'm from Burkesville," Sufi said. "I don't trust so easily. But Ten said she knew the man."

Silence. Tenna chewed at a knuckle.

"Then what," Jess said.

"The place we were in was the garage. He made us lie down in the back of a van and then I felt something on my neck."

"An anesthetic patch," murmured Sufi, her fingers absently clawing at the pile of the carpet.

"When we woke up, we were in a house somewhere in the mountains. We could see nice gardens and a lake, and the snow in the hills. They kept us there for a while." Tenna traded another look with Sufi.

"Delia Marati has a house in the mountains," Jess said.

Sufi nodded. "She came to see us, tried to tell us there had been a change of plans and we were going to be taken on an excursion." She snorted. "She must have thought we were stupid."

They wouldn't make eye contact. God, this was hard. Jess knew she'd never make a counselor, that was for sure. It was like extracting teeth.

"How did she get you on her ship?" she asked after a suitable interval.

"They landed a shuttle in the garden," Sufi said. "It had Tabora Mining's logo on the tail. They loaded us into that and we transferred onto another ship in orbit."

That made sense. Tanaka would have access to a shuttle. They wouldn't even have had to go through the space port.

"What did they tell you at that stage?"

Another exchanged glance. "Nothing," said Tenna, while Sufi nodded.

"And when you got to Luciana?"

"Nothing." Tenna shuddered. "They kept wanting to touch my hair."

"What about you, Sufi?"

The girl shrugged. "Same. We were brought out to meet this horrible fat man. Yuck."

Fat man? "Did they say a name?"

"No," Tenna said. "He was awful, with those glittery piggy eyes and slobbery lips."

Jess could imagine. Probably some rich bastard who couldn't wait until Tenna was sixteen.

Tenna's eyes filled with tears. "It was horrible, Mum. All I wanted to do was go home."

She reached an arm out to both girls, pulled them close in a tight, three-way hug and let her own tears mingle with theirs. When the sobs subsided, Jess pulled away a little but they were touching, arms around each other. "We're safe and none of us was hurt. Now we have to learn to let it slide away and not affect us." Easier said than done, she knew.

"Mum, I don't want to go back to school. Not *that* school, anyway. I couldn't." Tenna shivered.

Sufi nodded. "I don't want to go back to that school or to Burkesville, either. But I do want to see my mother. Commander Ditmar said she's been informed I'm okay."

"Yes, she has, Sufi," Jess said. And that was another thing. She'd have to find somewhere else to send Tenna but it would probably have to be an ordinary school, at least until she could get back on her financial feet. "School; well, we'll sort something out when we get home. If your mother and father allow it, you can stay with Tenna and me, Sufi." She'd manage, somehow. Sell the apartment, find somewhere cheaper.

The girl absolutely beamed. Sufi hugged Jess, strong, smooth young arms flung around her shoulders. "Ma wants the best for me, I know it."

"For now, you two stay here. There'll be something on the holovid for you to watch. I need to talk to Uncle Santh."

***

Hudson raised a hand. "Stop, stop. I'm not making any sense of this."

The IS broke off its reading in mid-sentence. "*Would you like me to start again from the beginning, Admiral?*" the IS asked.

"No. I'll leave it for another time."

He tapped his fingers on his desk. Waiting was the worst. Saahren should be contacting him any time now. He'd had a chance to read the report, a chance to talk to Haskett, and Bloom, if need be. If he was court martialed, what then? He dismissed the idea of commanding the Nordheim Militia out of hand. Even if he could have stomached working for Ottenshaw, he was a Fleet admiral, used to commanding fighting ships, not running a customs border.

If the worst came to the worst, he could afford to buy a freighter. He'd invested wisely over the years and though he wasn't rich, he could live comfortably with what he had. Sylvie's parents had left him their property, too. He still owned that.

"*Admiral Saahren, Sir.*"

His heart bounced. "Put him through."

Those eyes, so dark they looked black, bored into a man's soul. No smile. "Sir?" Hudson said.

"Thanks for the reports. The Ptorix ambassador has been to see the President, mouthing threats about invasion of Ptorix space. But the Ptorix have their own laws against slavery and as you suggested, the fact they'd allowed the GPR to mine was convincing." Saahren grinned, a brief upsweep of his lips. "President Goya tried to bluster his way through it until we suggested releasing the pictures you sent. The GPR has not raised a complaint about your 'invasion' of their planet, by the way."

Get on with it, man. Do I face a court martial or not?

Saahren seemed to read his thoughts. "The upshot is that you will retain your position but I'm supposed to warn you to obey orders in future. Frankly, I expect some initiative from my senior admirals, but maybe that's just me."

Relief flooded through Hudson's body. He sagged against his chair and let out a gusting sigh. "Thank you. I'd hoped. And feared."

"Understood. If you'd fired on the Ptorix in their territory it would have been a different story. I think we would have been forced to offer you up as a sacrificial lamb. However, we had one small piece of good fortune; Haskett had a stroke and Grand Admiral Kaspar has taken his place."

Hope soared in his heart. With Haskett gone, he stood a chance. Kaspar was much less hide-bound. "Excellent news, I have to say."

"Yes." Saahren smiled, a broad grin showing teeth. "Bloom was all for placating Anxhou but Kaspar cheerfully told Bloom to keep his nose out of Fleet business." The smile faded. "My only concern is that we can't actually bring the woman Marati to trial. Unfortunately, this is seen as a civilian matter under the jurisdiction of the planetary authorities. Is that going to be a problem?"

"If she's brought to trial, there's every chance she'll get off." Hudson tapped his fingers on the desk. "I have an idea Nordheim's President Ottenshaw may be involved in some way, and he may be open to blackmail. His wife has starheart earrings which came through Delia Marati."

"Blackmail?" Saahren shrugged. "Why not? It wouldn't be the first time. But there's not much we can do about it but hand her over to the authorities." One eyebrow arched. "Unless you can think of something else?"

Hudson certainly could. A solution he had had in mind for some time. "I'll deal with Marati, Sir, and the pirates. The matter will be finalized."

Saahren had his chin between two fingers, his eyes as cold as space itself. "I'll trust you to deal as you see fit, Admiral."

Hudson smiled. *Permission granted.* "Thank you, Sir."

The screen went blank. Hudson sat back in his chair and rubbed his hands.

Chapter Forty-three

Jess borrowed a conference room for this particular discussion where she could talk to Santh in private. She sat in one of the fifteen chairs grouped around an oval table and willed the butterflies to vacate her stomach.

The door swished open and Santh stepped inside, wary as a kid reporting to the principal. "Jess."

"It's okay, Santh. I've talked with Hudson." She waved her hand in an arc. "Pick a chair, any chair."

He sagged onto a seat opposite her, head bowed, shoulders drooped. "I was going to tell you but I was afraid you'd be angry. No, that's wrong. I was afraid you'd hate me."

"I guess I did, for a minute. But I've had time to think about it and I guess I always knew you had a special relationship."

The strain showed in his eyes, the lines etched into his handsome face. She'd guess he hadn't been sleeping well. "We didn't want you to know. Because of Tenna." He looked at his hands, laid palm-down on the table. "We resisted until you were away the whole time, with Tenna in hospital."

Just as Hudson had told her. "Did you love him?"

Tears glistened in his eyes. "With all my heart. I would have done anything for him; anything." He sighed. "Look, you deserved better, so much better. That was the only thing that made me sad. You're my best friend. I found that out when Troy died. I feel bad about how it's affected you. I'd never want to hurt you."

"Oh, Santh. It's okay, I'll get over it. Apart from being the best first officer I've ever flown with, you've always been there for me. The thing is, I don't have a ship anymore. And I expect Tanaka won't be in business anymore either."

His grin was a little bit tentative, a little bit shy. "What about Hudson? I told you, Tenna needs a father."

She rolled her eyes. "Give me a break. I hardly know the man." Although that wasn't really true. She and Hudson knew each other pretty well, after all they'd been through together.

Santh smirked. "Is it okay if I don't believe you? I think you're a great match."

She sighed. "Look, forget it, will you? Right now I'm going to be looking for a job."

His eyes lit up. "Ah. Well, I might be able to help you there." The hand he slipped down under the table reappeared with a rock. "This is an uncut starheart, an absolute beauty." He rolled the stone over the table. "Spit on your finger and wet it."

Jess did as she was told, wetting a little window into the stone's centre. Oh, wow. The heart of the stone blazed, pulsing beams of red and orange and yellow, with shots of purple and blue. "This is amazing. It makes Ottenshaw's wife's earrings look like trinkets. Santh, this thing is worth a fortune." She met his gaze. "Can you keep it?"

"Yes. I even asked Admiral Hudson. It was earmarked to go to the GPR bastards but he said I could have it for services rendered. I want to share it with you."

Oh, man. This would solve her problems; buy a new ship, maybe get her off Nordheim altogether. The surge of euphoria drained away. "No, I can't. You went through the pain to get this." She pushed it back across the table.

He pushed it back. "Half each, Jess. If you don't owe it to yourself, think of Tenna. I'm her uncle, you know."

The stone sat on the table between them, black and ordinary now the moisture had dried. A new freighter, Sufi and Tenna and school. Maybe she could even be classy enough for an admiral.

"It's incredibly generous of you. And it sure would help."

He smiled and pocketed the rock. "I'll take that as a yes. We can take it to Kentor to get it cut."

"We could if we had a ship."

"Oh, yeah. I was going to ask. What happened to *Maid*?"

"Marati blew her away." He didn't know, hadn't been told. For that matter, she didn't know what had happened to him. "Maybe it's time to swap war stories, Santh. I'll go first."

The telling took at least an hour. "I can't believe these GPR bastards," Santh said at last. "They despise us but they use us."

"They're not the only ones," Jess said. "Marati, Tanaka. They're our people, quite willing to trade in human bodies for their own ends."

"How does Tanaka fit in?"

"I'm not sure. We need to talk to Hudson."

As if on cue the ship's IS interrupted. *"Admiral Hudson requests your presence in his office, ma'am, sir."*

She exchanged a look with Santh and shrugged her shoulders. "Dunno. Let's go and see."

Hudson sat with his back to the door, in conversation with Captain Sundra who was on the bridge. He turned when they arrived and pointed at his visitor's chairs. "I thought you should witness the next few minutes."

"Witness what?" Jess sank onto a chair, eyes on the screen. Wow. Now that was what you called a bridge, a circular room bristling with screens, manned by probably fifteen people. A command chair took pride of place in the centre, itself surrounded by screens. The entire bulkhead at the other end of the room held an enormous screen so that it looked like you could see into space. *Cordoba* lay out there, a few klicks away.

Hudson didn't turn. "You'll see."

The view switched to the hangar bay. Jess' muscles tensed. That was Marati, under guard, but Marati being escorted to an airlock. What the fuck was happening? Other people appeared. That was her ship's captain and some of his crew. He was going to let them go, for fuck's sake.

She reached across the desk and put a hand on his arm. "Hudson, what—"

He glanced at her, a glint in his eyes. "*Trust me.*"

If he let that bitch go, if he let her get away with it, she'd never forgive him. But he'd said, in bed last night, she wouldn't get away with it. And yes, she did trust him. He kept his word. Her heart hammering, she waited.

Marati turned her head, searching. When she located a nearby sensor she smiled, a triumphant, smirking, supercilious smile. Jess' hands curled into fists as hate boiled in her gut. What she'd give to claw the bitch's eyes out.

"You're letting her go," she hissed.

He didn't even look at her. "Nothing she has done gives me, a Fleet admiral, the right to detain her."

She clutched at his arm, fingers digging in. "Hudson, you can't do this."

"I must." In her head he said, "*Wait.*"

The vision changed. The yacht slid out of Defender's airlock and into space, its flank illuminated by the nearby star. She picked up speed, the engine cowls glowing red, building up power for the jump to shift space. Jess bit her lip. *Come on Hudson, do something.*

The ship appeared to shiver, a strange trick of perception as the shift drive took over. That was it, home and free. Jess clenched her jaw, ready to protest. A brief, bright blossom replaced the speeding ship, followed by an expanding ball of debris.

"Yes." Jess pumped the air, her heart singing with savage glee, as fragments vaporized on *Defender's* shield.

Jess opened her mouth and closed it again. "*Did you tamper with the shift drive?*"

Hudson's eyes betrayed nothing but sincere regret. "Looks like they didn't maintain their main drives well enough. The change to shift drive is easily the most dangerous part of space travel. A couple of ships are lost every year in that way."

Captain Sundra appeared on a second screen, frowning. "You saw what happened, Sir?"

"Yes. Most unfortunate. These accidents happen too often."

"Agreed. Sloppy engineering." Sundra grunted. "I'll send out an armored tug, but I don't expect there will be any survivors."

"You're right, but we'd better follow procedures." Hudson sighed. "I suppose I'll have to file a report."

Jess searched Hudson's face. Technically, if he'd had the shift drive rigged, he'd executed Marathi, but he'd want to keep that quiet. *Let's move on.* "What about the slave ship?"

His lips jerked in a tiny, humorless smile. "I think we'll adjourn to the bridge for that." He rose to his feet and gestured to the door.

The call rang out 'Admiral on the bridge' as soon as Hudson stepped through the door. Captain Sundra stood at ease in the center, hands behind his back.

Hudson stopped beside him. "Ready?"

Sundra nodded.

"We are at present outside Confederacy space, GPR space and Ptorix Khophirate space," Hudson said to Jess and Santh. "Which means article seventeen of the Confederacy Fleet's rules of engagement comes into play. In summary, a commander catching a ship in the act of piracy outside any governing jurisdiction has the right to do what he wishes with the vessel and its crew. Technically, *Cordoba* is a GPR ship and I could, if I wished, turn the vessel over to the GPR authorities. But I'm not convinced these people will be punished as they should be. They have committed acts of piracy and slavery against our citizens. It is my judgment that an example should be made of them as a warning to others. All remaining prisoners have been transferred to *Cordoba*, including the GPR guards from the Orroyex moon."

He glanced at Captain Sundra. "In your own time, Captain."

"Sir." Sundra turned to his bridge. "Batteries one, nine and seventeen, confirm status."

The replies came back. "Standing by."

"Ten seconds."

Jess and Santh weren't the only ones watching the countdown on the edge of the view screen. Five... four... three... two... Jess felt the slightest tremor as the missiles launched. The sensors tracked their progress, yellow streaks on the screen.

"Impact in three... two... one... zero. Maximum power, port shields."

The missiles hit with pinpoint accuracy, engines, midships, bow, one by one. *Cordoba* bucked, broke in half, then disintegrated into an expanding cloud of rubble.

Savage joy surged up Jess' spine. Beside her, Santh hissed an exultant, 'yes'. Bastards. Good riddance. She put a hand on Hudson's shoulder. He grinned down at her. Oh, to hell with not in front of the troops. She pulled his head down to her level, said, "I love you," and kissed him.

She'd expected him to resist but he didn't. The infuriating man put his arms around her and kissed her as he might have in his own quarters; lips, tongue, a hand at her waist the other sliding down to her butt. Her insides turned to mush. When he let her go she was a quivering mess.

Somebody smothered a laugh.

Chapter Forty-four

"I've still got a heap of questions," Jess said. Hudson's hands still rested lightly on her hips. "And so has Santh."

Hudson gazed from one to the other. "You're friends again?"

She nodded and Santh managed a sheepish grin.

"Come back to my office, and we'll talk."

He sat behind his desk, while she and Santh resumed their chairs. "What can I tell you?"

"How it fitted together. Tabora, Tanaka, Marati. Slaves, starhearts, pretty girls." Jess glanced over at Santh, who nodded.

"Tanaka, as you know, traded with the GPR, providing them with goods they couldn't produce themselves. But Tanaka is a greedy individual. The GPR wanted miners and he agreed to provide them."

Santh stirred. "For starhearts. They're beautiful but a lot of men died for those things."

Hudson shook his head. "Oh, I don't think any mention was ever made of starhearts. I don't think Tanaka ever received any. The GPR asked for skilled, off-planet miners. I doubt Tanaka even asked what for."

"No, I reckon you're right. Tanaka was always after money, nothing else," Jess said.

"So at Tabora they picked men with no listed dependents, no family. Just like you and Ace." Hudson flicked a glance at Santh. "Nobody was supposed to have come looking for you two. The records said you shipped out and lots of people routinely did. My people checked the records extensively. None of the people taken had family or close friends."

"I remember that from when I signed on at Tabora. They asked me those questions." Santh scowled. "So that was why."

"Yes. Tabora controlled its own records so it was easy to hide. Now, perhaps you two can help me with Grimani, *Beaconsfield* and *Kimberley*?"

Jess replied. "Troy was a good captain and *Kimberley* was one of the few equipped to take the body tubes. But Tanaka knew Troy well. He must've realized Troy wouldn't play the slavers game." She turned to Santh. "You took the entire shipment to Kentor and they were transferred from there. Isn't that right?"

Santh nodded. "Guess so."

"The only thing I don't quite get is how Rocket Rawlings and Alfons fit in," Jess said.

"Yeah, I've had a think about that," Santh said. "Rocket was cargo master on *Beaconsfield*. When the ship stops, they wake everybody up, then transfer them over to *Cordoba*. He could probably live with it if they were people he didn't know. But he did know Alfons and it got to him."

Jess nodded. "Makes sense. He babbles when he's drunk, Troy figures out the connection. Presto; two dead men."

"But what would Troy have known to make him wonder about Alfons?" Hudson said.

"I don't think I'll ever know all the answers." She rested her chin on her hand, elbow on the desk. "But Troy had broken into Tanaka's before I did. He'd set up an access to the warehouse. Maybe his being edgy when Tenna was ill wasn't only about Tenna. Maybe he found out something about *Beaconsfield* and the meeting with Rocket just confirmed his suspicions."

"Maybe Tanaka tried Troy out about the Kimberley shipment and he became suspicious," Santh said.

Jess shrugged. It fitted.

Santh scratched at his hair. "But Admiral, Marati gets the starhearts. How does that work?"

Hudson steepled his hands. "Correct. Tanaka is paid in some other way. Jewels?" Raising his eyebrows he looked at Jess.

She tried to swallow a smile. "Yes. We brought some ordinary sparklers in for him more than once." She shivered. If she'd known then what she knew now... "In fact, last trip I said it seemed an awful lot for what we'd delivered. He said they owed him for something else."

"Yes, the slaves."

"So where do the girls fit in?" Santh asked.

"The GPR prides itself on its adherence to nature, to the fact it does not allow genetic engineering or the use of implants. But Confederacy humans have more variety because the gene pool is larger. So they wanted Confederacy women to improve their genome. I don't know if you noticed but they tended to be unusual women. Redheads, blondes, green eyes, that sort of thing."

Jess' lips curled in a sneer. "Delia Marati would've fitted in well if she'd been a hundred years younger."

A ghost of a smile flitted across Hudson's features. "I'll guess and say that somehow Marati found out the GPR was obtaining starhearts. She agreed to provide them with suitable women but that was the price."

Santh leant forward. "But how does Tanaka fit into that?"

"He doesn't."

Jess folded her arms and frowned at Hudson. "But I heard her and Tanaka talking at the dinner party."

"I think Marati knew about Tanaka's slave trade but I can't prove it. She was close enough to Tanaka to know about Dekstra and Grimani. I wouldn't be surprised if she worked with her GPR friends to obtain miners just so they could get starhearts for her. I don't doubt Marati obtained services from him, such as the shuttle that delivered Sufi and Tenna to *Dreamweaver* for their trip to Luciana but he was not directly involved. Marati wanted those starhearts for herself. I think she also bribed Ottenshaw. He is part owner of 'Tender Hearts', through a maze of other companies, of course."

Jess snarled and Santh's lips drew back.

"I think Marati knew this. I think she offered him starheart earrings for his wife as an incentive, shall we say, then convinced him it was in his best interests to turn a blind eye to her operations."

"What an out and out, devious bitch," Jess said.

"Yes. She was a clever woman."

"*Hudson*," Jess said in his head, "*was that explosion an accident or—*"

"*Of course it was an accident.*"

It was all she was going to get. Oh well. Jess huffed a sigh. "What now?"

Hudson shrugged. "Now we go back to Nordheim. I won't be facing a court martial."

Jess beamed at him. He'd be so relieved. He'd taken so many risks for her and for Santh.

He smiled, eyes twinkling. "I expect I'll be running Nordheim's militia for a short while until someone else is selected for the job. I can't do much about Ottenshaw, but Tanaka will be under arrest by the time we get back." Lowering his voice to a growl, he added, "As will some of the senior staff on the Tabora platform.

"I'll also start an investigation into the fellow who shot Grimani. I have no doubt he and a few others in the Militia are beholden to Tanaka."

Santh's grin was positively feral.

"Do you think Longford was involved?" Jess asked.

Hudson shook his head. "Longford was narrow-minded, unimaginative, and by the book. I have no doubt he was squeaky-clean honest; so honest he wouldn't smell a scam if he stepped in it."

Jess grinned. "You're right. That was why it was so easy for everybody to get around him."

The soft sound of the ship's environmental systems were drowned by the klaxons signaling imminent departure. The barest shudder shook the big ship. Transferring to shift drive. She gazed at Hudson, straight into his beautiful blue eyes. All he had to do was look at her and she felt a sexy thrill.

"Er, excuse me, you two," Santh said. "I think it's time I left." He stood, smirking, but paused. "Will you be married on Nordheim? Can I be involved?"

Jess scowled at him, hoping the blush wasn't obvious. "Oh, get out of here, Dekstra."

Hudson steepled his hands to hide a grin.

Santh waltzed out of the door, chuckling as he went.

"So," Hudson said. "What are you going to do? Buy another freighter?"

"I'm not sure," Jess said, shaking her head. "Except that I'm not staying on Nordheim. It's time to move on, take Tenna and Sufi somewhere where they can get a good education and leave all that's happened behind them." Forget about Troy, make a new life.

"I have an empty house on Sandford," Hudson said. "It's a semi-rural planet with some good schools. You're welcome to stay there." He paused, watching her, then went on, "We could work on it, you and I. In between tours of duty, of course."

Her heart raced. Her with Hudson? "I…"

"If it doesn't work, you can buy a place of your own." He rose to his feet. "I'm due at a meeting. Think about it."

**

Orham City Nordheim, two months later

Jess gazed around the apartment one last time. The furniture had been hers but now the Wickrams had moved in, it already had a different feel. Funny how quickly that happened. She felt like a foreigner in what had been her home. She searched her heart. No, no regrets, no sadness, none at all. Maybe she'd come back to Nordheim sometime but it would be as a visitor. "Ready to go, girls?"

Tenna pulled a face, looking at the ceiling. "Yes, Mum."

Tears sparkled in Nulleni Wickram's eyes. "I can't thank you enough. For the apartment, for Sufi." She hugged Jess, her arms wrapped tightly around her.

"I don't need the place anymore, do I? And rest assured Admiral Hudson and I will look after Sufi as if she were our own." She still couldn't quite believe she'd accepted Hudson's proposal of marriage. Her with a Fleet Admiral.

Sufi stood beside her father, who tried desperately to hold back his own tears. "I'll be back in the holidays, Mum, Dad." She was blinking back tears, too.

His face crumpling, her father seized her in a brief embrace, then pushed her way. "Make us proud."

The lieutenant standing at ease near the door cleared his throat. "We should be going, ma'am."

Jess picked up her coat and bag. "Good luck to you both. Mister Wickram, you'll find Santh will be a good boss. If he's not, you let me know."

One last hug and they were off, out the door to the shuttle waiting on the landing platform. The machine lifted and banked over the city, around the space elevator tower and up to *Defender*. The planet receded behind the aircraft, shrinking to a blue and green, white-striped ball.

So much had happened. Ottenshaw was still in office, of course. He'd wheedled his way out of any attempt to charge him over the underage brothel. Claimed he didn't know a thing about it, he'd dismiss a few minions. At least Tanaka had been sentenced to fifty years' jail for slavery.

She hoped Santh would be all right. She'd bought a half share of a freighter with him, so she could keep involved. His new boyfriend, the doctor he'd met on Tabora, seemed like a great guy. He'd given up the mining platform and set up a practice in Orham City.

In the view screen *Defender's* massive side wall filled the display. Funny, it was almost like a re-run of her first time on the ship, not too many months ago. But this time he'd be waiting for her. And she'd stay.

The End

Thank you for reading **Starheart**. If you enjoyed the book, I'd really appreciate it if you would leave a short review wherever you made your purchase. Writing is a lonely business and every author loves to get a little bit of encouragement.

The Iron Admiral: Conspiracy

Peace in the Galaxy is in the balance

Amid rising inter-species tensions, brilliant systems Engineer Allysha Marten takes one last job to rid her of debts and her cheating husband. On the mysterious planet Tisyphor she meets a security guard who wins her trust and her affection. Like her, he suspects that there's more to the operation on Tisyphor than reopening an abandoned mine. Together, they uncover a plot that threatens to plunge the Galaxy into inter-species war. As they scramble to prevent the coming holocaust, Allysha is horrified to learn that her new lover is ex-Admiral Chaka Saahren, the man the Ptorix call Chozhu the Destroyer, the man responsible for the death of her father, along with millions of other innocent civilians.

In a race against time, Saahren must convince Allysha to set aside her conflicted emotions about him to help him prevent the coming conflagration. And perhaps while he's doing that, he'll win back the only woman he's ever loved.

The Iron Admiral: Deception

Grand Admiral Chaka Saahren has the rewards of rank...
...but he doesn't have Systems Engineer Allysha Marten. Determined to keep her safe, Saahren will go to any lengths to win back the woman he loves. Allysha agrees to temporary employment by the Fleet, hoping to avoid at all costs the man she believes responsible for the death of innocent civilians, including her estranged father.

Sean O'Reilly has a plan...
...and it involves hijacking Allysha and convincing her, one way or another, to do just one more job—a job that would clear his debts and save his hide.

Allysha Marten must come to terms with her feelings...
...in the face of a reality that suggests she is a pawn in a growing power struggle, one where she will need all her skills and cunning to outwit a heinous plot that could result in the loss of billions of human lives.

Greta van der Rol loves writing action-packed adventures with a side salad of romance. Most of her work is space opera, but she has written paranormal and historical fiction.

She lives not far from the coast in Queensland, Australia and enjoys photography and cooking when she isn't bent over the computer. She has a degree in history and a background in building information systems, both of which go a long way toward helping her in her writing endeavors.

To find out more about Greta and her books, please visit her website at http://gretavanderrol.net/

Made in the USA
Lexington, KY
14 October 2014